'Catesby is a spook who never takes the easy option, and the elaborate minuets he dances around the equally elaborate terpsichore of his opponents provides great satisfaction for the reader. We attempt to second-guess both Catesby and his crafty creator, and are soundly outfoxed at every turn' Barry Forshaw, *Independent*

'Ted Wilson, writing out of deepest Suffolk, is a magnificent addition to the English tradition of writing about this dark side of politics and government' *Tribune*

'Wilson is now firmly ensconced in the new firmament of espionage writing' *Independent*

'Wilson's characters and their consciences come alive to lend the book its power' *Kirkus Reviews*

'Current favourites of mine include Edward Wilson, who crafts outstanding spy stories that beg the question of just how much of what he is relating is actually true' Quentin Bates

'When one reads Edward Wilson one feels sure one is only one step away from the truth of what really happened in that place and time. The result is a chilling conviction that history as it happened is not what we have been told' Nesta Wyn Ellis

'High-calibre writing throughout, and an array of extraordinary characters. Not to be missed' *Shots*

'Another excellent convoluted maze of an espionage thriller from Edward Wilson' *Our Book Reviews Online*

'The characters and details are woven so tightly and creatively into historical events that I dare you to separate fact from fiction' *Texas Book Lover*

The Envoy

EDWARD WILSON is a native of Baltimore. He studied International Relations on a US Army scholarship and later served as a Special Forces officer in Vietnam. He received the Army Commendation Medal with 'V' for his part in rescuing wounded Vietnamese soldiers from a minefield. His other decorations include the Bronze Star and the Combat Infantryman's Badge. After leaving the Army, Wilson became an expatriate and gave up US nationality to become a British citizen. He has also lived and worked in Germany and France, and was a post-graduate student at Edinburgh University. He is the author of five novels, *A River in May*, *The Envoy*, *The Darkling Spy*, *The Midnight Swimmer*, and, the fourth in the Catesby spy series, *The Whitehall Mandarin* – all published by Arcadia Books. The author now lives in Suffolk where he taught English and Modern Languages for thirty years. He's currently working on his sixth novel.

EDWARD WILSON

The Envoy

ARCADIA BOOKS

Arcadia Books Ltd
139 Highlever Road
London W10 6PH

www.arcadiabooks.co.uk

First published in Great Britain by Arcadia Books 2008
This B-format edition published 2009
Reprinted 2014
(fourth impression)

A catalogue record for this book is available from the British Library.

ISBN 978-1-906413-12-5

Printed and bound by CPI Group (UK) Ltd, Croydon CR0 4YY

Arcadia Books supports English PEN *www.englishpen.org* and
The Book Trade Charity *www.btbs.org*

Arcadia Books distributors are as follows:

in the UK and elsewhere in Europe:
Macmillan Distribution Ltd
Brunel Road
Houndmills
Basingstoke
Hants RG21 6XS

in the USA and Canada:
Dufour Editions
PO Box 7
Chester Springs
PA 19425

in Australia/New Zealand:
NewSouth Books
University of New South Wales
Sydney NSW 2052

For Julia, Tim and Edward

She's all States, and all Princes I;
Nothing else is;

John Donne, 'The Sun Rising'

Who is so safe as we? where none can do
Treason to us, except one of us two.

John Donne, 'The Anniversary'

Under the spreading chestnut tree,
I sold you and you sold me.

George Orwell, *1984*

Prologue

May, 1948. In a small posting, like the one in Nice, the consul is on call twenty-four hours a day. Kit was asleep in his one-bedroom apartment on the rue Marengo. It was a very nice dream involving a passionate mouth. The phone rang just as things started to get interesting. Kit rubbed his eyes and let it ring. He fumbled for the bedside lamp. He turned it on and looked at the alarm clock: two a.m. He let the phone ring three more times; they could wait. He assumed it was the *commissariat de police*, the local cops – yet again – for the US Navy was in port. Kit finally picked up the phone and answered in French. '*Bonsoir,* what sort of shit are our sailors causing now?'

There was an awkward pause before the caller spoke. The language was French, but the accent was angry American and wanted to know who was on the phone.

'It's me, Kit Fournier. Is that you Mr Patterson?' Patterson was DCM, Deputy Chief of Mission, at the US Embassy in Paris.

'Yes, Kit, it's me. You didn't sound like you were fully awake.'

'I am now, sir.'

'Listen, something serious has happened and you need to get moving. Is the car gassed up?'

'I think so – but I've got some spare cans anyway.'

'There's been an airplane crash in the Ardèche – and it looks like a US citizen may have perished. The gendarmes have found an American passport naming the holder as Lady Hartington.'

'Sounds like she's a Brit. Maybe the gendarmes got it wrong. They don't always recruit geniuses you know?'

'No, Kit, I think they got it right. Lady Hartington used to be known as Kathleen Kennedy, Joe Kennedy's daughter. Her British husband was killed in the war, but she kept the title. Did you ever meet her?'

Kit cast his mind back. He was still at school. It was a late spring day in 1940 and America was still at peace, but the Brits were getting hammered in France. 'Yeah, I did meet her, but only

1

briefly. They came down for the Maryland Hunt Cup. Kathleen and her brother Jack were staying at Zeke Coleman's place.'

'Do you remember her well enough to identify the body?'

Kit closed his eyes tight and thought, Why me? He hated dealing with dead bodies. After a moment, he said, 'I think so, she wasn't a great beauty, but she was a bubbly girl.'

■

Kit ended up giving a lift to the British consul who dozed for most of the first part of the journey. The Brit's own car, a 30s Citroën, had blown its head gasket. From time to time Kit studied his passenger's face. The burns were hideous; one ear had melted into a jagged swirl like a broken conch shell. Kit assumed it was a war face from a burning ship or plane – or a tank that had 'brewed up'.

The British consul began to yawn and stretch as Kit weaved his way through the streets of Aix-en-Provence. The pollarded plane trees that lined the boulevards were already in full leaf. Aix smelled of lavender and drains. 'How are we for time?' The Englishman's voice was standard Foreign Office languid, but the vowels were flat and he said 'uz' instead of 'us'. The only English accents that Kit recognised – upper-class and Cockney – were from films. And his passenger certainly didn't speak either of those. Nor did he sound like the British officers he had briefly encountered in the Far East.

'We're doing OK,' said Kit.

'I could murder a croissant and a bowl of café au lait.'

Kit parked the car on a square with peeling green benches and a memorial for the '14–'18 war. An elderly woman wearing a white apron was standing outside the *Café des Sports*. She looked at the *corps diplomatique* badge on the bumper of Kit's Ford and frowned. The two consuls chose an outside table. The woman's expression softened when she saw the Englishman's face. She seemed to know what had happened. When the Englishman ordered for both of them in perfect French his regional accent disappeared. As the woman padded off to the kitchen, Kit turned to his companion. 'I don't recognise your accent.'

'In French?'

'No, in English. Where are you from, if you don't mind my asking?'

The Englishman looked amused. 'Rotherham.'

Kit was none the wiser. His fellow consul might just as well have mentioned one of Jupiter's lesser moons. For Kit, England was just as strange and foreign.

∎

When they crossed the Rhône at Montélimar, a gendarme on a motorcycle waved them down. Kit's big American Ford stood out like an elephant in the French countryside. The gendarme informed them that the bodies had been removed from the village hall at Saint-Bauzille and transferred to the district council offices, the *préfecture* at Privas. The gendarme then saluted and gave them a motorcycle escort for the last twenty miles. Kit was embarrassed by the attention and stares of roadside peasants. The Englishman's ironic smile made things worse.

Arriving at the *préfecture*, they were greeted with some ceremony by a high-ranking gendarme and a very elderly man in a black suit with a Legion of Honour in his buttonhole. The old man introduced himself as the mayor, but everyone else referred to him as 'the chief'. There were also reporters with notepads, but the gendarme kept them at bay.

Kit and the Englishman were ushered into an office that was lined with dark polished wood. There was a crucifix on the wall behind the desk and a framed military citation describing an action that had taken place in Quang Nam Province in 1886. Christ, thought Kit, this guy really is old. The mayor invited them to sit down. The door opened and an elderly woman in black entered the room bearing a tray of coffee and petits fours. The loose heels of her espadrilles slapped loudly on the polished floor. Kit wondered if the *patronne* from the cafe in Aix had somehow followed them – they could have been twins. The woman poured the coffee into Limoges china cups and left. Kit felt engulfed by a wave of happiness and peace. He would have been content to spend the rest of his days in that dark room listening to the clock tick and smelling the furniture polish and must of age. He wondered if he could have it all dismantled and re-erected – including the old man and his Legion of Honour – in the garden of his home in Maryland. The ultimate tourist souvenir.

As they sipped the coffee the mayor explained that there were only four bodies, not eight or ten as originally reported. 'This confusion,' he said, 'may have been because this type of aeroplane has seats for eight passengers. But there were only two passengers – and with the two pilots – that makes four.' The old man turned to the Englishman. 'Three of them were carrying British passports. But you must confirm their identities before we will sign a permit allowing the repatriation of their remains. Are you capable of doing this?'

'I have been telegraphed detailed physical descriptions of the two pilots – a Mr Peter Townshend and a Mr Arthur Freeman. The passenger, Peter Fitzwilliam…'

The Frenchman interrupted. 'The passport identifies the bearer as Earl Fitzwilliam.'

'Yes, that was his title. In any case, Fitzwilliam was a prominent figure in French horse racing and breeding. I not only have recent photographs of him, but his trainer is coming down from Paris to help identify the body.'

'Very good.' The mayor turned to Kit. 'And the young lady, how sad. Her passport bears the name Lady Hartington, but it is an American passport.' The Frenchman sounded like a naturalist describing a rare hybrid butterfly. 'And I believe her father was a close friend of Roosevelt and a former American ambassador…' the old man's eyes flicked to the Englishman, 'to Great Britain.'

'Yes,' said Kit, 'that is correct.'

'And can you identify her?'

'I knew her personally.'

'That is very good. Her father is at this moment on the way to Privas – and it might be kind to spare him the pain of seeing his daughter. Her face is…' The Frenchman frowned and made a gesture against his own face suggesting disfigurement.

Kit felt sick at what he was going to have to do. He was also surprised to hear that Joe Kennedy was in France. Patterson hadn't mentioned it.

'We have had to turn our conference room into a temporary morgue. The bodies are now being transferred into zinc-lined coffins that we had sent from Montélimar. It enables them to be packed in ice.'

The old man, reflected Kit, clearly thought of everything

The mayor steepled his fingers and continued. 'There are no embalming facilities in the region. Personally, I find the practice barbaric and unnatural.'

Kit nodded agreement.

'There is,' said the Frenchman, 'also the matter of taking an inventory of the belongings of the deceased. We follow strict guidelines. Everything must be witnessed and countersigned.'

'Thank you,' said Kit as he finished his coffee. He left the petits fours untouched.

'When you are ready, you may view the deceased.'

∎

Kathleen's face wasn't as bad as the old man had suggested. Her jaw was crushed and bruised purple – and there was a wide gash down the left side of her face. But the worst thing was the way her lips were half open as if trying to utter a cry. Kit could also see that her teeth had been broken and shattered by the impact. He gently touched her forehead and said, 'Sorry.' That's the thing about being born a Catholic: you always feel guilty even if it isn't your fault. You can stop believing – it's all infantile nonsense after all – but you can't stop the guilt.

The Englishman came over to the coffin and stood beside Kit. 'She's in much better shape than my lot. The gendarme says she was seated in the back of the plane – and got less impact. You ought to see the pilots.'

'No thanks.'

'They were both ex-RAF. They must have known they were going to die, but still remembered to stuff handkerchiefs in their mouths.'

'What's that for?'

'Stops you from biting your tongue off when you crash.'

∎

On the other side of the room, the gendarmes had set up four trestle tables. Each table was laden with the belongings of one of the deceased. The pilots' tables were nearly empty. Fitzwilliam's contained only a small suitcase and its contents – but Kathleen's table was heavily burdened and overflowing.

The men's belongings were quickly dealt with. The most valuable thing was Fitzwilliam's signet ring – there was also a lot of cash. Kit stood by while the gendarme officer counted out every note and coin. When it was all finished, Kit signed his name under the Englishman's as a witness.

Kathleen's belongings were going to take a lot more time. The gendarme began with the most valuable items: a number of necklaces and heirloom brooches that were on loan from her dead husband's family. It didn't seem right to Kit that she should have taken them to glam up for a weekend with a married man on the French Riviera.

When the jewels were all inventoried and signed for, the gendarme began on the clothing – and there was a lot of it. Kit's brief memory of Kathleen had slotted her as a wholesome 'skirt and sweater girl'. She reminded him of the Mother Seton girls with their white bobby socks and saddle shoes kicking through mounds of autumn leaves on North Charles Street. But the contents of her suitcase suggested that 'skirt and sweater' was no longer her image. The poor gendarme was aware of the solemnity of the occasion – and tried not to smile as he waded his way through silken mounds of negligees, brassieres, stockings and knickers. There were also camisoles embroidered with her initials, KKH, and a pair of black lacy suspender belts. Kit heard a door open as he signed another inventory, but didn't turn around. The remaining items were even more intimate: a douche and a contraceptive diaphragm. These weren't the toilet items of a fresh-faced convent girl.

The voice behind Kit spoke with a strong Boston twang. 'What the hell do you think you're doing?'

Kit handed the diaphragm back to the gendarme as he turned to face the man asking the question. He recognised Ambassador Joseph Kennedy at once. Kit knew, instinctively, that he was in the wrong place at the wrong time – and that nothing he could say or do was going to make any difference. 'Good afternoon, sir, my name's Kit Fournier, I'm the US consul in Nice.'

'I didn't ask who you were – I asked what you think you're doing?'

'I am very sorry, Ambassador Kennedy, to have to inform you…'

'You don't inform me of anything, young man. Where's my daughter?'

Kit pointed across the room to the coffin. For the first time, he became aware of the smell of chrysanthemums. The funereal flowers seemed suddenly to flood the room. 'She's there, sir, next to the wall.'

Kennedy walked over to the coffin, glanced quickly down at his daughter. Then he half-turned and looked at Kit. 'Why are you still here? Get the hell out and don't come back.'

■

A week later Kit was sitting in the office of Jimmy Patterson, the Deputy Chief of Mission at the Paris embassy. Patterson leaned back in his chair and smiled. 'I feel sorry for you, Kit. He's not an easy man to deal with – and, poor you, you were only carrying out your consular duties as survivor assistance officer.'

'It doesn't matter. I can understand how Kennedy must have felt.'

'He's an almighty powerful man, Kit, and men like that are even more dangerous when they're grieving. First of all, let me give you some instructions. One, don't ever, ever mention what you saw and heard in Privas on 14 May. Two, Kathleen Kennedy Hartington was not involved with Peter Earl Fitzwilliam who was, of course, a happily married man. Ambassador Kennedy's daughter was just a friend of the family and, after a chance encounter with Lord Fitzwilliam in London, was offered a seat on a chartered plane to the south of France to meet her father. That's the line, got it?'

'Got it.'

'Now, Kit, what are we going to do with you?'

'What do you mean?'

'I think that, in your own interest, a little career change might be in order.'

'Does Kennedy want me kicked out of the diplomatic corps?'

'Not quite, but it might be an idea to lie doggo for a while.'

'Long unpaid leave?'

'No, Kit, you can still be a diplomat, but I think you need to add another string to your bow.'

'Oh, I know, one of those God-awful courses learning some obscure language that no one can pick up after the age of five.'

'You are a good linguist, but that's not what I had in mind.' Patterson looked closely at Kit. 'You were in the OSS at the end of the war.'

'Yeah, but I wasn't any good at that cloak and dagger stuff – I was too young and naive. The only reason I ended up in the unit was because my dad pulled strings.'

'By the way, how is your dad?'

Kit knew that Patterson's question had overtones. His father had retired from the army a few months after the war ended – and there were rumours that he had 'gone a bit funny'. He spent a lot of time trying to organise medical help for atomic bomb radiation victims in Japan. 'Dad's fine,' said Kit.

Patterson could see that he had touched a raw nerve and returned to Kit's career prospects. 'You know, Kit, there has never been a clear line between diplomacy and intelligence gathering. To a certain extent every envoy is a spy, and…'

'And what?'

'And I think, Kit, that if you're not prepared to get your hands dirty, you're not going to survive in this business.'

'Ergo?'

'Ergo, take my advice. Listen, Kit, your old outfit, the OSS never disappeared; they're just operating under a different name – and recruiting like mad. With your experience and background you'd be perfect.'

Kit realised that he wasn't being offered a choice. 'Would it mean that my career as a diplomat is over?'

'No, far from it, you'll still be an accredited diplomat carrying a black passport – only your post will be called "cover"– "diplomatic cover". Who knows, you might even get two pay cheques.'

Kit smiled. 'And will it keep Kennedy and his pals on the Seventh Floor off my back?'

'That's for sure.'

∎

The Agency's next training intake was scheduled for September. Kit spent several weeks of accumulated leave on a walking tour in the south of France. He returned to Paris at the end of August so he could say goodbye to various friends before catching a boat train to Le Havre, from where he had booked a liner berth to New York. On his last night in Paris, Kit ran into Porfirio Rubirosa at Abélard's – not one of Rubi's usual hangouts. Kit had first met Rubirosa in Santo Domingo where his father had been US military attaché. Kit was only eleven at the time and Rubi, then a captain in the Dominican army, had become a family friend. At the time Rubirosa was married to President Trujillo's daughter – and had very little to do. He treated Kit like a little brother, teaching him to ride and shoot. Rubi's excursions with young Kit were partly genuine kindness, but also gave him a cover to visit various ladies. Kit spent a lot of time leading Rubi's rider-less horse around in circles.

The Dominican idyll came to an end in 1937 when Kit's father confronted Trujillo directly about the massacre of Haitian migrants by armed Dominican vigilantes. His father was sure the army was involved – up to twenty thousand Haitians had been killed. There was a grotesque test to determine who was Haitian. A gunman held up a piece of parsley in front of a suspect. To a French-speaking Haitian, who knew it as *'persil'*, the Spanish equivalent, *'perejil'*, was unpronounceable. Rubirosa, to his credit, was not in any way involved for at the time he had been an undersecretary at the Dominican legation in Berlin, where he supplemented his salary by selling visas and passports to Jews. Meanwhile in Santo Domingo, Kit's father was relieved of his post and sent back to Washington. It wasn't the first time or last time that conscience would damage his career.

Kit wasn't only surprised to see Rubirosa at Abélard's; he was surprised to see him in Paris at all. 'I thought,' said Kit, 'you were Dominican ambassador to Argentina.'

'Argentina, the polo is fantastic – the best in the world. But the peasants play this game called *pato*, where you ride a pony bareback and chase live ducks that you have to catch and kill with your bare hands. It's very dangerous, especially for the ducks.'

'But, Rubi, why are you not there? What brings you to Paris?'

'Things haven't been too good with Doris…'

'What a pity,' said Kit. Doris Duke, Rubirosa's third wife, was reputedly the third richest woman in the world.

'…and, to be honest, I don't think Trujillo was very happy with the way I was doing my job in Buenos Aires. What about you, Kit? When are you going to become an ambassador?'

'I'm not. I'm sailing back to the States tomorrow.'

'From Le Havre?'

'That's right.'

'Let me give you a lift in the new Ferrari.'

■

The next morning Rubi really opened her up on the long straight on the *route nationale* between Pontoise and Rouen. The Ferrari was a road car, but a real racing machine too. There were no luxuries, the seats were canvas instead of leather. Everything non-essential was stripped out. Rubi was capable of purity too.

Windblown, they stopped for a simple lunch in Rouen of foie gras and red wine. When Rubirosa got up to have a pee, Kit followed him to the *pissoir* – he had to see if it was true. And he might never have another opportunity to see the famous 'Ding Dong Daddy from Santo Domingo'.

It was a fine sunny day and the *pissoir* was in an open yard at the back of the cafe. It was, thought Kit, one of the nicest things about France – the way you could have a pee in the open air and watch the world go by. He tried not to make it obvious that he was leaning over to have a look. He even thought of making small talk about the route or the weather to try to prove he wasn't really looking. But when Kit actually saw it, he was stunned speechless – it really *was* almost a foot long. But the impressive thing was its girth; it was as thick as a man's wrist.

Despite his dissimulation, Porfirio saw that Kit had stolen a look at his cock. Rubirosa began in English. 'You know there's an operation for these things. It's called, reduction phalloplasty. It certainly would make playing polo and driving fast cars a lot more comfortable. Porfirio did up his flies and then pinched Kit's cheek with his thumb and forefinger. 'But boy, I don't think your rich *gringas* would still want to sleep with me.'

∎

They followed the *route départmentale* for the rest of the journey. The road twisted and turned as it followed the sinuosity of the Seine valley. The sun was straight before them, blinding and leading. It made Kit think about power: Rubirosa's power, Kennedy's power. Theirs were obvious forms of power. But, thought Kit, what kind of power can I have, can I wield? He was about to cross a great ocean to find out.

London: November 1951

Lord Cherwell knew what sort of language appealed to the Old Man. And the importance of keeping it all on a single page, otherwise things didn't always get read. As soon as the Prime Minister picked up the memo his eye was drawn to the key paragraph:

```
If we are unable to make the bombs ourselves and have
to rely entirely on the American army for this vital
weapon we shall sink to the rank of a second-class
nation, only permitted to supply auxiliary troops
like native levies who were allowed small arms but no
artillery.
```

The Prime Minister adjusted his reading glasses and went back to the top of the page:

```
The McMahon Act (1946) forbids Americans to disclose
any atomic secrets to foreigners.
```

Churchill then picked up a pen and drew a question mark next to the offending passage. 'Surely,' he said, 'by "foreigners", they do not mean us. What about our wartime agreements?'

'They have been superseded. We should gain nothing, Prime Minister, by referring to them now.'

'Are you really saying,' Churchill's voice was ringing with indignant irritation, 'that the Americans would refuse to give us any information about bomb design, still less an allocation of bombs?'

'Whether we like it or not,' Cherwell spoke softly but firmly, 'this seems to be the present position.'

The Prime Minister frowned and regarded the memo's final point. The words seemed to taunt him like a cold-eyed gambler offering another card.

```
A decision is wanted now.
```

Eniwetok Atoll, US Pacific Proving Ground: 1 November 1952 (Catholic Liturgical Calendar: The Day of the Dead.)

Operation Ivy; device codename Mike, M for megaton. At a half-second before seven-fifteen a.m., Mike, the world's first hydrogen bomb, was detonated. The explosion yielded 10.4 megatons, a force 693 times more powerful than the atom bomb that had devastated Hiroshima. The fireball was three and a half miles in diameter; the mushroom cloud rose to a height of twenty-five miles and spread to a width of a hundred miles – one hundred million tons of radioactive material was blasted into the atmosphere. The ground zero islands disappeared completely and were replaced by a crater large enough to contain fourteen Pentagons.

Leighton Fournier, Kit's father, witnessed the explosion from the deck of the *USS Estes*. He had used his position as a member of the ABCC, Atomic Bomb Casualty Commission, to wrangle an invitation to the test. His obsession with the new bombs was one of the reasons why his colleagues whispered that he 'had gone funny'.

> *At sea*
> *Near Eniwetok*
> *Marshall Islands*
>
> *1 November 1952*
> *Día de los Muertos*

Dear Kit,

I've just attended a preview of the end of the world. They gave us bigwigs radiation badges and dark glasses like welders wear, but the ordinary sailors had nothing. A few seconds before the end of countdown, everyone without protective glasses was ordered to go to the other side of the ship and face away from the blast. It was scary; my frightened animal self wanted to go with them. The last seconds of the countdown seemed to take forever as if Time had stopped in its tracks and was asking us to reconsider what we were doing. As soon as the flash occurred I instinctively covered my eyes and saw all the bones in both my hands. I turned away and faced the ship. All the ladders, the superstructure and all the gun turrets had turned from grey into sepulchre white – as if the Estes had become a ghost ship. When I turned my eyes back to the blast, the fireball was forming into a mushroom cloud. At first like a giant puffball streaked with red, then a white mushroom with a stem. The frightening thing was the way it just kept growing and growing. About fifteen or twenty seconds later the shock wave hit us and rocked the ship from stem to stern. My ears popped and popped again and then there was a boom behind us as the shock wave passed through us and headed out to sea. By now I thought it was all over, but that explosive cloud kept growing. It was now more like a giant doughnut then a mushroom. It was turning dark grey and black and heading towards us. A few minutes later, the skipper ordered us all below and the ship was completely buttoned up – every hatch and porthole secured. We were steaming away from the test site at full speed and the ship's topsides were being washed down with high pressure hoses and sprinklers. Gosh.

I arrived on Eniwetok Atoll four days before the test (long bumpy flight in a MATS C-54 Skymaster) and was treated with more hospitality than my humble status merited. I was feasted on steak and lobster and boated out to coral reefs to snorkel in clear turquoise waters amid shoals of brightly coloured fish. (Un paradiso terrestre? Yes, Kit, I am aware of the irony.) The scientists treated me like visiting royalty and proudly showed off their pet monster. The Mike device wasn't a 'bomb' such as you drop out of a B-29: it was a small factory, the size of a two-storey house bristling with cylinders, tubes and refrigeration units holding reservoirs of liquid deuterium (a form of heavy hydrogen that boils at – (minus!) 417 degrees Fahrenheit). But, my new friends assured me that once the principles of releasing that apocalyptic power are understood, it will take only months to produce a 'weaponised' miniature version of Mike.

The odd thing about the scientists was not just their intelligence, but their civilised awareness of the enormity of what they were doing. One of them said to me: 'Five billion years of evolution has led to this: the capability to destroy everything time has bought. And why? To threaten obliteration on a former ally that we have turned into an enemy – because we don't like their economic system.' I suppose, Kit, that we're all the same: willing pawns manipulated by the vast currents of history. Only maybe, we shouldn't be quite so 'willing'.

Much love,
Your silly old dad

> PS *The name of the island that we just blew up was Elugelab;*
> *'Flower' in Micronesian dialect.*

Leighton folded the letter and put it in his bag. He knew that it would be weeks before he could post it. All communication and news from the test site was embargoed for the next sixteen days. It was feared that the news might affect the US presidential election that was only a week away. Two days after the explosion Leighton took part in a flight over the test area for the purpose of taking air samples and monitoring radiation levels. The plane never returned.

Notes from the 1953 Bermuda Conference

The American proposal to drop atomic bombs on North Korea if the truce broke down shocked the British delegation. Churchill regarded the bomb as something new and apocalyptic; but for President Eisenhower nuclear weapons were nothing more than the latest 'improvements' in military weapons. The President was polite and friendly, but never smiled or laughed. Churchill was gloomy and full of pent-up anger and resented the way that John Foster Dulles, the US Secretary of State, behaved as if he was running the show. Every time that Churchill broached the idea of a summit with the Soviet Union to try to reduce the danger of nuclear war, Dulles put on a stern preacher face as if the Prime Minister was suggesting a deal with Satan.

There was, of course, something that everyone thought about, but no one dared say. At least not in public, for it would be a tactless breach of diplomacy. What would happen, say, if a hawkish Washington decided to end the Soviet problem with a pre-emptive nuclear strike? And it was a tempting option, for the US military planners knew that the Russians still lacked the capability to retaliate across the Atlantic. *But...* they could reach Britain – and that's where the revenging Soviet bombs would fall. The British people would bear the brunt of American rashness – and most of them would die.

London: June, 1954

The Defence Policy Committee authorises a British H-bomb programme.

Chapter One

London, 1956. Mice, thought Kit. Not tiny rodents, but MICE: money, ideology, coercion, excitement. Basic training for case officers: the four means that you use to recruit an agent or persuade someone to betray their country. MICE, he thought, how apt an acronym. It wasn't always that simple. The 'E' could stand for ego as well as excitement, but ego could cause problems – like bragging. Of the four, most station chiefs preferred 'money'. When you get someone to take a bribe you have a paper trail for blackmail, then you get 'coercion' as a bonus – and that's even better than greed.

Kit turned up his collar and thrust his hands deep in his overcoat pockets. He felt a used Underground ticket, a mint, loose change – he liked English money, big and solid compared to greasy American nickels and dimes – and deeper down, the heavy lump of a snub-nosed Smith & Wesson .32. The London evening that swirled around him was dense fog and shadow. It was the worst smog of the winter and smelled of sulphur. A bus, led in front by a conductor waving a torch, rose out of the gloom. He remembered the gas-lit streets of his Baltimore childhood: Victorian gothic with negroes and armed cops. But this was another country and the past was dead – or almost dead. When Kit turned left off Oxford Street into Poland Street, it was like descending into a mine shaft.

He walked blindly into utter blackness, led only by the sound of laughter and shouting from the pub. A door opened and a powdered woman tumbled out framed by a ring of rancid yellow light. The scene reminded Kit of an Eliot poem. He ignored the pasty woman who asked for a light, and entered the warm fug. The pub had high ornate ceilings with Edwardian mouldings. The plaster was stained yellow by decades of tobacco smoke. It was easy to spot Driscoll. He stood out like an Olympic weightlifter in a consumption clinic. The unnecessary ID prop, a copy of *Merchant Shipping News*, was curled up in Driscoll's massive fist.

Driscoll looked tense and uncomfortable. A half-finished pint of beer rested by his elbow. Kit made his way through the pub crowd, smugly aware of how well he blended in, until he was next to Driscoll. He pointed to the pint: 'Can I get you another one?'

'No, thanks.'

Kit was surprised at the way Driscoll seemed to shrink within himself. Then Kit caught the eye of an artistic looking middle-aged man standing two paces behind Driscoll. The man – wearing a tweed jacket and black polo neck – smiled and gave Kit a conspiratorial wink that seemed to welcome him into Soho's world of furtive pleasure. Kit winked back. The man mouthed, 'Good luck.'

Kit had learned a few Gaelic phrases. He leaned close to Driscoll's ear and whispered the Republican motto, '*Tiocfaidh ár lá.*' It meant 'Our day will come'.

A cloud seemed to pass over Driscoll's face and he clenched his fist. 'You think it's funny?'

'No, I hope your day will come – and sooner than you expect.'

Driscoll unclenched his fist, but still looked suspicious. 'What's your name?'

Kit gave his alias without blinking. 'Shaw. What are you drinking?'

'Not this piss.'

'Guinness?'

'Their Guinness is crap too. I wouldn't mind a Jameson.'

Kit ordered two doubles and studied Driscoll out of the corner of his eye. He was good at watching people without appearing to look. Driscoll had the body of a superb athlete on the way down; one that had just started to turn blowsy and a bit paunchy. On the other hand, Driscoll's file was textbook perfect. Born in County Kerry, he came from a family with a strong Sinn Féin history. In 1950 Driscoll immigrated to the United States where he joined the US Navy and trained as a frogman. He won a medal in Korea. Afterwards, Driscoll left the navy convinced that he could make a fortune as a property developer in California. A business partner swindled Driscoll out of his life's savings and ran off with his wife. Driscoll then descended into alcoholism, petty crime – and not so petty crime too – and suicidal desperation. Finally, he came back home and joined the IRA – and that turned sour too. It was, thought Kit, almost a film script. An alarm bell faintly sounded.

This guy's profile is just *too* perfect – he must be a plant. But who planted him? He could be from MI5, SIS, Scotland Yard Special Branch or even MoD police. It was all a big game. Allies spied on allies and agencies spied on agencies. You scored a goal when you caught someone with cum stains on their cassock.

Kit watched Driscoll down the whisky in one gulp – almost like a Russian. Kit finished his own drink and ordered another round of doubles. He knew that he wouldn't get drunk because he'd swallowed a wineglass full of olive oil before setting out. The oil coated the stomach lining and prevented the alcohol from being absorbed. It was essential 'tradecraft' for anyone, agent handler or diplomat, who had any dealings *at all* with Russians – so much good vodka wasted. Kit watched beads of sweat form on Driscoll's brow as he drank. He almost felt sorry for him – Driscoll had a problem. 'How do you like London?' said Kit.

'London is shite.'

'Let's go for a walk,' said Kit.

The fog had lifted and the outside air had turned cold and clear. The pair headed north through a warren of side streets towards Regent's Park. Kit sensed that Driscoll was more relaxed in the open. 'I've read your citations from Korea, Mr Driscoll, you're a very skilled professional.'

'No big deal.' If anything, Driscoll had enjoyed the Inchon operation. It was better than being cooped up on ship smelling farts and sweat. Driscoll's underwater demolition team had cleared mines and laid beacons to guide the marines on to the sea wall. He won the Navy Cross for bravery, but after that everything turned to shit. Driscoll didn't even know what he'd done with the medal.

Kit paused and listened. There were footsteps approaching and someone talking. A man wearing a flat cap and a filthy mackintosh weaved into the lamplight. 'Fuckin' bastards,' he said, 'fuckin' bastards, bastards.' The man was bent over double, but was walking with a purpose. He nearly collided with Driscoll, but then continued on his way. Kit watched the drunk disappear into the shadows and then turned to Driscoll. 'I don't want to waste your time – or my time – do you want a job?'

'Is your name really Shaw?'

'Of course not.'

'I want to know who I'll be working for.'

'You'll be working for me.'

Driscoll turned away. They walked in silence until they reached Regent's Park. They crossed the road and followed a path into the greensward. The damp night air carried the roars of caged nocturnal predators from the zoo on the opposite side of the greensward.

Driscoll finally spoke. 'And who do you work for?'

Kit knew it was pointless to dissemble. The nature of the operation would only point in one direction. 'I work for the US government.'

'You're talking shit.'

Kit was taken aback. 'What do you mean?'

'Tell your bosses to fuck off.'

'Fine.' Kit reached deep in his pocket and felt the Smith & Wesson. He had shown his face – and Driscoll's life wasn't worth having his cover blown. He was going to take Driscoll down to the weeping willows by the boating lake. There wouldn't be any lovers or watchmen; the night was now a pelting shower of sleet. The police would write it off as an internal IRA feud – like the last time he had to terminate an agent's contract.

Suddenly there was nothing but flashing white pain. Kit was lying on his back, struggling for breath. The blow to the solar plexus had come totally without warning. He hadn't seen Driscoll move at all. Kit couldn't have reached for the gun even if the Irishman's foot wasn't pinning his hand. Driscoll meanwhile removed the Smith & Wesson from Kit's coat pocket. 'Very thorough,' he said, 'you've even got an American gun.' Driscoll pointed the pistol in Kit's face, 'But your fake American accent wouldn't fool anyone.'

Driscoll moved his foot and Kit struggled to his feet. His voice was little more than a breathless squeak. 'You're crazy. Who the fuck do you think I am?'

'It doesn't matter: MI5, RUC Special Branch. You want to turn me into a tout, an informer.'

Kit tried to smile: he should have seen what was coming. He had forgotten to remind himself that the world of espionage is a sick place: a wilderness of mirrors inhabited by haunted minds that see only mirages and lies. The more plausible a truth, the more cunning the deception. Kit spread his arms in a gesture of surrender and nodded to his breast pocket. He had to prove himself, otherwise it looked like Driscoll was going to kill him. 'Check my ID.'

'Hand it me.'

Kit slowly removed the slim leather case and flicked it open to show his photo, security clearance and job title. Driscoll took the ID with his left hand and studied it in the dim light. He then thumbed open the lock on the Smith & Wesson, flicked out the chamber block and emptied the bullets on to the ground. Driscoll stared for a second; then handed the unloaded gun back to Kit – followed by the ID. 'This seems genuine, but I still don't like your fucking attitude. Turn around.'

Kit turned. He waited to be coshed, but instead he felt Driscoll brushing the damp leaves off the back of his coat. 'Tell me more about this job.'

'We want you to do some diving, some snooping – and maybe even a hit or two.'

'What's in it for me?'

'Well for starters, you can stay on in the flat.' Kit knew that Driscoll had been homeless. 'Is it OK?'

'It's fine.'

'I know it's pretty basic, but we don't like our safe houses to be too fancy. We don't want the neighbours to gossip.'

'Didn't you hear me? I said the flat was fine. You should try sharing a shit hole in Armagh with a sheep for six months.'

'We've heard that things haven't been going too well.'

'We've made mistakes.'

'From what I've heard,' probed Kit, 'it all sounds pretty awful.'

'But it's worth it. Don't think I'll ever betray the cause. The auxiliaries beat to death two of my uncles in Dublin Castle.'

Kit remembered hearing some of his British counterparts refer to the Irish as 'Bog Wogs'. The engrained mutual bitterness surprised him – and he was ashamed of exploiting it. Once again, Kit thought of MICE. For Driscoll, it wasn't just money: he was a man with a grudge, another word for 'ideology'. 'I don't suppose,' said Kit, 'you've got any diving gear?'

Driscoll shook his head.

'You'll need some.' Kit slipped a roll of banknotes into Driscoll's coat pocket. 'That's five hundred pounds – as much as an English labourer makes in a year. You'll also need some of that money for buying a van and paying for hotels.'

'I still haven't said I'm going to do the job. And you haven't told me what it is?'

'We want you to help us drop the Brits in the shit – as deeply as possible.'

'In Ireland?'

'No, in England, in Portsmouth Harbour. And since you haven't asked, any work you do for us has to be completely sterile – no fingerprints leading back to Washington.' There were other rules too: the ones called 'sanctions' that formed the unspoken bond between handler and spy. Driscoll knew that if he blabbed or displeased, it wouldn't be MI5 or Special Branch who left their calling cards, but Protestant gunmen. Sanctions aren't betrayals, they're rules.

Driscoll blew on his hands and rubbed them together. 'So what's the deal?'

'Have you heard of Commander Lionel Crabb?'

'Of course, everyone knows Crabby. He's a real character and a damned good diver too – the best the Brits have got.' Driscoll paused. 'You want me to hurt him?'

'Only if he gets in the way.'

Driscoll stopped and peered into the darkness.

'Something wrong?' said Kit.

'I don't like killing other divers – even if they are Brits.'

'Like I said – only if he gets in the way. The job isn't about killing Crabb, it's about fucking up Britain's foreign policy.'

'I still don't understand what I'm supposed to do.'

'In the middle of April,' said Kit, 'a Russian cruiser called the *Ordzhonikidze* and two destroyers are going to dock in Portsmouth harbour. The *Ordzhonikidze* is carrying First Secretary Nikita Khrushchev and Soviet Premier Nikolai Bulganin on a goodwill visit to Britain. The people I work for want to destroy that goodwill.'

'How does Crabb fit into this?'

'A British intelligence organisation intends to send Crabb on a spying mission to see what the *Ordzhonikidze* has under her hull. The dive is a serious breach of diplomatic protocol. If the Russians find out, it could cause an embarrassing international incident.' Kit paused and waited.

'There's more to it than this,' said Driscoll. 'Otherwise, you wouldn't need me. You would just tell the Russians directly.'

'Yeah, there's a lot more to it.'

'What is it you want me to do?'

Kit looked directly at Driscoll. The Irishman's eyes were hidden in the gloom, his damp pale face shone like a skull in the weak light. 'I want you to put limpet mines on the bottom of that cruiser – and I want Crabb and the British government to get blamed for it.'

Chapter Two

She was looking out to sea. Kit knew it was her, even from a distance. She seemed a head taller than the fishermen's wives who milled about between the sheds on Aldeburgh beach. Simple, understated, elegant. She was wearing a headscarf, a white turtleneck sweater and dark glasses: American incognito via the Latin Quarter. She reminded Kit of Jack Kennedy's wife. The Kennedy marriage was one of those mistakes that you can't do anything about, like when Jack got starboard and port confused and steered his PT boat across the bows of a Jap destroyer. Never mind.

Kit didn't speak until he was almost behind her; near enough to smell her perfume: jasmine, citrus and sandalwood. He imagined her, still half-dressed, touching the fragrance to her wrists, her neck, the backs of her knees. When he finally spoke, her name nearly stuck in his throat. 'Jennifer.'

'Kit.' And then the perfect teeth smile and Left Bank *bisou-bisou* kisses. It wasn't pretentious or affected; it was just the way she was. The fishermen's wives continued gutting the morning catch – not staring, but watching all the same.

'I hope you haven't been waiting long.'

'Not at all, you're five minutes early. Shall we go for a walk? It's supposed to rain later.'

'Jennie, I live my life awaiting your commands.' Kit offered his arm and they crunched off over the shingle to the sea. The firm pressure of her hand on his arm made his heart race and his head spin. His legs felt disconnected. It was hard work being happy – especially when you know it's not going to last.

'It's always lovely to see you. I just hope the embassy is safe without you. I would hate to think that American national interests might be sacrificed because you've come to Suffolk to see me.'

'I'm not that important.'

'That's not what my dad says.'

'That's because he's been talking to my mom – she exaggerates.'

'False modesty, Kit, does not suit you. Everyone knows you're a rising star.'

'Gosh, I didn't know that. Can you give me a list of their names? And send a carbon to the Ambassador, please.'

'My name would be at the top of the list.'

'Thank you, but praise from a host country national sometimes arouses suspicion.'

'Oh, so you know about that.'

'Know about what?' said Kit.

'That I'm a "host country national", as you put it, that I've become a British citizen.'

'You're not citizens, you're subjects.'

'Don't be silly. And don't look at me like I'm a traitor. It's because I'm married to Brian. And because of his position... well, you know how it is. By the way, you'll find the walking on shingle easier if you dig your heel in first.'

'Not a good surface for escaped prisoners – the bloodhounds and redcoats would have you in no time. I feel like Magwitch.'

'By the way, you *are* going to stay for dinner? I'm sure we can find Magwitch a pie.'

'Of course, I'm dying to meet Brian – the man who won *la belle reine de pays Chesapeakais*.'

'I'm not *belle*, but Brian is very much looking forward to meeting you. I think you'll get quite a grilling.'

Kit flexed his arm to squeeze his cousin's hand close to his side. 'Is there anything you don't want me to say?'

'Of course not, talk all you want. I haven't any secrets, I hate secrets – you know that. Why are you laughing?'

'How did you survive in the cipher section?'

'That was different,' said Jennifer, 'only a job. The secrets I hate are personal ones, like hiding things from someone you love.'

'Like adultery.'

Jennifer breathed in, as if Kit had uttered a swear word. 'The worst thing about adultery is the secrecy. The lies are worse than the act. Unfaithfulness is worse than murder. Maybe those people who stone adulterers to death are right.'

'You scare me, Jennifer.'

'Why on earth?'

'Why? You sound like you've converted to Islam.'

Jennifer drew her scarf across her face, then laughed and let it down again. 'But I can show my face to you. You're close family – and immune to impure thoughts.'

'Well thank goodness for that. I'm glad you don't think I'm going to…' Kit let the sentence hang in the air.

Jennifer turned away. 'I love the sound of sea on shingle. Just listen – it's like dead sailors whispering, but their voices are so pebbly clear you lose the words. I can't remember the Chesapeake Bay saying anything. The sand and marshes muffle the waves.'

'What about the bell buoys – and the foghorn on Thomas Point light?'

'Oh, I loved Thomas Point – that octagonal white clapboard house on stilts. I used to imagine living there. I must have been ten when I saw it for the first time. It was in June, just after school broke up. As a treat, Peter and Robert sailed me round it in *Stormy Petrel*. How they fussed over their little sister – and how I wanted to be fussed. The sky was perfect azure. I remember all those gulls nesting in the girders beneath the house and on the roof too. And my brothers were the most handsome *beaux* any girl of ten could imagine – brown, lean, golden gods. They even smelled good. Now, I'm babbling.'

'Oddly enough, I remember Robert more than Peter. He once tried to teach me to box – it wasn't a success. I don't think he liked me much.'

'Robert was an acquired taste. Of course, mother doted on Peter. Fortunately, Robert couldn't care less – he positively enjoyed being the less favoured.'

'You know, I spent an evening with your parents last time I was on leave.'

'They mentioned it in their last letter. How was it – honestly?'

'Pretty awful.'

'I thought it might have been.'

'Your dad was all right – but he always is. By the time dinner was finished, I was, of course, too drunk to drive back to our place so they put me up for the night – in Robert's room. Out like a light, until I was woken about three in the morning by the sound of breaking glass. I got up to see what was wrong. Your mom, of course, was drunk and had knocked over a table.'

'Normal.'

'I didn't go downstairs, but waited in the shadows of the landing in case she needed help. But she was OK – I heard her open

another bottle. And then it got weird; she was talking to someone. I knew it wasn't your dad because I could hear him snoring.
It was Peter.'

'What did she say?'

'She was complaining about your living in England – and having married an impoverished scientist.'

'She exaggerates. Brian, by British standards, is very well paid.'

'That's what she meant. In any case, your mom wanted Peter
to come over and sort you out.'

'Totally predictable. She's a broken record on that one.'

'Oddly enough, Peter didn't say a thing.'

'That's not funny, Kit.'

'Sorry… maybe, I wasn't listening hard enough.'

'Stop it.'

Kit took her by the shoulders. 'Let me see your face, Jennie.
Yes, you can't hide it – the faintest crack of a smile.'

'OK, I'm not immune to your black humour. But you shouldn't
make fun of other people's grief.'

'I stand corrected. Let's get on to safer ground. Tell me about
your husband.'

'Brian is absolutely lovely.'

'I thought he was a scientist.'

'Kit, you're starting to be a bit tedious.'

'Sorry.'

'Brian, as you probably know, works in the Atomic Weapons
Research Establishment on Orford Ness. That's why we moved to
Suffolk from Aldermaston.'

'I bet he's something really important.'

'Well, I suppose he is; he's head of project. Brian is an excellent
scientist and is admired by everyone who works for him.'

Kit lowered his voice and pressed his cousin's hand. 'What do
you think of his work?'

'I don't like it – and Brian doesn't like it either. It must be awful
for him. He's a very gentle man and part of him loathes working
on the thing.'

'Does he tell you that?'

Jennifer paused. 'Not in so many words.'

'Do you argue much about it?'

'Stop being perceptive.' Jennifer picked up a flat stone and
skimmed it across a pair of waves. For a second the North Sea

had turned into the Aegean. Jennifer's body scored the grey sky with the clean lines and Attic grace of a perfect Artemis. Kit felt hopeless desire bore into his brain like a hot drill.

'You...' Kit looked away from his cousin. He couldn't find words to complete the sentence.

Then Jennifer was talking. 'Well, if you really want to know, I think the whole thing is a silly waste of money. You can't imagine the cost.'

Kit's mind was still elsewhere: in a faraway land of cypresses, cicadas and hills scented with wild thyme. He wanted to say, 'Artemis, leave it all and come with me.' Instead he simply said, 'I don't know the details, but I'm sure the bomb programme is costing a lot.'

But Kit did know the details, for one of his operatives had done a FININT 'black bag job' – Financial Intelligence burglary – at the Ministry of Supply and photographed the budget figures with a Minox spy camera. Kit was surprised at the amounts involved. The cost was staggering: the British government really wanted an H-bomb. The operative, posing as an electrical installation inspector, had done a marvellous job and copied over a hundred pages of expenditure estimates. Kit not only knew Brian's salary, but also his travel and subsistence expenses. But there was one figure that left Kit totally confused. It came under a subheading titled Red Snow: the estimate was fifty-four million pounds. There were no explanatory details.

'In any case,' said Jennifer, 'British tax money needs to be spent on schools and hospitals – and indoor toilets too. What do you think, really think? Does Britain need a bomb?'

'You've already got one, fifty actually. It's called Blue Danube – and it's been in service for three years.'

'You know what I mean, Kit, the fusion weapon – the H-bomb, the one that Brian's working on. Do we need it?'

Kit was surprised by her admission. He wondered if his cousin was a security risk. 'I don't know. The problem is that Whitehall doesn't trust Washington. The British government knows there are a lot of American generals, and politicians too, who wouldn't mind fighting a nuclear war in Europe to get rid of the Soviets – and the sooner the better.'

'Before the Russians deploy TU-95s and R7s?'

'You scare me, Jennie, you shouldn't know these things.'

'Everyone should know them, Kit.'

They continued to walk along the shingle beach. Jennifer had got one fact wrong: the Tupolev 95 was just coming into service. It was the first Soviet long-range bomber capable of striking the United States. But the Pentagon was more worried about the development of the R7, a Russian intercontinental ballistic missile that would be impossible to shoot down. Consequently, there were crazies, like General Curtis LeMay, who were agitating for a pre-emptive strike while the US was still immune to Soviet retaliation. If the Russians knew that was about to happen, the US airbases in East Anglia would be their first target. England would be obliterated in a nuclear holocaust.

Jennifer seemed to read her cousin's thoughts. 'How many British dead, Kit?'

'Forty million – and Europe too, the people, the paintings, the music, the vines of Burgundy, the olive groves, all those lovely languages and mellow buildings. The whole fucking lot turned into a radioactive ash heap.' He turned to his cousin, but she was walking away. 'Jennie?'

'I need some fish for tonight.'

'I'm sorry.'

'You get wonderful fresh fish here. Look, there's a boat landing – it's Billy and his uncle.'

The beach boats were clinker-built oak and broad beamed. None had cabins or shelter of any kind; they were open to rain, wind and salt spray. They weren't elegant: they were designed for battling North Sea waves after being dragged down a shingle beach and launched into cold angry surf. According to the season, they long-lined, trawled, laid lobster pots or set herring nets.

Jennifer checked her purse. 'I've got enough. Let's see what they've got.'

As the boat ground on to the shingle, a man in a greasy smock ran forward with a cable and threaded a hook through a ring low down on the bow. Meanwhile someone started a donkey engine and the cable went taut. As the boat was winched up the beach, other men ran forward and placed boards black with axle grease under the bows to help her slide over the shingle.

'They're marvellous,' said Jennifer, 'I love them. They're like a ballet troupe. When there's a heavy sea running, they have to be awfully quick. If they get knocked sideways by a big wave, they can capsize. That boy, Billy Whiting, is a wonderful singer. He's been in the chorus for two Benjamin Britten operas – and even had a solo. He's got a wonderful temperament. I'd love to have a son like him.'

'Jennifer, you're crying. What's wrong?'

'It's you, Kit, and all the others too. You and your bombs, you and your fucking bombs.'

'Jennie, please …'

'Don't touch me. I'm all right. Let's see what they've caught.'

Chapter Three

The meal began with Suffolk slip sole *à la meunière* and went on to spring lamb with minted new potatoes and garden peas. Kit supplied the wine, vintage claret 're-looted' from the cellar of a *Reichsmarschall* by the 101st Airborne, and a bottle of '33 *champagne fine* cognac from the embassy. Jennifer went to bed early: she felt tired and dizzy. After dinner, Brian and Kit took their brandies into the garden. Kit turned and looked at the house. The thatched roof and chimneys were black silhouettes dimly sketched against the night sky. 'Beautiful place – very oldie England.'

'It's not old at all. It's fake Tudor, built about 1900. It used to be a gatehouse. The lord of the manor wanted to show off and pretend the workers were picturesque as well as servile. But fortunately Jennifer loves it.'

'How did you end up living here?'

'The Ministry requisitioned it – and a lot of other houses – during the war. This cottage and a few others were kept on to billet staff working on the island.'

Kit looked around: there was nothing but blackness. Thick forest enclosed the garden on every side. 'It certainly is... quiet.'

'At first, I was a little concerned – I feared that Jennie might find it too lonely here. I even suggested we find a place in the village, but she assured me that she loves seclusion.' Brian paused. 'Could this place remind her of home, of Rideout's Landing?'

'The farm was isolated, but being on a river it seemed...' Kit didn't finish the sentence. He sensed that Brian wanted to know more about his wife's background, but it wasn't a past that he wanted to share. Brian had Jennifer's body, why did he want the other stuff too. 'In any case,' said Kit, 'there were always lots of people around.'

Brian sipped his brandy, then said almost apologetically. 'Jennie doesn't often talk about her family. It's as if she's cut off her past by changing countries and nationalities.' The Englishman paused; he wasn't used to probing the feelings of others. 'I suppose it might have something to do with her brothers.'

'She'll never get over it.' Kit stopped and listened. 'What's that noise? Stray dogs?'

'Muntjac deer. They bark – especially when they're mating.'

'You've got your own deer park. You must feel like an Elizabethan grandee.'

'Hardly. The muntjac are a foreign species – like the North American grey squirrel. The Victorian toffs who introduced these animals were too vain and too stupid to understand how much damage they would do to the native fauna. The grey squirrels raid birds' nests and have driven out our native reds.'

Kit smiled at the image of American squirrels chasing British 'reds' and almost made a McCarthyite wisecrack. But he bit his tongue for he sensed that Brian neither liked nor trusted him – and that drink made him aggressive. Kit steered the conversation to the calmer waters of flattery. 'You seem very knowledgeable about natural history.'

'When I was a boy I used to love walking on the moors, places like Blackstone Edge that you've probably never heard of. Much of the flora was very primitive, such as clubmosses and ferns, the sort of species you would have found hundreds of millions of years ago when life was just beginning. I found it exciting to learn about them and imagine that I was a time traveller.'

'What about Orford Ness?' said Kit, thinking of Brian's nuclear workplace. 'It looks pretty desolate from this side of the river.'

'That shingle spit may look desolate, but it's full of marvels.' Brian gave a rare smile, 'The *real* secrets are plants like the yellow horned poppy with blossoms the size of soup plates – big golden banners waving against all that cold wind and salt spray. And sea pea too, exquisite little mauve flowers clinging on with deep strong roots. Places like Orford Ness and the northern moors are the real England – not the suffocating pampered gardens on the stately homes circuit.'

Kit began to realise there was more to Brian than the gruff North Country scientist. But it didn't make Kit like him; it only made him more jealous. 'Are there animals too?'

Brian smiled again, 'Just the MoD security police and their attack dogs. Frightening chaps – all the locals are terrified of them. There's also a huge colony of hares. They must have swum over and, without lurchers and shotguns to harry them, they've multiplied like mad. The security fellows sometimes use the hares for marksmanship practice. I'm not sure I approve, but they always give us one for the pot. I've developed quite a taste for saddle of hare. Jennifer, as you know, is a dab hand with game – not squeamish at all, almost like an Englishwoman.'

'She used to go hunting and fishing too. We even used to eat those grey squirrels. Get Jennie to cook you a pair.'

'A brace,' said Brian, 'in England we never say a *pair* of game or game birds – we say a brace.'

'Thank you.'

'Jennie tells me that your fathers were classmates at West Point. That's the American Sandhurst, isn't it?'

'Not exactly, it's a four-year course and you get a degree as well as a commission. In any case, our dads – both being Maryland boys – became friends.'

'And Jennie's father married your father's sister.'

'Younger sister, Aunt Janet.' Kit wondered how much longer the interrogation was going to last. He wanted to know if Jennie had told her husband about Tombstone Frank, a shared ancestor who had made a living digging up bodies from Greenmount Cemetery and selling them to Johns Hopkins Medical School. Frank later improved the freshness of his cadavers by preying on drunken sailors. Kit feared that the psycho gene had been passed on, but not the entrepreneurial one.

'And,' Brian was still probing for something, 'you were all brought up as brothers and sisters.'

'Sort of, our house was seven miles away – half an hour's bike ride or an hour by boat.'

'Sounds idyllic – I wonder why Jennifer never wants to go back.'

'Maybe,' said Kit, 'she's afraid of ghosts.' Suddenly, there was a rustling sound from the hedge next to the road – and then a long blood-curdling shriek with hisses. 'Bon appétit,' said Kit raising his glass. 'That must have been an owl.'

'Well done. It's a barn owl. We studied them when we developed radar. The barn owl has asymmetrical ear openings – the opening in one ear is higher than in the other ear. This means they can hunt in conditions too dark even for their wonderful eyes. They pinpoint their prey by the difference in decibels. They know they're getting closer when the volume in each ear begins to even out. On the way to Orford in the morning, just as the sun is rising, I often see them hunting in the hedgerows. A glorious sight.'

Kit didn't know what to say. He knew that Brian was competing – but he wasn't sure why.

Brian coughed and cleared his throat. 'I'm sorry,' he said, 'about earlier on.'

'About what?'

'I shouldn't have made those remarks about the USA not coming into the war until it was half over. Americans must be fed up with hearing that old chestnut.'

It had, thought Kit, been pretty damn insensitive. He should have seen the blood drain out of Jennifer's face. Kit tossed back the last of his brandy. 'In France, they say the same thing about *les résistants de la dernière heure.*'

Brian was silent in the dark shadow. Kit realised that he hadn't understood a single word .– now he was competing too. He remembered how Brian had frowned whenever he or Jennifer had swapped a French phrase or quote.

'I wouldn't mind another drink,' said Kit.

'The bottle's in the house.'

'By the way, Brian, your point about the war loans was a fair one. It doesn't seem fair that we make Britain pay up, while we shovel millions of pounds of Marshall Plan aid into Germany.'

'In the end it could destroy British manufacturing.'

Kit smiled. 'But it could have been a lot worse.'

'How?'

'If Roosevelt hadn't tricked the Japs into attacking Pearl Harbour, we might not have come into the war at all – and then we would have made even more money out of it. We could have made war loans to *both* sides.'

Brian grunted a laugh. 'I probably shouldn't tell you this, but Jennifer warned me about you. She said you liked to play the professional cynic, the devil's advocate.'

'Did she?' What, thought Kit, was the game now? Something like: *Despite your kinship and shared past, Jennifer is closer to me than she ever was to you.*

'But she is very fond of you.'

'Thanks.'

The men turned to walk back towards the house. The light from a kitchen window began to cast shadows over their faces. Kit looked at Brian in profile and tried to analyse what attracted Jennifer to him. He was handsome in an English rough tweed sort of way: tall, raw-boned, strong jaw and big hands. In fact, Brian bore a striking resemblance to Group Captain Townsend – the RAF officer whom Princess Margaret had been forced to ditch. Brian's hair was also curly and black, except – the light from the window struck at an angle and revealed something hidden in normal light – for the grey roots. Kit was mildly abashed: this blunt no-nonsense Englishman dyed his hair.

When they entered the kitchen, Kit saw that the washing-up was done and everything put away. Jennie hadn't been tired after all. Kit wished he hadn't come.

'Sleep well, I'm off to bed.' Brian was smiling again. 'Make yourself at home – and help yourself to the brandy. It's your brandy anyway.'

'It's not a war loan – it's a gift, a genuine gift.' Kit knew that his voice sounded brittle.

'Thanks.'

Kit watched Brian's back disappear into the darkness of the inner corridor. A second later, there was a faint loom of light as a door opened – then the door shut and the light was gone. He thought he heard Jennifer's voice, but couldn't make out the words. Kit blotted out what was going to happen next. He hoped that he could find the brandy bottle; he hoped it would help him sleep.

■

The daffodils were coming out around the Roosevelt Memorial in Grosvenor Square. It was a bitterly cold March morning. Kit checked his watch: twenty past seven, too early for most people on his pay grade. He liked to arrive before the others so he could check the pigeonholes and in-trays of his colleagues while they were still bleary-eyed over breakfast coffee and the international edition of *The Herald Tribune*. He didn't like to be left out of any loop and always wanted to be au fait with other people's agendas. Nor was he above the odd act of petty malice. If some other FSO, Foreign Service Officer – especially the commercial attaché – had been giving him a hard time, Kit would ransack the offending officer's pigeonhole for something marked 'urgent' and dispose of it in the burn bag or shredder. The best thing wasn't hearing that the officer had been told off, but watching him spend hours afterwards emptying his trays and drawers trying to find the missing document. Kit always asked what was wrong and offered to help.

He felt his breast pocket to check his ID. The outer embassy doors were locked until nine. The doormen were always 'locally sourced' Brits – indigenous personnel – because it cost too much to fly over Americans for such low-paid jobs. Most of the doormen were middle-aged 'gorblimey' types who wore blazers with British regimental badges as a sort of tribal defiance. They took their jobs very seriously and always scrutinised Kit's ID as if it were an expert KGB forgery. The US Marine guards, on the other hand, who controlled access to inner sanctums, secure comm rooms and archive vaults, always called him 'sir' and waved him through. If the marines were 'covered', wearing their anchor-and-globe white peaked caps, they clicked heels and gave him snappy salutes. Kit liked the deference and thought that if, say he retired to a *palacio* in Mexico, he would keep dress-uniformed marines as servants and grooms: 'Saddle the horses, Corporal Cracker, Doña Jennifer and I are riding to Mass and then on to the village to distribute dinner scraps to the poor.' 'Of course not, Cracker, not *all* the poor – only the deserving ones.' But this was a grey London dawn and the marines weren't there to tend his horses. Dream on, *chico*, dream on.

Kit spent the first part of the morning being the POLCOUNS, Counselor for Political Affairs. It wasn't just 'diplomatic cover'. The post was a real job and his pay reflected the extra responsibility. If the officer was up to it, holding a genuine post as a senior diplomat as well as being CIA Chief of Station was extremely useful: you knew what both hands were doing and why. Kit supposed that, after the Ambassador and the DCM, he ranked third in the embassy hierarchy. And yet he kept a very low public profile: his photo never appeared in the press and he was never interviewed. If the BBC or a journalist wanted to talk to someone from POLCOUNS, Kit always sent his deputy. Nor did he attend Royal garden parties, Ascot or Henley. He only turned up at functions that were for working diplomats and policy makers. The sort of cosy events where everyone knew everyone else and what they were up to. In general, Kit preferred the shadows because that's where you could get things done and influence policy.

∎

A lot of Kit's day-to-day work was dealing with documents that had been summarised for him by his junior staff. Kit underlined key sections and exclamation-pointed the margins next to anything that needed following up. Anything stupid or useless was crossed out or scribbled over with DRIVEL, DROSS or CACA COMPLETA. But he always made clear and perceptive notes on the wide margins that he demanded. Kit enjoyed the work – especially when his margin comments turned into memos and the memos finally wormed their way into US foreign policy. It was creative – like directing an epic film or designing a town.

At half past ten Kit had an appointment with the DCI, Director of Central Intelligence, Allen Welsh Dulles and his brother, John Foster Dulles, the Secretary of State. Both men were his bosses – and, arguably, two of the most powerful men in the world. Who was more powerful? Khrushchev? Nehru? Mao? Certainly not Eisenhower – he only did what the Dulleses told him to do. Kit knocked on the big oak-panelled door of the Ambassador's office and waited. He knew the Ambassador wouldn't be there. He was meeting captains of industry in Birmingham. The commercial attaché had drafted a speech for him and the Ambassador had surreptitiously come to Kit asking him to 'translate it into English'. Kit knocked again louder and John Foster bellowed, 'Come in.'

The brothers were sitting at a big oak table, *American* oak, an antique bequeathed from Thomas Jefferson's Monticello. There were no aides, no secretaries, no briefing folders – just a jug of ice water and glasses. No nonsense. At the Foreign and Commonwealth Office, you sink into plump armchairs while the Foreign Secretary fills your cup from an Echinus Demotter tea service and offers Fortnum and Mason shortbread from a Georgian silver salver. But this was the *US* foreign policy machine: hard polished oak and ice water.

'Good morning, Secretary Dulles,' Kit hesitated as he considered protocol, then turned to the CIA brother and said, 'Good morning, Allen.'

Neither man rose for a handshake. Kit hadn't expected them to: handshakes and bear hugs were for public occasions, like airport arrivals, when the cameras were clicking. Allen spoke first, 'Nice to see you, Kit.'

Kit sat down and propped his briefing folder on the floor against a chair leg; he didn't want to defile the empty expanse of gleaming table. He looked at Foster and was surprised by how much he had aged. He knew that he was the older brother by five or six years, but the age difference now seemed ten or fifteen. Allen was fiddling with his pipe: the pipe and his moustache made him look distinguished in a British academic sort of way. The press called him 'the gentleman spy' and he liked to live up to the persona. Allen knew he looked better in profile, and tended to pose that way for photos. But when he looked straight at you, with those cold eyes magnified by those frameless glasses, he looked exactly like the Soviet Foreign Minister, Vyacheslav Molotov. For an eerie moment, the resemblance was so stunning that Kit half thought that Foster was playing an elaborate practical joke and had substituted his Russian counterpart in his brother's place. But as soon as Allen Dulles spoke, he turned American again. 'We were just talking about your dad. He was the most solid of the Georgetown gang and we miss his counsel greatly.'

If you miss him so much, thought Kit, why didn't you send a wreath? No body had been recovered, but there had been a big requiem mass at the Basilica of the Assumption in Baltimore. The truth, Kit knew, was that his father had become a marginalised figure, a wilderness voice spouting soft-hearted views about détente and disarmament. Kit felt a flush of paranoia. Was the reference to his dad an accusation? Did Allen Dulles think he was sprouting inherited dove feathers? Kit put on a smile that carried a hint of irony, of betrayal. 'We miss him too.'

'How's your mother getting on? Clover says she's taken up painting again.'

'She's fine. She says she'd like to spend six months a year in France – she loves painting the rivers of Charente and she's researching a book on Berthe Morisot.' Kit immediately felt like an ass for mentioning his mother's book: neither of the Dulleses would have heard of the female French impressionist. Kit feared he was coming across as a pantywaist.

The younger brother finally managed to light his pipe. 'You know, Kit,' said Allen, getting down to business, 'we're worried about Downing Street.'

Kit looked at Foster for confirmation. 'You mean Eden?'

The Secretary of State nodded and the younger brother

answered, 'Not just him, but mostly him. Your latest reports highlight concerns about the Prime Minister's health. Anything new?'

'Yes, I finally managed to access Eden's medical records.' By 'access', Kit meant a break-in to photograph documents. Once again he had used Stanley, the same operative who did the Ministry of Supply job. Stanley, an artful South Londoner in his late fifties, was an unfathomable well of talent: electrician, safe-cracker, cat burglar, spotter of ringed gee-gees and loving grand-father. He also had the most trustworthy face Kit had ever seen. The private clinic, where the Prime Minister's medical records were filed, was a Stanley masterpiece. He broke into the clinic the night before and faulted the electrical system. Before parting, he left a message on the receptionist's desk in perfect handwriting titled 'Re: Electrical fault' and asking her to ring his own tele-phone number. The next morning the receptionist assumed the message was from a colleague and rang the number. By the end of the working day, Stanley hadn't quite finished the ring main cir-cuit, but was more than happy to stay on to get it done. They left him a set of keys to lock up. As soon as the staff had left, Stanley cracked the safe containing confidential patient information and started snapping away with the 8x11mm Minox camera.

'Well,' said Foster, 'are you going to enlighten us?'

'It seems,' said Kit, 'that the original 1953 operation was botched even worse than we had thought. Sure, a cholecystectomy isn't the sort of thing you do for a merit badge in first aid, but a com-petent surgeon should have managed...'

Foster looked puzzled. 'What is a cholecsyt...?'

'Removal of the gall bladder,' said Allen, winking at Kit.

'It ought,' said Kit, 'to have been a fairly routine operation, but the knife slipped and Eden's bile duct was severed. This is a big mistake. The duct drains bile and other waste material from the liver directly to the small intestine. If the bile duct isn't connected up, it leaks poison into the system and eventually kills the patient. So a couple of weeks later, there was a second operation to ligate the duct and save Eden's life. But this was just a temporary solu-tion because it meant the poisons would backlog in the liver caus-ing malignant jaundice, acute atrophy of the liver and death.'

'So why,' said Foster, 'is Eden still counted among the living?'

'I don't know. You would have to ask the FBI.'

'What do you mean?' Foster was genuinely perplexed, but his brother kept winking at Kit.

'There was a third operation that took place in June '53 in Boston, the one in Massachusetts. The surgeon was Dr Richard Cattell, a world renowned repairer of biliary ducts. As you know, sir, the CIA are not authorised to carry out covert operations in the United States. If you want to know the outcome of Eden's Boston op, you'll need to ask the FBI to carry out a black bag job on Cattell's clinic. I know the Feds can do this, but they need written permission from the Attorney General.' Kit was teasing. Everyone knew that interagency rivalry between Hoover's FBI and the CIA was so poisonous that such cooperation was unthinkable.

'Calling on your impressive medical knowledge,' said Allen, 'what do you think happened?'

Kit smiled. 'I suppose Cattell repaired Eden's bile duct by carrying out an end-to-side hepaticojejunostomy using a 16-F rubber Y-tube as a stent.'

'Did you just make that up?'

'No, I telephoned my sister – she's a medic and knows about Cattell's work.'

Allen let out a sigh and turned to his brother. 'Isn't it typical, Foster? The Brits whinge about us, but when they make a botch of something it's the American cousin who has to repair the damage, be it on the operating table or the battlefield.'

Kit looked out the window over the London skyline. There were still many empty gaps: demolished bomb sites waiting to be rebuilt. The words of Allen Dulles, and his pompous arrogance, made Kit want to scream abuse at his bosses.

'What really concerns us,' said Foster, 'and the President has mentioned it too, is Prime Minister Eden's state of mind. Is he mentally and emotionally fit for the job?'

'That's a good question. According to his medication records, the Prime Minister regularly takes dextroamphetamines. This is a stimulant that produces a feeling of energy and confidence. Otherwise, he wouldn't be able to do his job. Cattell's operation saved Eden's life, but he never made a full recovery.'

Foster cut straight to the point. 'Has the Prime Minister ever seen a psychiatrist?'

'No, definitely not. But whether or not he *should* see a psychiatrist is a different question.' Kit was immediately ashamed of his cheap wisecrack. Anthony Eden had lost two brothers in the First World War and a son in the Second. He himself had won the Military Cross in 1916 for saving the life of a wounded sergeant in no-man's-land. Neither of the Dulles brothers had ever heard a shot fired in anger. As for Eisenhower, the President may have heard angry shots but only from a distance and from the safety of a rear-echelon headquarters. The Dulleses might have scorned Eden's foreign policy, but neither brother spoke a foreign language. Sure, Allen could order a meal in French and a schnapps in German, but Eden was fluent in both languages as well as Persian. The Prime Minister could also tell stories and swap proverbs in Arabic – and was confident enough in Russian to converse over a dinner table.

'If,' said Foster, 'the Prime Minister had to be replaced, whom would you recommend?'

Kit smiled wanly. The principle that diplomatic missions were to abstain from interfering in the internal affairs of the host nation was Geneva Convention bullshit. 'Well, there are only two horses in the race: Butler and Macmillan. And Macmillan, I am sure, would be the one more conducive to US interests.'

Foster was nodding approval. 'And,' said Allen, 'he has an American mother.' And Kit was pleased too. The most important part of his job was telling his bosses what they wanted to hear.

'Tell us more about Eden,' said Foster, leaning forward. For the first time, Kit was rocked by a whiff of stench from the Secretary of State's appalling bad breath. Was he a ghoul that ate corpses for breakfast?

'Sometimes, he gets pretty weird in cabinet.'

'Explicate.'

'Tears, tantrums, paranoid outbursts about his ministers ganging up against him. He also has an annoying habit of making late night phone calls. Eden is an inveterate worrier.'

'How do you know these things?'

Kit took a notebook out of his jacket pocket, wrote down the name of a minister he had compromised in a honey trap and passed it to the Secretary of State. The security situation was a sensitive one. But Kit wasn't worried about a British or Russian bug. The FBI carried out anti-bugging security measures on a routine basis with the best expertise and technology in the world. The problem was the FBI itself: the Bureau almost certainly left behind their *own* listening devices. Therefore, it was perfectly all right to discuss secrets and sensitive issues you didn't mind sharing with the FBI – but the identity of Kit's horny minister with strange preferences was not one of them.

Allen smiled when he saw the name on the note, then said, 'Can we move on to the press issue? There doesn't seem to have been much progress.'

'Well, sir...'

'We're not very happy, Kit.' The Secretary of State pulled a newspaper cutting from his jacket pocket and pushed it across the table. 'We don't want any more of this.'

Kit looked at the clipping. It was a front-page editorial about nuclear policy from Britain's best-selling tabloid. Each question was starkly highlighted: ARE WE TO SIT PASSIVELY WHILE GRAVE DECISIONS ARE TAKEN IN WASHINGTON? ARE WE TO WAIT FOR OUR FOREIGN POLICY TO COME TO US FROM ACROSS THE ATLANTIC? WHOSE FINGER DO WE WANT GUARDING OUR TRIGGER? AT LEAST LET IT BE BRITAIN'S OWN FINGER.

'What are we going to do about it?' The Secretary of State was still speaking. 'We're not asking you to subvert a British newspaper – we merely want the American point of view to be fairly represented.'

'The British press,' said Kit, 'is not an easy culture to influence.' He knew he couldn't say more: he could see Foster had gone into high-minded Methodist preacher mode. It would be a waste of time telling him how you could pop down to the King and Keys and buy any hack for a double whisky, but two hours later they write the opposite of what you want. They don't understand the principles of bribery. It was different in South America: you could buy a newspaper and the print works for the cost of a second-hand Ford.

Allen weighed in. 'Look, Kit, my brother must be thinking about what Cord Meyer has managed to pull off back in the States. Operation Mockingbird is a great success. Cord has more than four hundred journalists in the bag – and not just hacks, some of these guys are Pulitzer Prize winners. We think you could do something like that here.'

Kit knew it was impossible, but he didn't say a thing because you only tell them what they want to hear. He was saved further embarrassment by a knock on the door.

Foster looked up. 'Come in.'

A WAC, Women's Army Corps, cipher clerk entered carrying a telex message. 'A cable from Washington, sir.'

Foster took the message, looked at it and said, 'Thank you, corporal. It doesn't need an immediate reply.'

'Very good, sir.'

Kit watched Allen eye up the cipher clerk's calves and ankles as she left the room. The Director looked up and winked at Kit before turning to read the message.

Kit looked at the Dulles brothers while they pored over the cable. He realised he had not only sold his soul to the devil, he had financed the mortgage too. Why? MICE again: it wasn't the money and certainly not the ideology, but both 'E's' – ego and excitement. He liked the sense of power; even over life and death. It was an ugly vice, but an addictive one. Maybe if he'd been bigger framed and better at sport, maybe if he had been a successful lover, then he wouldn't be here.

Kit left his inner thoughts to eavesdrop on the hushed conversation between the Dulleses. The cable was from Eisenhower and it was about the forthcoming visit of Khrushchev and Bulganin to England. The President wanted the Secretary of State to 'sound out' the Foreign Secretary and Prime Minister on their agenda for the Soviet visit – and to show 'US disappointment and concern' over any suggestion of 'negotiations' that excluded Washington. Kit knew that things were heating up. There were serious differences between the two allies on Cold War policy. The Americans were for military and political containment; the British policy was for détente and diplomacy.

Allen Dulles looked up and smiled. 'By the way, Kit, thanks for those budget figures you sent us on British nuclear research. That was a fine piece of work. It confirms our views that the Brits have decided to go all out for a hydrogen bomb.'

'Which,' added Foster, 'is in our view a big mistake. Britain simply doesn't have the economic and industrial base to develop her own independent nuclear deterrent.'

'The best strategy,' said Allen, 'is to frighten the shit out of them about the Russian threat so that they'll beg us to move more of our own bombs here.'

The making of foreign policy, thought Kit, is not a pretty business. It's a selfish amoral trade. As an envoy, the interests of your closest ally don't mean a thing; your job, your only job, is to further your own country's national interest. You don't just fuck your enemies; you fuck your friends too.

'Kit,' said Allen Dulles, 'you seem lost in thought.'

'Sorry, sir.'

'Tell us more about Philby. From our side of the Atlantic it all seems most bizarre.'

'Philby,' Kit laughed. '*Everyone* knows that Kim is the third man: the press know it, Parliament knows it, Graham Greene knows it – who the hell do you think Harry Lime is supposed to be?'

It wasn't Philby, but the hypocrisy that made Kit laugh. While Nazi bombs were raining down on London in 1940, the Dulles brothers were corporate lawyers brokering lucrative investment deals for wealthy clients with the German war machine. Treason wasn't a word carved in stone, it was a dye that came out in the wash. Kit hid his feelings and smiled at the Director.

'It seems,' said Foster, 'that the only people who won't admit that Philby is a traitor are the British government. I've heard that he still works part-time for MI6. Astonishing.'

The Cambridge spy ring – Guy Burgess, Donald Maclean, allegedly Philby and at least two others who were still undercover – was the reason why London was the only US Embassy in the world that had FBI agents in permanent residence. The Burgess-Maclean spy scandal was a running sore that showed no signs of healing. On matters of high security, like nuclear weapons, US officials would never trust their British counterparts again – and the FBI was there to make sure of it.

The Secretary of State leaned forward with a grave face, the loose folds of flesh about his throat quivered as he spoke. 'Is Philby a pederast, a sodomite?'

To Kit's ear, the biblical expressions seemed echoes from the paternal pulpit of the Dulles childhood. 'Philby,' he replied, 'is definitely not homosexual. Who knows what he does in bed with his wife and girlfriends – I'm not sure it's relevant.'

The Secretary of State didn't seem satisfied. 'They are, you must admit, a strange bunch.'

Kit wondered whether if by 'they' he meant the spies, the sodomites or the British in general. He decided not to comment.

'Listen,' said Allen, 'we've got to have lunch with the Foreign

Secretary. But before we go, can you tell my brother about that party you went to in New York last year?'

Kit touched his ear and mouthed, 'Bugs.'

'Don't worry. Go on, tell us the whole story and don't leave anything out.'

Kit could see that Allen Dulles wanted to make mischief. The Director knew that their conversation was being recorded by the FBI and he wanted to create a little havoc. Kit didn't like playing the court jester, but this was part of the job too. 'I've got a classmate who's a lawyer married to an extremely wealthy heiress. They have a penthouse on the Upper East Side where they throw some wild parties. If I'm in town, I get invited. The people you meet at these parties are always rich, always glamorous – and usually beautiful. I feel like an intruder, but I like watching what goes on.' Kit whispered to Allen, 'Are you sure about this?'

'Go on, Kit, back to the party.'

'It was a good party, but I sensed something in the air – a hint of something sordid. As I implied, these parties often have an edge. I'm not a puritan, but...'

The Director nodded.

'I could tell there was something there that made me uneasy – and I don't just mean cannabis, cocaine or furtive fellatio in a cloakroom. These things are, in their own way, normal.'

'Not in the US Embassy, I hope,' said the Secretary of State.

'Not to my knowledge, sir.'

'Let him finish, Foster.'

'There were two young men there that didn't seem to belong – eighteen, maybe younger. They both had fine blond hair and bad teeth. I couldn't tell where they came from: they spoke only to each other, but there was something in their manner that was coarse. They kept to themselves in the shadows – and after a while I forgot they were there. I didn't like the atmosphere and thought about leaving, but then Porfirio Rubirosa turned up. I guessed it was him when I saw the Hispanic caterers begin to chop their knees with the sides of their hands.'

'Why were they doing that?' said Foster.

Allen sighed, 'You are one of life's innocents, Foster. It's Spanish sign language for someone with an enormous cock – in this case, Ambassador Rubirosa.'

'I see.'

In any case, Porfirio came over to say hello and we chatted amicably – in French, of course, to stop the caterers eavesdropping. We talked about racing cars and Trujillo, mostly racing cars. Trujillo, by the way, is developing a urine incontinence problem. Then Rubi was dragged away to meet the ladies – the women would have lynched me had I detained him any longer. So I was left all on my lonesome – and that's when I saw her.' Kit paused.

'Who was it?' asked Foster.

Kit searched for words. 'A mysterious woman, very mysterious.'

The Director sniggered. 'Did you fall in love?'

'No, sir.'

The older brother was getting restless. 'What's the point of this story?'

'Don't rush him, Foster.'

'She was wearing,' said Kit, 'a red dress with a low-cut neck, but her cleavage was hidden by a feather boa. I don't think she was drunk, but she didn't seem very steady on her high heels. She was wearing little black lacy gloves and black lacy stockings to match.'

'Was she beautiful?'

'No sir, she was not beautiful. But the fact that she was surrounded by such beautiful people made me feel sorry for her. She wasn't young either – late fifties. Now, my father used to say that a gentleman is someone who makes a fuss of such a woman, makes her feel the centre of attention – the young pretty ones don't need any help. Ergo, I went over to have a chat.'

'The model,' smiled Allen Dulles, 'of a US Foreign Service Officer.'

'She smiled when she saw me coming over, nice dimples. I filled her glass with champagne – Rubi for some reason had left me holding a three-quarters full bottle. I began polite small talk. She didn't say much; she just made little mewing noises. I wondered if she might be Brazilian. She had black eyes and, as far as I could tell, the skin beneath her make-up seemed dark.'

'An ageing Latina,' offered Allen, 'did you consider she might have been a relation of Rubirosa?'

'No, sir. For when I looked at her face – close up – I realised who she was. In fact, the truth of her identity hit me like a sucker punch in the solar plexus. I was out of breath and got the shakes.

The woman could see it too and it made her face turn hard – she knew that I knew.'

Allen Dulles was smiling behind his folded hands, enjoying the story. 'What did you do, Kit?'

'I wanted to run – out of the apartment, down twenty floors of service stairs across the Hudson River and all the way to the Canadian border. I knew something that I wasn't supposed to know. But I couldn't move. I just stood there holding the ball like a second string quarterback about to be trashed by some brick shit-house of a defensive end. I looked into those black eyes, saw the jowls tighten – and a hint of stubble under the face powder. Sir, I was no longer looking at a woman. I was face to face with J. Edgar Hoover, Director of the FBI.'

'Did Hoover know who you were?'

'I think so. He told me to fuck off and that I was playing out of my league. I thought it best to clear off. I said goodbye to my friends and left.'

'So you don't know what happened next?'

'I've since heard that the party turned pretty raunchy and that the blond boys gave Hoover a hand job – but I can't confirm that part.'

John Foster Dulles looked at his watch, told his brother that he'd won the bet and he owed him ten dollars. The meeting was over.

■

It was almost midnight when Kit left the embassy. He'd stayed until all the FBI personnel had signed out. The officer in charge of embassy night security was a marine captain from a steel town in Pennsylvania. He came from a working-class Polish immigrant family. The captain was sharp and bright – and wanted a career in the intelligence branch. Kit advised the officer to train as a linguist. He liked the young captain and had pulled a few strings to help him get posted to the Defense Department Language School for his next assignment. The captain was planning to study Vietnamese. He'd heard that Southeast Asia was a hot tip for the future: 'It's where all the action's going to be.' Kit thought he was right.

The captain was grateful to Kit and didn't hesitate to let him into the cramped basement closet where the FBI kept their tape machines. The marine officer knew that Kit could be more useful to his career than a couple of FBI agents who wore white socks with black suits and spoke with mid-Western accents. The tape was easy to find. It was still on the reel-to-reel machine, obviously the only recording the FBI had done that day. It also looked certain that the recording had been done automatically and unmonitored by a human listener – good. Kit pulled on a pair of surgical gloves to avoid leaving fingerprints and rewound the tape. He put on the headphones and then fast-forwarded to the Hoover conversation. He then cut out the incriminating section with scissors. Kit knew that the Dulleses would, to an extent, protect him, but he didn't want a lifetime of FBI harassment just because Allen Dulles wanted to piss off Hoover. Kit finished the job by splicing in blank tape to replace the section he had removed. He then rewound to the beginning and erased the rest of the tape, making it look as if the technician had made a mistake. Kit knew that the agent concerned, unsuspecting foul play, would then send the tape to a lab in Washington that had the technology to recover the lost recording. The lab would probably think that FBI London had done the splicing themselves. When the London jerks got the tape back and discovered the empty spliced-on bit, they would think that the lab had fucked up the tape and was trying to hide the fact. Kit smiled in anticipation of the bureaucratic shit-flinging fight that would follow.

■

When Kit got back to his flat it was one o'clock in the morning. Unlike the other embassy staff, he lived in a working-class borough of the East End. In fact, it was 'a manor' controlled by a well-known family of villains. It suited him perfectly. Kit paid 'the brothers' a few pounds a month 'to keep an eye on his place' – and they did so with a vengeance. The Manor was full of eyes and ears that instantly picked up anything out of place. That brand of surveillance and assurance of safety was better than anything Scotland Yard's Diplomatic Protection Squad could offer. But the villains and Cockney neighbours who kept an eye on Kit and his flat had no idea that he was a diplomat. As far as they were concerned he was François Laval, a Canadian shipping agent from Montreal.

The flat, in a rabbit warren of run-down streets, was a safe house that he paid for with his own money – in Canadian dollars. Kit's 'official address', where everyone at the embassy supposed he lived, was on the top floor of a Georgian terrace in Pimlico. He had sublet it to a junior doctor who, because of her hospital schedule, was seldom there. The doctor knew that she was paying less than half the going rent. In exchange, she had to follow a script if anyone turned up looking for Kit or made enquiries. She had to give the impression that she was a secret girlfriend – possibly one that was cheating on her husband – and pretend to be very embarrassed and a bit angry too. Meanwhile back in the East End, anyone who snooped around looking for 'the Canadian geezer' was in for a nasty surprise. The Montreal shipping agent was a perfect cover – it explained his American accent and fluent French – and his irregular comings and goings. And 'the brothers', of course, assumed the shipping agent stuff was 'pure porkie' and that Kit was a fellow villain engaged in smuggling.

Kit loved his bolthole. As soon as the got in, he took off his tie and draped it around a plaster death mask of Baudelaire that he'd found in a junk shop on the rue Saint Jacques, not far from the Panthéon. He poured a brandy and bade a toast to the pale mask of the French poet.

The room shook as a train rumbled past. Kit's flat backed on to a railway embankment. All the embassy staff on similar pay grades rented smart townhouses in Kensington, Chelsea or Hampstead, but Kit preferred the rough edges and accents of the East End. He liked to get away from people like himself: educated, arrogant, privileged assholes.

Most days, the couple in the downstairs flat were the only sane people he ever met. The husband was a reserve centre forward for a first division football club. He had to supplement his football wages by working as a draughtsman and a signwriter. He also played the clarinet and went to Labour Party meetings – mostly to complain about Gaitskell wanting 'to sell out the workers'. His wife, an immensely strong and shrewd woman, had become a seamstress in a fashion house after leaving school at fourteen. The proprietors noticed that she had an eye for colours and began to trust her with commissioning designs. Kit found the wife reserved and a little suspicious, but the man was always friendly and open. He called Kit 'old china'. What's that mean? China plate? Must be slang for mate. Kit smiled: 'We're mates.' They had two kids under five – and the wife was pregnant again.

Kit lit the gas fire and settled in an armchair with his brandy. He liked the neighbourhood; he even liked the brothers. Sometimes he met them for a drink at the Blind Beggar – they never let him buy a round. Maybe they were cultivating him as a future gang member. The thought was flattering. The brothers were bad guys, very bad, but certainly weren't the worst. A new gang was surfacing in Stratford who, it seemed to Kit, were truly evil. The brothers, of course, were evil too, but they compensated with a certain sleek beauty and style. The new gang had no beauty, no style: nothing but raw psychopathic cruelty. Their idea of a 'don't try that again warning' was to nail their victims to the floor with six-inch nails and cut off their toes with bolt cutters. In any case, their protection rackets were nudging too close to the Manor – and there were dark rumours down at the Blind Beggar.

There was something about dangerous men that was queerly thrilling. Kit found this thrill in the presence of the two younger brothers, both of whom were boxers of almost professional standard. When you looked into their eyes there was nothing there; nothing but black bottomless wells of emptiness. Not the faintest glint of fear, humour or doubt. If they decided they had to kill you, they were going to kill you. Asking for mercy or forgiveness was as pointless as feeding a dead cat. Kit was beginning to understand that the Brits were a hard people – capable of violence as well as endurance. But they were quiet about it. North and South Americans were violent too, but in a more affable way. Once, when he was a boy, a drunk had stumbled from a bar in Managua and embraced him hard. The drunk breathed rum fumes into his face and spoke Spanish with a strong Nica accent. He whispered into Kit's ear: 'What's the difference, *chico*, between cutting up a gringo and cutting up an onion?'

Kit was frightened. He looked around for his parents, but they were buying something from a flower stall a hundred yards away. He was so terrified that he feared wetting himself. He tried not to tremble and to be polite. 'I don't know, *señor*, what is the difference?'

'When you cut up a gringo, you don't cry.' The drunk then threw his head back and roared with laughter before disappearing back into the bar.

It was a turning point. Ever since that day, Kit had felt deep shame. He had nearly peed himself: he was a coward. When he went back to boarding school, he gave up cross-country running for American football and learned to box. He had to prove that he wasn't a coward after all. And volunteering for the OSS had been part of the same pattern. Kit knew deep down that it wasn't just the Kennedy confrontation that had caused him to volunteer for the Agency – he had been heading that way in any case.

The induction course for new agents was just as much about forming the minds of the recruits as it was about imparting spy-craft. You were first told that the United States government will *never* 'order or authorise assassination in a clandestine opera-tion'. Kit remembered the intense look on the instructor's face as he said those very words. The instructor then paused and examined the eager upturned faces of America's future spy elite. 'And, gentlemen,' he said, 'that – along with "the cheque is in the post" and "I promise I won't come in your mouth" – is one of the world's three biggest lies.' What the ban on assassination really meant was that you *never* write anything down. All planning and coordination must be mental and deniable.

Later they learned to refer to killings as 'wet ops'. The ideal assassination, of course, was one that could be passed off as an accident. And the most efficient form of 'accident' is a fall of more than seventy-five feet. ('Elevator shafts, stairwells, unscreened windows and bridges will serve. Bridge falls into water are not reliable. Ideally, try to ensure that no wound or condition not attributable to the fall is discernible after death.')

Kit's first attempt at a 'wet job' took place in Germany during his last posting. Horst had turned out to be a double agent: dou-ble in the sense that he seemed to be taking money from both the Stasi and the CIA. It was impossible to turn him over to the West German authorities: a court process would have compro-mised agents in the field. Kit and a major from the US Army Intelligence Corps decided to take Horst for a drive along the Rhine in Horst's own car at two in the morning. The German's hands and feet were bound and he must have thought they were planning to kill him by making it look like he had fallen asleep and driven over a cliff – and he was determined to make sure it didn't happen that way. As they were driving along an auto-bahn, Horst's car sputtered to a stop. 'Fuck,' shouted Kit, turning to Horst in the back seat, 'your fucking gasoline gauge doesn't work.'

Horst smiled: he had been waiting for Kit to find out.

'What are we going to do?' said the major.

'Listen, Roger, would you mind walking back to the village to chase up some gas – or a telephone – while I look after this piece of shit.'

Kit listened to the major's feet as they crunched away into the darkness. After five minutes Kit got out of the car to have a pee. Just as he started pissing, a voice began to shout from the other side of the autobahn. '*Horst, kommt hier – macht schnell!*' Somehow Horst had managed to undo the ropes that were binding his feet and hands. Before Kit could even do up his flies, Horst was out of the car and running towards the voice.

Kit shouted, 'Fuck,' and took off running after his prisoner. He was still ten feet behind when Horst climbed over the autobahn guardrail to get across the central reservation to reach whoever was calling to him from the opposite lanes. Except there wasn't a central reservation: they were on a viaduct. Neither Kit nor his German counterpart from the BfV, the West German FBI, heard the body land on the gravel streambed two hundred and fifty feet below. They waited for five seconds; then the BfV colleague called across the dark void. 'Kit, you still want me to drive around to pick up you and Roger?'

'Yes, please.'

It was textbook perfection. The police and local press reported it as a 'tragic accident' – motorist ran out of fuel and fell to his death while seeking help. Two days later workmen were busy raising the barriers to prevent such an accident from happening again. There were, however, other repercussions. Kit's cover was blown – and he was never sure how. In the end, there were more deaths and Kit had to leave Germany – which was one of the reasons he preferred sleeping in a safe house in the East End.

■

'How long is Brian going to be away?'

'I don't know.' Jennifer looked out to sea and the wind blew a twist of hair across her mouth. 'He couldn't say for certain – at least a week, maybe two.'

Kit skipped back as a breaker crashed and surged over the shingle. The wind was blowing the tops off the waves. 'Bracing,' he said.

'I love it. It clears the head.' Jennifer pointed to a black hull that was rising and plunging against the stiff south-westerly gusts.

Kit tightened his jacket against the cold wind. 'What's this desolate place called again?'

'Dunwich. It used to be one of England's biggest cities, but it fell into the sea. Coastal erosion.'

'It is spooky here.' Kit suddenly halted and pointed to the top of the sandy red cliff, 'Look at that.'

'Oh, no!' Jennifer turned away and shut her eyes. 'I'm not going to look.'

Kit continued to regard the ribcage of a human skeleton that hung like a tree root out of the cliff face. 'Should we tell anyone?'

'No, it happens all the time. It's the last remaining corner of the churchyard. One more winter of cliff-fall and all the graves will be gone.'

'When Caddie was in her first year at medical school, they gave her a brown wooden box containing an entire skeleton. None of the bones were stuck together – it was like a jigsaw puzzle.'

'I remember. She used to ask me to pick bones at random out of the box and hold them up so she could guess what they were. I hated it – but I wasn't going to show her I was chicken.'

'Remember that time she took us to the medical museum at Johns Hopkins – all those bottled foetuses...'

'Please, Kit, that's enough... not at a time like this.'

Kit wondered what she meant, but didn't ask.

'Have you got much more work to do?' said Jennie, changing the subject.

'I've got to go back to the airbase tomorrow – boring ODA stuff.'

'ODA?'

'Office of the Defense Attaché. It's not even my job – the assistant attaché who should be doing it has the flu.'

'Have you got to count the atom bombs?'

'God no, it would take too long. No, I've got to give a talk on the Status of Visiting Forces Agreement.' Kit paused and pretended to look cross. 'Who told you we've got atom bombs in the UK?'

'No one, just a guess. So what is this visiting forces thing?'

'It has to do with legal jurisdiction in matters concerning US military and indigenous personnel.'

'Indigenous personnel?'

'That's anyone who isn't an American. In this case, the British.'

'So Brian is an "indigenous personnel".'

'That's right.'

'And when I have my ba...' Jennifer stopped and faked a cough to cover her verbal slip.

Kit took in what she had almost said, but pretended not to have noticed. Nonetheless, the half-spoken word hit him like a hammer between the eyes. He began to shake all over, but hoped that if Jennifer noticed she would think he was shivering because of the cold.

'So what does the agreement mean for the poor Brits?' said Jennifer.

'Well, if an American airman runs over a dog or robs a shop or rapes a girl, he can only be handed over for trial in a British court if we agree.'

'That doesn't sound fair.'

'Well, in most cases we would hand him over, but we keep a get-out-of-jail-free card, just in case. Like my own legal immunity as a diplomat.'

'Have you had to use it yet?'

'All the time – I'm the biggest villain you've ever met.'

'Hmm, I thought you had a wicked heartless side.' Jennifer looked at him sideways. 'I bet that you can really be naughty when you put your mind to it.'

'I don't have to put my mind to it – it comes naturally.'

'What are your plans for this evening?'

'I've got a room in the BOQ at the Woodbridge airbase. I'll probably eat in the officer's club or wander into the town.'

'That sounds awful. Let me cook you dinner. You can stay. I'll make up a bed in the spare room.'

'It's too much trouble. I'll be fine.'

'And I'd be very disappointed.'

'Well, I've got to be at the airbase pretty early.' Kit felt his heart pounding. He didn't want to stay with her: it was too dangerous.

'I'm an early riser too – and it's only a twenty-minute drive to the base. I insist you stay.'

'Thank you.' Kit kissed his cousin's forehead. 'I will stay, but I might be a bit late. I have to go back to clear something up.'

'I bet it's those indigenous personnel again.'

'They do get in the way, you know. See you soon.' Kit blew a kiss and hurried back to his car.

∎

The sign, RAF Bentwaters, as well as the Union Jack on the flag-pole, were polite sops to the host nation's sovereignty. The commanding officer was also British: an RAF Wing Commander on the verge of retirement. The Wing Commander was the sole occupant of an out-of-the-way office where he spent his mornings tying flies – nymphs, emergers, hoppers – for trout and salmon. In the afternoon he pushed all the office furniture to one side and practised his putt, trying to achieve that smooth pendulum stroke that means more consistency. Few Americans at the base even knew that the Wing Commander existed and fewer had ever seen anything like him. For aside from this splendid native warrior with Brylcreemed hair and handlebar moustaches, the base was totally American down to bowling alley, crew cuts, baseball diamonds and soda fountains. Kit hated the place, but had business to do.

The intelligence section was located in an underground – 'nuclear proof' – bunker. The military police sergeant passed Kit's ID under an infrared scanner and required him to sign the visitor's book. He then phoned through and a second later the door buzzed and the bolts slid back. The S2, a lieutenant colonel with a Texas accent, had laid the freshly developed photographs on the briefing table. The air reconnaissance section had taken the photos during a brief break in the weather. 'Poor visibility,' drawled the S2, 'is always a dawg-gone problem in this part of the world, but we done got them.'

Kit easily recognised the main features of river, marsh, shingle spit and sea, but the details he wanted most required expert interpretation. He found the part of the Orford Ness AWRE site that interested him most and moved the viewing device into place. The lens magnified the photo details and created a three-dimensional effect. 'As I said before, colonel, it's the excavations and construction in this grid square here that are causing wonder and concern. What's your opinion?'

The S2 opened a file and took out an enlargement of the area concerned. 'As you can see, sir, they're digging down deep, but they're building up berms around them too. It's not going to be a nuclear bunker like the one we're in now.'

'What are they building then?'

'Well, sir, I had to call in some help from an engineer that worked at Los Alamos and on Bikini Atoll too. As I always say, there's no sense in buying a dawg, if you're going to bark yourself.'

'What did the dog say?'

'That dawg sure knows his stuff – he said I was right. He said these structures are not intended to – and would not – withstand a nuclear strike from the outside. Then he said that these structures are meant to withstand a nuclear blast from the *inside*. They are what's known in the nuclear testing trade as containment bunkers.'

Kit bit his lip and stared at the photo. He felt the delicious haemostasis of an adrenalin rush. That sheer bliss minute when source confirms source; that moment when all the diverse pieces of an intelligence jigsaw suddenly slot into place – and prove what you always knew by creative intuition to be absolutely true. 'I'll need these photos.' Kit had stuffed them in his briefcase before the S2 could protest or ask for a receipt. Before leaving the base, Kit sweet-talked a waitress at the officer's club into giving him a large bag of ice: he had two bottles of '47 Montrachet that needed chilling.

■

Kit had guessed correctly again. It was a white wine meal: *moules marinières* followed by grilled cod that had been long-lined off Aldeburgh. He wasn't surprised to see Jennifer limit herself to a single glass of Montrachet, but he wasn't going to let on that he knew the reason why. 'Come on, Jen,' he said trying to refill her glass, 'you've always been a girl that likes a drink.'

'No, one is quite sufficient.'

'I know what it is, Jennie. You're afraid of becoming a lush like your mom.'

'That's a cruel thing to say.'

'I'm sorry. I should be more sensitive.' Kit paused and smiled. 'Is something wrong? You're looking a little pale.'

'Kit, stop it! I'm fine, blooming in fact.'

'You've got a secret.'

'I've got lots of secrets.'

'Last time we met, you said you hated secrets.'

'Kit, you're more than a dog with a bone – you're a dog who knows where all the other bones are buried.' Jennifer paused and smiled. 'That's why they made you a spy?'

Kit wasn't surprised that she knew, but hoped that it was a secret kept within the family. 'Does Brian know?'

'No – and I would never tell him.'

Well, Jennie since you know my secret – along with your dad, your mom and all the liquor store staff in Talbot County – why don't you tell me yours?'

'It's only because Brian should be the first to know.' Jennifer smiled. 'But you must know anyway.'

Kit clinked glasses. 'Congratulations.'

'It's taken us a long time.'

Kit remembered a crude joke that a doctor friend used to tell about giving advice to obtuse couples wanting to start a family – but it wasn't a joke she would like.

'So, Kit, you must keep it a secret.'

Kit leaned forward and kissed her forehead. 'I'm very happy for you – it's wonderful news.'

'Well, maybe I will have a little more wine.' Jennifer poured half a glass. 'This is a lovely wine. Where did you get it?'

'It's a present to you Jennie, from the American taxpayer. I stole it from the embassy.'

'Couldn't you get in trouble?'

'When I get strapped into an electric chair next to the Rosenbergs, it won't be for stealing plonk.'

'Don't joke. That trial made me sick.'

Kit looked away. The Rosenberg trial didn't only make him sick; it frightened him.

Jennifer put a hand on her stomach as if trying to caress her unborn child. 'The Rosenbergs had children, little ones. I wonder what they said to them.'

Kit hadn't been a player in the Rosenberg stitch-up, but he had seen a secret CIA memo suggesting that the Rosenbergs have their death and prison sentences commuted in exchange for making a public statement condemning the Soviet Union as an anti-Semitic state that aimed to prosecute and exterminate all Jews under its jurisdiction. Lies weren't lies when you called them 'psychological warfare opportunities'.

Jennifer looked at her cousin through the candle flame. 'Why are you being so quiet?'

'Because I'm ashamed.'

She reached forward and put her hand on his. 'I know about you, Kit. I know more about you than you think.'

'Then why am I so ashamed?'

'You're ashamed about not being able to tell the truth about yourself – or anything.'

'Maybe I hate the truth more than the lies.'

'Like why don't you have a girlfriend. Oh, Kit, you've turned so red.'

'Why don't you shut up?'

Jennifer picked up a breadcrumb and put it on her plate.

'I'm sorry I snapped at you.'

'Have some more wine.'

Kit looked at his cousin's hands as she filled his glass. Her bright red fingernails reflected in the candlelight and enhanced the rich gold of the wine. Jennifer wore little makeup, but her toe-nails and fingernails were always perfectly groomed and painted a deep vermilion – as if stained with the blood of prey. It was, of course, unbearably erotic.

'Do you like Brian?' she said.

The question caught Kit off guard. 'I really like him. He's extremely bright, very talented and very in love with you.'

'He likes you too.'

'You said he was out of the country. Any place interesting?'

'He hasn't gone abroad – he's at sea. They go off quite often, but I don't know what they do.'

'Didn't Churchill call it, "rum, sodomy and the lash"?'

'I'm sure that Brian is not inclined in that direction.' Jennifer laughed. 'I'm *very* sure of that.'

Kit felt the knife twist and poured himself another glass of wine. At the same time, another corner of his brain filed 'frequent sea trips' under 'query'. 'I hope he's on warmer waters than the North Sea.'

'I don't think they told him where he was going. It all seemed very hush-hush.'

'Does Brian tell you much about his work?'

'He does tell me some things, maybe too many things.'

Kit covered her hand with his. 'Listen, Jennifer, you must never tell anyone that. Not a word. Governments are crazy and para-noid about the bomb business – anyone involved in a project, or anyone near to those involved, is a suspect. You don't want to end up like the Rosenbergs.'

'Kit, I want you to listen,' Jennifer paused, 'I don't like what Brian does, but there isn't a way out.'

'I know.' Kit knew that Brian had one of those jobs that were for life. You couldn't get out because you knew too much. Likewise, there was no such thing as an ex-spy: your brain, your memory was an archive full of secrets. If you tried to run away they locked you up or killed you.

'I can't ask Brian, but I can ask you.'

'Maybe you shouldn't.'

'Tell me, Kit, what are they doing on Orford Ness?'

'I don't know. Why should I?

'Don't lie, you do know.'

Kit looked at his cousin. He was so hungry with desire that he would have told her anything – even for a chaste kiss. He tried to recover: his job was to make *her* a traitor. 'OK, the real answer is that I'm not sure what they're doing, but I've got some ideas.' He paused. He was afraid to look through the candle flame; afraid that he would throw himself babbling at her feet like a pagan before an idol.

'What is it, Kit?' Her voice was dry like rustling paper.

'They shouldn't be doing that shit here... not in England, not even in the Australian desert. It's too dangerous.'

'Brian says it isn't dangerous – they haven't got live warheads.'

'Oh, does he say that?'

Jennifer touched her throat: it was a nervous gesture she made when worried. 'What do you mean?'

'I can't say exactly – we haven't got enough information. But the problem isn't just Orford Ness – their entire policy is stupid...'

'Which policy, Kit, which one exactly?'

Kit dug his nails hard into his palm. He shouldn't tell her; it was giving away too much, but it might help win her over. 'The fusion weapon, Jennie, the fucking hydrogen bomb – the one that blasts seven hundred Hiroshimas in one go.'

Jennifer nodded: she knew. 'I wish,' she said, 'that Britain would turn into a little neutral country – like Sweden or Finland – and just watch all this insanity from the sidelines. Instead of bombs, we could have art centres, cycle paths, poetry clubs, nursery schools,' the tears were running down her cheeks, 'and fertility clinics.'

Kit stroked her hair and wiped away her tears. 'Maybe, Jennie, maybe some day.' If only, he thought, if only that were true. If Britain ever tried to become a neutral country Washington would sell off sterling and wreck the economy.

Jennifer finished drying her eyes and handed the handkerchief back to Kit. 'I'm all right now. Sorry, I was silly.'

'You're not silly. But maybe we shouldn't complain about US Foreign Policy. It's the fucking family business. The company profits paid our school fees and bought your first party frock.'

Jennifer smiled. 'I thought our money came from bootlegging and body snatching.' The smile faded. 'It's so frustrating – nothing changes anything. If Brian's project fails, the Americans will just move their own H-bombs into Britain. Won't they?'

Kit didn't answer. This outcome was precisely what Eisenhower and the Dulles brothers intended – and his job was to help bring it about. 'I wish,' said Kit in a half whisper, 'that I could just run away.'

'Why don't you? How could I help?'

'I haven't said this to anyone. A few years ago I wanted to quit the service, but Dad convinced me to stay. He said that if all the sane sensible people left, the asylum would end up completely in the hands of the lunatics. I thought that he was exaggerating, but I now know there are people making nuclear policy this very day who in any other walk of life would end up heavily sedated on a high security ward swapping cigarette butts with lobotomised child murderers.' The awful thing, thought Kit, was that his father had been right. He had to stay in government service: you could only change things – or make things *less bad* from inside. It was a bitter birthright. 'You know what, Jennie, we pay the price for being different.'

'Different from what?'

'From other American families – those no-neck oafs who chase the dream from one coast to the other. The ones who just graze and get fat and have brats that graze and get even fatter. We're not like that – we're professional players.'

'I don't want to be.'

'You can't escape, Jennie, you're chained to the gun carriage.'

'That's what Dad used to say every time we had to pack up and follow him to Manila or Panama or Guatemala.' Jennifer paused. 'You want something from me, Kit, what is it?'

'I want you to spy on your husband.'

'Are you serious?'

'Very.'

'You really want me to spy on Brian?'

'Yes.'

'You're actually looking at me – the first time this evening.'

Kit knew what she meant. He was notorious for avoiding eye contact. He had been often told off for it during his training: they said it made an agent look shifty and furtive. He looked away again.

'I can't believe you're serious. I couldn't,' she said, 'do anything like that. You know so little about women. No wonder you don't have a girlfriend.'

'You think I don't like girls.' Kit reddened. He could tell that Jennifer was looking at him in a strange way. He felt her leg press against his under the table; she was teasing, taunting. Then her leg was gone: maybe it was an accident.

'Have you ever recruited a woman spy before?'

'No.'

'That's obvious. You need lessons. So let's start again, why oh why would a happily married woman – very much in love with her husband…'

Kit tried not to flush. He wondered if she was trying to hurt him on purpose.

'…why would such a woman be tempted to spy on her spouse?'

'Because her husband is a scientist in charge of a nuclear research project that could result in the death of her own unborn child among millions of other victims – and cancers and genetic deformities for the lucky survivors.' Kit looked at his cousin. 'Sorry, Jennie, that sounds really corny.'

'No, Kit, you sound sane.' Jennifer leaned forward and touched her cousin's hand. 'Listen, I know how serious the situation is – but I just want peace – for myself.'

'Forgive me,' he said. 'I was wrong for asking. Pretend it didn't happen.'

'Don't apologise. I hate the thing on Orford Ness. I want it to go away – but I can't betray my husband. Now I sound corny.'

'Corny, but sincere.' He paused. 'Damn, I'd almost forgotten – I've got a present for you.' Kit got up, returned with a package wrapped in brown paper and handed it to Jennifer. 'I don't think the bookseller in Charing Cross realised how valuable this is.'

Jennifer cut the string and folded back the paper. '*The Portrait of a Lady*.' She leaned forward to kiss Kit. 'You know this is my favourite novel.'

'And a first edition too. The dealer had two of them – but I'm being selfish and keeping the other one for myself.'

Jennifer caressed the book and the leather binding. 'It's priceless.'

'You know, Jennie, I was just thinking, these first editions are so rare, they would make ideal code books.'

'Stop it, Kit. Can't you just appreciate a rare book as a thing of beauty?'

'Codes are beautiful too. When you worked in the cipher section, did you ever use the polyalphabetic tri-graph?'

'Yes, but I can't remember how they work?'

'Dead simple – and the perfect code too, totally unbreakable if you haven't got the decryption key.'

'Are you still trying to recruit me?'

'Not really, but I remember how much you liked cipher work.'

'I always liked decoding – it cleared the brain. I can just about remember the polyalphabetic – you used it with one-time pads.'

'That's what you are *supposed* to use. The trouble with one-time pads is that they kind of give the game away. Ordinary Joes don't walk around with flash paper pads containing randomly generated letters in groups of four. If the local '*policie*' find one of those in your possession, it's off to the torture chamber. Ergo, I prefer books – provided they have at least three hundred and sixty-six pages.'

'One for each day of the year.'

'You'd make an excellent spy.'

'So page one is your encryption code for 1 January.'

'No, that's too obvious. It's better to begin the year with a date that's only known to the agent and his handler – say, when one of them lost his or her virginity.'

'The date would only be secret if they lost their virginities with each other.'

Kit smiled. 'I hadn't thought of that. So, as far as we're concerned, we'd better find another date. When's the baby due?'

'The beginning of September.'

'Good, so page one of *The Portrait of a Lady* will be 1 September. But if we were encoding a message for today we would need to know how many days have passed since 1 September – our New Year's, so to speak.'

Jennifer fetched a calendar from the dresser and counted. 'Two hundred and three.'

'Good, let's go to page 203 and find our encryption key.' Kit found the page and laughed. 'How serendipitous.'

'What does it say?'

'"She would do the thing for him, and he would not have waited in vain."'

Jennifer smiled. 'Sometimes I think you're the devil.'

'No, but he pays my salary. Now, let's say that one of the "jays" was caught in flagrante with the French *assistante* at St Ignatius School for Boys.'

'Unlikely.'

'True, but all the more reason to send a secret message to the Curia Generalizia. My job now is to encrypt the name of the unfortunate Fifi.'

'Mademoiselle La Touche.'

'That's the one. To encode FIFI, I use the first four letters on our page of the day which are SHEW.' Kit took a notebook and pencil from his coat pocket. 'There are twenty-six letters in the alphabet, which means that F is five.'

'You're wrong, F is the sixth letter.'

'No, my dear, *you* are wrong. You forgot that A is zero – so B is one and F ends up five. A lot of recruits make that mistake. At any rate, when you encrypt, you add the letters – S, eighteen plus F, five equals twenty-three and the twenty-third letter is X. Likewise, H plus I equals fifteen or P, E plus F becomes J – but after that we have a problem, W plus I comes out as thirty.'

'And there isn't a thirtieth letter of the alphabet.'

'Which means you have to loop back to the beginning – A is twenty-six, B is twenty-seven, therefore thirty is E.' Kit wrote down the figures to demonstrate the calculation.

Jennifer looked at the notebook. 'The encrypted message you send me would be XPJE.'

'Exactly.'

'How do I decrypt to discover the name of the poor La Touche girl?'

'You subtract the key – SHEW – from the encrypted message. In other words, X, twenty-three minus S, eighteen becomes five or F.'

Jennifer took the pencil. 'But when E, four has W, twenty-two deducted you end up with minus eighteen.'

'When you have a minus sum, you have to add twenty-six, thus minus eighteen becomes eight.'

'And letter eight is I – and that makes FIFI! This is fun!'

'Good. The beauty of the polyalphabetic cipher is that the encryption code changes every day.'

'What happens when you run out of pages?'

'We choose another book – *Madame Bovary* or *Anna Karenina*, say.'

'I prefer Isabel Archer, she didn't commit adultery.'

'How can you be sure?'

'She wasn't like that, Isabel was a good girl.' Jennifer stroked the novel. 'I do love this book.' She opened it to the last page and read, '"She had not known where to turn; but she knew now. There was a very straight path..."' Jennifer looked up. 'But the ending is left up in the air. The book doesn't tell us where Isabel's "straight path" is heading.'

'I think I know.'

'No, Kit, you don't know.'

'Let me help you clear things away.'

Just as Kit was about to go off to the guest bedroom, Jennifer said, 'What do you want?'

He looked at her. She was facing him squarely. There was nothing coy or seductive in her stance: it was completely open and honest. Kit looked away; he was frightened. 'I... I don't know.'

'I wish I could help you.'

Kit knew that he had said the wrong thing, that he had missed something and that it wasn't going to come around again.

When Jennifer spoke again, her voice had changed. 'I might send you a few messages just to see if the cipher works. At least, I can *play* at being your spy.'

■

When Kit woke he could hear Jennifer bustling about in the kitchen. He looked at his watch: it was just after six. He hoped it was like that when Brian was there too. He hated the thought of her lingering in bed to please him. Why, he thought, do men wake up with erections: the dawn hard-on? Were they visited by succubi and incubi who teased them in the dark watches of the night? As he dressed he tried to remember his dream: something about Jennifer's oldest brother. Not just rescuing him and getting him to the airfield in time, but actually digging up the body and bringing it back to life. There were different versions of the dream before – but they always ended the same. The brother, Peter, always went floppy and dead again – like an inflatable dinghy with a bad leak – before he could get him back to Jennifer. If he could only get Peter home in time, Jennifer could pump him up again. Kit wondered if it had something to do with early morning erections. It all seemed Freudian as hell.

Kit washed, dressed and went to the kitchen. A big kettle was gurgling on the Rayburn and toast was browning under a gas grill. 'I believe,' said Jennifer, 'that you've become a tea drinker.'

'Yes, I've gone native. I go to soccer games too.'

'Goodness, they might have to reclassify you as an indigenous personnel.'

'We try to blend in with the locals.'

'Whom do you support?'

'I haven't decided yet. I went to see Queen's Park Rangers play Ipswich, and I much preferred Ipswich. Maybe I could watch them when I come up here. What about Brian?'

'He's a Manchester United fan – tribal loyalty.'

'I can't stand them.'

Jennifer poured the tea. 'Isn't it odd, a couple of Americans like us talking about English soccer teams?'

'Proletarian sport is one of the nicest things about their culture. I could become obsessed by it.'

'Kit, when you say things like that you sound an even worse snob than you are.'

'I must change.'

'Damn.'

'What's wrong, Jennie?'

'No eggs.'

'I don't need an egg.'

'But I insist. I won't be long – the man at the end of the lane keeps hens. Five minutes.'

Before he could protest, Jennifer was gone. But as soon as she was out of the house, Kit was searching the marital bedroom. He checked all the drawers for documents, diaries or address books. Not a thing. He went to the wardrobe and searched the pockets of Brian's suits and jackets, but there was nothing other than old ticket stubs and petrol receipts. He then began to check the chest of drawers where Jennifer kept her things. He opened the top drawer: it was where his cousin kept her stockings and underwear. He gently extracted articles of the most intimate lingerie and buried his face in the fine silk. He wanted to breathe the most private and secret essences of Jennifer into his lungs, but there was so little time.

As he returned Jennifer's underwear to the drawer, Kit noticed some other things lurking at the back – half hidden. They were not 'normal' or even conventionally 'sexy' articles of underclothing. The strange apparel and other objects belonged to a completely different order of things. 'My God,' he said, 'my God. Who would have thought this?' At first, Kit was shocked to his core. Then he was oddly excited by the discovery – and then ashamed that it did excite him. He closed the drawer: it was like closing the first half of his life.

Chapter Four

When Kit got back to London, he found it difficult to get Jennifer out of his mind. Her face kept materialising like an apparition on official documents and memos. It was a long day that had ended with a late-night clandestine meeting with the cabinet minister he had compromised in a honey trap. The woman in question was stunningly beautiful, but needed elocution lessons. She had also begun 'dating' someone on the other side – bad news.

Once again, it was past midnight when Kit got back to his flat. He'd had to stay late for a top secret briefing about the results of the most recent hydrogen bomb test in the Pacific. The briefing had been given by Sterling Cole, Chairman of the Joint Congressional Committee on Atomic Energy. Cole's message was chilling. The H-bomb test on Bikini had been three times more powerful than the scientists had predicted. The crew of a Japanese fishing boat – 'eighty-five miles outside the declared danger zone' – had been afflicted with serious radiation sickness. After Cole finished, the press attaché gave a talk about how important it was to stop 'H-bomb panic' from spreading through the British press and to the public at large.

Kit lit the gas fire that had been installed in the old Victorian hearth. It hissed and spat under the mantelpiece before it settled down. There were still London homes with coal fires – and the fumes still killed. The Great Smog of 1952 killed over four thousand Londoners in ten days; there were even cattle asphyxiated at Smithfield Market. But the Clean Air Act was on its way – those coal fires were going to be history. Pity in a way, thought Kit. He liked to think of Falstaff fondling a wench at the Boar's Head warmed by a 'sea coal' fire. Four thousand Londoners killed by coal smoke. How many would an air burst over St Paul's finish off?

An H-bomb over St Paul's wouldn't just melt Wren's great bronze dome: it would vaporise it. In one second the temperature of the blast would reach a hundred million degrees Celsius. A fireball, a mile in diameter, would unleash a wall of wind sweeping all before it at seven hundred and fifty miles per hour. Cars, trucks and buses would be tossed into the air like autumn leaves – tyres alight and petrol tanks exploding. Gulls in flight over the Thames estuary would drop from the sky in flames. Ten seconds later, the suction from the blast would reverse the wind direction and create a vast mushroom cloud. A super-heated three-hundred-mile per hour hurricane would boil the Thames into a cauldron of steam. At three miles distance clothing would burst into flames or melt. No living thing would survive within sixty-five square miles. That was one H-bomb – and yet Kit knew that London was targeted with eight.

And London was, in megaton-speak, 'lucky'. Kit remembered a Pentagon briefing that had started as surreal, then quickly took off into the absolute *un*real. It began turning funny when General Curtis LeMay pointed to a map of Moscow pinpointed with four hundred H-bomb targets. *Four-fucking-hundred!* A junior White House staffer had the temerity to ask why. Kit remembered how LeMay puffed his cigar and smiled. 'The Russian bear's a big beast. We need,' said the general, 'to take his leg off right up to his testicles. On second thought, let's take off his testicles too.' Kit remembered how fond his father was of quoting St Thomas Aquinas. It wasn't only a matter of *Jus ad Bellum*, but of fighting a 'Just War' with 'Just Means'. If, thought Kit, twelfth-century ignoramuses were able to work that one out, what does that say about us? When did our own savagery begin? Sherman marching through Georgia? Hamburg and Dresden? Hiroshima and Nagasaki? When did deliberately killing civilians become an acceptable means to achieve military and political goals? Collective punishment. You can't get the top brass, so you kill little kids instead. Why is it OK for us to do it, but not the other guys?

Kit poured himself another glass of brandy. None of those qualms mattered. He was a servant of the State and had a job to do. He remembered how the DCI had faulted him for not having recruited any journalists to spout the American line. It was a subtle game. The strategy was to target progressive and centre-left publications. No sense in preaching to the converted. An anti-American paper changing its tune was the more effective form of propaganda. And you shouldn't ignore book reviewers and publishers either – they were often strapped for cash and vulnerable. Good reviews for 'good' writers and vice versa. Sometimes it verged on the ridiculous. His predecessor had 'subsidised' a London house to publish a Swahili translation of the complete poetry of T.S. Eliot. If that doesn't stop Africa from going communist, nothing will.

■

Kit went to the bedroom to undress. The walls were bare, except for a statue on a plaque of the Virgin Mary. Pepita, the Indian woman who looked after Kit when the family had been stationed in Managua, had given him the statue. She was his favourite of several nannies. The statue was pure Latino tat. The Virgin was painted with luminous white so that her image glowed in the dark. A symbol of purity. Pepita would always say, 'Remember, Kit, she is always looking at you.' A few years later, Kit realised that Pepita's words were a veiled warning about masturbation. The warning worked. Puberty arrived as a horny storm, but Kit was always dissuaded from self-love by the glowing nocturnal image of Pepita's Virgin. *She's watching.* Then somehow, the Virgin became an object of desire and that desire became manifest in the person of his cousin, Jennifer. Jennifer – body, mind, soul, voice – became Kit's Holy Virgin. And then Jennifer went with another man – and did strange things. Kit poured another brandy, a final one he hoped. It was all complicated in a way that he could never explain to anyone, could never explain to himself.

Kit stared into the mirror above the chest of drawers. His eyes were bloodshot and his face had the drawn look of a monk in an ascetic order. Maybe that was his role: a modern Knight Templar serving the Holy State. But he wasn't any good. He hadn't recruited a single journalist or publisher. And worse, he hadn't spotted Burgess and Maclean. He'd worked closely with both of them when they were stationed in Washington, but hadn't detected a whiff of treachery. Sure, Guy was a queer and a drunk, but that isn't particularly unusual in the trade. And Maclean, a devoted family man, seemed an even less likely traitor. Kit still blamed himself. He had been briefed about them, but he trusted his intuition and his intuition was shit. A year after he defected, Donald Maclean made a statement to the press. Kit kept a copy of it taped to the corner of the mirror: *I am haunted and burdened by what I know of official secrets, especially by the content of high-level Anglo-American conversations. The British Government, whom I have served, have betrayed the realm to Americans. I wish to enable my beloved country to escape from the snare which faithless politicians have set. I have decided that I can discharge my duty to my country only through prompt disclosure of this material.*

∎

As Kit sat over his morning tea and toast, he opened his first-edition copy of *The Portrait of a Lady* to the appropriate page. He found a piece of lined paper and wrote out the message in standard four-letter groups for encoding. IWAN TTOB UYAS MALL BOAT TWEN TYTO TWEN TYFI VEFE ET. He then copied out the encryption key for the day from the novel: ONES COUS INAL WAYS PRET ENDE DTOH ATEO NESH USBA ND. Kit encoded quickly. He didn't need to add up; he knew the seven hundred and thirty-six combinations of the tri-graph by heart. He then wrote the encoded message, WJEF VHIT… on a blank sheet of paper and popped it in an envelope. It was risky sending it that way. If Brian opened the envelope he would never be able to break the code, but he would know that someone was communicating in code. Next time he met Jennifer, Kit would show her how to hide encoding within a seemingly innocent letter. For example, lay out the letter so the left-hand margin contains the encoded message.

Kit put on his best lounge suit, white shirt and grey silk tie. It was St Patrick's day and there was a reception at the Irish Embassy. He wondered if he should wear a green tie or green socks or a green jockstrap. It was all so stupid. He supposed they'd all have to wear cardboard shamrocks in their lapels or something similar. It was one of the most drunken occasions of the diplomatic year. Everyone enjoyed watching the Brits trying to interact with their hosts as if the Easter uprising and partition had never happened. That bit was always great fun and almost made it worth going. The Russians were fun too – and really did get drunk, no olive-oil prophylaxis beforehand. Irish whisky was too good to waste.

∎

There was a lot of traditional Irish food to soak up the booze: so most people stuck to the booze. Vasili, Kit's counterpart in the Soviet Embassy, raised a Waterford crystal tumbler of single malt to greet the American. Kit had known Vasili for ten years. The Russian was now KGB Chief of Residency, the Soviet equivalent of CIA Chief of Station. At the top level, there was no coyness or pretend secrecy about one another's job or identity. They were all members of the same club, even though they went out on the court to thrash each other. And, like gentleman players, they were polite to each other in the clubhouse afterwards. And, like aspiring professionals in any sport, they charted each other's progress through the rankings. Vasili had done much better since the death of Stalin and the execution of Beria; likewise, Kit had profited from the replacement of Dean Acheson – a pompous ass largely responsible for teeing up the Cold War – by Foster Dulles, who was an even worse ass but less hostile to Kit's career.

Vasili winked and gestured for Kit to come over. Kit flashed him a middle finger, then looked up to see the Irish Ambassador frowning directly at him. Kit nodded and smiled blandly, then made his way to the drinks table and served himself. He then circulated past the Uruguayan chargé d'affaires, who was speaking in German to the Papal Nuncio, and found himself next to Vasili. The Russian, by way of small talk, began by asking, 'How are the British getting on with their hydrogen bomb?'

Kit laughed and gestured with his thumb towards a British cabinet minister, then whispered, 'Why don't you fucking ask him?' It was the same minister that Kit had compromised in a honey trap.

Vasili glanced at the minister and said deadpan, 'I don't think he would tell me.'

'But his girlfriend might.' Kit not only knew that the Russians knew, but he knew that the Russians knew that he knew. In other words, his comment revealed nothing that wasn't already known. Otherwise, he wouldn't have said a word. Kit wasn't sure how the Russians knew about his honey trap and it worried him. There were rumours that a Sov attaché had got involved too. The rumours complicated things and Kit longed to know if they were true. He gave Vasili a playful nudge with his elbow. 'She's a good looker, isn't she?'

Vasili didn't reply and kept a straight face. He wasn't going down that dark alley with anyone who wasn't a very senior colleague. It was the sort of thing you only talked about in the hushed offices of the Lubyanka in Moscow. Kit knew this, but liked teasing the Russian. To lighten the tone, Kit asked, 'How many of your embassy staff are *not* KGB?'

Vasili pursed his lips and looked thoughtful, 'Just over half – but who knows about the other half? Maybe they're just pretending to be cooks and drivers, but are really undercover KGB spying on us. Who knows? KGB is not, my friend, so much a job title as an existential concept.'

An essential part of Kit's job was transcribing these conversations. If they weren't too juicy, he dictated them to a security-cleared shorthand typist. But he had a feeling this was one he'd have to type himself. He knew that Vasili had to do the same – and not put a foot wrong. The tightrope that Vasili walked didn't have a safety net. There were fifteen members of the original Bolshevik government. By 1940, ten of them had been executed and four others had died. That management culture permeated the entire state apparatus. The NKVD, the predecessor to the KGB, had arrested almost twenty million and executed seven million. And yet, thought Kit, the survivors of all that terror were so infinitely human. How could they love music, poetry, art – and friendship too – with such passion? Was it because the abyss was always there and each minute had to be caressed and savoured like a precious wine? Compared to them, thought Kit, we are so shallow, *so* insipid. Did Donald Duart Maclean see that too?

'You and your friends,' said Vasili, 'aren't so close any more.'

'Thanks to you guys. But we're not getting divorced, we're staying together for the kids.'

'You mean like Little Boy and Fat man – you're staying together for the bombs.'

'Don't be silly, we don't share that stuff any more. After Comrade Burgess and Comrade Maclean, we wouldn't trust the Brits with a recipe for chocolate chip cookies.'

'Vasili looked slightly confused; he'd learned English English. 'What are cookeesh?'

'They're what the British call *biscuits*.'

'So they are the same thing.'

'No, not the same. The recipes are different.'

'Are the American recipes better?'

'Much more advanced, let's say.'

'And why,' said Vasili, 'won't you tell the British how to make these better cookeesh?'

'Cookeees.' Kit paused and made eye contact. 'I've already told you – their sous chefs can't be trusted with kitchen secrets. So the Brits are going to have to find their own recipes.'

Part of Kit's job was misinformation. He knew that Vasili would assume that he was lying about the US-UK rift – the hidden 'truth' being the contrary, that Anglo-US military cooperation was improving. But it had, in fact, become even worse under Eden. It was bluff, double and triple bluff. In the intelligence world, 'truth' and 'factual reality' seldom coincide. The Cambridge spies were *underused* by the Russians because, for years, the KGB had believed that the members of the spy ring were perfidious triple-dealing Englishmen who had been planted by the British Secret Service. The officers handling the Cambridge ring had risked being shot by their KGB bosses because the secrets they gleaned from the spies were too good, too perfect, to be 'true'. If everything adds up and is confirmed by other sources as true, it doesn't mean 'truth' – it means a vast conspiracy to deceive.

'Good whisky,' said Vasili, and drained his glass.

'By the way,' said Kit, 'do you still see our friend, Monsieur Poêle?' Mister Pan, Peter Pan, the statue in Kensington Gardens. It was the place where Kit and Vasili exchanged information via dead drop spikes. There was, from time to time, intelligence that was mutually beneficial to both superpowers – to the detriment of a third. The exact spot was next to a little-used path between the statue and the Serpentine. The dead drop spike is a metal container about the size of a fountain pen. One end has a sharp spike for sticking in the ground, the other a little green loop for retrieving it. The hollowed out spike is used for concealing messages or microfilm. If Kit had something to pass on, he would go for a walk in the gardens and suddenly discover that a shoelace needed tying – and then press the spike into the soft grassy turf with the palm of his hand. The sign that dead drop mail was waiting was a piece of chewing gum stuck on the armrest of a bench near the park entrance.

'I haven't seen Monsieur Poêle for some time. Is he well?'

'He's feeling a bit under the weather.' Kit waited to see if Vasili had got the joke: rain, snow, pigeon shit. Finally, it registered and the Russian groaned. 'He might,' said Kit, 'appreciate a visit.'

'Have you heard,' said Vasili, 'the one about my friend Boris?'

'No.'

'Boris hasn't been feeling very well lately – and he's been making some mistakes, so he's called back to Dzerzhinsky Square to see the chief. The chief says, "How are you feeling, Boris?" Boris says, "To be honest, I'm not feeling too good today." "Well, Boris," says the chief, "would you like to hear the good news?" "Yes," said Boris, "what's the good news?" "The good news, Boris, is that you feel better today than you will tomorrow."'

■

The next day Kit woke with a hangover and a letter from Jennifer. She encoded the first part, BCIU QAWG NCIK, which Kit decoded to, IVEF OUND BOAT. The rest of the letter was written in the clear.

> *It's a lovely boat and, I think, a very seaworthy one. Billy Whiting, the boy who does chores for us, found it lying ashore at Aldeburgh. It's a traditional East Coast boat called a Blackwater Sloop – I love the name. Billy says it needs some work, but that he and his uncle can manage it. What should I do?*
>
> *It was lovely to see you – you always make me laugh. Brian's back. He's working very long hours and seems troubled about something. I think there's some sort of crisis on Orford Ness.*
>
> *I hope you come up to have a look at the boat. Sorry this is so brief.*
>
> *Take care,*
>
> *Much love, Jennifer*

Kit was pleased that Jennifer remembered how to use the code. He re-read the letter, the words 'crisis on Orford Ness' rang a very loud alarm bell. What were they up to? Kit knew he was expected to penetrate the security on Orford Ness, but didn't know how it was possible. He wasn't allowed to use anyone acting under 'official cover' – this excluded all US military and government employees. Kit thought about Driscoll, but knew that an Irish navvy with an IRA background had as much chance of getting an AWRE security clearance as a KGB officer in full dress uniform.

Kit carried Jennifer's letter over to the sink, lit a match, burned the letter and washed the ashes down the drain. Then he struck another match to light the gas cooker so he could boil a kettle for tea. I must be turning into a Limey, he thought. Kit took the lid off the tin of leaf tea, but waited for the water to boil so that he could 'warm the pot'. Making tea was the English equivalent of a Tridentine Mass. But what about Stanley, thought Kit? A site like Orford Ness must be begging for electricians.

■

Facial appearance is only part of an effective disguise; there's also walking, gestures and voice. But, thought Kit, the most important part of a disguise is sharing the attitude and thoughts of the person you are impersonating. If you could do that, it changed you far more than a false moustache or a fake limp. In a corner of his bathroom mirror, opposite the Maclean statement, Kit had taped another quote: *The essential character of a nation is not determined by the upper classes, but by the common people, and that the common people of all nations are true brothers in the great family of mankind.*

Kit stared at the words. He secretly admired the man who had said them, but it wasn't an easy belief for him to take on. The words were from the unpublished autobiography of Paul Robeson, the black American singer. Kit's admiration for Robeson had to be 'secret', for part of his job was stopping the autobiography from being published. Robeson's book, banned in the US, was now doing the rounds of publishers in London. Robeson had fallen foul of HUAC, the House Un-American Activities Committee, for saying things like 'our basic democratic rights are under attack under the smokescreen of anti-communism.' Consequently, Kit's bosses, the US State Department, had taken away Robeson's passport and issued 'stop notices' at all ports and border crossings.

It hadn't been difficult to find a corner of the South Lambeth Goods Depot that was quiet and abandoned – particularly if you parked there at lunchtime. Kit's favoured place was next to a pair of derelict water tanks next to a siding that was never used; years of stale grass had grown and turned rank between the rails. A sparrow hopped between the sleepers foraging for seeds. Kit opened his briefcase and took out his make-up box. He set up a mirror on the car dashboard and within five minutes had turned himself into an American of mixed race. For a second or two Kit admired himself in the mirror: the dark skin improved his looks. He then locked the car and set off on foot to his agent rendezvous.

Kit found himself humming a song he'd picked up from Stanley, 'Meet Me in Battersea Park.'

> See the people riding on the roundabouts and swings,
> Children so delighted at the puppets on the strings.

Kit arrived at the usual park bench and sat down. He checked his watch: Stanley was running late. That was unusual, the Londoner always got there first. The bench was on the edge of the park and looked out over the Thames. On the other side of the river a red-coated Chelsea pensioner limped along the embankment. The pensioner finally found a bench and sat down. He leaned on his stick and stared across the water. Kit felt that the pensioner, with a leg full of shrapnel from Ladysmith or Mafeking, was watching his every move. Kit opened a copy of the *Manchester Guardian* – it was part of his cover – and started reading an article about the implications of Khrushchev's speech denouncing Stalin. All change, thought Kit, all change.

Kit looked at his watch again: six minutes late. Maybe Stanley wasn't going to show. And in any case, he might not fancy a job in Suffolk. Kit looked across the river; the pensioner had been joined by another and they were talking. The paranoia began to ease and Kit folded the *Guardian*: the newspaper was a prop, part of the cover story he had put on to deceive Stanley. Kit knew that Stanley, despite his criminal activities, was both a patriot and a man of the left. He would never have touched a job if it meant working for a foreign power, especially the Americans. Therefore, Kit had devised a cover story that included an English wife, a friendship with Paul Robeson and connections with British socialism. Kit never mentioned a political party by name, but let Stanley make his own assumptions. The targets of his break-ins – bomb budget figures and the Tory PM's health records – would be valuable assets to any of the government's socialist opponents. Wouldn't it be funny, Kit thought, if the left wing of the Labour Party ended up getting blamed for the burglaries? He could imagine Allen Dulles slapping his thigh and howling with laughter.

There was the sound of someone kicking a football on the field behind the bench. Then the voice of a child, 'Come on, Grandad, *please* try to get the ball.'

'Now, listen Albert, I've got to have a talk with this gentleman.'

Kit heard tiny footsteps brushing through the grass at the back of the bench, then a child's voice whispering in his ear. 'Mister, would you like to play piggy in the middle? You can be piggy.'

Kit turned and faced a boy who looked about four. He wasn't used to children and felt awkward around them. Before he could think of something to say, Stanley came to the rescue.

'Albert, you young tearaway, let that poor man be.' Stanley then knelt down and pointed into the distance. 'Look, Albert, you see those two elm trees over there. Pretend they're fullbacks – I want you to dribble back and forth between them practising that two-step move I showed you.'

Kit watched the child trot off towards the trees. It all seemed so strange – child, grandparent, park, play. What, thought Kit, was the name of this strange planet? The sounds of organ music and laughter from the funfair carried across the greensward. The park was dotted with prams: punctuation points of life. How, thought Kit, do you find the code word that lets you in?

Stanley called out to his grandson. 'Use both feet – that's it!' Then turned to Kit and said, 'They're on to me.'

'How do you know?'

'They tried to put the frighteners on me – bastards.'

'Who were they?' Kit was playing dumb.

'It was them. You always know it's them – they stick out like bleeding thumbs.'

Kit knew that by 'them' Stanley meant the security services. In the underworld you called a gang or a villain by name, but the heavy hands of the State were always 'them'. It was as if they were evil spirits and saying their name aloud – MI5, Special Branch, SIS – would invoke a curse. 'What happened?' said Kit.

'They were waiting for me when I came out of the Bread and Roses – parked in a big Humber. But I ignored them and continued on my merry way – and the car starts following me at walking pace. When I turn into Elmhurst Street, the Humber turns too, and two blokes jump out and start to walk on either side of me. But I just walk along whistling with my hands in my pockets pretending they're not there. They didn't like that – and about three seconds later, they lift me up and throw me against an iron railing. It hurt and I've still got the bruises. So I say, "What that's for?" And one of 'em says, "Shut it, Stanley." For a while, they just kept staring at me. Then the other one said, and he had a voice just like a vicar, he says, "We're disappointed in you, Stanley, we never thought you would do something like this. We strongly advise that you stop." And that was it – the driver turned around and picked them up – and I haven't seen them since, but I think they're watching. That's why I brought Albert – they know I wouldn't bring the kid if I was on a job.'

'Have you ever worked for them?'

'Might have.' Stanley seemed embarrassed. 'Nothing much, did the phones at the Egyptian Embassy.'

'I'm sorry it turned out this way.' Kit reached into his pocket and took out a roll of pound notes.

'What's that for?'

'It's a token of appreciation, a bonus, for what you've done.'

'I don't want it. I liked working for you. It felt good to get at those bastards – they just want to keep us down.'

Kit shoved the roll of notes into Stanley's coat pocket. 'Just take it.'

'What's the matter? You seem angry.'

'I'm not angry at you.' Kit stared at the river. The tide had changed and there were brown whirlpools heading seawards. He wondered if it was possible to choke to death on self-loathing. Stanley was a villain and safe-cracker, but one that knew all the words of 'The Red Flag' and 'The Internationale'. Kit remembered Stanley telling him how he had fought the Fascists on Cable Street and had his skull cracked in a baton charge by mounted police. The duping of Stanley required more than a trick of spycraft; it required an acid of bleak cynicism that corroded the soul.

Chapter Five

As Kit walked past the Roosevelt Memorial, he noticed that the daffodils were in full bloom. A reminder that in one month the Russian light cruiser, *Ordzhonikidze*, would dock in Portsmouth Harbour bringing First Secretary Khrushchev and Premier Nikolai Bulganin to Britain for the goodwill visit. As soon as Kit got to his office he sent for the most recent underwater espionage files – not the sort of stuff you can take home to peruse of an evening over a glass of wine. Even in the embassy itself, he had to sign a dated and timed top secret document receipt.

The previous October the *Sverdlov*, another Soviet light cruiser, had been to Portsmouth for the Spithead naval review. Both British and US Navy intelligence were surprised by the ship's manoeuvrability and wanted to find out her secret. The underwater espionage was a joint CIA-MI6 operation, codenamed SM/CLARET, that involved both British and American divers. MI6 had enticed Commander Lionel 'Buster' Crabb out of his boozy retirement for a fee of sixty guineas, a quaint unit of British currency worth twenty-one shillings. It hadn't taken Kit long to learn that ordinary people exchanged pounds, but gentlemen traded in guineas. But it was only afterwards that Kit discovered that 'the gentlemen' from MI6 hadn't told their boss, the Prime Minister, what they were doing. It was a totally unauthorised op. It didn't take Kit long to realise that MI6 had used the CIA as camouflage. If something had gone wrong, they would have blamed the Americans for spying in British waters. The ensuing shit storm would, of course, have destroyed Kit's career.

In the end, it nearly did go wrong. The Russians got suspicious and sent a swimmer over the side. But fortunately, the divers had already accomplished their mission. They discovered two propellers set in sunken recesses in the forward hull. The *Sverdlov* was one of the first warships that had been fitted with bow thrusters. The extra props were not only useful for dockside manoeuvres, but would help the cruiser to take evasive action under fire. Kit knew it was a significant intelligence find and was certain that British Naval Intelligence was leaning on MI6 to find out more.

Kit flicked through the SM/CLARET file. One of the CIA divers reported that Crabb wasn't fit enough to do this sort of work: he was overweight, a slow swimmer and consumed too much oxygen. Apparently, Crabb had had some difficulty with his breathing apparatus and was forced to surface. 'This,' wrote the CIA man, 'probably accounted for the crew becoming alerted.' Kit closed the file. Poor Crabb, he thought.

In the end, Kit received a verbal reprimand for the *Sverdlov* affair. The reprimand wasn't for spying on the Russian ship, but for having used 'official cover', American CIA trained frogmen. The real message from his bosses in Washington was: *Don't leave any fingerprints and provide tons of 'plausible deniability'*. There was a whole manual, and a very secret one, entitled 'Embassy Directed Covert Operations in a Host Country'. During SM/CLARET Kit had violated almost every guideline on 'compartmentalisation' and 'anonymity'. His mistake had been to trust his British counterpart. Meanwhile, the Brit was wiping MI6 fingerprints off the spy mission, but leaving all of the CIA's. It was a brilliant example of 'dry-cleaning'. Kit felt no resentment: it was all part of the game. But next time it was going to be his turn – that's why he had hired Driscoll.

The next file that Kit looked at was US Naval Intelligence stuff: the folder was packed with 8x10 glossy photos. Many had been snapped by adrenalin fuelled helicopter crews hovering just a few feet over Russian ships. Assholes, thought Kit. A miscalculation, a sudden gust of wind, a rotor catches a piece of rigging – and a Soviet ship's drenched with blazing aviation fuel and dead Americans and dead Russians burning all over the decks. What happens next? Are we all crazy? Kit began reading the ship details.

The Ordzhonikidze *is an Admiral Sverdlov class cruiser. She displaces 17 thousand tons and is 689 feet in length*. Kit did a quick calculation – nearly ten swimming pool lengths. Could Crabb still manage it? *The* Ordzhonikidze *carries 12 six-inch guns and 12 four-inch guns* – as, thought Kit, any fool can see from the photos. The important questions are the mysteries that lie beneath her hull. What sort of sonar does she have? Had they replaced the old Tamir and Mehta systems? Could they now detect US nuclear submarines and destroy them with nuclear depth charges? What sort of torpedo tubes does she have? Are there underwater ports for sowing mines? Could these mines be nuclear? And why was the ship so fast – was the stern propeller of some new design?

Kit pushed the file aside and leaned back in his chair. The bottom of that ship, if not the Holy Grail, was still an intelligence treasure trove. He knew for certain that the Brits were going to try again: the temptation was too strong to resist. And it would have to be another unauthorised operation. The Prime Minister would never sanction it: the risks of a serious diplomatic incident were too great. Especially as the UK was leaning towards a policy of détente with the Soviet Union – and a botched spying incident would blow it. And wouldn't, thought Kit, it serve them right. He had begun to feel good again. He had left the sickly twists of conscience behind. He was back in a professional world where there were no innocent bystanders, just willing players wearing team strips. Being hurt and hurting others was part of the game.

MI6 hadn't approached Kit about the *Ordzhonikidze*. They knew they couldn't expect a CIA cover story for a second dive. But Kit still felt annoyed about being left out. The stuff on the bottom of that ship was the bread and butter of intelligence gathering. And what were the Brits going to do with the *Ordzhonikidze's* secrets? They didn't have the resources to build countermeasures. There were only two horses in the arms race. There was no point in the op if they didn't share the intelligence with the Americans.

Kit picked up his desk calendar and looked again at the dates. The timeframe was limited to three days and all the main players – including Crabb and his handler – were known. Kit knew that they would stay at the Sally Port Hotel again. And he knew, roughly, where Crabb would begin his swim – there were only three places in the crowded dockyard where a diver could get in the water unobserved by a ship docked on the Railway Jetty.

The only light in the office was a desk lamp, but the ghostly glow of the London night crept through a window and lurked on the carpet. Kit looked into the shadows and decided that the Driscoll op needed another twist. He opened a desk drawer, peeled off a piece of flash paper – when your contact burns it, there's no ash – and began to write the message. When he was finished, he unscrewed a dead drop spike and popped the note into its hollow core.

Kit walked over to the bookshelf and took down his copy of *USSR Biographies*. The volume was only 'confidential', so he didn't have to keep it in the archive vault. 'Who the fuck,' he said aloud, 'was Ordzhonikidze?' He flicked through the volume: Ordzhonikidze, Sergo 1886-1937. Kit wished he hadn't bothered. It was depressing reading. The ship's namesake had been a lifelong and loyal friend to Stalin. At first, Ordzhonikidze had been well rewarded and rose quickly through the ranks to govern the Ukraine. In 1936 his loyalty came under question. Rumours spread. A year later he was dead. A death certificate, stating suicide, was signed by the Health Commissar himself, Dr Kaminsky. A short time later, Kaminsky was arrested and executed. I suppose, thought Kit, you were damned if you did and damned if you didn't. And then, a dozen years later a keel is laid down in Leningrad shipyard – Stalin still very much alive – for an umpteen-gun, seventeen-thousand ton cruiser to be named the *Ordzhonikidze*. If, thought Kit, there is a God, I bet He's just like that.

■

It was well after dark when Kit left the embassy. He found his way out through a service entrance in the back and had to dodge around ranks of stinking dustbins. He emerged into a dimly lit close called Three Kings Yard. He turned left into Upper Brook Street, also dark and deserted except for a single black taxi. Kit walked west to Park Lane where there was brightness and traffic, then turned right towards Marble Arch. He looked across the road. Speaker's Corner was quiet – all the loonies were back on the ward. The Corner was, however, a great idea. It was a quaint heritage thing that gave simpletons the illusion that freedom of speech really did exist in 1950s England. But where, thought Kit, can I get a copy of *Ulysses* or *Lady Chatterley's Lover*?

Or, even better, get a journalist to write about 'The Man in the Mask'? It was Kit's favourite scandal. Once or twice a month, a cabinet minister attended a dinner party at a very exclusive address. The podgy minister, aside from the black leather mask that hid his identity, was completely nude. He served the rest of the guests naked and ate his own dinner out of a dog's bowl. For some time, Kit had been trying to discover the identity of the masked minister, but no luck. This was one mystery on which Establishment ranks were closed and lips were sealed. Not even his honey trap minister would talk about that one.

When Kit got to Bayswater Road there were a number of well-dressed couples laughing in haw-haw voices and trying to hail taxis. Kit walked westwards against the convivial evening flow. Hyde Park, dark and deserted, stretched out on his left. Kit suddenly felt cold, as if an icy dead hand had slipped under his shirt and caressed his spine. He turned up his collar, something wasn't right. Kit stopped at Lancaster Gate. He looked north into the twisting labyrinth of streets. The pale Georgian terraces, scabbed and peeling, stooped in genteel seediness. He wondered if the hotel was still there – and the odd-shaped room where he had been very happy, and then very sad. The twisted memory vanished, something else wasn't right. Kit knew that he was being followed.

Kit hadn't seen his trail, he had *felt* him. When he was a trainee at 'the farm', Kit had been taught never to stare at the back of a person you were keeping under observation. There was a strange sixth sense inherited from our animal ancestors. We might not see, smell or hear the predator, but we feel that stalking eye crawling up our exposed spine to the back of our necks.

Kit walked the few remaining yards to where Elms Mews angled into Bayswater, then looked at his watch and shook his head. He was pretending that he was waiting to meet someone. Kit folded his arms and tapped his foot in pretend impatience. Meanwhile, he glanced back the way he had come. About fifty yards away, a young man of middle height was reading a bus timetable. Kit waited five more minutes, then checked his watch again. The young man was now reading a menu in a restaurant window. Why, thought Kit, don't you just wear a flashing sign saying you're on a surveillance op. Kit was certain that the young man was a watcher from A4 – the MI5 branch responsible for trailing suspicious foreigners around London. Kit felt the red mist descending. How *fucking dare* they put a tail on him? It wasn't just a breach of diplomatic etiquette; it was a personal insult too – not so much to be under surveillance, but to have the task assigned to some incompetent office junior. OK, asshole, let's see how you handle this one?

Kit crossed the road and set off into Kensington Gardens. The path towards the Peter Pan statue was poorly lit, but was wide and straight so his tail shouldn't have any trouble keeping him in view. Kit listened to a cacophony of alarm calls from the various waterfowl on Long Water. The Romans, he remembered, used to keep geese as sentinels. Kit reached into his coat pocket and found the dead drop spike. He stopped, peered around as if to make sure he was unobserved; then stepped off the path and bent over as if to press the dead drop spike into the earth. Instead, he palmed the spike up his sleeve, and set off briskly towards the Serpentine. When Kit was sure he was no longer being followed, he doubled back using the thick waterside foliage as cover. As Kit suspected, his trail was on his hands and knees searching the grass with a pocket torch. The fool had fallen for one of oldest tricks in the book: faking a dead drop in order to shake a trail.

Kit sat down beneath a rhododendron and waited. He wondered how long it would take Blanco's boy – for he was now more sure than ever he was from El Blanco's stable – to realise he'd been duped. The CIA's nickname for Dick White, the Head of MI5, was El Pene Blanco – or just El Blanco. In any case, Kit knew that his watcher had made a serious professional mistake. Once you've been assigned a surveillance target, you don't do *anything* else. You stick to him like shit on a poodle. If the target leaves a briefcase of nuclear secrets in a taxi, you don't run after the taxi – you keep trailing your man. Unbroken surveillance, 'eyeball', is sacred. If your target plucks a baby out of a pram and throws the child in the river, don't jump in to save the kid. It's just a cheap trick to shake your trail.

Kit could hear the young man getting annoyed. 'Shit. Where the fuck is it?' Finally, he saw the agent stand up and brush his hands and knees. Kit watched to see what the young man would do next. He put the torch in his pocket, said 'fuck' a few more times, then retraced his steps to the Bayswater Road. Where, thought Kit, were the rest of the surveillance team? Was he acting alone? Unbelievable, but it seemed to be the case. Now it was Kit's turn to become a one-man surveillance tail.

It was easy. The young man was totally unaware that the tables were turned. The only thing that concerned him seemed to be the fact that he had fucked up his first important assignment. Kit saw his annoyance as he stopped to kick a dustbin when he emerged from the gardens. The agent than set off north-east towards Regent's Park: walking eyes down, hands in pockets. He stopped at a phone box on Edgeware Road. Kit knew it was going to be a difficult conversation, having to explain to the senior duty officer that he had lost his trail. Kit watched him leaning against the steamy window glass. The call took about two minutes, the young man nodding his head as each point was confirmed. The young man then made another call. This, thought Kit, was the looking-for-sympathy-and-consolation call. Wife? Lover? Maybe his mother – he was so young.

The young man left the phone box and headed towards Marylebone. Kit liked the way Norman French lurked mispronounced in English place names. The Americans did it too – Detroit, Des Moines. All those old French priests and explorers lying unremarked beneath strange feet and unknown voices. Kit returned to the living when he saw the young man check his watch, then watched him disappear into an Underground station. There must, thought Kit, be one last train. It would, he knew, be difficult to continue trailing the young man without being recognised. The platform and train would nearly be deserted. The game was over – or was it?

Kit stayed out of sight on the street as the agent bought a ticket – then followed him into the station. He didn't stop to buy a ticket; he wasn't going to need one. The upper station hall was totally deserted, but the echo rumble of a train covered the sound of Kit's footsteps as he ran towards his target. The young man was at the top of a steep escalator. The hard thump in the middle of his back must have caught him totally unawares. A reflex action made him try to grab the handrails, but the force between his shoulder blades was too powerful – it so winded him that he could not even cry out. Kit watched him tumble and somersault to the concrete floor below – once or twice reaching out, trying desperately to grab anything to break that awful fall.

Kit registered the body at the bottom of the escalator. It looked misshapen and broken. He thought he heard a moaning sound, but it might have just been hot air rising from the deep tunnels. He turned and left quickly – the shock of what he had done already making him shake and feel unsteady at the knees.

■

It was another late night and another half-bottle of brandy. Kit tried to justify what he had done. MI5, he reasoned, are a bunch of shits. It was their guys who had roughed up Stanley. They were the British equivalent of the FBI. As such, they were only allowed to operate within the United Kingdom itself. Their job was counter-espionage. They ought to be following Russians around, not Americans. How long, thought Kit, had the man trailing him been in the security service? He certainly seemed awfully green. Kit remembered the odd thing again; the strange sound the young man was making just before he pushed him down the moving stairs. It was a convulsive, liquid sound that seemed to come from deep inside. Had he been ill? Suddenly, Kit realised what the strange sound had been, the young man had been crying. He had been trusted with an important mission and failed. Maybe there was an older brother who was a dead war hero – and the young man's one dream had been to live up to that memory. Kit poured another brandy. When he was drunk he felt better about himself.

Kit corked the bottle and got into bed. It didn't matter, he thought, MI5 were total shits. One of the first things that El Blanco did after being appointed was to establish F Branch. Their job was to infiltrate trade unions and political parties – they even spied on the Labour shadow cabinet. Kit knew this was true because he ran agents who did the same thing. One of F Branch's big successes was burgling a senior member of the British Communist Party and photographing the names and personal details of all fifty-five thousand members. Now they just needed to press the button and round them up – then deep six them or despatch them to that inhabited anthrax island in the Hebrides.

Kit turned off the light and tried to go to sleep. It didn't work. He felt like shit. He hated hurting people, but he kept doing it. He could see the glow of Pepita's luminous Madonna. Sometimes, he hated being alone. He wanted to be cuddled like a child. He wanted Pepita. When Kit finally fell asleep his pillow was damp with tears.

Chapter Six

The next day Kit's secretary passed on a strange message. Someone had rung from a phone box claiming to be Kit's 'spiritual adviser' and recommending they meet 'at the customary place' at 'the customary time'. At half past three, Kit left the embassy and hailed a black taxi. He thought about telling the driver to take him straight to the rendezvous point, but then he remembered what had happened the previous evening. He was weary of counter-surveillance games and all the other puerile spy games. But he had to continue playing them because he was trapped in a deadly adult playground from which there was no escape. Kit told the taxi driver to take him to Harrods. The store with its many entrances and exits was one of the best places in London to shake off a tail. And then from Harrods, a quick hop on the Underground to South Kensington.

■

Brompton Oratory is a late-Victorian Italianate monstrosity where the rich Catholics of Kensington and Chelsea confess their sins: 'Bless me, father, for I support Apartheid and care more about my cat than the children of the black workers in my South African gold mines.' Except, thought Kit, that they probably don't see that as a sin. Kit crossed himself with holy water and looked around for his 'spiritual adviser'. He spotted Vasili as the Russian came out of a confessional. Vasili crossed himself and went to a side chapel in a deserted corner of the Oratory lit only by candles. Kit watched him genuflect before a seventeenth-century altar that the Victorian architect had looted from a church in Brescia, then go to a pew where he bowed his head and muttered his penance. Kit followed and knelt in the pew directly behind. He leaned forward and whispered, 'What did you confess?'

'I said that I was unfaithful to my wife.'

'Are you?'

'Oddly enough, no.'

'In that case, you should have confessed telling lies. Your absolution is invalid.'

'Shit, maybe I should go back and tell him.'

'I shouldn't bother. Just don't,' said Kit, 'lie to me... more than you have to.'

The side chapel smelled of spilt candlewax and incense. For a second, Kit saw Pepita's coffin in the country church near her family's home. He remembered the rosary beads woven through her strong brown fingers; the lush fleshy tropical flowers heaped high. And hundreds of candles, each villager carrying one. Kit was ten years old when Pepita died of a burst pancreas. She was in great pain, but kept working thinking it was just a cramp that would go away. His mother found him another nanny a week later.

'I went,' said Vasili, 'to see Monsieur Poêle, but he had nothing for me.'

'I couldn't leave anything – I was being followed.'

'They shouldn't do that – you're supposed to be allies.'

Kit was desperate to tell something to Vasili, but the Oratory worried him. It was becoming notorious as a DLB – dead letter box – for the Soviet Embassy. Oddly, however, no one ever bugged it. None of the competing secret services involved wanted to frighten agents away from Brompton Oratory. There seemed an unspoken agreement to keep the venue clean – otherwise agents and handlers would have to disperse all over the metropolis and things would be more difficult for everyone. Spies, like everyone else, want an easy life at the office.

Vasili turned around and looked at Kit. 'Who have you pissed off now?'

'I think you know.'

'I know,' said Vasili, 'that it is a very long list.'

He shifted to safer ground. 'We're worried about British policy.'

'What's new? We're worried about American policy, French policy, Chinese policy. Is this all you want to talk about?'

'No, but I might be giving you something later – and I want you to know why I'm passing it on.'

'And what do you want in return?'

'First of all, I want you to listen.'

'So talk.'

'My personal view – the one I feed to Washington – is that the British ruling class, especially the Prime Minister, suffers from a collective form of madness.'

'We like Eden.'

'I'm sure you do.'

'What do you call this British madness?'

'Schizophrenic delusions of post-imperial grandeur.'

'I didn't know that you were a qualified psychiater.'

'Psychia*trist*, Vasili, you're getting your languages confused.'

'Thanks.'

'Schizophrenia is the inability to differentiate between fantasy and reality. The scary thing about schizophrenics is that they never lie. They really believe what they say is true. The British still think they are a world power – and that's why they keep doing stupid things, irrational things.'

'What sort of things?'

'You know, the military bases east of Suez, the oversized fleet, large troop deployment in the Middle East...'

'And,' Vasili leaned his face close to Kit's and whispered hoarsely, 'trying to develop their own hydrogen bomb.'

'Yeah, that too.' Kit fiddled with a hymn book: the H-bomb business was too sensitive to discuss with any Russian, particularly their KGB chief in London. The Rosenbergs went to the high voltage toaster for less. Kit answered in safer, more general terms. 'British military expenditure is way out of proportion to their status as a power. They should spend the money making life better for the people of Britain. That, Vasili, is what socialism is all about. Not the sort of militaristic shit your country does.'

'We need military might to defend our people against your aggression.' Vasili paused and smiled. 'And please don't tell me what socialism is about – tell President Eisenhower. Let's cut the bullshit. Tell me, Kit, what have you really got to say?'

'We want to teach the British a lesson about their post-imperial delusions.'

'You mean,' said Vasili, 'that you want to show them that they are no longer a world power – because all the strings are pulled from Washington.'

Kit shrugged. 'That's right – and let's see what happens when Hungary or Poland get out of line.'

Vasili frowned. 'So how do you intend to give this lesson?'

'You know the *Ordzhonikidze*, the cruiser that's bringing First Secretary Khrushchev to Portsmouth next month.'

'What about her?'

'We'd love to know all her secrets – particularly the ones she's got hidden beneath her hull.'

'If there was anything secret below the *Ordzhonikidze's* water-line, we would not risk bringing her into an English port, as well as mooring her in a Royal Navy dockyard.'

Kit smiled; he knew Vasili was lying. 'Sure, maybe there are no secrets to find, but boys like playing games. Now, if the Brits had invited us to play with them, this conversation would not be taking place. But they've decided that it's their ball and their soccer field and we've been PNG'd.' The abbreviation was embassy slang for being made Persona Non Grata.

Vasili's face remained a blank throughout. There was no hint of surprise or indignation, but when he finally spoke his tone seemed bored and weary. 'Are you telling me,' his voice fell to a faint whisper, 'that the British are going to send a frogman to espionage the bottom of the *Ordzhonikidze*?'

Kit nodded and passed Vasili an envelope containing the details.

The Russian folded the envelope into his breast pocket. 'You've just stabbed your closest ally in the back.'

'No, our closest ally stabbed herself in the back.'

'You are warning us,' Vasili's tone suddenly became animated, 'of what would be a serious breach of diplomatic etiquette. I'm not sure I believe you – maybe you want to make trouble between us and the British. I know that Prime Minister Eden would never...'

'The Prime Minister knows nothing about it. It's an MI6 decision, an entirely unauthorised op. Maybe they're a bit out of control.'

Vasili folded his hands and closed his eyes as if recollecting something private. Finally he smiled and said, 'Remember the story I told you about Boris?'

Kit nodded and said, 'It might end like that one.'

'No, it won't: your societies are too soft. The British Boris will end up with a pension and a new set of golf clubs.'

Kit knew it was time to go. He shook the Russian's hand, then got up to leave.

Vasili tapped the side of his coat where he had placed the envelope. 'Remember, Kit, I owe you one.'

'Thanks, I might need it one day.'

Vasili was alerted by something in the American's voice. He lowered himself back into the pew. 'What do you want Kit? Is it professional – or personal?'

'I don't know.'

■

Two days later, Kit found himself on his way to an appointment with Dick White, the Director of MI5. His summons to MI5 wasn't totally unexpected. Kit, still convinced that he had been trailed by one of White's 'watchers', had written a letter of official complaint to the Foreign and Commonwealth Office. He didn't identify himself as the surveillance target – nor did he provide details of what had happened. The letter observed diplomatic conventions and was signed and sealed by the US Ambassador.

Kit was more than a little surprised at how quickly the letter had winged its way from the FO to MI5 – that meant there were undercurrents. The letter inviting him to meet the Director had been motorcycle-despatched by a Royal Signal Corps Corporal – one so smartly booted and uniformed that he made the US Marine guards look slovenly. The letter was brief and offered the Director's 'sincere apologies'. It also expressed a desire to discuss the 'general issues involved with the aim of preventing such incidents from happening again'. In truth, Kit suspected it was a ruse by the British Security Service to get him on their own turf for a private grilling. They even sent a long sleek Humber Pullman to pick him up – for a lift to an address that didn't exist.

The building, functional and bland, had neither nameplate nor street number. But Kit knew it was called Leconfield House and occupied a squat rectangle between Curzon Street and Clarges Street. He was met by a man wearing a tweed suit and highly polished brogues. He stared at Kit through a monocle and said that 'K' was a little delayed, but would see him as soon as possible. The man, who smelled of whisky, left Kit in an office piled high with newspapers and magazines. Kit noticed the communist *Daily Worker* piled side by side with the *Daily Telegraph*. There were also arts and literary journals – and student newspapers from a variety of universities. It was funny, Kit thought, we all get the same stuff and probably collate the same information for the same reasons. There must be dozens of obscure quarterlies that only survive because the security services need to take out subscriptions to spy on their contributors. There was a thin partition separating

Kit from the next office, from where there was the sound of snoring – but it was, to be fair, *after* lunch.

A door opened. It was the Director, Dick White – El Blanco himself. The name was doubly apt for the Director had a great shock of fine white hair. He so looked the part of a senior civil service mandarin that Kit wondered if he had been appointed by a casting director. White shook hands and led Kit up a narrow staircase to his own office. Kit was surprised to find the Director's office was more small and drab than his own. A single window that needed washing looked out over the chimney pots of Mayfair. The only decorations were an Ormolu clock on a mantlepiece and the Security Service's coat of arms hanging above it. Kit had never seen the crest before – maybe it was a secret and you had to be invited to Leconfield House to have a peep. The coat of arms was a triangle and each corner of the triangle formed three miniature triangles. The top triangle boasted an all-seeing eye – like the pyramid on the back of a US one-dollar bill. The two base triangles enclosed M and 5 – M eye 5. The relationship of the symbols to another secret organisation was comically blatant.

The Director saw Kit looking at the coat of arms. 'I think,' he said, 'we're going to have to get around to changing that, it's a little too…'

'Masonic?' said Kit.

The Director smiled wanly and nodded agreement.

'Thank you, Director White, for taking the time to see me.'

'I've wanted to meet you for some time, Kit. I met your father during the war. He was, I believe, the most senior agent to jump into France with a Jedburgh team.'

'He was a complex man,' said Kit. He wondered if Dick White knew that his father had been one of the first to enter Oradour-sur-Glane after a unit from the SS division, *Das Reich*, had torched the village after massacring every single man, woman and child as reprisals. The men were shot, the women and children herded into the church and burned alive.

'I was very sorry to hear what happened.' The Director meant his father's death.

'Thank you.' Kit stared at the Director's necktie knot so he wouldn't have to think about his father. He was pleased to see that White used a four-in-hand. The casual simplicity of the knot warmed Kit to Director White. At prep school, the nouveau riche kids – the sons of 'the crass commercialists' – always tied Windsor knots. Maybe they thought it was 'better' because it was more difficult to tie. Ironically, Khrushchev and all the other Soviet leaders sported Windsor knots: Khrushchev's, in particular, was always a perfect isosceles triangle, the epitome of Windsor knot art. The Russian leader, of course, hadn't been to an East Coast prep school so he didn't know the subtle messages of dress code – but Dick White did.

'I also wanted you to come here so that I could apologise in person for the surveillance incident and to reassure you – and your embassy colleagues – that it will never happen again.'

'Thank you,' said Kit.

'You are entitled to further details,' the Director paused, 'and an explanation of what went wrong.'

Kit knew that Blanco was sparring and looking for an opening. He knew that White *had* an 'explanation' and was looking for an excuse to provide it. Kit decided to give him one. 'It all seemed very strange. Firstly, that your agent was acting alone – no foot backup, no second eyeball, no mobile backup.' The terms Kit used were a tacit admission that he wasn't just a diplomat, but it was obvious that Blanco knew this already. 'Your man also seemed, if you don't mind my saying so, very inexperienced.'

'You're absolutely right. It wasn't, of course, a genuine operation – it was a training exercise.'

Kit had seen that one coming. He let Blanco continue.

'We use live unwitting targets for training exercises, I'm sure you do too.'

Kit nodded.

'The training officer concerned overstepped his boundaries and has been reprimanded.' The Director paused. 'He decided, very wrongly, to spice things up by choosing a surveillance target from a *real* embassy rather than, say, a junior bank clerk from Barclays. Unfortunately, neither the trainer nor the trainee realised that their actions were a breach of diplomatic protocol.'

'I apologise for not looking more distinguished. Next time I leave the embassy I'll wear a cocked hat and a ceremonial sword.'

The Director gave Kit a sideways look. 'Ours always do.'

'But then, you're British.'

White paused and toyed with a letter opener. 'I hope you don't mind my saying that I've read your file?'

Kit smiled. 'It's to be expected – I've read yours.'

White's next question was totally unexpected. 'Do you like us?'

Kit thought he meant MI5 and gestured at the office. 'Do you mean...'

White smiled and clarified. 'Do you like the *British*?'

'I admire the British very much – perhaps too much, considering my role.'

'I thought,' said White, 'that what happened in Saigon in '45 might have turned you against us. I can't say I blame you if it did.'

Kit hadn't expected that one. Blanco certainly knew the file. He looked hard at the Director. 'Are you,' said Kit, 'inviting me to speak my mind?'

'Please do.'

'I thought that your General Gracey was a cretin who far over-reached his authority. I hold him responsible for the death of my cousin Peter.'

'I didn't know that Major Calvert was a relation. I'm sorry.'

'I must admit that I'm bitter about what happened – and it's not just Peter's death. We were sent to Vietnam to help Ho Chi Minh fight the Japanese – and he won. Or, I should say, the Vietnamese people won. But as soon as the dust settles, it's the same old British-French colonial carve-up. The people of Vietnam were betrayed – and so were we.'

White folded his hands and looked pleased. Kit was annoyed that he had shown so much emotion, but still felt a need to explain. 'We were very young then, I was barely in my twenties, all of us Roosevelt New Deal idealists. We thought we were the vanguard of a New World order – we all supported the United Nations charter and world government. No more war, no more exploitation of beautiful brown people just because... how does that rhyme go – *Thank God that we have got / The Maxim gun, and they have not.*'

'And like many idealistic young men before you, you felt betrayed by those in command?'

Kit smiled. 'I think we were entitled to. Don't you understand the enormity of Gracey's actions? He freed and armed Jap POWs to hunt down the same Vietnamese who, as our allies, had fought the Japanese. That paved the way for the French to come back and the nine bloody years to Dien Bien Phu.'

'The outcome was unfortunate.'

'And it's going to happen all over again – there's going to be another war.' Kit paused and smiled. 'But don't worry, that one will be our fault.'

White stared hard without blinking. 'Idealism can lead people to do strange things.'

Kit sensed that he was talking about Burgess and Maclean. But there was another elephant in the room: Kit's act of violence to the agent who had followed him.

Kit looked away embarrassed, afraid to show his self-loathing and guilt. 'I hope he wasn't badly hurt.'

The Director paused as if the matter were something that was best left unanswered. Finally he said, 'He won't be playing tennis for a while. He broke his arm in two places. Pity about the tennis, he was one of the best amateurs in the country. In any case, we've sent him home on extended convalescent leave. His parents need him there.'

Kit sensed there was more to the story. He was about to offer an apology, but White cut him off.

'There's one other child in the family, a younger sister who adores him. She's bright as a button, but has a disease that affects her coordination – she trips and knocks things over a lot. Oddly, she loves tennis, but is totally hopeless at it. Her brother used to spend hours gently swatting balls to her over the net, ninety per cent of which she would hit out of court or miss completely. But her brother insisted it was worth it, because when she did manage one back, her face would glow.' The Director paused and looked at something on his desk. 'It's all very sad, because her disease is a wasting one and she's become worse. They have to feed her through a tube – she's expected to die within days.'

Kit's mind flashed back to that night. The dots suddenly joined up. The watcher's distressed phone call from a box in Edgware Road had nothing to do with botched surveillance; he was phoning home. And later the young man's tears at the top of the moving stairs: Kit had nearly killed him during a moment of private grief.

The Director looked away. 'I don't suppose any of this is very relevant.'

Kit got up to leave.

■

Kit turned down the offer of a lift. Grosvenor Square was only five minutes on foot. But Kit didn't go back to the embassy: he just wanted to walk. London seemed wild. The strong equinoctial wind from the south-west threw dust, soot and scraps of paper high across the town – a brisk spring clean after a dull forgetful winter. The wind whipped short sharp waves across the Serpentine and swept grey frothy scum on to the lee bank and across the footpath. Across the water, ducks bobbed in the rushes under the windward bank like gale-bound boats. Boats, thought Kit, he must see Jennifer about that boat. Being afloat was a cure for madness.

Kit, turned-up collar and hands in pockets, sat on a bench in Kensington Gardens looking at Monsieur Poêle playing a flute. The Peter Pan statue was, like Brompton Oratory, a notorious pick-up point for spies. An icon of childhood innocence and wonder despoiled by dead drops, brush-passes, honey traps, agent handlers, hidden cameras and an umbrella or two with a ricin poison hypodermic hidden in its tip. His trade turned everything into shit.

Kit knew that Blanco had done exactly what he had wanted. He had pressed all the right buttons: his father's death, Saigon – and that poison toad of paranoia that mocks with yellow eyes in the depths of Kit's own soul. Blanco is master. He knows that every spy carries a sediment of self-loathing and self-doubt – and he knows how to stir it with a big spoon. Kit closed his eyes and imagined a map of London, England and Europe. He wanted to get up that very moment and start walking: across Westminster Bridge, down the Old Kent Road, Bexley, Dartford, Canterbury, Dover – 'Foot-passenger, sir?' 'Yes.' 'Single or return?' 'Single, please.' At some point, he would meet up with other pilgrims on the way of Saint Jacques de Compostelle – but he wouldn't tell them his secret. Nor would his pilgrimage stop there or at Gibraltar – or Tangier or the desert beyond. Not until every drop of poison – or life – had been sweated out.

There were voices behind him. It was not a language he knew, but it was guttural and full of hard consonants. One voice seemed angry, urgent and demanding; the other disdainful. Bombs no longer fell on London, but her streets were infested with spies who were crawling out of the rubble like vermin looking for fresh corpses. Kit felt an urge to tell the arguing men to shut up, but when he turned around they had started to walk away. Perhaps, he thought, they had gone to drown each other in the Serpentine. Kit got up to walk back to the embassy. 'I must,' he said aloud, 'see about that boat.'

■

The Blackwater Sloop was heavier and more seaworthy than any boat Kit had ever sailed in the Chesapeake Bay. Kit liked the long keel and the big foredeck, plenty of room for hanking a jib or dealing with an anchor. 'Let's have a look down below,' said Kit.

Billy Whiting stepped down into the cockpit, unlocked the hatch and lifted out the washboards. 'She's a bit mouldy,' said Billy, 'and the bilges need pumping out – rainwater mostly – she's been laying ashore for two years.'

Kit slid the hatch cover forward, lowered himself into the cabin and sat on a side berth. There wasn't enough headroom to stand up, but the below-decks were still spacious for a twenty-one foot boat. The brass fittings needed polishing, but the woodwork gleamed of dark varnish and white gloss paint. Everything was tidy and functional: a two-burner spirit cooker on gimbals, a folding chart table, a miniature coal stove, paraffin lamps, barometer, clock, a shelf for books and an old-fashioned brass voice hailer. Kit could already imagine lying at anchor in a remote creek during a still night: gentle tide trickle, curlew cry, the piping of oyster-catchers – 'Sounds and sweet airs that give delight and hurt not'. Childhood. Kit longed for childhood – and all its wonder and clean innocence. He looked up into the cockpit. Billy, framed in profile against a perfect blue sky, was staring at something on the river. Kit stood up and stuck his head out of the companionway so he could see too. A Thames barge with brown sails was tacking through the narrow bend in the river where the Alde turns west. 'Where's she going?' said Kit.

'She's taking London bricks up to Snape, then she'll load up with sugar beet for Reedham.'

'Doesn't she have an engine?'

'Not that one, if she needs to she can pick up a tow from Ralph Brinkley when she gets abeam of Iken. The river gets squiggly and narrow up there, but those barges can tack on their own length. They handle beautiful.'

Kit watched the barge tacking through the narrows. The low dark hull disappeared as she finally rounded the bend, but the sails were still visible above the riverbank. Meanwhile, a pair of American fighter jets were scoring the sky with vapour contrails. These British, thought Kit, who are they? They warm themselves by open coal fires, they relieve themselves in outside toilets, they still ship cargo under sail – and yet five miles away they are trying to build a hydrogen bomb. Kit watched the great tan sails gybe with the cool practised grace of a ballerina pirouetting into an arabesque. An hour ago the passing sails of that Thames barge had kissed the Atomic Weapons Research Establishment at Orford Ness with its wind shadow.

Billy had stopped watching the barge; he had found an old rag and was polishing a brass cleat. 'All this stuff,' he said, 'will come up pretty fine with a bit of Brasso.'

'What do you think of this boat, Billy?'

Billy paused and ran his hand over a coaming. 'She's one that Webb built in the 1930s at Pin Mill. These boats just *feel* right.'

'She's not bad, but she's got two cracked frames that need replacing. I want rock elm planks – which might not be easy to find.' Kit looked at the boy. He could see him weighing everything up. 'How handy are you, Billy?'

'Not bad.'

'Have you ever bent planks with a steam box before?'

'No, sir.'

'Can you learn how?'

Billy paused, then nodded his head.

'Good. Don't take any short cuts. I want this boat to be perfect. OK?'

Billy slowly nodded, his eyes bright with pride.

'And when you've finished that, I want all the seams re-caulked.'

Billy smiled, 'I've done lots of caulking – and I'll tidy up the rigging and brightwork too.'

'Are you sure you'll have time – with school and,' Kit paused because he sensed it was something he shouldn't mention, 'your singing lessons?'

Billy turned away and looked out to sea. 'I used to get a lot of stick about it at school – I had to use my fists to put them right on more than one occasion. But now the whole school – and the little kids from the primary too – are going to be in Mr Britten's new one. Hardly any adults, just kids.' Billy laughed.

'What's so funny?'

'This new opera sounds like it's going to be a right mess. The littlest ones are going to be bashing about with hand bells, sandpaper blocks and slinging mugs around. Meanwhile the rest of the kids are going to be singing, playing recorders and blowing bugles. I expect all the dead fishermen will come out of the sea and walk up Aldeburgh beach to see what all the racket's about.'

'What's it going to be called?'

'*Noye's Fludde*, but it's nowhere near finished.'

'Sounds like the story out of the Bible.'

'Some might think that, but there's been other floods too.'

'You had a bad flood here, didn't you?'

Billy's eyes narrowed and became hard: another raw nerve. Kit ignored the warning sign to keep off. 'I've heard about that '53 flood. How bad was it here?'

At first Billy ignored the question and concentrated on polishing the brass. Then he said, without looking up. 'It drowned my big sister – and her baby. She got confused in the night and must have run the wrong way. We found her and buried her – but the little one,' Billy swept his arm across the North Sea horizon, 'is still out there somewhere.'

'Her husband survived?'

'Louise didn't have a husband. She got up the duff when she was sixteen. The father was some Yank from the airbase. He'd cleared off long before Louise had the baby. No one ever told him what happened.' Billy paused, then said in flat tones, 'And we don't want him to know. It's nothing to do with him.'

Kit sensed the topic was closed. 'I suppose,' he said, 'we'd better tell Mr Gardiner that I'll buy the boat.'

After climbing down to the ground, Kit walked around the stern of the boat for one last look before setting off. For the first time he noticed the carved nameplate bolted on to the transom: *Louise of Ipswich*.

■

'Have you done much sailing, Brian?' Kit found making small talk with Jennifer's husband excruciating. Even the most innocent remark seemed to give offence.

'Not very much, in fact none at all. Manchester is not famous for its yachting.'

'But,' said Jennifer, 'you are going to take it up – you'll love it.'

Brian put his drink down and got up to stir the fire. Kit detected a scowl. Brian hadn't been brought up to feign enthusiasm or hide feelings. He'd be a lousy diplomat – or spy.

Jennifer got up and massaged the back of Brian's neck as he tended the fire. 'Poor thing, you're so tired.'

Kit turned away, embarrassed by the intimacy. Supper had been a strained experience too, but he could hardly have avoided accepting the invitation. He also loathed the idea of sleeping under the same roof – and knowing what might be taking place less than half a dozen paces from his own bed. Kit knew it would for him be a sleepless night – lying there listening and afraid to listen. He cursed himself for not having bought a packet of barbiturates. They were knock-out powders intended for slipping into the drinks of enemy agents – and on nights like this, Kit's imagination was the worst enemy of all. He looked at Jennifer. She was sitting in a deep armchair with her eyes half-closed. The firelight softened her features. Her face seemed more relaxed and content than it had for years. Kit forced his mind into double-think. He could love her happiness, but still hate the reason for it. Double-think was how you survived: his job had taught him that. The ones who couldn't do double-think were killed – like Peter – or went loopy. There was even a special hospital, Sheppard Pratt, for intelligence agents who cracked up. You couldn't risk them mouthing off secrets to 'normal' loonies from outside the Agency.

Kit sensed Jennifer was about to say something. It was an extrasensory thing they had shared since early childhood. She began to speak without moving or even opening her eyes. 'There's something I've always wanted to know,' her voice sounded like a spirit speaking through a medium, 'but until now I've never felt strong enough to ask.'

Kit knew what was coming. 'Don't, Jennie, don't.'

'No, Kit, I want you to tell me. How did Peter die?'

Kit wanted help. He looked at Brian who was staring at the fire with his hands folded. Why, Kit thought, don't you do something? Get up and put your strong protecting husband arm around her and say, 'Not now, dear.' Or even take her off to bed and do your lousy things. Kit felt nothing but rage and loathing. He wanted to pick up the fire poker and bring it down on Brian's dense head. Kit turned to Jennifer. 'You already know the facts. What more can I tell you?'

'Was the sun shining? What was Peter wearing? When was the last time he smiled? Lots of things, I want to know them all.'

Kit stared at the carpet. It was an Indian carpet, a moth-eaten and worn relic of the Raj. It brought back Gracey, his Ghurkas, the confusion and mess. 'It was,' said Kit, 'an unsettled day. There were lots of clouds, but the sun kept breaking through. The countryside around the airport was totally flat and bleak – so empty, it was almost ghostly.'

'And Peter?'

'Peter wasn't in a smiling mood. He was still furious about being PNG'd – and on top of all that, his expatriation flight from Tan Son Nhut had already been cancelled twice. After the second cancellation, we went back to the Villa Fevier, our local HQ, for lunch and a beer. Peter was restless. He felt like he was in limbo and just wanted to get going. Meanwhile, everything seemed to be falling apart. There was gunfire and columns of smoke from the villages around Saigon.' Kit turned to Brian, 'As you know, General Gracey had released and re-armed Japanese prisoners of war who were now burning Vietnamese villages.'

'Gracey had to restore order.'

'Well, Brian, he wasn't doing a very good job on that particular afternoon, because the Viet Minh retaliated by burning French warehouses on the docks and had set up so many roadblocks that travel without a military escort was impossible.'

'Tell me,' said Jennifer, 'about Peter.'

'After lunch we set off back to the airfield because there was finally word of a flight out. I'd been driving up until then, but Peter said he'd take over because he knew a short cut through the golf course. It was a dirt road, very bright red dirt, with drainage ditches on either side. Peter was wearing an ironed khaki uniform with his major's oak leaf on his collar. He'd grown a moustache – and it suited him.'

'I know. He sent Mom and Dad a photo. We all thought he looked like a film star.'

'Well, I remember thinking at the time, this is a bit like being in a film. We hadn't gone far – maybe four hundred yards – when we saw the roadblock. It seemed stupid. Why were they blocking a road like that? The only people who used it were probably the golf course greenkeepers. It wasn't much of a roadblock, just underbrush and saplings. Peter might have thought we could drive straight through it. There were kids – maybe fourteen or fifteen years old – on his side of the Jeep. Peter shouted at them to get out of the way. Of course, his French was so damned good he sounded like the real thing. I think he realised his mistake – even before he realised the kids had guns. You see they would never have shot at an American – we were the good guys back then. And because of that, a lot of French officers had taken to wearing American uniforms to protect themselves. I suppose the kids were really pissed off, thinking that Peter was one of those fake *Amerloques*.' Kit paused and smiled. 'You know for a second, it was really kind of funny. Sometimes things are so bad they cease to be tragedy and turn into farce. Do you know what I mean?'

Jennifer nodded, her face sensual in the firelight and a tear tracking down her cheek. Brian was stationary in the shadow.

'And Peter knew it too. His face curved into the broadest smile that I've ever seen – and then he started to laugh. The sound was like a million church bells on an Easter morning. He was still laughing when the back of his head flew off in fragments.'

Brian got up, severe in the shadows. 'I think you've said enough.'

'Shut up.'

'How dare you speak to me like…'

Jennifer was up now too, her calming hands on her husband's shoulders. 'It's my fault, Brian, I wanted to know. Please, let Kit finish.'

Kit stood up and offered Brian his hand. 'I apologise. I shouldn't have spoken to you that way.' They shook hands. Kit found Brian's hand as large and hard as seasoned oak.

Jennifer was sitting again and staring into the fire. 'There was no hope then.'

'And no pain either, there are a lot worse ways to go.'

'And what happened to you, poor Kit?'

'The Jeep veered off the road and into the ditch. I was thrown clear. As soon as I got up, I started shouting in bad Vietnamese, "*Khong ban* – don't shoot, I'm American, not a Frenchman." It seemed to confuse them – and I managed to run halfway back to the Villa Fevier before they started shooting. If I wasn't such a coward, Jennifer, I would have stayed with Peter.'

'There was nothing you could have done.'

'But we might not have lost his body.'

'Was there ever any news?'

'Only rumours and dozens of exhumed graves. All pointless. We'll never find him.'

Brian was still looming in the shadows. 'Do you blame us for what happened?'

'I blame Gracey and the people who let him get away with it. He refused to let us fly US flags from our Jeeps – and he was personally responsible for ordering Peter out of the country.'

'Why was he ordered out?'

'Peter made contact with the Viet Minh. He wanted to broker a peaceful handover of the Saigon region to a Vietnamese government. We thought we were following anti-colonial US policy. General Gracey, on the other hand, saw his job as holding the fort until the French could get back.'

'So you were on the side of the communists?'

'Some people might put it that way, but Peter thought we were on the side of the Vietnamese. That's the horrible irony. Peter was killed by the very people whose cause he supported.'

Brian emerged into the light. 'You make it all sound very innocent and idealistic. But, Kit, we all know the truth. Would you like a top-up?'

Kit offered his glass.

'The truth is,' Brian poured the whisky, 'you want to push us old fogeys out of the way so the world can be America's own playground. You want it all your way – and some of us don't want that to happen.'

Kit smiled. 'National interests, even of close allies, do not always coincide.'

Jennifer started to bank up the fire so it would keep in until the morning. 'I hope you two have finished talking foreign policy. I grew up with it.'

'Sorry, Jennifer,' said Brian. 'I just think it odd that Kit felt so strongly about the foreign occupation of Vietnam, but won't admit that Britain is an occupied territory too.'

'You're quite wrong, Brian, I *do* admit it.'

■

Kit lay awake in the spare room listening to the plumbing as the other two prepared for bed. The last plumbing noises ceased and the bedroom door gently shut. This was going to be the hardest hour. Those large firm hands troubled Kit. The fingers weren't tapered and graceful like a musician's, but strong and rough like a blacksmith's. Brian's fingers were made for tearing and poking. Kit tried to stop the obscene images from turning in his mind, but they kept coming. His brain had become a porn film that wouldn't stop: sometimes rewinding, sometimes fast-forwarding – then slow motion, grinding to a still. Jennifer: wide-eyed, panting and penetrated. And worst of all, enjoying it.

Kit covered his head with a pillow; he was so afraid of hearing something. Then he took the pillow away, sat up and listened to the dark watches of the night. There were owl noises in the garden. He prayed that there would be only silence from the marital bedroom. But there wasn't. It wasn't the noise of bedsprings, but the noise of the bed frame itself – as if the wood and joints were being strained. Then quiet again. Kit counted the minutes longing for the silence to remain unbroken. The noise was very faint at first: a soft mewing sound, then it became louder, but more muffled. It sounded like someone being hurt. He knew it was Jennifer.

■

It was late the next morning before Kit was back at his desk. The Suffolk trip had left an overflowing in-tray full of non-covert diplomatic stuff. The most bizarre was a note from Jeffers Cauldwell, the cultural attaché, marked urgent. The note consisted of one word: Elvis. 'Who,' said Kit aloud, 'who the fuck is Elvis?' He was about to phone for an explanation when the door opened and Cauldwell entered – as always, *comme il faut*. The elderly Ambassador, Aldrich Winthrop, regularly referred to his cultural attaché as the perfect image of a diplomat in terms of appearance and manners. Kit noticed that since being assigned to London Cauldwell had swapped Brooks Brothers charcoal-grey for Bond Street pinstripe. He was also wearing perfectly polished black wing-tips – what the British call brogues. Cauldwell was a dandy, but a tough dandy. He had been a star quarterback in high school and had commanded a PT boat in the Pacific: one that didn't get cut in half by a Jap destroyer. After the war, Cauldwell went to Harvard and got a degree in English Literature when he wasn't hanging around with the louche arts crowd in New York. He got to know Tennessee Williams, Jackson Pollock and Ginsberg.

'Who the fuck,' said Kit, 'is Elvis?'

The cultural attaché perched himself on the edge of Kit's desk and smiled. 'Are you serious? You really don't know who Elvis is?' Cauldwell spoke in a refined Deep South drawl that diphthongised every vowel. The cultural attaché was one of Kit's oldest friends in the diplomatic service. They had been on the same FSO induction course and worked together in Bonn and Berlin. When Kit was the first to get promoted, Cauldwell told him that it didn't change a thing: the Cauldwells would always be socially superior because they had owned more black people than Kit's family had. Kit wasn't sure that he was being ironic – and it worried him.

'Elvis,' repeated Cauldwell.

Kit leaned back, put his fingertips together and thought hard. 'The name vaguely rings a bell that has white trash reverberations.' Kit smiled, 'Is Elvis one of your relatives? Are you trying to get him into West Point?'

'Very *drôle*, Kit, very *drôle*. I actually thought you might be some help, but it looks like the PAO has left you out of the loop. And here was I thinking that you knew everything.'

'I only know important stuff, not utter drivel – so who is Elvis?'

'A cultural phenomenon – an androgynous white trash who sings with African rhythms and pumps and grinds with Latino hips. A good enough looking boy in a greaseball sort of way – but inclined, I suspect, to flab. He is, I must admit, a pretty damn good singer, but the important thing about Elvis is his ingénue sexuality. He's like a male Lolita. The sex he offers isn't real, but trashy, innocent and almost pre-pubescent. He is obscene in a uniquely American way. The prettiest street urchin in Athens or Tangier could never do an Elvis – those boys are too knowing, too corrupt. And, unlike Elvis, those boys will never make a million – or be on the Ed Sullivan show.'

'So what's the problem?'

'Personally, I don't think there is one. But the Information Service people are worried about the Elvis image.' Cauldwell put on his half-frame reading glasses, opened his briefcase and took out a vinyl record. 'Listen to this when you have a chance – it's called "Heartbreak Hotel".'

'Thanks. I'll file him in my collection between Elgar and Fauré.'

'Don't be a snob, Kit. Elvis is going to be very big – and the honchos at USIS are wetting themselves on how to deal with it. As you know, our job is to push cultural products that give a favourable image of America – like Broadway musicals and all that Doris Day crap. We've got to package Elvis in a way that doesn't offend – and then wrap him in the Stars and Stripes. I wanted some ideas from you.'

'Why, Jeffers, don't you guys push our best artists and writers instead of populist stuff.'

'Don't be silly. Our *best* writers and artists are usually insane, alcoholic, drug addicted, politically beyond the pale like Pound – or given to illegal sexual practices.'

'What about Whitman and Melville?'

'They're OK, they're long dead.' Cauldwell paused. 'By the way, are you sure your office isn't bugged by those assholes in the basement?'

'Absolutely.' Kit was certain for two reasons. One, he had the sweepers in on a regular basis. Two, he used his friendship with the marine captain to gain further access to the FBI cupboard to check what and who they were monitoring. But since the captain was soon to be assigned to the DoD Language School at Monterey, Kit would have to be more discreet in the future.

'That's good. In my own office I feel like Winston in *1984*.' Cauldwell paused. 'Listen, Kit, I've got to talk to you about something.'

'Go on.'

'You know about Henry?'

'I think I met him in the pub – doesn't he play violin in some big London orchestra?'

'That's the one.'

'Seems like a nice guy.'

'Well, Kit,' Cauldwell seemed to be weighing his words, 'Henry and I have sort of moved in together.'

'Have you told any one else?'

'No.'

'Good. You have to be discreet. There's nothing wrong with having a flatmate or a lodger – but don't volunteer the information unless one of the assholes tries to make an issue of it.' Kit looked closely at Cauldwell. 'I've got an idea, but I don't suppose you'd go along with it?'

'What then?'

'Why don't you find a girlfriend as camouflage? You wouldn't have to bed her, you'd only need to take her to a few official functions – and that would stop tongues from wagging.'

'Oh for Chrissake, Kit, I'm not Hollywood horseflesh, I'm a career diplomat. Give me some dignity. Some of your ideas are really crap.'

'I'm only looking after your interests. At the moment we're lucky at this embassy. The Ambassador and the DCM are both civilised and liberal gentlemen, but there's a cold brutal wind blowing from the other side of the Atlantic. McCarthy wasn't the finale, he was the prelude.'

'I know that and I'm grateful for your concern.'

'Good.' Kit smiled and winked. 'Now just suppose, Jeffers, that…'

'Suppose what?'

'Suppose you *had* to do it with a girl. Someone was holding a gun to your head. Who would you choose?'

Cauldwell folded his arms and laughed. 'Well as far as the female staff of this embassy are concerned, I think I would prefer to take the bullet.' Cauldwell then paused and looked into the distance as if gazing upon an imaginary picture gallery. 'If I really had to do it with a woman, I'd choose that sister of yours.'

'You must be joking, they're both terrible! Which one did you mean? Caddie? Virginia?'

'No, neither of those names rings a bell.'

'I haven't got any other sisters.'

Cauldwell snapped his fingers. 'Her name was Jennifer. I met her at one of your dad's parties in Georgetown – a real beauty, coltish and slim-hipped.'

Kit felt a tremor run down his spine; he wanted to punch Cauldwell in the face. 'She's a… she's not my sister, she's my cousin.'

'You seemed very close – in appearance and manner. Some families are like that.'

'We were very close.'

'What's she doing now?'

'She married an Englishman – they live in Suffolk. So you can forget having a date with her.'

'You sound almost angry.'

'I'm just pretending.'

Cauldwell got up as if to leave, then glanced down at a document on the desk.

Kit swiftly covered it with a folder. It was a naval intelligence report on underwater espionage. 'Do you mind?'

'Don't get ratty, Kit, I've got a top secret clearance too you know?'

Kit slid the folder down a couple of inches so Cauldwell could read the full classification heading: EYES ONLY + NEED TO KNOW. It meant severely restricted access regardless of the officer's security clearance.

'Shit,' said Cauldwell, 'you make me jealous. I wish I had a job like yours.'

Kit hefted a thick wad of documents in his in-tray. 'Most of this POLCOUNS stuff is mind-numbing – and when do I get invited to film premieres and glamorous soirées?'

'I wasn't referring to your diplomatic job.'

Kit frowned and leaned back in his chair. 'You're not supposed to know about my other job.'

'But Kit, *everyone* knows. It's an open secret.'

'OK, but open secrets are still secrets.'

'Like Lord Boothby and the Chancellor of the Exchequer's wife?'

'Absolutely. And I would keep quiet about that one – we're not supposed to know.'

'I'm glad I'm not part of it,' said Cauldwell. 'Women have strange tastes.'

Kit felt a tremor pass down his spine.

'Did you know,' said Cauldwell, 'that Boothby is fucking Ronnie Kray too?'

'Really?' Kit was genuinely surprised. 'How do you know?'

'I've got my agents too.'

'Maybe we *should* swap jobs.'

'By the way,' said Cauldwell, 'does cousin Jennifer live anywhere near Aldeburgh?'

'Fairly near, about ten miles.'

'That's interesting, could be very handy.'

'Why?'

Cauldwell waited and smiled at Kit. 'It's in reference to that job of yours we're not allowed to talk about.'

'Go on.'

'You realise that Henry has to travel a lot with the orchestra – Europe, Far East and Russia too. In the music world, they tend to club together according to type of instrument. Brass hang around with brass, woodwinds with woodwinds – and strings, of course, with strings. They all know each other. It's an intimate world of foreign hotels: loneliness happens and so do indiscretions. Does the name Natalya Voronova mean anything to you?'

'Should it?'

'It should. Natalya Voronova is one of the best cellists in the world – and she isn't very happy.'

'Why isn't she happy?'

'She doesn't get on with her husband – she doesn't love him.'

'Is he a cellist too?'

'No, he's a nuclear scientist in Semipalatinsk.' Cauldwell pulled an envelope out of his pocket and handed it to Kit. 'All the details are in there – including the dates Voronova will be playing at the Aldeburgh Festival.'

'Thanks.'

Cauldwell walked to the door. 'By the way, Kit.'

'Yes?'

'Have you ever killed anyone with your bare hands?'

'No.'

'I have.'

Cauldwell had gone before Kit had the chance to search the cultural attaché's face for the trace of a joking smile.

Chapter Seven

Kit had taken the train to Portsmouth via Brighton. He shared the compartment with a French au pair who was returning to Nantes for Easter. Kit put on his East End 'legend': that he was a *Québécois* who worked for a shipping firm in London. He was feeling nervous about what he was going to have to do and wanted light relief. In fact, the adrenalin rush of an op always excited him and made him a little silly. Kit had really begun to like being François Laval. As he entertained the au pair with stories of Laval's life and travels, Kit began to prefer his fictional self to his real self. The escape from self was like an intravenous shot of mood changing drug. Between Brighton and Worthing they caught a glimpse of the sea. Kit offered the au pair a shot of brandy from his hip flask. The drink seemed to widen her eyes and swell her lips. The sea was gleaming in the April sun. Kit started and the girl joined in:

> *La mer*
> *Qu'on voit danser le long des golfes clairs*
> *A des reflets d'argent, la mer*
> *Des reflets changeants sous la pluie*

They embraced and kissed as the train passed through a tunnel. Kit felt her mouth open beneath his: her tongue was groping and hungry. Emboldened Kit began to slip his hand up her dress – there was no resistance – until he felt the damp inviting warmth of her sex. Maybe this was what he really wanted. He was more intoxicated by his disguise than the brandy. For one glorious liberating moment, he was François Laval: a normal man with normal desires.

As the train slowed on the station approach, the au pair smiled and confided that their meeting was a great coincidence. They both had the same first name. Hers was Françoise. Later, as they parted on the platform, she looked at Kit in a strange way. 'Who are you?' she said. 'You don't have a Quebec accent, you have a normal French accent.' As Kit watched her disappear in the crowd bustling towards the ferry, he felt the fake François Laval fall from his shoulders and turn into dead ash.

It was a short walk from the station to the Sally Port Hotel. Kit had booked two rooms – even though he might only need one. Driscoll was arriving under his own steam in a Humber van. Kit hoped he'd remembered to swap the number plates and would drive carefully: a police check would thwart the whole thing. The plan was to meet in a lorry park late that afternoon. Driscoll would change into his frogman suit in the back of the van – and then Kit would drive him to the King Stairs at least an hour ahead of Crabb and his handler. It was going to be an awkward social situation – like turning up to a dinner party to which you had pointedly not been invited.

Kit checked into the Sally Port under the name of Paul Martin. It was best to use simple names for cover legends: ones that didn't stick in the mind or were easy to pin down. The world was full of Martins and Browns and Wilsons – surname anonymity. In Vietnam it was even better. Eighty-five per cent of the population had the family name of either Nguyen or Trinh – so you knew people by their first names, which weren't their first names at all, but their last names. A spy needs to know the culture. And in the spy trade, names are the most valuable currency of all – more valuable than nuclear secrets. You might have the recipe for hydrogen bomb cookies, but you can't bake those cookies unless you have the engineering and industrial base to build the right oven. But names were gold dust – that's how Burgess and Maclean had done so much damage, they knew the names. And the irony is that no one has *more* names than a spy.

The window in Kit's room faced north-west and gave a good view of the harbour. The *Ordzhonikidze* and two accompanying destroyers had docked that morning. The cruiser was lying alongside South Railway Jetty with her stern facing the harbour entrance. The two destroyers, *Sovershenny* and *Smotryaschy,* were rafted beside her like nursing pups. Most of the *Ordzhonikidze* was hidden from Kit's view by cranes and warehouses, but her masts and aft gun turrets were visible. Kit took a pair of binoculars out of his travelling bag for a quick look. There was nothing much to see: her rotating radar dishes had been covered with grey tarpaulins. A useless security precaution, for US

Navy reconnaissance aircraft had already provided the agency with high resolution photographs of every diode and bolt – and the Russians knew it. The tarpaulins were just theatre props to impress the Brits.

Kit focused the binoculars on South Railway Jetty. He was surprised it hadn't been cordoned off from the public. Crowds of sightseers were freely strolling along the quay – many strewn with cameras and taking snaps. The *Ordzhonikidze* had become an instant tourist attraction. Kit shifted the glasses back to the cruiser. A sailor with black hair and a gymnast's body was waving and blowing kisses to someone on the quay. He wondered if it might be his French au pair. No longer his.

He could almost hear her singing to another man. And why shouldn't she? Kit felt a pang of jealousy and longing. He wasn't a proper man; he was nothing more than an eunuch of the State, like the sterile workers in an ant colony. At some point, the State had ceased to be an ideology or even a nation. It was a way of being that consumed – not the ordinary soldiers and sailors, they were free to blow kisses – but the State's own masters.

■

Driscoll was slumped in the driver's seat of the van reading a tabloid newspaper. The Irishman was wearing a donkey jacket and a flat cap. He looked every inch a genuine English workman. Kit thought, however, that the flat cap wasn't quite right. Brits of Driscoll's generation went bareheaded to show off their pomaded quiffs. Kit was carrying a heavy black leather bag. He shifted the bag to his left hand and tapped on the van's window. Driscoll reached over to open the passenger door.

Kit got in. 'Everything OK?'

'Yeah.'

Kit looked around the lorry park. The state of the vehicles was a sad reflection of the British economy: some were from the 1920s. There was even an old Thorneycroft lorry with solid tyres and an open cab with a wooden door. The driver was muffled up with scarves and had a pair of goggles dangling from a piece of string. The ancient lorry seemed to be used for hauling coal and the driver's face was coated with black dust. He was probably waiting to pick up a load from the docks. It reminded Kit of that blustery day with Jennifer on Dunwich beach and the collier beating down to London. A moment of purity. And now he was in a filthy van that reeked of sweat and stale tobacco. Kit watched the Thorneycroft driver unscrew a thermos and pour himself a cup of tea while making furtive glances in their direction. 'Anyone speak to you?'

'No.'

'Good.'

Driscoll looked at the driver. 'He gave me a nod, but backed off. The one good thing about Brits is that they keep their distance. They can tell when you don't want to talk. The Irish don't care – they'll talk your leg off even if you're not listening.'

'Bad for security.'

'I know.'

'Listen,' said Kit, 'there's a change of plan.'

'I don't like the sound of this.'

'I want you to do the business when the flood tide is at its strongest.'

'Shit, do you think I'm some sort of Olympic swimmer?'

'You won't have any problem getting there.'

'But how am I going to get back?'

'You'll manage, but if you can't, I've marked some alternative ex-filtration points on your chart.'

'It's a stupid state of tide to do a job like this.'

'I know, but I want to keep you as far away from Crabb as possible.'

'So I won't have to kill him.'

'That's right.'

'Good. He may be a Brit officer, but I don't like killing other divers – we're like brothers, but you wouldn't understand.'

'You're right, Driscoll, I don't understand anything.'

Kit couldn't tell Driscoll the whole truth about the dive. He couldn't tell him that the Russians knew that Crabb was going to be spying and supposedly doing worse things to their ship. Likewise, Kit had deceived Vasili. He had told him nothing about Driscoll. The whole point of Kit's double deception was to convince Vasili and the Sovs that the mines had been planted by Crabb. Kit knew that the Russians would be expecting Crabb at slack water because the ageing diver wasn't fit enough to do the job at any other time. Kit reasoned that the Russians would be least vigilant when the tide was running strongest: they couldn't maintain constant guard underwater, not enough divers and oxygen tanks. Therefore, a hard running tide was Driscoll's best chance of escaping capture or being killed.

'You want me,' said Driscoll, 'to have a look at the bottom of the hull for sonar and mine laying ports?'

'You won't have time. You've got to get in and out really quick.' Kit undid the black leather bag. 'The only thing I want you to do is put these on the hull.'

Driscoll stared at two identical lumps bulging in their black waterproof covers. 'I didn't think you were serious. You made me think we weren't going to go that far.'

'Will you do it or not?'

'I'm not sure. You're asking me to do something which is just too fucking serious. I don't want to cause another world war.'

'We're not going to sink that ship, and there wouldn't be a war even if something went wrong and we did.' Kit hoped he wasn't giving away too much. 'Look, the purpose of this op is to ruin Britain's reputation as a responsible world power. With any luck Russia will break off diplomatic relations and the British government will fall – and that would be a big step to a united Ireland. I thought that's what you guys want.'

Driscoll lifted one of the limpet mines out of the bag. 'Mark ones. The timers have a maximum delay of seventy-two hours – we should put these on just before she sails, otherwise she might sink in the harbour.'

'Don't worry, the timers have been altered. I've already set them.'

Driscoll picked up a mine. 'They're heavy on land, but light as a feather in water.'

'Why's that?'

'You're not a diver, are you?'

'No.'

'Limpets have neutral buoyancy, which means they almost float. Otherwise, the magnets wouldn't be strong enough to hold them to a hull.'

Of course, thought Kit, the clear logic of destruction and war. If only we organised our lives and loves as cleverly as we organised the killing of others. 'I think,' said Kit, 'you'd better get changed. I'll drive.'

Driscoll still had the mine in his hand and was looking at it as if it were an evil genie. 'I hope you know what you're doing.'

As Kit helped Driscoll get into his diving suit, something else began to bother him. He realised that the diver's first loyalty was to Irish Republicanism. And although there had been a falling out with one IRA commander, Kit suspected there may have been reconciliation with another. The movement was riven with sects and factions – a fact exploited by the British. Could Driscoll, thought Kit, have passed on something about the dive? And what if his new IRA unit had been infiltrated by MI5?

■

The tide was flooding hard when they reached King's Stairs. It would be another three hours before slack water. Kit was certain that Crabb and his handler would wait until the tide had begun to slacken. He was sure that Crabb would follow the same routine as when they spied on the *Sverdlov*. A quick swim up to the ship on the waning flood, then back again on the new ebb. It was effortless: just a matter of drifting with the changing current – perfect for an elderly frogman. Also perfect for any Soviet divers waiting in ambush.

Kit parked as near the harbour steps as he could. It was broad daylight, but it didn't matter much if they were seen. It was normal to see divers carrying out underwater maintenance on the crumbling jetties in the spring after the winter gales. In any case, Driscoll was out of the van and into the dark swirling waters in less than half a minute. Kit watched the black-masked head bob through the rotting piles of the King's Stairs jetty. Driscoll, thought Kit, looked more like a seal than a human. He wondered if he'd ever see him again.

Sending Driscoll in on a fast flowing tide was a calculated risk. Kit also assumed that the Sovs had Crabb under surveillance and wouldn't send down their own divers until they had been warned that he was going in. On the other hand, Kit was perfectly aware that he himself might be under surveillance – and that in a very few minutes Driscoll might find his head being cut off by a Ukrainian Olympic weightlifter.

Kit picked up the tabloid that Driscoll had been reading. Grace Kelly had just married Prince Rainier III. They had to get married twice because Monaco, like France, required a civil ceremony before a religious one. The Chancellor, Harold Macmillan, had just come up with 'something completely new for the savers of Great Britain'. It was called 'a premium bond', not 'a pool or lottery'. You got your money back – without interest. Like the bedroom in a bored marriage. Kit tossed the paper into the back of the van and gazed out into the harbour.

Kit fought off a wave of self-doubt and fear; his hands were clammy and sweaty. He was only doing his job, carrying out US foreign policy. Washington disapproved of the Soviet goodwill visit. In fact, 'the Seventh Floor' – diplomat slang for the Secretary of State – was appalled that the British government was moving towards a policy of unilateral détente with the Soviet Union. Kit's job was to destroy the Khrushchev-Bulganin goodwill visit and to poison Anglo-Russian relations. The West must speak with one voice and strike with one fist – and both had to be American. Kit fought off another wave of self-loathing. He wondered if Caesar's envoys had ever felt the same – and yet the Gauls and the Celts had never built a single aqueduct bubbling with clean water or laid a single straight road of good stone.

Kit knew, or at least prayed, that the limpet mines would never go off. His note to Vasili had suggested that MI6 were using Crabb to plant mines. Crabb was, after all, a renowned limpet mine expert and had won the George Cross for de-mining British ships during the war. Kit felt sorry for Crabb. He knew that the Russian divers were just as likely to kill him as capture him. But the important thing was that the Russians search the hull of the ship to see if Crabb had left anything behind. The Sov divers would have to be totally incompetent if they didn't find the limpets. Kit fervently hoped that Vasili had taken his warning about the mines seriously – and that the information had been passed on to the captain of the *Ordzhonikidze*.

But what if they didn't find the mines? Kit had already made up his mind that he would own up to the Russians and send Driscoll back to show them where he had placed the mines. Kit's own life and career were far less important than the risk of starting a nuclear war. He'd lied to Driscoll. The consequences of sinking a Soviet ship and drowning their leaders would be far more than the diplomatic isolation of Britain. And what would happen to him then? Prison in the USA or USSR – or a bullet in the head. Kit put his hand deep in his overcoat pocket and felt the pill bottle – or cyanide? It's a rough trade. Especially for Catholics who believe that suicide is a mortal sin. Worse than murder, Kit. Taking a life that God gave someone else is bad enough, but destroying the precious gift He gave to you alone is spitting in Creation's face. But anyone with half a brain knows all that stuff is a load of shit. Double-think, Kit, keep practising – you're getting good at it.

But, fingers crossed, the Russian divers would find the mines – and there would be one hell of a diplomatic incident. It would be bad for Britain, but not as bad as Kit had told Driscoll – the idea of the incident helping bring about a united Ireland was an exaggeration and a lie. And the mines themselves would never be mentioned in the press – all that would be too sensitive and not in the national interest of either country. The Russians would probably accept Eden's explanation that MI6 had been acting totally without authorisation – which was true. But what assurance was there that it would never happen again? Was the elected British government capable of controlling its Secret Intelligence Service? And that, thought Kit, *is* a damned good question. In any case, relations between Britain and the Soviet Union would be poisoned for decades to come – and that would suit Washington fine. Kit was doing his job.

∎

Kit checked his watch. Driscoll had been gone for nearly an hour and a half. Twenty minutes later than the worst case ETA. Maybe he'd been spotted and had escaped by swimming up river with the tide behind him. Maybe, thought Kit, he ought to drive around to the ex-filtration point he had marked on the chart. It was near a posh yacht club. Kit could imagine the scene: 'I say, d'you mind if I borrow your man? I want him to look at the rudder pinions on my yawl.' Kit shielded his eyes against the late afternoon sun. The water had gone a glittery silver gold. He strained to see that black seal's head – but nothing. I'll give him, thought Kit, another fifteen minutes and then drive to the yacht club.

From King's Stairs it was only possible to see the stern of the outermost Soviet destroyer. Kit took out his binoculars. There was a boat alongside the destroyer with a big blond sailor curling a rope. No frogmen or nervous officers looking over the side. Then it came, borne on the wind, a sharp popping sound – like a rifle shot. It could have been anything. Like what? Kit looked at his watch again; the fifteen minutes of grace had gone. He thought about the second room at the Sally Port Hotel: 'I'm ever so sorry, but my colleague from the shipping agency has been delayed by some urgent business in London.' 'Yes, he's Canadian too.' Kit opened the van door and looked out towards the end of the jetty. It wasn't a seal, it was Driscoll. He was struggling: the tide was dragging him sideways towards the jagged underwater pier pilings, but he kept fighting against it and coming closer to the stairs. After one more struggle, Driscoll finally found a firm footing and pushed the mask off his face. He was breathing hard.

Kit walked to the concrete steps on the side of the jetty. The tide was now two feet higher covering all but the top step. He gave a hand to Driscoll and helped him stagger ashore. 'That fucking tide, you can't imagine that fucking tide.'

'We'll talk later, get in the back of the van.'

Kit started the engine and spun the van around. Just as they got to the harbour gate, a large saloon car turned in off Queen Street. Kit recognised Crabb's handler in the driving seat. He was an MI6 operative who went by the stupidly obvious alias of Smith. Kit saw 'Smith' give him a surprised glance and then turn around to say something to Crabb who was already in his diving suit.

'What took you so long?' said Kit.

'They knew I was there. After I finished the job, I saw a diver above me in the gap between the nearest destroyer and the cruiser. There were probably others. I don't think anyone saw me so I went deep and swam under the keels of both destroyers and out into the middle of the harbour – that's when the tide caught me. I came to the surface once and someone took a pot shot.'

Kit stopped as soon as he saw a public phone. He dialled a number to a phone that was almost certainly tapped – but things had gone too far for that to make any difference. As soon as Vasili answered, he said the agreed word in Russian, then in English, 'Cookees.' The phone clicked as Vasili hung up. Kit leaned his head against the glass of the phone kiosk; he felt nauseous. 'Poor Crabb,' he said, 'poor Crabb – whoever you are, give him peace.'

■

When they got to the Sally Port Hotel, Driscoll was dry and combed. He looked like an almost respectable businessman from a rough background – which fitted in perfectly with the hotel's ambience. There was no one at reception, so Kit leafed through the hotel register to check out the other guests. 'Shit,' he said.

'What's wrong?'

'Don't ask. We're not staying here.'

When they got back to the van, Kit paid off Driscoll – and

gave him ten pounds extra. 'Forget about checking out the sonar. There's definitely not going to be another dive tomorrow – or the next day. Ditch the van as soon as you can and take a train back to London. Your Kilburn digs are still fine – stay there until you hear otherwise.'

'What if I want out – after this shit?'

'It might be safer to stay in.'

'Is that a threat?'

Kit closed his eyes and breathed deeply. 'Why the fuck, why the fuck can't you take friendly advice?' He looked at Driscoll. 'Do you think I like doing this shit?'

'Then why do you do it?'

'Maybe I've got six kids and a big mortgage? Maybe I need the money so I can go to college and become a lawyer?' Kit took a notebook and pencil out of this pocket. 'Or maybe I can't get out either. Here, I want you to draw me a sketch of exactly where you placed those mines.'

'What difference does it make?'

'Just draw.'

Driscoll drew the underside of the *Ordzhonikidze* with fast sure strokes and put circles with x's inside them to show the mines. 'They're both here – under the port quarter. It's best to hole the hull in the same area – it sinks them quicker.' He moved the pencil towards the bows. 'By the way, there is a pair of large underwater doors here – big enough for laying large mines or putting out divers.'

Or, thought Kit, for saying hello to uninvited guests.

■

Kit got Driscoll to drop him off in a run-down area near the main station. There were numerous bombsites: cleared, but still not rebuilt. The British hadn't been whacked as badly as the Russians or Germans, but the Americans hadn't been whacked at all. A lot of his colleagues kept forgetting that.

It was a lousy hotel, but it was too late to be choosy. The desk clerk was smoking and dropped fag ash over the register as Kit signed it in the name of William Stewart. The room was loathsome. The sheets hadn't been changed and – an especially nice touch – there was a pubic hair on the pillowcase.

Kit hadn't bothered to check the names of the other guests. It wasn't likely that Crabb and MI6 would lower themselves to such a dump. Besides they were all staying at the Sally Port. The thing that alarmed Kit most of all was that there were five of them. Crabb had signed in his own name, his handler had used his usual alias – and then added names for three more rooms in his own handwriting. Who were the other three? That's why Kit had cleared off: he wasn't going to stay in a hotel packed with SIS.

■

The following day dawned wet and overcast. Kit said 'no thanks' to breakfast and checked out. He left his bag in left luggage at the station and went for a walk along the docks. He constantly felt eyes in the back of his neck. Despite the rain, there were still large numbers of sightseers milling about on the South Railway Jetty and gawping at the *Ordzhonikidze*. If you walked to the edge of the quay, the Russian warship was almost close enough to touch. Kit looked down into the dark oily water between the grey hull and the jetty pilings: bottles, wood waste, drowned rats, chip papers and rubbish indescribable jigged along the ship's water-line. For a second, Kit imagined a human face rising out of the filth. How can we do this to anyone? Kit suddenly jerked upwards and backed away from the quay's edge. Had someone pushed him? He turned around. There was no one there at all – but the eyes were still boring into the back of his neck.

Kit pulled his collar up against the wet south-westerly wind and walked to the southern end of South Railway Jetty. He turned around and looked at the stern quarters of the *Ordzhonikidze*. Driscoll was right, it was there that she looked most slender and vulnerable. Kit wondered if the mines were still clinging to the cruiser's undersides. Part of him wanted to run back to the ship and shout a warning to the nearest sailor. Kit turned away and looked south. The edge of the jetty was about two hundred yards from King's Stairs. He was surprised to see that Smith's saloon car was still there – along with another identical one. They were obviously pool vehicles. Smith was leaning against a car's bonnet talking to a tall man wearing a trilby. Both were looking out into the harbour. Had there been another dive?

Kit turned around and retraced his steps into the town. He stopped at a restaurant called The Lighthouse for a lunch of fish and chips and strong tea. 'Yes,' he always told his American friends, 'they really do put vinegar on their French fries.' Now Kit found himself dripping the vinegar too.

Kit looked at his watch. There was still time for more snooping before the London train. Kit walked down Queen's Road then turned towards King's Stairs. He saw that the saloon cars were gone. He continued towards the jetty and harbour steps. The only evidence of drama was a scattering of cigarette butts around where the saloon cars had been parked. The only sounds were ship's whistles, the mournful toll of bell buoys and gulls. Nothing.

It was risky, but Kit wanted to have one more look at the Sally Port Hotel. As soon as he turned the corner, he saw there were lots of cars. Some with police markings, but most were unmarked government pool cars – some looked like MoD police. Kit walked briskly down the street on the opposite side from the hotel. There was a hastily drawn sign stuck to the front entrance of the Sally Port: Temporarily Closed. Kit passed close by a uniformed policeman talking to a man in civilian clothes. The only words he picked up were 'funny stuff' and 'Russians'.

■

Before he boarded the train, Kit made one last phone call. Vasili's voice had laughter in it: 'Chocolate chip cookies,' he said. Kit hung up the phone and breathed easy. Thank God, they had found the mines.

The London train was half-full. A large number of soldiers and sailors were heading back to London for weekend leaves. They all seemed half-asleep. The British wore uniforms with reluctance, but with natural poise. Americans, on the other hand, tried too hard. There were other differences too. The Americans had 'unknown soldiers', the British had 'unknown warriors'; the US military used 'power', the British wielded 'might'. There was something about the British that was inexplicable, something primal and tribal. Kit leaned back in his dusty train seat – why did train carriages always seem coated in a thin film of dust? Maybe it was because of the coal. There were men on the tracks in boiler suits – men old enough to wear flat caps and jaunty scarves. Wherever you went in Britain, they were always there: a Greek chorus leaning on shovels. The engine chuffed and the train lurched forward. Ten minutes later Kit was – for the first time in three days – sound asleep.

Kit woke up after Basingstoke and set off to find the buffet car. He needed a drink, but the buffet was closed. It happened on the way back to his seat when he was passing between two carriages.

The hard push in the centre of the back came a second before the words. 'You fucking bastard.' Kit felt his forehead slam hard against the glass window of the train door. His left arm was bent up hard against his back. He felt a blast of cold air as the door opened. It was a long drop and the blackness was passing in a loud whirl of chaos. Kit pulled free and flung himself away from the abyss. He was now facing his attacker. It was Smith. He didn't have time to duck. Smith landed a straight right on the side of Kit's mouth. The wind blew the door shut.

Kit collapsed on to his haunches with his hands over his head to ward off further blows. Smith started to wade in with kicks, but his foot got caught in the folds of Kit's coat. Then a train guard opened the door between the carriages. The guard had a gold watch chain and a silver moustache. 'Gentlemen,' he said, 'gentlemen, please. May I see your tickets?' The guard's manner suggested that stopping passengers from murdering each other was just another part of his job.

Smith gave Kit a last look. 'Don't worry, Fournier, we're going to get you.' He then opened the carriage door and disappeared towards the front of the train.

The guard then helped Kit to his feet. 'Let's get you back to your seat, sir.'

■

The news of Crabb's disappearance broke ten days later. The Kremlin press office called the incident 'shameful espionage'. The Soviet Embassy in London informed the British Foreign Office that it 'would be grateful to receive an explanation'.

Kit now had a copy of the FO's explanation on his desk and read it a second time trying to tease out the coded significance of each word. 'Commander Crabb was engaged in diving tests and is presumed to have met his death while so engaged. The diver, who, as stated in the Soviet note, was observed from the Soviet warships to be swimming between the Soviet destroyers, was presumably Commander Crabb.' Kit smiled. The reference to 'diving tests' was the flimsiest of fig leafs. In the very next sentence the Foreign Office virtually admits that Crabb was spying. 'Presumably' was merely inserted as a diplomatic caveat to avoid pleading guilty to a serious breach of international law. 'Yes, your honour, it was my finger on the trigger and *presumably* I shot the bastard.'

Kit found the last sentence of the British statement the most revealing. 'His approach to the destroyers was completely unauthorised and Her Majesty's government desire to express their regret at the incident.' No more wheedling 'presumablies'; the key phrase is 'completely unauthorised'. It's a bit like inviting a couple around to dinner. Five minutes after they arrive at your house, your guest's wife goes to powder her nose and one of your servants follows her up the stairs and sticks his hand up her dress. If you had done it, the friendship would be over and you might get punched on the nose, but since it was one of your staff – behaving in a 'completely unauthorised' manner – you've got a way out. Of course, you now have to dismiss the horny servant. Kit knew the Prime Minister had no alternative. Eden was going to have to sack the Head of MI6, Major General John Sinclair. Kit had bagged the biggest beast of his career. The self-loathing was still there, but there was exhilaration too. Is that why people became assassins? Little vermin with small dicks wanting to make their marks. He wondered if Allen Dulles would be pleased. Kit wished that he had drowned himself in Portsmouth Harbour.

Neither the British nor the Soviet statement mentioned the *Ordzhonikidze*: the cruiser was the elephant in the room. Nor would the limpet mines be mentioned – ever. That file wouldn't see the light of day for another hundred years. But other powers and other intelligence services would pore over each word of the British apology like scholars of Biblical exegesis – and come to the conclusion that something was being held back. In terms of coded diplomatic language, the Foreign Office statement was far too repentant to be an apology for something as relatively minor as a bit of underwater spying. And everyone in the trade knew it.

•

Kit invented a mugging incident to explain his split lip and black eye. Only Cauldwell was sceptical about the cover story. 'I bet you took on two Sov agents with your bare hands and crippled both of them.'

'Actually, there were three of them.'

'What a hero.'

'And now I've got to go back to Washington so the President can give me a medal in the rose garden.'

'Really?'

'No, I'm fibbing. It's just a routine consultation at the State Department. I'll be gone about eight days.'

The Washington trip bothered him, but he wasn't going to show it. Kit didn't know why he'd been summoned and wasn't looking forward to it. Another bad omen was the fact that he was being called in for an 'interview' by counter-intelligence. The reason could be anything from a minor breach of security regulations to suspicion of spying for a foreign power. It could be bad shit – and you were never told in advance the reasons why you were being interviewed. Counter-intelligence always wanted to keep their interviewees on the back foot so they couldn't fabricate alibis. It also worried Kit that the interview was scheduled to take place the very day of his flight to the States – they might decide to send him back in handcuffs.

■

The interview room was in the embassy cellar. There were no windows, no wall coverings – not even a carpet. Nothing but exposed heating pipes, an overhead florescent light, metal desk, metal chairs, polygraph lie-detector and tape recorder.

'How you doing, Kit?' The interviewer, Bill Shepherd, limped over to shake hands. 'Nice to see you.'

'Fine, nice to see you too, Bill.' Kit knew that Shepherd's limp came from an injury sustained parachuting behind communist lines in Korea. No one in the Agency, absolutely no one, enjoyed more respect than Bill Shepherd. Kit was relieved to see that his interrogator would be an old friend. Bill and he had been GI Bill classmates at the University of Virginia after the war.

'Sorry about this,' said Bill, as he finished threading a tape through the recording machine. 'I hope we can get through this as quick as possible and then go for a beer.'

'Bill.'

'Yes.'

'Spare me the "make a friendly rapport with the prisoner" shit. We've both done the course on interrogation techniques – so give me some professional dignity.'

Shepherd sat down and sighed. 'Listen, Kit, I was being genuine – it wasn't a trick. To be perfectly frank, I feel totally fucking embarrassed by this.'

'Sorry, I'm feeling a bit touchy. Let's just get on with it.'

'The most embarrassing bit comes now.' Shepherd took a Bible out of his briefcase.

'You can't be serious – you mean I've got to fucking swear.'

'Yeah, I know, it's stupid, but the shadow of McCarthy is still with us. Thomas Jefferson must be turning over in his grave.' Shepherd picked up the Bible and turned on the machine. '30 April 1956, the US Embassy, London, England. Minister Counsellor Kitson Fournier, you are being interviewed under section five of the National Security Act. By agreeing to this interview, you are waiving your rights guaranteed under the Fifth Amendment to the US Constitution. Any statements you make may be cited as evidence and used against you in any future proceedings. Do you agree to proceed with this interview?'

'Yes.'

Shepherd winked and held up the Bible. 'Do you solemnly swear to tell the truth, the whole truth and nothing but the truth?'

'Yes.'

'Did you make a total of two telephone calls from public phones in Portsmouth, England to the Soviet Embassy on 17 and 18 April of this year?'

'Yes.'

'To whom were you speaking on these occasions?'

'Refer to DCI.' It was a standard response indicating the answer had to be withheld on security grounds. The question could only be answered with the permission of the Director of Central Intelligence.

'Did you make and file a transcript of these telephone conversations?'

'There were no conversations as such. They were simply coded signals consisting of a single word or two.' Kit frowned and pointed to the recording machine.

Shepherd pressed the pause button. 'Listen, Kit, I'm not supposed to stop this thing. It's not SOP. I'll have to write a note.'

'Bill, who the fuck are you working for? British intelligence or US intelligence?'

'What do you mean?'

'Don't play the innocent. You know what I mean – the only people who have phone taps on the Soviet Embassy are the Brits. We don't. I know that because I tried to tap the Sov lines as soon as I got here – and was told off.'

'OK, Kit, it's shared intelligence.'

'They're pretty selective about what they share.'

'And so are we.'

'Listen, Bill, this interview is a sop to the Brits. The British Foreign Office has been leaning on the Ambassador to beat me up a bit and put me back in my box – so they called you in.'

'How do you know?'

'I'm guessing.'

'Listen, I'm just given a brief and background information to carry out a section five interview – the intelligence isn't sourced or evaluated. Shall we carry on?'

'OK.'

Shepherd pressed the record button and the wheels started turning. 'What were you doing in Portsmouth on April 17 and 18?'

'Refer to DCI.'

'Would you consent to being monitored by polygraph for the rest of this interview.'

'Yes.'

Shepherd attached the lie-detector sensors. The polygraph measured heart rate, blood pressure, breathing and hand perspiration. When Kit was finally wired, the questioning continued. 'Have you ever paid for sex with a prostitute of either sex?'

'No.'

'Have you ever taken illegal drugs?'

'I visited an opium den in Saigon in 1945. I mentioned this when I was interviewed for a top secret clearance in 1951 – so it should still be part of my records.' Kit knew it was an entrapment question.

'Have you ever attended a meeting of a socialist, communist, fascist or national socialist party?'

'No, not in the sense of an official party function. But I have attended numerous social functions with persons who are members of such parties.'

'Was your attendance consistent with carrying out your official duties?'

'Yes.'

'Are you currently engaged in a sexual relationship?'

Kit frowned. It was another cum-stains-on-the-cassock question from the puritan legacy that lumped together sexual sin, witchcraft and national security. 'No, I am not having a sexual relationship of any sort.'

'Could you describe your financial situation?'

'I am entitled to draw up to thirty thousand dollars a year out of a family trust fund managed by Medler and Gower, but I haven't withdrawn any money from it since leaving university. I live well within my government salary and, in fact, nearly fifty per cent of my net pay is reinvested by Medler and Gower in a personal fund.'

'For what purpose.'

'I don't know – maybe to give to a charity. I don't think about money very often – in fact, I consider the topic vulgar.' Kit was completely aware that the purpose of this line of questioning was to establish a pattern on the lie-detector readout for the purpose of comparison with the questions that really mattered.

'Do you ever buy works of art?'

'The last painting I bought of any value was one called *Mestizo* by the Brazilian artist, Portinari.' Kit smiled. He was full of admiration for the deft way that Shepherd had sprung the pseudo-McCarthy trap. 'I would like to amend my previous answer where I said that I only met members of socialist and communist parties when carrying out official duties. Portinari, whom I met and conversed with at an art exhibition, is a member of the Brazilian Communist Party. I've also met the artists Kahlo and Diego Riviera, whose politics could be described as left wing, at a family party in Georgetown. ' How, thought Kit, Senator McCarthy would have loved this – East Coast blue stockings with red paintings. But it was better to own up than be caught in a lie.

'What attracted you to the Portinari painting, the *Mestizo*?'

'The subject's face, as the title *Mestizo* suggests, contains features of all the races – Indian, African, European – that inhabit the Americas. I also like his calmness and dignity.'

'Could you describe the painting as homoerotic?'

Kit wanted to say, probably a lot less than the image of Jesus on the cross, but knew it would only make things worse. 'I don't see it that way.'

'How do you see the painting?'

'I've already said – as the universal everyman of the New World.'

'Some critics would describe the painting as socialist realism – like those brawny workers you see on Soviet propaganda posters.'

'I think they'd be wrong. The *Mestizo* has a lot more subtlety and complexity. In any case, I bought it for my father, who always said he admired Portinari.' Kit waited for the next question. He knew he'd been skewered. If anyone on the House Un-American Activities Committee got hold of this interview, his career would be finished. You weren't allowed anything that didn't conform. You were condemned by the very paintings on your walls and the books on your shelves.

Shepherd continued. 'Have you ever passed on information to a member of the Soviet Mission that could be detrimental to the security interests of the United Kingdom?'

This was the question that Kit had been waiting for. This was the reason he had gone without sleep for forty-eight hours and taken a mild dose of barbiturates before the interview. He was going to lie and the polygraph readout would continue as flat and bland as a pancake. 'No, I have not.'

Shepherd turned off both machines. The interview was finished and Kit was more certain than ever that the tape and polygraph results would soon be on their way to the British Foreign Office – and thence to MI6 and MI5. The whole episode reeked of host country pressure.

'Sorry, Kit,' said Shepherd, 'I really put you through it. I had to.'

'Aren't you going to ask for a urine sample?'

'No, I'd have to watch you do it.'

'Seriously?'

'Yeah, in case you swap someone else's piss for yours. And there's no way I'm going to ask you to whip your cock out without a half dozen medical witnesses to sign a disclaimer.'

Kit was relieved. A barbiturate bearing pee sample would have sunk his boat. 'Come on, Bill, who do you think pushed for this interview?'

'I honestly don't know.' Shepherd paused, then looked closely at Kit. 'You were lucky you weren't PNG'd. Come on, let's go for that beer.'

'It'll have to be a quick one. I'm flying to Washington this evening.'

Chapter Eight

'War without death.' Uncle George smiled and picked up a document file from his desk. An old friend of George's was a Brigadier General in the US Army Chemical Corps and passed on copies of the latest research. 'They've just carried out trials using volunteers from the 82nd Airborne Division. Listen to this.' George opened the file and read, 'The next time I saw Sergeant Lynch he had left the ward and was taking a shower in his uniform while smoking a cigar.'

The enthusiasm was worrying. Kit looked into George's watery blue eyes and tried to detect signs of incipient madness. Perhaps, he thought, the Chemical Corps friend had passed on samples of the drugs too.

'Don't you see, Kit, this is the dawning of a new era. Nuclear bombs are soon going to be as obsolete as the crossbow. We'll saturate the battlefield of the future with chemical clouds of this wonder drug. It won't burn lungs or harm bodies, but it will change consciousness. Trained killers will turn into lotus-eaters. War without death.'

The project that Uncle George was enthusing about was MK-ULTRA, the Agency's mind-control programme. Nothing was ruled out: hypnosis, mental telepathy, psychic driving, hallucinogenic drugs, mescaline, psilocybin, marijuana, heroin, induced amnesia, prolonged paralysis and intense auto-suggestion were all part of the mix.

'The problem is,' said Kit, 'how do we stop our own troops from being affected by the LSD?'

'We're working on that one. There might be an antidote.'

George, Jennifer's father, was an uncle by marriage. He was a retired colonel and had been a classmate of Eisenhower's at West Point. George never got a general's stars, not because he lacked ability, but because he lacked guile and duplicity. In most ways, Kit preferred George to his own blood relations. He didn't seem to have a dark side. Whenever Kit visited the States, he preferred staying on the farm with George and Aunt Janet. And they liked having him too. In a way, he felt they needed him as a surrogate son.

Kit put his hand on George's shoulder and gave an affectionate squeeze. 'I'm really grateful that you picked me up at the airport and brought me here. With Mom in France, I didn't want to be stuck alone at Maury House.'

'What about your sisters, are they still in New York?'

'Yes, they're sharing a flat in Greenwich Village. Caddie's qualified now and Ginny's still trying to make a name for herself.' There was, thought Kit, a certain serendipity to the careers of his sisters. Caddie was a doctor who specialised in venereal diseases and Ginny wrote avant-garde plays and hung around with beat-nik poets. In some ways, their worlds overlapped.

'Have they got boyfriends?'

'I don't know, but somehow I doubt it.' Kit wasn't greatly inter-ested in the sex lives of his sisters. They did go to bed with people, but more, Kit thought, out of clinical or psychological curiosity than love. Caddie must be an impossible partner. Kit imagined potential lovers being examined for genital warts, primary chan-cres and urethral fistulae. She also liked showing off her collection of medical photographs illustrating the latter stages of terminal syphilis and advanced cases of granuloma inguinale. And it was Caddie, bless her heart, who had told Kit about eproctophilia: a condition where people become sexually excited by flatulence.

'Well,' said George, 'I'm glad that our Jennifer's settled. Do you see them?'

'Quite a bit. I've bought a boat that I'll be keeping near where they live in Suffolk.'

'If Janet was a better traveller, we'd go see them.'

Kit smiled. It was Uncle George's coded way of saying that his wife wasn't sober enough to make the trip. 'How is she?'

'Not bad. Having you here's a help – but don't think that means you have to stay here all the time.'

'I love being here.' Kit meant it. It was a way of being close to Jennifer that no husband could ever experience. He could see where she came from and what had shaped her – all the way back to the womb. It was all there: the river, the bay, the rickety old jetty where a pre-pubescent Jennie sat wearing muddy knickers with her feet dangling in the water and minnows nibbling at her toes; the marsh whirring with hummingbirds; musical soirées and candlelight; the long rambling wooden house with polished oak floors bearing the furtive footstep echoes of Mad Betty, the ghost of an early nineteenth-century maid. And her father – a scarred soldier who tried to gentle and calm everything he touched.

'I'm trying,' said George, 'to grow Chinese artichokes this year. Very rare plant. We love Jerusalem artichokes, but they make Janet fart. I've just found this book called *Five Acres and Freedom*. You don't need much to survive. We could all be self-sufficient, you know – and tell General Motors and Standard Oil to go to hell.'

'You'd better be careful, Uncle George, you'll end up in front of the House Un-American Activities Committee.'

'Screw them. What's more American than the frontier spirit and looking after yourself? Capitalists aren't real Americans – they're parasites.'

'You remind me,' laughed Kit, 'of when you were in that play.'

'That's was all your sister's idea.'

'Perfect casting though. You stole the show.' George had played the old counsellor, Gonzalo, in *The Tempest*. Ginny had directed it with a local amateur drama group.

'Well at least I didn't forget my lines. Listen,' George drew himself up straight.

> *All things in common nature should produce*
> *Without sweat or endeavour. Treason, felony,*
> *Sword, pike, knife, gun, or need of any engine*
> *Would I not have; but nature should bring forth,*
> *Of its own kind, all foison, all abundance,*
> *To feed my innocent people.*

George sat back down. 'I fear I may be boring you.'

'Far from it. Do it again.'

'Now, sir, you mock me.'

'Actually, George, you were fantastic in that play.'

'Was I?'

Kit nodded. He could tell that George enjoyed the praise. The harmless little vanity made Kit warm to him even more. 'You know I've got to go to Washington tomorrow?'

'Would you like to borrow the car?'

'No, Anne Truitt's giving me a lift from Easton.'

'Oh, I like Anne. Are you going to be staying with them in Georgetown?'

'No, I'm going to be staying with Cord and Mary Meyer.'

'Hmm.'

'That sounded like a very serious hmm. What's hmm mean?'

'You mean you don't know? What sort of intelligence agent are you?'

'I don't know. Unfortunately, we don't pick up the latest salacious gossip over in London town. It sounds like something's wrong *chez les Meyer*.'

'The junior senator from Massachusetts.'

'Poor Cord. He doesn't deserve this.'

'The Kennedys have moved in next door – that big place, Hickory Hill.'

'Thanks for filling me in. If my bedroom door opens in the middle of the night, I'll have to remember not to moan "Jack honey" in a throaty Vassar purr.'

'My generation weren't saints either – so I'm not going to pass judgement.'

■

The cherry trees were no longer in blossom. Washington springs came early, then flopped into long sweaty summers that stretched from May to October. The British Foreign Office classified the town as a semi-tropical posting. Kit had no affection for the capital: a Potomac fringe of grand white government buildings, a handful of wealthy enclaves – then miles and miles of slum housing and poverty sprawling further than the eye could see or a taxi driver would venture.

The State Department Building was the ugliest piece of architecture that Kit had ever seen. It was a long seven-storey slab of beige brick and concrete with metal window frames. Kit showed his ID to a policeman in a glass cubicle. The cop pressed a buzzer and Kit entered the entrance lobby. The floor was highly-polished reddish-brown linoleum tiles that made your shoes squeak and echo. The State Department coat of arms was mounted on the wall facing the entrance. There were also photoportraits of Eisenhower and John Foster Dulles. Kit pressed a button to summon the elevator and checked his tie and hair on the gleaming stainless-steel doors while he waited for a lift to 'the Seventh Floor'. There were plans to renovate the lobby into a fake eighteenth-century reception hall. And that, thought Kit, would be worse: the epitome of nouveau riche vulgarity. From time to time he penned memos begging that the plans be scrapped. He could hear the sneers of the French Ambassador already.

Kit exited the elevator and walked down the corridor to John Foster Dulles's office. In the reception area outside the office was an oil painting of Key House. It had been painted in 1903 by the grandson of Francis Scott Key who wrote the national anthem. The style of the painting was about a hundred years out of date even in 1903, but Kit always looked at it with affection because the beautiful eighteenth-century house was set in an early American Arcadia. The house lies on a slight rise above the Potomac River; the thickly wooded banks are turning autumnal; there are dogs and horse-drawn carriages in the foreground, boats with sails in the background. The house was demolished in 1949 to build a four-lane freeway.

A door opened and an assistant undersecretary of something or other told Kit to 'go straight in'. Foster Dulles seemed much more relaxed on his home ground than he had in London. This time there were aides dancing in attendance to take notes and fetch documents. After the usual small talk, Dulles got straight down to business. 'It seems, Kit, the next few months are going to be a very challenging time for Anglo-American relations – probably the most difficult this century.'

'Things were,' said Kit, 'pretty bad over Indochina.' Kit knew that Dulles had been in favour of using atomic weapons to stave off a French defeat at Dien Bien Phu, but Anthony Eden's firm opposition had defeated the plan.

'The problem with Anthony,' – Dulles pronounced it Ant'nee, an affectation that annoyed the British – 'is that he never understood the danger of a Red Asia.'

A cloud of foul breath drifted across the desk. Kit tried not to breathe in.

'But,' the Secretary of State continued, 'the problem has now shifted to the Middle East. What do you think Eden's trying to pull off in Egypt? He doesn't seem to be handling Gamal Nasser very well.'

Kit looked closely at Dulles. 'I've had a few indications, but…'

'Indications about what?'

Kit looked around nervously at the others in the room. Dulles made a gesture and the aides left the office. As soon as they were alone, Kit continued. 'Last winter I was invited to a drinks party at the private home of the Minister of State at the Foreign Office. When I went to have a pee, I noticed a telephone in the hall between the minister's bedroom and the bathroom. So I did the natural thing, unscrewed the earpiece and put in an MOP transmitter.'

Dulles frowned.

Kit continued. 'At first, most of the stuff we picked up was "cabbages and kings" – that's what we call worthless chatter – but eventually the FO minister received a late-night call from the Prime Minister.' Kit took two sheets of paper out of his briefcase and handed them over. 'That's the transcript of the telephone call.'

Dulles adjusted his bifocals and began to read aloud from the transcript. '"What's all this poppycock you've sent me about isolating Nasser and neutralising Nasser? Why can't you get it into your head that I want the man destroyed?"'

It was odd to hear the Prime Minister's words spoken with an American accent. For a few seconds Kit wondered if Dulles was speaking his own thoughts. The illusion was broken when the Secretary of State looked up at Kit. 'I didn't realise that Eden could get so mad. What brought this on?'

'The Prime Minister thinks Nasser is stirring up trouble in Jordan and other neighbouring countries. And some of it may be down to medication: Benzedrine and sleeping pills aren't a good combination.' For a second Kit thought about MK-ULTRA: they were experimenting with the same drug mix to induce hysteria. 'Read on, sir, it gets better.'

'"I don't care if there is anarchy and chaos in Egypt. I just want to get rid of Nasser…"' Dulles finished the Eden transcript and looked intently at Kit. 'You can see where this is heading, can't you?'

Kit felt very uncomfortable under the heavy Dulles stare. 'Are you suggesting, Secretary Dulles, that the British are planning to assassinate Nasser?'

'That's a question that we should be asking you – you're supposed to be our eyes and ears in London.'

Kit was used to sharp criticism: harsh words were background music in the corridors of power. 'I'm sure that assassination plans exist, but...'

'But you haven't been able to penetrate the secrecy around them.'

'It depends on how you define penetrate.' Kit began to feel resentful. It wasn't Foster's job to question his role as an intelligence officer. On the other hand, you can't tell the US Secretary of State, the second most powerful man in the world, to fuck off. 'I know that experiments have been carried out at Porton Down...'

The Secretary of State's face looked blank.

'Porton Down is the British Ministry of Defence laboratory for chemical and biological warfare. In any case, there have been recent experiments involving nerve gas, ricin and poison-tipped darts. They carry out practice assassinations on sheep.' Kit paused and remembered his father's tales of how tethered farm animals were used to measure blast and radiation effects at the US nuclear test sites. *We use animals*, he said, *to harden our souls for cruelty to our own species.*

'If a Nasser assassination is planned, how likely is it to succeed?'

'Less than ten per cent. Most of Britain's undercover intelligence assets in Egypt have been blown and rounded up. Their only hope is a handful of dissident army officers.'

'What a pity. We would not be adverse to such an assassination, but we can't be seen to have anything to do with it. We have to protect our reputation in the Arab world. But it would suit our policy just fine if the British got rid of Nasser – and then,' Dulles smiled for the first time, 'we would condemn them for having carried out a beastly and illegal act.'

Kit was surprised by Foster's open cynicism, but then he realised that it was the first time that he had ever been alone with him. Perhaps the high-minded pulpit persona was something the Secretary of State saved for more public settings – or for his kid brother. Different people, different faces.

'The problem,' continued Dulles, 'is that Nasser thinks he can play ball with both sides. He accepts Soviet military aid with one hand while his other hand is grabbing American aid to build the Aswan dam. We're not going to let Nasser get away with that. We're going to pull out of the Aswan project.'

Kit wasn't surprised. Development aid wasn't about helping

the world's poor; it was about blackmailing Third World countries to follow US policy. Without the Aswan dam, Egypt would end up an economic cripple. No food, no power, no jobs. The Gringo Dollar was just as deadly as poison gas and nuclear bombs. If a country gets out of line, you wreck their economy and starve their kids.

'Well,' said Dulles, 'we know that Nasser is going to be mad as hell. But since he won't be able to get back at us, he's going to take it out on the Brits instead. What do you think?'

'I suspect,' said Kit, 'that Nasser will kick the British out and seize the Suez Canal.'

'And how are the British going to respond?'

'Eden will go bananas – he might even take military action.'

'And that,' said Dulles, 'is where we are going to fall out with our British cousins. We're going to have to tell them that it's finished, that their empire is over.'

Kit looked at the Secretary of State with detached amazement. Dulles came from a family of diplomats: John Foster was, in fact, the third member of his family to occupy his present post. And yet, thought Kit, this man goes about international diplomacy with all the grace of a trained chimpanzee putting out a grass fire with a wet sack.

Dulles took out a penknife and began to sharpen a pencil as if it were his personal view of world history. 'They have to understand that "Pax Americana" is the only song that the West is going to sing. As things develop, we'll keep you informed of what lines to take and who, on the British side, to groom and cultivate.'

Kit began to get up for he assumed the interview was over.

'Stay there for a second.' The Secretary of State frowned at his pencil and shaved off another sliver. 'It is not in the interest of the United States that Britain possesses an independent nuclear deterrent. We'll keep you briefed on what line to take.'

'Thank you, sir.'

'But I won't keep you, Kit, I believe you've now got a meeting with my brother over in the Kremlin.'

■

The Kremlin wasn't *that* Kremlin, not the one in Moscow. It was State Department slang for the dreary complex of office buildings on E Street that housed the CIA. There were plans to move to a pleasant site called Langley across the river in Virginia – where the DCI could watch deer and other woodland wildlife through his office window while he plotted overthrows of disobedient governments.

The DCI seemed flushed and ebullient as Kit entered his office. Kit suspected that Allen Dulles had got laid over his lunch break. The Director's womanising was gossip so stale that it was no longer mentioned.

The DCI got up and held Kit in a manly bear hug. His jacket carried a whiff of cheap perfume. 'You did a fantastic job in Portsmouth Harbour.' Dulles hugged him tighter and for a second Kit thought his boss was going to kiss him on both cheeks like a French general handing out a Croix de Guerre.

'I hope I didn't go too far.'

Dulles let him go. 'No, not at all. But any more British non-sense about unilateral détente with the Sovs has been truly scuppered. The Russians will never again trust perfidious Albion. And, by the way, I've just heard that John Sinclair has resigned as Head of MI6.'

Kit already knew, but feigned surprise.

'I hear,' continued Dulles, 'that Sinclair's replacement is Dick White, the fellow who was running MI5.'

'I've met him – we call him Blanco.'

'What's your impression?'

'Smooth and devious – not to be underestimated.'

'Add your impressions to his file before you leave.'

'Sure.'

Kit watched the DCI walk back to his desk and noticed the limp. Like Lord Byron, Allen Dulles had a club foot – not a fact that either man had tried to make known.

'The thing about our British cousins,' said Dulles, 'is that they seem to be becoming more secretive and furtive. Which is a pity, because they're pretty damned good at knowing what's what on Arab Street. There's a certain sort of upper-crust Britisher that likes nothing more than to dress up like a Bedouin and learn the lingo – T.E. Lawrence, Wilfrid Thesiger, St John Philby. I suppose we could be crude about the reason why – but even some of the girls, like Gertrude Bell, get into it. And, I have to admit, they do it with dash and style. Replacing them in the Middle East won't be easy.'

'Are you going to send me somewhere to learn Arabic?'

'No, Kit, but I want you to keep us posted on Eden – and also keep an eye on Macmillan and Butler. See which one is more, shall I say, *congenial* to our interests. Did you know that Macmillan's mother was an American? It seems we've crossbred most of their ruling class. As for Wallis Simpson… your Baltimore girls get everywhere.'

'My mom never liked her.'

'Clover can't stand her either.' Dulles lowered his voice. 'It might, you know, be jealousy. Wallis is, of course, ugly – and they all wonder what her secret is. Have you heard of something called the Singapore Grip?'

'I believe it is achieved through endless hours of exercise over a number of years. It probably helps if one trains the appropriate muscles from an early age and refrains from bearing children.'

'Exactly. In any case, we digress. What more can you tell us about the British H-bomb.'

'They still haven't got one.'

'I know, Kit, but they have got something up their sleeve – and are being very furtive about it. The stuff you send us about recruitment patterns at Aldermaston is priceless. There has recently been a shift away from pure research recruitment to applied science and engineering. Ergo…' The DCI paused and waited for Kit to complete the analysis.

'Ergo, they already know the science of creating a thermonuclear fusion device, but are now looking for specialists who know how to glue one together.'

'That, Kit, is the *obvious* conclusion, but my intuition tells me there's a lot more to it. In any case, I understand you're keeping a close eye on the Atomic Weapons Research Establishment in Suffolk.'

'Yes, it's on a long bleak spit called Orford Ness. I've had aerial reconnaissance photos taken – and, quite fortuitously, I have a cousin who is married to the chief scientist at the Orford Ness site.'

'How serendipitous. But I think I knew that already.' Dulles paused. 'This cousin of yours – is she, by any chance, George Calvert's daughter? I think her name's Jennie?'

'That's the one. We're still good friends.'

Dulles aimed a trademark wink at Kit. 'That Jennie's a real beauty. Have you recruited her as an agent?'

Kit felt his mouth go dry. 'Not quite an agent, perhaps an unwitting asset.'

'Good.'

'I've also bought a boat that I'll be keeping on the river at Orford. In fact, I'll be able to see the research labs from my mooring.'

'Excellent. We can pay for that boat if you like.'

'No thanks, I'd like to keep it as a personal possession.'

'Foster loves boating too. Have you been to that island of theirs on Lake Ontario.'

'No.'

'Foster becomes a different person up there. He chops wood, fetches water, catches fish and cooks them. It's his *dacha* – he ought to invite Khrushchev. By the way, did you know that Khrushchev has just announced that the Sovs are going in for missile delivered H-bombs?'

Kit nodded.

'The Russians are way ahead of us on rocket science, there are even rumours of a satellite launch in the offing – but that, I am sure, is wild exaggeration. But we still have a lot of catching up to do.' Allen smiled. 'And that's why Britain, three and a half thousand precious miles closer to Moscow, has to be our nuclear front line and a base for *our* nuclear weapons. A separate British H-bomb would create practical problems of command and control – and would also invite policy differences.'

'What, sir, if the Brits don't want to go along with this?'

The DCI gave Kit a cold look that carried a hint of anger. 'The British are going to have to learn to like it or lump it. No time for sentimentality about thatched cottages, quaint accents and unarmed cops on bicycles. Sometimes, Kit, I fear that you might be going native?'

Kit smiled. 'I drink tea, sir, but I draw the line at pints of luke-warm bitter.'

'Good. But there's one more thing.'

'Yes.'

'Our listening station in Tromso has been picking an unusually heavy amount of traffic in the North Sea – and SIGINT hasn't been able to decode anything. So the level of security seems unusually high too.'

'British?'

The DCI nodded. 'And Russian too.'

■

Kit could see that Cord and Mary Meyer were having problems with their marriage. Their façade of happiness and mutual respect was too perfect. Both were too well brought up to discomfort a visitor by revealing the slightest flaw in their relationship. Kit knew they were showcasing the marital harmony: he would have felt more comfortable if they had thrown crockery at each other.

After a simple dinner – Chincoteague oysters, steak and salad – Mary went to work in her studio where she was trying to adapt oil and canvas to the sort of severe minimalism that Anne Truitt was developing with sculpture. Both Kit and Cord knew it was best not to comment. They shifted themselves to Cord's study to drink Scotch on the rocks.

Kit was a little surprised to see that Cord had framed his Bronze Star and Purple Heart decorations and had them hanging on his study wall. He knew that Cord had been rattled by his experiences as a marine lieutenant in the Pacific – and thought he would have thrown his medals in a drawer just like everyone else. Cord had lost an eye and been left for dead when a Japanese grenade landed in his foxhole. A week later, Cord's twin brother had been killed on Okinawa. There was a savage symmetry: you lose an eye and then you lose a twin. Spooky. Cord smiled wanly and stuck a thumb at the framed medals. 'My dad had that done when I was in hospital. Can't really throw them away.' Kit had the queer feeling that his mind had been read. That was spooky too. Cord offered the Scotch and steered the conversation away. 'How do you like England?'

'It's an acquired taste, but I am acquiring it. Still, I would have preferred Paris or staying on in Bonn. My German was getting pretty good. Are you still stuck on E Street?'

'I get abroad quite a lot because of the Radio Free Europe stuff, but I have to be based here for reasons of control.'

Kit knew that Cord was the CIA's undercover press czar. He oversaw a vast global network that churned out pro-America propaganda. His operation was a work of near genius. Cord's philosophy was to recruit progressive and left-of-centre journalists to take up the American cause. He also fed funds to anti-communist trade unions. Cord was incapable of hypocrisy; he sincerely believed in what he was doing. He was an anti-communist liberal who believed in world government and the United Nations. Cord had written an intensely moving account of his war experiences called *Waves of Darkness* that veered towards pacifism. Kit thought it was a fine book, but maybe too intense, too sincere. At times, Kit wanted to grab Cord and shake him. 'Tell me a joke, say something ironic.' But he knew that Cord wouldn't have seen the irony.

'By the way,' said Cord, 'did you know that Jack Kennedy lives just up the road?'

'Oh, does he? I didn't know that.'

'Jacqueline and Mary have become good friends.'

'That's nice.'

∎

Kit was woken in the middle of the night. Moonlight poured in through the open bedroom window. It must have been an owl: a screech owl that was hunting in the large Virginian gardens. He looked at the luminous dial of the bedside clock: quarter to three. He was thirsty: the whisky had dehydrated him and he had forgotten to fetch a glass of water for the night.

Kit got out of bed as quietly as possible and found his dressing gown without turning on a light. He didn't want to disturb the sleeping house. He opened the bedroom door slowly, but it still sounded like a raised coffin lid in a horror film. Otherwise, Kit liked the Meyers' house: it was large and gracious, full of wide corridors and landings with varnished oak floors. He liked the smooth cool feel of old oak planks under his bare feet. A large bow window flooded the landing with light from the full moon. The window looked out over the circular drive that came to the front of the house. There was a car parked on the gravel; it hadn't been there before. Were there new visitors who had come late?

Kit leaned his forehead against the window and stared at the car. It was a dark blue Plymouth with Massachusetts licence plates and a US Senate parking permit stuck on the bumper. Kit noticed that the car's right front fender was badly scratched and dented. Jack, he thought, isn't any better at driving cars than PT boats.

After a minute or so a car door opened – gratingly loud in the still night air. Mary was wearing a paint-stained artist's smock and white peddle pushers. She certainly hadn't dressed for her date. The car engine started; she turned to wave, but didn't watch the Plymouth disappear down the drive. She was looking straight at Kit. They remained staring at each other for nearly a minute: there was no anger or resentment in her look. It was infinitely sad – and just seemed to say, over and over again, *I don't know why, I don't know why...*

■

When Kit got back to England the weather was fresh and cool. It felt invigorating after the humid Washington swamp. He liked the way the strong cleansing winds blew torn clouds across London and began to hate the confines of the office. He needed a trip to Suffolk so he could get his boat in the water.

Kit's job meant he could leave London whenever he wanted. Ambassador Aldrich was aware of the situation and didn't object to Kit dumping his routine diplomatic duties on the Deputy POLCOUNS. The deputy was a shrewd Virginian named Perry. As Kit handed over another folder, Perry frowned. 'You know something?'

'What's wrong?' said Kit.

'Can I be frank, sir?'

'Of course.'

'It seems that you offload all the boring shit on me.'

'But now, Perry, I'm going to reward you.' Kit smiled and took something out of his in-tray. 'This is not just for your astute analysis of the situation, but also for the assertive way you have stood up to the person who is about to write your annual OER. Here.' Kit handed his deputy a gilded invitation card.

Perry read aloud, 'To celebrate the recent marriage of Marilyn Monroe and Arthur Miller.'

'It's going to be London's biggest celebrity bash of the year – and now you're going instead of me.' Kit looked closely at his dour deputy. 'This, Perry, could be the making of you. When Marilyn lays eyes on you, she'll think, "I've had Joe DiMaggio's brawn and Arthur Miller's brain, now I want raunchy down and dirty sex." Princess Margaret will be there too – and God knows what might happen if she feels the same dark desires. Hmm, but we don't want an incident that might embarrass the Ambassador.' Kit reached for the card. 'So on second thought...'

Perry quickly put the invitation in his pocket. 'I'll manage.'

'Good.' Kit picked up three more files and handed them over. 'Have a look at these and add your own conclusions – UK dollar reserves, UK oil imports and Anglo-Egyptian relations. Two-hundred-word summaries of each for the Seventh Floor with copies to me, the CM and DCM.'

'Thanks a lot.'

Kit paused and waited to catch his deputy's eye. 'Actually, this is *very* important shit. It means I seriously trust you.'

'I'll do my best.'

Kit watched his deputy betray a slight flush of pride as he turned to leave. As Perry shut the door, Kit fished another invitation out of his in-tray. It was one that Cauldwell had managed to provide. It was a VIP invite to a concert at the Aldeburgh Musical Festival. The event featured Soviet artists and would give Kit an opportunity to meet Natalya Voronova – the cellist with the nuclear scientist husband.

■

Louise, Kit's Blackwater Sloop, was ready for launching the week before the Whitsun Bank Holiday. Kit went down to Slaughden Quay the evening before with blankets, tins of food and bottles of wine. The boat was suspended by strops in a launching trailer. In the morning they would attach a tractor to the trailer and push her down the ramp and into the River Alde. The boat swayed on her harness when Kit climbed aboard with the provisions. It was like being at sea already. Kit stowed the food he had bought in cabin lockers, then folded the bedding on a berth in the forepeak. The rough texture of the blanket reminded him of childhood camping trips. When he finished tidying things down below, Kit went topsides to check the rigging and anchor. Everything was perfect. Billy Whiting had done a fine job. Kit ran his hand over the fresh varnish of the mast and looked out to sea. It was exciting: not the sordid excitement of war and spying, but the fresh pure excitement of childhood.

Slaughden, a half-mile south of Aldeburgh, was on a narrow neck of shifting shingle, hardly more than a hundred yards wide, where the river almost touched the sea. The fragile isthmus was guarded by a nineteenth-century Martello tower mellowed by age and salt wind into a gentle ruin. Beyond the Martello lay ten miles of shingle spit and marsh – for all intents an island. Kit squinted and looked south. There was nothing but sky, banked shingle, wheeling gulls, grey sea and gleaming river. But hidden from view in the middle of that bleak wilderness, the Orford Ness Atomic Weapons Research Establishment squatted like a poisonous desert toad. It was an ugly blot, but ugly blots were the prices countries paid for not being mugged with a nuclear cosh – maybe. Who knows?

The following day Billy Whiting helped crew *Louise* down to her mooring at Orford. The day was bright, but fresh and cool. The clear weather brought a brisk breeze from the north-east. It was a fast passage even against the flooding tide. Kit made note of his new neighbours: gulls, terns, curlew, oyster-catchers, heron, swans, avocet. Billy pointed out a mud bank south of the Martello tower that was fast disappearing under the tide, then made his way to the foredeck where he sat enclosed in his own world. Kit felt the sun warm on his face and listened to the regular gurgle along the hull. The river was empty except for a broad beamed open boat trawling for shrimp – small brown ones with a nutty flavour. You ate them with brown bread, butter, lemon and a pint of bitter. Billy and the fishermen exchanged hardly perceptible nods for greeting. They were a reticent people.

An hour later, the low dull buildings and bunkers of the research establishment began to appear above the riverbank. Orford Ness lighthouse, painted in broad bands of red and white, seemed cheerfully out of place. The opposite bank was greener with sheep grazing in the salt marshes. Further inland the land rose in gentle wooded slopes. The weathered stone of Orford Castle and the square spire of the church reflected beige, pink and dove's breast grey in the morning sun. It was, thought Kit, like sailing into a watercolour.

After picking up the mooring, Kit rowed Billy ashore. They met Jennifer on Orford town quay. She was wearing a floral dress and a broad brimmed hat with a blue ribbon. She looked so English. When Kit leaned to kiss her cheek he was wrapped in a scent of verbena. As he pulled away, he noticed the mark on her neck – ever so faint and grey. His heart pounded. He tried to imagine that the mark was a smear of makeup or ash. 'We're going to a chorus rehearsal. Would you like to come?'

Kit looked puzzled.

'It's a new Benjamin Britten opera, we're just getting started. Billy's been cast as Jaffet, Noah's son, but I'm just a member of the congregation. It's a lot of fun – all children and amateurs. Ben wants it that way – just like they did miracle plays in the Middle Ages. Please come.'

Kit now remembered. He turned to Billy who looked embarrassed and was shuffling his feet. 'I don't know,' said Kit, 'I'd feel like an intruder.'

Jennifer put an arm around Billy. 'How can we teach Billy not to be ashamed of being good at things?' Kit watched the boy turn red. It was obvious that Billy was in the throes of a schoolboy crush.

'OK,' said Kit, 'but I'll put my fingers in my ears when it's Billy's turn to sing.'

Billy flashed a sly smile. 'Don't you dare.'

Beneath the magnificent oak beams and window tracery, the interior of Orford Church was plain and austere. Like most Suffolk churches, it had been stripped and whitewashed by Cromwell's puritans. The rehearsal was being conducted by Britten's companion, the tenor Peter Pears. Kit had heard of Pears, but was surprised at his size and strength. He had hands the size of dinner plates. Pears explained to the chorus that they had to imagine they were the congregation of a twelfth-century Suffolk church. Pears said that he would pretend to be Noye and slowly walk through the church to the stage while they sang the first hymn. He then made a signal, the orchestra began and a moment later the voices rose. Kit felt the hairs on his spine raise. It was a simple hymn and there were no professional singers: just ordinary folk. Power was passing from the priests to the people.

Lord Jesus, think on me
And purge away my sin;
From earthborn passions set me free,
And make me pure within.

After a few minutes Kit silently slipped out the back of the church. He didn't belong there. As he began walking down the hill to the quay, the chorus began Britten's setting of *Eternal Father*. The voices behind were roaring louder than an angry sea – for every one of them had known the words by heart since childhood.

O hear us when we cry to thee
For those in peril on the sea

Kit shielded his eyes from the sun and looked out beyond Orford Ness – beyond the mean ugliness of the bomb makers – at the gleaming relentless sea. The voices now stormed louder, *O hear us*… How many of theirs lay out beneath those waves? They alone knew because this mad island belonged to them – and them alone.

■

Kit rowed back to the boat. He was going to spend the next two days exploring. The weather was now warmer and the wind had dropped. Kit cast off and drifted from the mooring under sail. A half-mile below Orford, the river was split in two by an island full of lagoons and loud bird life, Kit steered into the branch that bent inland to the west. The river there twisted from bend to bend and required frequent gybes. At each change of course there was a solid thunk of block and tackle as the boom swung from one side to the other. Kit had a chart spread on his knees. He was looking for a tributary river called the Butley, but it seemed difficult to find. At last, he spotted a place where the river wall fell away. The entrance was marked by two withies – narrow sticks stuck in the mud – almost invisible to someone without local knowledge. Kit was beginning to realise that sailing in Suffolk was a business just as secretive as being a spy.

Once inside the Butley, it was easy to see where to steer. On the left bank was an abandoned brick dock that was crumbling into ruin. According to the chart, there had been a brisk nineteenth-century trade swapping London horse manure for Suffolk wheat and barley. But the river had long since returned to splendid isolation. There was little wind now, but *Louise* continued to glide upstream on the last of the rising tide. Kit felt the boat was being drawn forward by an invisible thread.

The river seemed in turns desolate, wild and mysterious. A mile from the entrance, the land on both sides of the river rose and became thickly wooded. There was a valley with a grazing herd of roe deer that scattered to cover at the sight of a sail. Kit finally decided to drop anchor when he saw a shed and jetty. Both structures looked long abandoned and deserted. In any case, it was so unexpected – like discovering a hunter's hut in a wild rainforest.

As soon as the boat was fast and the sails furled, Kit decided to explore. He was happy. He couldn't remember the last time he had played. Kit cast off the tender and rowed towards the jetty. He noticed a bank thick with mussels, but it was too late in the season to eat them. There were, however, broad beds of samphire. Kit grounded the boat and cut three bundles to add to his supper, then continued to the jetty. He made fast and climbed on to the boards – making sure not to put his foot through a rotten plank.

The shed had been built on an island of marshy land amid a lawn of sea lavender. It was connected to the mainland proper by plank bridges that leapfrogged from islet to islet until they reached the riverbank. What a fantastic hiding place. Kit tried the shed door. There was a padlock, but the clasp was fitted to wood that had turned rotten and hung uselessly against the door frame. He opened the door. Aside from the dust, cobwebs and desiccated wasp nests, it wasn't in bad repair. There were old cane fishing rods, nets, table, chairs and a tea service. The calico curtains had rotted away to transparent lace. Kit closed his eyes and had a vision of moustached gentlemen in boaters, Edwardian ladies with hoop skirts and high buttoned boots, a flurry of parasols and a bounding Labrador. For a second, he felt a kiss and a loose lock of hair brush his cheek. He reached out, but no one was there – just gull cries and plummeting swallows. None of it was real, only the pain lingered. Kit rowed back to *Louise* and went for a swim.

Kit cooked a meal of omelette, samphire, fried potatoes and green salad. Afterwards, he sat in the cockpit as the tide ebbed and the boat settled into the mud. He had brought along George Crabbe's poem 'The Borough'. Peter Grimes, an Aldeburgh fisherman, had been shunned for suspected murder.

> *There anchoring, Peter chose from man to hide,*
> *There hang his head, and view the lazy tide…*

Kit put down the book and watched a pair of oyster-catchers strut across the exposed mud. Their black and white plumage and the way they swayed on their long legs made Kit think of drunken gents in evening dress. Their braying communal piping sounded like a whole club bellowing, 'Waiter, more champagne, more champagne…'

That night Kit lay in the forward berth with the hatch cover open so he could watch the wheeling stars. He liked the rough kiss of the wool blankets and the gurgle of water against the hull as the tide rose and refloated the boat. And for the first time, Kit heard the night call of the curlew: *curr-leek-leek, curr-leek-leek*. It was a plaintive mournful sound and the oyster-catchers didn't seem to like it much. The oyster-catchers retaliated with their *more champagne* piping at full throat. This, in turn, brought in more and louder curlew: *curr leek-leek-leek, cu-r-r-r-leek!* Kit didn't want to sleep. He wanted to stay awake all night listening to England.

> *Be not afeard this isle is full of noises,*
> *Sounds and sweet airs that give delight and hurt not.*

During his first day back in the office Kit stared at his overflowing in-tray. He had begun to hate his job with a passion and wondered how much more he could offload on Perry. Kit remembered visiting George at his office at the Pentagon a few months before his uncle was due to retire. George's in-tray at the time was even more overflowing. Kit remembered all the documents festooned with red TOP SECRET tags, urgent notices and complex distribution lists that needed initialling and passing on. Kit remembered that George had looked at his watch and said, 'Gosh, it's already quarter past four. Time for a drink.' He then picked up his in-tray and emptied it into the burn bag for the daily incineration. George saw the amazed look on Kit's face and said, 'If it's important enough, it will come round again.' Then he pulled open a desk drawer and took out two glasses and a bottle of bourbon.

But Kit knew that things in London were different. The issues that the Dulles brothers had outlined in Washington were moving to the point where they were going to boil over and burn hands. The Portsmouth operation was still a raw wound too. Prime Minister Eden was pilloried in Parliament and had finally admitted, 'It would not be in the public interest to disclose the circumstances in which Commander Crabb is presumed to have met his death.' On the surface, it was an extraordinary and frank confession that dirty tricks had occurred. It was interesting, thought Kit, that Eden had more or less admitted that Crabb was dead. The more he thought about it, the less certain he was that Crabb had perished. Was the Prime Minister laying a false trail? Or, thought Kit, am I deceiving myself to avoid guilt for another death?

Kit opened the daily briefing folder prepared by his own staff. It was a news digest that saved him wasting time reading newspapers. Jerry Lewis and Dean Martin were splitting up; Marilyn Monroe and Arthur Miller were getting hitched. The American military assistance group in Vietnam had suffered their first death. An airman, Richard B. Fitzgibbon Jr, had been murdered by another US serviceman. Elvis Presley's 'Heartbreak Hotel' was now a 'golden record'. French paratroopers had launched a clean-up operation in Algiers by blowing up two buildings in the Casbah. An acquaintance from the French Embassy had recently told Kit that their officers in Algeria had become fond of quoting Abbé Arnaud Amoury, the bishop who led the thirteenth-century crusade against the Albigensians. At the sack of Bézier, a general had asked the Abbé how they could tell the difference between '*les bons catholiques*' and '*les hérétiques*'. Abbé Arnaud replied, '*Tuez les tous* – kill them all, God will sort them out in heaven.'

Kit flipped through the rest of the news and turned to the confidential briefing pages at the back. Vyacheslav Molotov had been sacked as Soviet Foreign Minister. Kit was surprised it hadn't happened sooner. There were rumours that Molotov had tried to get rid of Khrushchev and that he supported the heresy of a united Germany. Kit continued reading. According to a *Pravda* article, Molotov hadn't been fired after all – he had simply been 'reassigned as Ambassador to Outer Mongolia'. It reminded Kit of one of Vasili's indiscreet revelations. During a visit to Burma, Khrushchev was given a jungle tour using traditional transport. As they trundled off, Molotov remarked to an aid: 'Look at that – an elephant riding an elephant.' A wisecrack too far. Kit decided to go for a walk in the June sunshine – it would be nice to see Vasili again.

■

Kensington Gardens was full of nannies pushing prams. Kit wondered if the French au pair from the Portsmouth train was among them. He was surprised by how much he wanted to see her again. As Kit continued walking towards the Peter Pan statue, the pram traffic increased. He looked at the circling nannies and tried to spot one that looked French. Then what? 'Do you know by any chance a Mademoiselle Françoise...' No, it was a stupid idea. In any case, he found what he was looking for. The chalk mark on the rubbish bin looked fresh. It meant confession time at Brompton Oratory.

Kit spotted Vasili in the Marian side chapel where he had seen him last. Vasili was reading a book and his lips were moving. It looked almost as if he was praying. Kit slid into the pew next to the Russian. Vasili continued to read and to mouth the words. Kit glanced at the book. Despite the Cyrillic letters, he could see that the text was typeset as poetry. Vasili closed the book and said, 'Pushkin.'

Kit had been ready to make some joke about the embassy in Ulan Bator, but sensed that the mood wasn't appropriate. They shook hands and sat in silence. Finally Vasili said, 'I often wait here expecting to see you, but you never come. I've been told not to ring the embassy any more.'

'Even from a public phone?'

'Yes. Since the Portsmouth business, everyone is nervous.'

'What happened to Crabb?'

Vasili shrugged his shoulders, then said, 'Let's go for a drive in the country. I want to see fields and cows – and pretty milkmaids like in the novels of Thomas Hardy.'

'It's against the rules.'

'Well, let's just go for a walk.'

The two walked north towards Hyde Park. The streets were busy and neither said a word until they were sitting on a bench by the Serpentine watching the ducks. 'The limpet mines,' said Vasili, 'were American ones.'

'I'm not surprised. You didn't really think that MI6 would use British mines – it was a false flag op. If anything went wrong, they wanted us to get blamed.'

'Why did they do it? What did these – how do you describe them – crazy or mad...'

'Crazy.'

'What did these *crazy* British secret agents want to achieve?'

'They wanted to go all the way. They wanted to sabotage détente between Britain and the Soviet Union. They wanted to bring down Eden's government... I suppose they wouldn't have minded a military coup.'

'I see.' The Russian nodded slowly.

'Listen, Vasili, rogue agents are a real problem in the West – not just in Britain. The French secret services are even worse – that's why no French government dares pull out of Algeria. The Secret State breeds monsters who get drunk on power. They think that if they sink an *Ordzhonikidze* – or burn a *Reichstag* – they can create a crisis so dire and dangerous that the generals will have to take over. We didn't only save your ship – we saved the British people as well.'

Vasili looked away, almost embarrassed. 'You're not a good

actor, Kit. Your lines are too well rehearsed. Try to be more natural and spontaneous.'

Kit looked at the Russian. 'Why don't you believe me?'

'Because the results of the Portsmouth Harbour incident – a wrecked Soviet friendship visit, a broken UK détente policy, a weakened Eden government – are all aims of United States foreign policy.'

Kit breathed deeply. 'Your problem, Vasili, is that you see conspiracies everywhere. I thought you had enough of that under Stalin.'

'Do not, my American friend, lecture me on a tragedy that affected me, my family and every Soviet citizen.' Vasili's voice was shaking with anger. 'You have no right, no right…'

Kit looked at the gravel beneath his feet. He felt as significant as a cockroach. 'I'm sorry.'

Suddenly the Russian was laughing. 'Why are *you* sorry?'

'Listen, Vasili, if you think I'm lying, keep asking Commander Crabb until he confesses.' Kit was a little ashamed that he was condoning torture, but they were all players.

'What?'

'Crabb, the British diver, you captured him, didn't you?'

'Crabb's dead.'

'Where's the body?'

'It'll turn up – bit by bit.'

Kit felt his head was on fire. He wiped a drop of sweat from his brow. 'How did you kill him?'

Vasili turned away and looked across the park. The great oaks had finally begun to unfurl their leaves. 'Commander Crabb's mission was to examine the ship's propellers. British Naval Intelligence wanted to know why our cruiser was so fast.'

Kit felt his sweat and blood turn cold. He had heard nothing about a plan to examine the cruiser's propellers. Why did Vasili know this?

The Russian continued. 'While Commander Crabb was looking at the propellers, the *Ordzhonikidze's* engines were fired up. Then the giant propellers were put in gear – first forwards, then reverse.'

The manner of the diver's death was horrible, but there was something that shocked Kit even more. 'How did you know that Crabb was sent to spy on the propellers?'

The Russian didn't answer. He simply looked across the Serpentine with a face of stone. But Kit didn't need to know more. The penny had finally dropped; a big bent British penny. It wasn't the third man or the fourth man – everyone knew about Philby and Blunt – it was the fifth man. That mythical beast bred by paranoia whose existence was denied by all except a few conspiracy crackpots on E Street. Kit looked closely at Vasili. 'You've penetrated the British Secret Service at the highest possible level – and you want me to know it.'

Vasili's face softened. 'You are a man, Kit, who loves poetry. That's the most important secret we share. May I recite you some Pushkin?'

Kit nodded.

Vasili looked across the Serpentine. His eyes glazed over as if the London pond had turned into the vast waters of Lake Ladozhskoye on the outskirts of nineteenth-century St Petersburg. The words came in a melodic flood with sorrow chasing laughter – and ended on a note of dry weary resignation. 'Now,' said Vasili in English, 'I have taken my flute to pieces and returned it to its case.'

A young mother was showing her toddler how to feed scraps of bread to the ducks. The child dropped a piece of bread near the water's edge. A duck darted forward to grab the bread, the child reached out to stroke the shining feathers and the duck beat a noisy retreat. The toddler looked disappointed and ready to cry. The mother kissed the child and explained the way ducks were – then put the child back in the pushchair and wheeled away.

'We have geese in Siberia that come to England for the winter and smaller birds too called,' Vasili paused and pursed his lips to make sure he got the pronunciation right, 'waxwings.'

'How do you know these things?'

'Sometimes I come here with a bird book to learn the names. Birds and animals are far more cosmopolitan than we are. At Stalingrad rats would eat dead German for breakfast, dead Russian for lunch and dead Romanian for supper – they were far better fed than the soldiers. Humans aren't very clever, considering the size of their brains.'

Kit decided that Vasili sounded more profound in Russian than in English. The spell was broken. There was a dry American side to Kit that had little time for philosophical platitudes – unless they were his own. He suddenly wanted to bring their meeting to a close. 'Have you anything else to tell me?'

Vasili took a deep breath. He seemed to be shaking his head.

Kit knew that something was wrong. It was a cool day, but beads of sweat were forming on Vasili's brow. 'Are you all right? Would you like a drink?'

'No, Kit, I'm not all right.' The Russian paused. 'Remember the story I told you about Boris having to go to the Lubyanka? It's something like that. "The good news, Vasili, is that you feel better today than you will tomorrow."'

It suddenly occurred to Kit that his Russian counterpart might be making a pitch for defecting or turning double. Handling that sort of thing was the trickiest task in the business. He remembered his training: keep listening, stay open and always be available. Kit counted to a hundred; he made to get up to leave, then said, 'I can help you.'

Vasili looked closely at Kit and laughed, then leaned close to his ear and whispered, 'It's not what you fucking think – defectors are weak assholes. They'll never be happy anywhere.'

Kit stayed silent. There was something about Vasili that was uncanny. It was as if the Russian could see straight into his mind. It gave him the creeps. It was like playing chess with one of those masters who knew every move you were going to make before you had even thought about it.

'No, Kit, I'm worried because I've got to tell you something that no one must know about – not even Khrushchev or Bulganin.' Vasili paused and looked at the ground. 'It's my decision – and it's the decision of a loyal Soviet citizen. But if it goes wrong, I'll be called back to Dzerzhinsky Square – the first stop on the way to Donskoi crematorium. That reminds me, did I ever tell you how they executed my old boss, Lavrenty Beria?'

Kit shook his head even though he knew the story.

'There is a big wall lined with thick wooden planks – birch.' Vasili smiled. 'You have to be careful shooting in a concrete cellar – the bullets, they could bounce around and hit a guard or witness. We are a careful people. There's a big hook bolted to this wooden wall – like you hang a carcass on in a butcher shop. This is where they bring Beria. He has his hands tied behind his back. There's extra rope hanging down from the knot tied around his hands. The rope reaches to the backs of his knees and makes him look like a monkey with a long tail. They use this to tie him to the hook. Beria begins to speak, "Let me talk to Georgy." He meant Malenkov. He kept writing to Malenkov during the trial begging mercy and forgiveness. He knew the letters would make Malenkov cry – and they did. But Beria just won't shut up – so Roman Rudenko wraps a towel around his head to stop him talking. You can still see the towel moving over his lips and hear muffled sounds coming out. Rudenko pulls the towel tighter and the lips stop moving. Then General Batitsky aims his pistol at Beria's forehead – but just before he pulls the trigger, the towel slips down over Beria's right eye. For a second or two, that eye is staring all over the place like a trapped animal looking for a way out. There isn't a way out. Finally, the eye seemed to grow so large that Batitsky thought it was going to pop straight out of Beria's head. It was looking straight at the gun barrel when the general pulled the trigger.'

'I don't want that to happen to you.' Kit was surprised by how much he really meant it.

Vasili smiled. 'It's the way the system works. I can't complain – my chief knows I'm meeting you. Of course, if it goes wrong he will deny all knowledge. The chief said this to my face – he laughed and slapped me on the back as he told me.'

For a second, Kit thought that Vasili might be playing a game. Then he looked at the Russian's face. There was no artifice: only the world-weary sorrow of a man staring into the abyss.

'Kit,' the Russian's voice seemed on the edge of tears, 'something awful has happened.'

Chapter Nine

The following week there was a reception at Winfield House, the Ambassador's new residence in Regent's Park, to welcome the new DCM – Deputy Chief of Mission. Kit's new boss was a 'Yalie' named Birch. Generally speaking, Kit didn't get along with Yale graduates. He wasn't a Protestant and his origins were too far south and too far removed from business. The American ruling class was a complex of rival tribes. Tribe membership was determined by family and region, but also by school and university. Princeton alumni – like F. Scott Fitzgerald and the Dulles brothers – were affable and dressed well, albeit in an old-fashioned way. Harvard men exuded well-bred intellectual aloofness, but weren't afraid of unconventional and radical ideas. Harvardians were snobs who despised snobbery. The service academies – West Point and Annapolis – produced athletic war heroes and shrewd bureaucrats. Yale, however, was only about one thing: the power of money.

One out of every hundred Yale undergraduates is 'tapped' for the Order of Skull and Bones. This elite comprises the richest and most powerful students at the university. The initiation rituals of the society are supposed to be secret – and so are the names of its members, but everyone knows who they are. Total anonymity would be pointless and counterproductive. The essence of their power is that the members are known by rumour rather than by published list. The sham secrecy is intended to create an aura of mystery and awe. You might 'know' that someone is Skull and Bones, but you don't know how lethal and far reaching is the hidden web of tentacles at their command. Kit was careful never to criticise Skull and Bones even in private conversation – lest his words be reported back to a member. He despised his own cowardice for he knew he had fallen into their trap. Skull and Bones don't care if you like them – or even respect them. They want you to fear them. Kit was more afraid of Skull and Bones than he was of the KGB or the FBI. Birch, the new DCM, was Skull and Bones

– and Kit knew that he would have to step carefully and to watch his back.

As soon as he was settled in, the new DCM invited Kit to his office for a 'chat'. Birch was in shirtsleeves and leaning back in his chair. His desk and office walls were decorated with photos of his family, his naval flight squadron and the Yale varsity baseball team – nothing fancy or pretentious. Kit knew about the Birch family, but had never met them socially. They were Northerners who had become rich during the Civil War – and then stupendously rich in the 1920s and 30s. Birch's father had been a notorious Wall Street rogue – and a friend and client of John Foster Dulles between the wars. Kit had also heard rumours that the DCM's father had been one of the gang who had dug up and stolen the bones of Geronimo, the Apache chief. The grave robbery was a stunt carried out by a group of Yalies when they were young lieutenants stationed out West. It was rumoured that Geronimo's remains were now part of the Skull and Bones initiation ritual. The reasons for the DCM's rapid rise slid neatly into place. Maybe the State Department was frightened of Skull and Bones too.

Birch waved and said 'Hi' as Kit walked into the office, then got up and walked around the desk to shake hands. Birch put his arm around Kit's shoulder as he pumped his hand and said, 'How you doin', nice to see you.' While all this was going on, Kit noticed two personnel folders lying on the DCM's desk: one was his own, the other was Cauldwell's. Birch pulled up a chair for Kit then went back behind his desk and picked up a perforated teleprinter sheet. 'Have you read the cable about Aswan?'

'Yes I have. I was also briefed about the situation when I saw Foster in Washington last month.'

Birch seemed a little startled, as if he wasn't sure that Kit should be referring to the US Secretary of State as 'Foster'. Kit dropped the name intentionally in order to put his status cards on the table. 'Well,' said Birch, 'now that the White House has formally endorsed the plan to withdraw funds from the Aswan project, we've got to see how Nasser reacts.' The DCM looked closely at Kit. 'We've now heard that it is certain that Nasser is going to nationalise the Suez Canal.'

Kit nodded. The news wasn't unexpected, but he felt uneasy about the way Birch had said it. It was obvious that the DCM had access to top secret cables that weren't passed on to him. It was, Kit realised, the first time he had been left off a top secret circulation list.

'For the next few weeks,' continued Birch, 'we have to keep a close watch on British reactions and keep Washington informed.'

'I think Washington has to realise that the reactions of the British people and the reactions of the British government are not necessarily going to be the same.'

'I suppose,' said Birch, 'you are something of an authority on British popular opinion.'

Kit thought there was a note of sarcasm in the DCM's voice. 'What makes you think that?'

'Well, living as you do in a working-class area of London's East End, you must have your ear close to the ground.'

Kit felt his blood turn cold, but tried to hide his shock. It had, of course, been inevitable that his safe house address would eventually be blown. It happened to all safe houses, that's why you needed to keep changing them. The shocking thing was that Birch, so newly arrived, had so quickly set up a net to spy on his own subordinates. Kit recovered his composure and gave Birch an easy smile. 'I did the same when I was in Bonn. I think it's the duty of an envoy to understand the host country. You can't do this from a diplomatic ghetto of dinner parties and privilege.'

Birch looked closely at Kit, as if he were an outsider who had infiltrated an elite club. 'What you say is true, but a lot of people in our business find such ideas...' the DCM paused, searching for a word, 'uncomfortable.'

'Some people call it "going native". But if you don't "go native", you'll never find out what the natives think and what they're up to.'

'You're ex-OSS, South East Asian Command, aren't you?'

'Yes, but I was barely out of my teens.'

Birch looked at his squadron photograph. 'I was still in my teens when I was shot down. My crew didn't bail out in time.'

Kit knew about the incident – and he also knew that there were a lot of unanswered questions. But to be fair, only those who have been in those dark places really know the truth. And it's not always a truth that you want to wave around.

'But,' said Birch, 'how can you go native in England? Our

language is their language – our films are their films – Churchill is half-American. We're practically the same people. Look at their music – big band, Sinatra and jazz.'

Kit remembered the rehearsal of Britten's *Noye's Fludde* at Orford Church and decided that it was pointless to answer. He suddenly felt very depressed. In the end, Chesterfields, chewing-gum and Hollywood were going to win.

The DCM saw that he had made his point and picked up a file. 'How well do you know Jeffers Cauldwell?'

'Fairly well. We were on the same FSO entry course – and later we served together at the embassy in Bonn.'

'Do you see him socially?'

'I often see him at official functions and in the staff canteen.'

'That's not what I meant by social. I mean outside work.'

'On a few occasions, four I think, we've had a drink together in a pub. Usually to kill time when we're early for a reception or a conference.'

'What do you know of his personal life?'

Kit could see where the questions were leading and was deter-mined not to help. 'Very little. When we were on the FSO course, Jeffers used to spend a lot of time in the gym. He's a pretty good boxer.'

'Have you boxed with him?'

'No, I don't box.'

'Well,' said Birch, 'I've heard that Cauldwell is quite a gadfly on the arts scene too – and has an especially keen interest in modern theatre.'

'I don't consider that part of his personal life – he is, after all, cultural attaché.'

'Isn't Cauldwell a friend of Tennessee Williams?'

'I believe that Williams is an acquaintance, but not a close friend.'

'Did you know that Tennessee Williams is a homosexual?'

'Of course, it's common knowledge in the arts world – and beyond.'

'Does Jeffers Cauldwell associate with any other homosexuals?'

'I'm sure he does. In fact, we all do. The diplomatic world, and the arts world too, are very cosmopolitan.' Kit paused. 'And, of course, part of my job is keeping files on the sexual preferences of diplomats, civil servants and politicians.'

'Do you like doing that?'

'Not particularly.'

'I suppose,' said Birch, 'it is a bit tacky. But I'm a man of the world too – and I know these things happen.'

Kit wondered if the remark was a veiled reference to the Skull and Bones initiation. At one point, the initiate has to give a speech revealing in detail his complete sexual history. Sexual secrets are blank cheques – and each member of Skull and Bones carries a blank cheque with the signature of every other member. A secret cult based on blackmail bonding.

The DCM continued. 'I don't want to sound like a prude. My own views on private sexual behaviour are liberal, but the world around us is different. And, perhaps, not as cosmopolitan and permissive as you believe it to be. I don't want any of my senior staff to be vulnerable to blackmail.'

Kit was getting fed up with the endless circling around the question. 'Are you suggesting, sir, that Jeffers Cauldwell is homosexual?'

Birch folded his hands on his desk blotter and looked at Kit. The DCM's face had the ironic half-smile of a schoolmaster who had just trapped someone doing something wrong in the toilets. 'What do you think?'

'It's not part of my job to investigate embassy personnel, who are not in my department, as potential security risks.'

'Well, let's talk about someone in your department.'

'Who?'

'You.'

Kit was taken aback. 'What about me?'

'Why do people talk behind your back? Why do they think you're an odd fish?'

'You'll have to ask them.'

'I have and now I'm asking you.'

The aggressive questioning annoyed Kit, but he was used to it. It was part of US government culture. The military, the Agency and the State Department were not polite places. Being sworn at and getting 'bawled out' were a way of life for senior officers. Sometimes it was personal; sometimes it was just a character test. But Kit suspected that Birch's attack was personal. 'I'm not surprised that people talk behind my back. A lot of it is professional jealousy: a grade three who resents my promotion, a rival who wants to drop me in the shit because I did it to him. And the fact that I don't socialise and spend all my time working.'

'What do you do for sex?'

'Nothing.'

'Masturbation, prostitutes?'

'No,' he said, 'I don't do either.' Kit wondered if Birch was trying to edge him towards a Skull and Bones type sexual autobiography. 'I suppose I come from a culture where periods of celibacy – even life-long celibacy – are regarded as an ideal rather than a reason for suspicion.'

'You see yourself as *un moine soldat*?'

Kit smiled. 'Yes, a monk soldier.' He found it a useful persona to hide behind: a modern Knight Templar, a sole combatant recruited from the *noblesse*. An image as romantic as it was false.

'Is Jeffers Cauldwell a monk soldier too?'

'No.' Kit looked out of the window across Grosvenor Square. The terrace of shabby genteel Georgian houses on the western side was scheduled for demolition to make way for the new US Embassy.

'Is it true that Cauldwell's boyfriend has moved in?'

Kit completed the betrayal without even blinking. 'Yes.'

'What do you know about the boyfriend?'

'Not much. He's a concert violinist, highly respected. His name's Henry something.'

The DCM paused like a lawyer preparing to sum up. 'There are two issues here. The first is security. Cauldwell has access to classified information, including a list of Soviet artists whom we're grooming as defectors. We can't have someone in his position vulnerable to blackmail. Also, you must realise that male homosexuality is a criminal offence under British law – and, in a worst-case scenario, I'm not going to use diplomatic immunity to get Cauldwell out of jail for sodomy.'

'Cauldwell is very discreet – and he isn't vulnerable to blackmail. He's not ashamed of his sexuality – he's almost open about it. In fact, he's one of the soundest and sanest FSOs in the service.'

'You feel guilty, don't you? That's why you're sticking up for him.'

Kit looked at the floor and nodded. He was tired of people reading his mind.

'Well, Kit, you're going to feel even more guilty when you find out what I want you to do?'

'Thanks.'

'You're welcome. Cauldwell's lover is not just a violinist. His full name is Henry Westleton Knowles. His family are upper-class socialists. You know the sort – blue bloods with red hearts. And young Knowles is more than a talented musician – he studied economics at Oxford. What you might call a Renaissance man. In any case, Knowles seems to want a life outside music. He's just been selected for a safe Labour seat for the next election.' Birch paused; he was waiting for Kit to respond.

'You don't want to get Cauldwell – you just want to scare him. The real target is Knowles.'

Birch smiled as if he had just discovered penicillin. 'Compromising the Englishman is not just the icing, it's the cake itself. Knowles is an extremely able and ambitious young man. He's tipped to rise quickly in the Labour Party – and, heaven forefend, might one day be a minister in a socialist government. Meanwhile, we'll have the dirt ready for throwing or coercing.'

It was obvious that Birch took his intelligence brief much more seriously than had his predecessor as DCM. Kit realised that he was going to be losing a lot of his independence as Chief of Station. Or more? Had he been replaced?

'So,' said Kit, 'what do you want me to do next?'

'Provide verification and corroboration.'

'Fine.'

How ironic, thought Kit. He tried not to smile as he walked back to his office. It was a private joke and he didn't like to show his emotions. How ironic that Birch wanted to blackmail others for 'sexual deviation'? As part of his Skull and Bones initiation, Birch had not only publicly masturbated, but had also submitted to anal rape with Geronimo's thigh bone. How wonderfully apt. The revenge of the Native American warrior from beyond the grave.

■

Later that afternoon, Kit's secretary passed him a sealed envelope marked 'personal and confidential'. He opened it: there wasn't the usual tag indicating source or circulation list – and it wasn't a document normally considered 'confidential'. It was simply a transcript of a speech from the US House of Representatives.

Homosexuals in Government
Congressional Record
volume 96

Mr MILLER of Nebraska.
Recently Mr Peurifoy, of the State Department, said
he had allowed ninety-one individuals in the State
Department to resign because they were homosexuals.
Now they are like birds of a feather, they flock
together. Where did they go?
In the Eightieth Congress I was the author of the sex
pervert bill...

Kit scanned the rest of the document. It was the sort of right-wing bigot rant that embarrassed US diplomats who had to deal with sophisticated Europeans. At first, he thought it was from Birch. But something told him it wasn't. Perhaps it was someone's idea of a joke. But there was only one other person in the embassy who had that sort of sense of humour. Kit crumpled the paper up and threw it in the burn bag.

Chapter Ten

Kit decided to do the job himself: Judas didn't delegate either. Jeffers Cauldwell had a flat in Pimlico in a Georgian terrace near the Thames. Kit remembered Jeffers saying how nice it was to stroll over to the Tate on a Sunday afternoon and look at the Impressionists. He remembered a lunchtime visit with Jeffers to the National Gallery of Art in Washington. It was when they were students on the FSO course. The lectures on consular duties had left them badly in need of mental stimulation so Cauldwell suggested they pop over to the gallery. They were looking at Monet's *Cathedral at Rouen* when Cauldwell said, 'It's unfinished.'

'Why,' said Kit, 'didn't he finish it?'

'Because that would have ruined it. The whole point is to capture a moment, an *impression*. Look at the brushstrokes, see the way they whisk up from the canvas and break off. It's like the paint is still alive.'

As the taxi made its way along the Embankment, Kit stared out the window and covertly ran his hand through his holdall to make sure he had everything: skeleton keys, picks, tiny files made from mild steel, pocket torch, compact camera, flash, brass knuckleduster and his Smith & Wesson .32. Kit didn't like the way the driver kept studying him through the rear-view mirror. He waited until the driver's eyes were firmly back on the road, then slipped the Smith & Wesson from the holdall to his coat pocket. In the States the gun was known as 'The Saturday Night Special'. With its short blunt barrel, it was easy to conceal and quickly whip out to solve an argument or end a game of craps. It had probably killed more Americans than all foreign armies put together.

Kit stared out the window. The glass, smeared with rain and road grease, turned London into one of Cauldwell's dark unfinished impressionist paintings. The Thames was just an empty abyss. The taxi slowed for a right-hand turn into St George's Square. 'Which number?' said the driver.

'Twelve.' Kit gave the driver a note and waved away the change.

Kit walked up to number twelve and pretended to ring a bell. When the taxi had driven off, he set off towards Cauldwell's actual address – which was a few hundred yards away. If anything went wrong, he didn't want the cabbie blabbing to the cops about a fare he had dropped at the crime site. Kit stopped briefly in a dark alleyway to screw an adapted silencer on to the barrel of the Smith & Wesson. He knew that silencers were shit with revolvers. They didn't muffle the shot completely; silencers were designed for .22 automatics. But if worst came to worst and he had to plug Cauldwell and Knowles, he wanted to make the killings look like home-grown crime. A lot of London criminals used .32 calibres, but a .22 – and no shots heard by the neighbours – would point to the security services.

Kit emerged from the alley and continued walking in the light rain. The enhanced .32 was now heavy and awkward in his over-coat pocket – bouncing against his thigh like a gross penis. What frightened Kit most of all was the knowledge that he was capable of killing. If you don't have that knowledge – that grotesque self-confidence – then your threats are hollow and your bluff will be called. It's pointless to wave a gun in someone's face if they know that you don't have the balls to pull the trigger. They won't respond to your threats. Why should they? On the other hand, if they know you are crazy enough to do it, they'll do *anything* you ask. Fear of death, thought Kit, is the worst shit – it takes away all your dignity. He looked at his watch: it was ten past two.

∎

The mortise lock was easy to pick. Kit managed it with a skeleton key and a strong wrist. Lock picking was an art like playing a stringed instrument. You need strong fingers and wrists, but also an extremely sensitive touch – and a thorough knowledge of the inner mechanisms and quirks of the lock you are picking. The Yale was more difficult because of the spring tension, but soon yielded to a fine pick and file.

Kit eased the door open a crack, waited and listened. There were no lights and no sounds – not even a ticking clock. Kit felt around in the darkness. There were coats hanging from hooks and an umbrella stand – he knew that he was in a small vesti-bule that was probably under the staircase of the upstairs flat.

He pushed open a panel door and stepped into what he assumed was the sitting room. There was a front window that looked out on the street. A tiny sliver of light from the street protruded from where the heavy velvet curtains had been pulled together – otherwise the room was black. Kit tried to orientate himself. He guessed that the door to the bedroom would be opposite the window, but there would also be other doors leading to other rooms. Kit stepped carefully into the centre of the room. Then there was a sound – ever so faint, but real and alive. He froze and waited. Something was touching him, rubbing against him. Kit reached down and stroked the cat behind the ears. The tabby was purring so loudly that he was afraid it would wake the others.

Kit took the battery torch out of his holdall and switched it on. The torch was fitted with a hood that cast a thin direct beam. He spotted side tables and plant pots that needed avoiding. There were three doors leading from the sitting room. He assumed the middle one led to the bedroom. He made his way to the door on his hands and knees to distribute his weight and lessen the chance of creaking floorboards. It also enabled him to use his hands to feel for any board that was loose. The floor was covered in a blue Chinese carpet: it seemed very old, but very fine. In the centre was the ideogram representing happiness and long life.

When he got to the door, Kit put his ear near the bottom and listened. There was the measured breathing of a sound sleeper. He listened for a second breath. If Cauldwell was alone, the visit was pointless and he would have to retrace his steps. Kit waited. The measured breathing stopped and turned into a cough. He could hear someone stirring beneath the covers. The coughing continued. Then there was a voice, 'Are you all right?' It was an English voice.

'Is the water on your side?'

Kit listened as Cauldwell drank and the other said something too soft to make out. For some reason the nocturnal sounds reminded him of his parents. The muffled late-night sound of their voices from behind the bedroom door – his father insomniac and his mother trying to soothe. It was that bad time after the war when nothing could soothe or make him sleep soundly again. Kit waited for Cauldwell and Knowles to settle. When all was quiet, he stood up and placed his hand on the door handle.

He waited another ten seconds, pushed the door open hard and loud – then stood still in the dark.

'Who's there?' It was Cauldwell's voice.

Kit heard the bedsprings creak as the other sat up. 'What's going on?' The voice was full of refined public-school indignation.

Kit switched the torch on and shone the beam on Henry Knowles's face. He squinted against the light. There was no fear in his eyes, only annoyance at having been disturbed. He then played the beam on Cauldwell who was blinking and trying to block the light with his hand. 'What do you want?' he said.

Kit dropped the torch and took the gun out of his pocket. He groped against the wall with his free hand until he found the light switch and flicked it on. The overhead light was clothed in a Chinese lantern decorated with the symbol for 'happy home'. It was composed of the ideogram for 'house' containing the ideogram for 'woman'. Kit remembered that the symbol for unhappy was a house with two women. He wondered what a house with two men represented and aimed the pistol at the bed. Cauldwell squinted hard trying to make out who was in the room.

'It's me,' said Kit.

Cauldwell grabbed his spectacles from the bedside table and put them on. He gaped at Kit. 'It is you. Why are you here? What's the gun for?'

'To make sure you follow instructions.'

Meanwhile Knowles, stark naked, was out of the bed. 'What's the meaning of this?'

Kit pointed the gun at the Englishman. 'Stay where you are.'

Knowles ignored him, picked up a decanter half-full of water to use as a weapon. 'Get out of here now.'

Kit pulled the trigger and the decanter shattered. The silenced shot sounded like a heavy shoe dropping on a carpeted floor.

'Do as he says,' said Cauldwell, 'he will kill you. He's one of those.'

'Get back in the bed,' said Kit, 'and throw the covers off – and mind the broken glass.'

Knowles removed a shard from his pillow as Cauldwell gathered the blankets and threw them on the floor. Both men were now lying naked side by side. Kit shifted the gun to his left hand, picked up the camera and took two snaps. 'Is that all you wanted?' said Cauldwell as if he had half expected the visit.

'No, put Henry's penis in your mouth – and then reverse positions.'

Kit put them through the entire repertoire of same sex male love and continued taking pictures until the film and flashbulbs were used up. He then put the camera back in his holdall, all the while keeping them covered with the pistol. Kit could see that Knowles was a brave bastard. Cauldwell grabbed a blanket. 'Do you mind? We're cold.'

Kit nodded.

'I don't suppose, Kit, that these snapshots are intended for your own erotic gratification.'

'What do you think?'

'Who put you up to this? The DCM? Or was it that FBI shit in the basement? I don't suppose I'm important enough to involve E Street or the Seventh Floor.'

'You're fishing, Jeffers. I'm not going to tell you anything and you know it.'

'I think,' said Knowles, 'the wise thing to do would be to destroy that film. You've been badly advised. Blackmail is a criminal offence in this country. Why not just hand the film to me? Otherwise, I'm going to ring the police as soon as you've gone.'

Kit suspected Knowles was bluffing. He pointed to a phone on the bedside table. 'Ring them now. As soon as they finish booking me for unlawful entry, they can arrest you and Jeffers for sodomy.'

Knowles picked up the phone and started to dial. Cauldwell reached over and stopped him. 'Don't, Henry, it's not a good idea.' The phone went back on its cradle.

'Instead of calling the cops,' said Kit, 'why don't you make some coffee. None of us is going to get any sleep tonight.'

As Cauldwell ground the coffee beans and prepared the cafetière, Kit tried to engage Knowles in conversation – at the same time cradling the pistol in his lap. He wondered if the DCM had told him everything about the Englishman – or just filled him in on a 'need-to-know' basis. Kit's instinct sensed that Knowles was a missing piece in a jigsaw that was only half complete. He tried light talk. 'Have you ever played at the Aldeburgh Festival?'

'Several times. It's a regular venue.'

Cauldwell poured three coffees and sat down. Something in his manner suggested that the Aldeburgh question was an awkward one. 'You know that Henry is giving up concert playing, at least temporarily. He'll be standing for parliament at the next election. I'm sure the DCM didn't leave that one out.' It was obvious that Cauldwell was trying to steer the conversation away from Aldeburgh.

Kit ignored the remarks and addressed Knowles directly. He remembered a name that Jeffers had passed on during an office chat. Kit assumed that Cauldwell was merely bored and wanted to get in on the 'cloak and dagger' stuff. At the time, Kit hadn't taken the information seriously, but he did now. 'I don't suppose that you know a Russian cellist named Natalya Voronova?'

The Englishman looked as if he had just swallowed glass. He glanced across the table at Cauldwell. Cauldwell looked away and reddened. A heavy silence filled the kitchen. Bingo, thought Kit, bingo, bingo. Kit opened his holdall and took out the camera. He then opened the camera, removed the film and offered Knowles the undeveloped roll. 'You can have this, if you tell me everything you know.'

For a second Knowles looked at the film as if he were a Knight Templar being offered the Holy Grail in exchange for desecrating a crucifix. Then the Englishman looked straight at Kit without blinking. 'I have nothing to tell you. I only know Voronova as a name in a string section.'

■

The other photographs arrived at the embassy late the next afternoon. Those photographs – the ones taken by the U2 flight – were hot stuff too. Too hot to be despatched in a diplomatic pouch. They were sent via a military courier who carried the photos in a locked briefcase that was handcuffed to his wrist. The courier, a bespectacled Signal Corps second lieutenant with acne, was sitting outside Kit's office with a marine guard. The marine was chewing gum; the courier was reading the poems of William Carlos Williams.

Kit spread the aerial reconnaissance photographs on his desk and read the NSA analysis that came with them. It was the most highly classified intelligence material that he had ever been allowed to see. He felt his fingers tingle and burn when he touched each glossy print. It was the first over-flight of the Soviet Union using the new Kodak cameras. The target of the spy flight was an installation in the Central Volga region five hundred kilometres north-east of Moscow codenamed Arzamas-16, a city so secret that it didn't even appear on the map.

The photos were of such high quality that Kit could actually see the multiple barbwire fences, the watchtowers and distinguish the different types of Soviet Army trucks. He looked again at the NSA commentary: *outer defensive ring is twenty-five miles from centre and guarded by Russian Army paratroopers… inner defensive rings patrolled exclusively by Minister of Interior troops.* In other words, KGB. The installation itself was so secret that even crack Soviet soldiers were not allowed access. *The spaces between the multiple fences are plowed and patrolled regularly.* The ploughing – 'plowing' – was a nice security touch. It enabled patrols to easily detect footsteps and a breach of security. 'How,' said Kit, 'how the fuck did they do it?' He went through the photos again. The area was heavily wooded and there was considerable evidence of logging. Kit wondered what happened to the logs. Were they used for fuel? Pulped for paper – or milled for building material? A picture started to form in Kit's mind. Or were the logs…? How much, after all, did it matter? Then Kit remembered the last thing that Vasili had said to him: 'We are soldiers in an inhuman war.'

■

Jennifer met Kit at Wickham Market station; she was driving a new car, an Austin Devon A40, and wearing a white linen skirt. She looked pretty fine: pregnancy made her blossom even more. Kit put his bags into the boot: the door opened downwards and formed a neat platform. 'It makes a handy picnic table,' said Jennifer.

'What happened to the Hillman?'

'It was wrecked.'

'Who was driving?'

'That information is classified.'

Something in Jennifer's voice told Kit that there was more to it, an awkward side she didn't want to talk about. He let it go. 'I'm looking forward to getting out on the river. I hate being cooped up in London when the weather is like this.'

'What have you been doing?'

'Selling secrets to the Russians and blackmailing homosexuals.'

Jennifer laughed and gave her cousin a little slap on the hand. 'Can't you ever be serious?'

'Half serious, maybe.'

'The problem with you, Kit, is that we never know which half to believe.'

'Maybe I should start taking transparency pills so you can see into my mind. But could you endure such horrors?'

'Nonsense, you're all sweetness and poetry. You have no dark secrets – it's just a front you put on.'

'Let's make a deal, Jennie, I'll start taking those transparency pills if you do too.'

Kit sensed something tighten in his cousin. Then she laughed again. 'I'm not sure it would be a good idea. I wouldn't want to hurt anyone.'

Kit looked out the car window. The lane was blowing white with the fine lace of cow parsley; just before the forest there was a field scarlet mad with poppies. Kit watched a roe doe flee from the poppy field by leaping over a wire fence into the tangled darkness. 'Not wanting to hurt,' he said, 'is not the same as not hurting.'

'Sorry, Kit, I didn't quite catch that.'

'It's nothing. I was just mumbling inanely to myself – like my mom when she can't find her reading glasses. How's Brian?'

'He's been very busy lately. There seems to be a big problem on the island – I think there's a construction project behind schedule.'

Kit suddenly flashed back to the briefing he had received from S2 intelligence at Bentwaters airbase. It was about the strange things that the Brits were building on Orford Ness Island. How had the aerial photo analyst described them? *These structures are not meant to withstand a nuclear strike from the outside, but they are meant to...* Vasili's melancholy story was starting to make sense. Poor Boris.

∎

Jennifer dropped Kit at Orford Quay and tried to help him carry his bags to the pram dinghy he used as a tender. 'Don't,' he said, 'you'll get all muddy.'

'I like mud.' She kicked off her shoes and started to hitch up her skirt to undo her stockings.

'Don't, Jennie, people are looking. Think of Brian's reputation.'

She let her skirt down. 'I'm glad you didn't say mine. But you will take me for a sail sometime.'

'Any time.' Kit sat on the boot door to pull on his wellies and watched a heavy lorry laden with cement roll on to one of the landing barges that ran as ferries between the quay and Orford Ness.

'The locals don't like it,' said Jennifer, 'all that construction work means a lot of heavy traffic through the villages. Brian gets some strange looks when he goes to the pub.'

'Maybe it's his Mancunian accent.'

'You've noticed? Not many Americans pick up the differences. They think all the English speak either Cockney or posh.'

'It's my job to know one native tribe from another.'

'And you love it. Peter admired the way you picked up languages. In one of his letters he wrote about how you entertained your Vietnamese hosts by telling a funny story in their language and imitating the local peasant accent.'

'But Peter didn't tell you that I practised the story for an hour beforehand with an interpreter. It was all an act to make the British general think we knew the local situation better than we did. Just another cheap trick of the trade.'

'I wish you weren't so self-critical. I've always admired you.'

Kit felt his temples throb and his face turn red. The late-morning sun was high in the sky, the river behind her a blinding silver frame. He wanted her so much that he thought his chest would burst. He finished doing up his sea boots and carried his bags to the dinghy. When he had finished stowing his things, he turned around. Jennifer was still standing by the car. He went back. 'I think,' he said, 'my dinner jacket and shirt are going to be a bit crushed.'

'Let me do some ironing for you.'

'No, I prefer going to these things looking like a tramp. I like looking worse than the Russians. It gives me a chance to tease them about aping capitalist manners.'

'And not getting it right.'

'What a snob you are, Jennie.'

'I get it from you.'

'You get it from your mom.' Kit kissed his cousin, went back to the dinghy and pushed it into the water. Jennifer was still there waving as the tide swept him past the quay. Three more cement lorries rumbled down to the slipway hiding her in their shadows.

■

Kit thought that sailing to an Aldeburgh Festival concert by yacht would be a pretty classy way to arrive. In the early evening, after he had picked up a mooring near Slaughden Quay and started changing into black-tie dinner dress, he saw that others had the same idea. There were four other yachts with distinguished gentlemen who all looked like Harold Macmillan. Each of the Macmillans was struggling to do up a bow tie. Whenever someone they knew sailed past they called out, 'Air, hair lair.' Kit loved it – and every time he spotted a champagne cork arcing over the moorings, he called out, 'Air, hair, lair,' too.

∎

The main part of the music programme was devoted to the three great Russian cello sonatas by Prokofiev, Shostakovich and Rachmaninov. Kit loved the Prokofiev. The music started like a runaway freight train about to go off the rails. Throughout the concert he kept his eyes on Natalya Voronova and wondered how exactly she fitted in. She was an attractive woman with thick black hair and pale skin who played with utter passion and intensity. She frightened him. Kit knew that she would be shadowed by KGB minders and that it wouldn't be easy for them to talk at the reception afterwards. Even if she wanted to talk – maybe she was KGB herself. Most people had the wrong idea about how the Soviet surveillance system worked. They imagined slab-faced KGB thugs holding exquisite dancers and sensitive musicians on a tight short lead while they toured the West. It wasn't like that. The KGB minders were themselves talented and experienced performers. KGB shadows could have angelic faces and long fine fingers just like anyone else.

The piece that Kit had liked least was the Rachmaninov – and, oddly enough, he was the only composer of the three who had made his life in the West. Perhaps Vasili was right: Russians lose their soul when they leave Russia. That, thought Kit, was the good thing about being an American. If you wanted to find your soul, the best way to find it was to get the hell *out* of the country. They all did it: Whistler, Henry James, Josephine Baker, Eliot, Hemingway, Pound, Fitzgerald – even the Duchess of Windsor. And when they did go back, they usually killed themselves or ended up, like Pound, in St Elizabeth's insane asylum. Pound, thought Kit, had got off too lightly. The poet should have been shot for turning traitor and siding with the fascists. Still, there's nothing wrong with being a traitor if that's what you think you've got to do – but in the end, they have to shoot you and you shouldn't complain. The rules are clear and simple.

After the concert, Kit walked along the beach to the Wentworth Hotel for the reception. The beamy fishing boats were pulled up high on the shingle. There was little wind and the low breakers seemed to be grumbling to themselves while they turned and washed the smooth stones. Out to sea there was nothing except the green and white lights of a ship creeping south – and, every six seconds, the ghostly loom of a light vessel below the horizon. Kit remembered being on the same beach on the same spot with Jennifer the year before. He reached out and tried to touch her essence – as if it could be left behind in the night sea air. Other voices – Slav and Saxon – skipped over the beach from the hotel terrace. Kit crunched over the shingle towards the lights.

The Aldeburgh Festival people had a desk at the Wentworth where you signed in and picked up a name tag. The one reserved for the US Embassy representative was made out for *Counsellor Jeffers Cauldwell, Cultural Attaché, United States Embassy*. Kit explained that his colleague was unable to attend. 'I'll have to,' he said, 'take my chances incognito. Maybe I'll be mistaken for someone famous.'

'It doesn't matter.' The woman at the sign-in desk was 'air hair lair' with slightly bohemian undertones. She wore a necklace of chunky amber. 'No one else is displaying a name tag. The Russians, especially, are a rule onto themselves.' She lowered her voice. 'But confidentially, I think this name tag thing is very un-British. It's the sort of thing the Americans do at conventions and such.' She suddenly paused, then put a hand to her mouth. 'Oh, I am *so* sorry – how rude of me!'

Kit smiled. 'You're absolutely right – it's almost as bad as chewing gum. They both should be banned.'

The woman smiled wanly and Kit headed towards the drinks table for a glass of lukewarm flat bubbly. The reception, compared to your average diplomatic bash, was a pretty humble affair. The Aldeburgh Festival didn't have as much money to throw around as national governments. Kit looked around the reception room. There was no one that he knew personally. The only persons he recognised were Benjamin Britten, Mstislav Rostropovich and Sviatoslav Richter. Kit sipped the stale non-vintage champagne. Richter and Rostropovich were as handsome as film stars. Britten, on the other hand, was as understated as the Suffolk coast that he loved. The English composer was slightly stooped and might have been mistaken for a clerk in an ironmonger's.

'Excuse me.' There was a voice at Kit's elbow. He turned to find Natalya Voronova beside him. 'Are you Jeffers – Henry's friend?'

'No,' said Kit, 'Jeffers couldn't come. He asked me to take his place.'

Natalya seemed taken aback. Her voice became more accented. 'Ah... are you from the embassy too?'

'Yes.'

'American?'

'Of course.'

The cellist glanced around, as if to check for minders or eavesdroppers. It was a bad, clumsy move that a professional would never have made. It was obvious that Natalya had no training in intelligence work. 'I was,' she said, 'hoping to meet Jeffers.'

'He told me you were.'

'So you know?'

'I know everything.'

'Everything?' Natalya seemed confused.

Kit looked over her shoulder. A Russian was staring in their direction over a champagne glass, but as soon as he saw Kit's glance he turned away.

'Where are you staying?' said Natalya.

'On my boat.'

'On...?' She looked puzzled.

'On a boat, a yacht.' Kit racked his mind for the Russian equivalent, but couldn't find it. 'En français, c'est ce que l'on appelle un voilier.'

'Oh, a *boat*, one with sails! Is she big?'

'No, very small – just me alone.'

There was suddenly a lurking presence of other Russians and Kit knew that it was time to disengage and circulate. He didn't even dare suggest another meeting. As he moved on, Kit saw a pianist whispering in Natalya's ear. She was shaking her head and frowning. Meanwhile, vodka had appeared. Someone passed Kit a tiny ice-cold glass opaque with frost, and someone else filled it with ice-cold vodka. He noted that the English had started to leave. After two drinks, Kit headed back to the boat.

■

After rowing back to *Louise*, Kit rigged an anchor light from the forestay. Its purpose was to stop another boat or ship from running him down in the dark watches of the night. It probably wasn't necessary on one of the Aldeburgh Yacht Club's visitor's moorings, but Kit liked the warm yellow circle of light cast by the hurricane lantern. The light also attracted fish that rippled the water around the bows. Kit sat for a while on the foredeck – the music still playing in his head – and wished again that he was something other than what he was. His job was squalid – and it made his life squalid too. What would he say to the Great Inquisitor when He asked, 'Why, sinner, did you spy, murder, lie, deceive and bear false witness?' 'Because I never had piano lessons.' Somehow, thought Kit, his excuse wouldn't be good enough. And even that was a lie. There had been a woman – a Frau Niedermann – who gave them lessons when his dad was stationed in Lima. But Frau Niedermann had become ill – she might even have died, for the lessons never resumed. He wished he hadn't made jokes about her name. And their dentist was a German too. In South America, *all* dentists are German. Kit suddenly felt very tired. He went down below, undressed and brushed his teeth. Then he lit the paraffin lamp in the fore cabin and crawled into his berth. Cosy.

Kit always felt happy spending a night afloat. Somehow he felt safer and more secure than on land. The boat was his own self-contained little world. Kit opened a book, but after a few pages he started to fall asleep. He rolled down the wick of the lamp until it went out – and then listened to the sound of wavelets lapping against the hull. He was so near the sea that he could also hear the sough of waves gently breaking on Aldeburgh beach. He remembered that there was only a thin strip of shingle isthmus – like a tightrope – that protected the moorings from the full force of the North Sea. Kit soon fell into a sound dreamless sleep.

After what seemed hours, Kit found himself fully awake and staring upwards at the cabin roof. A weak glow from the anchor light penetrated the cabin from the portholes and hatch – enough for him to read his watch: two a.m. He didn't know what had woken him. There was no wind and the boat was lying calmly with the ebbing tide. Nothing seemed wrong. He lay still and listened. Then it began. Something was thumping against the hull – like a log or a body. Kit waited and listened as the object bumped its way along the hull towards the stern. He wondered if it was a small boat that had broken loose from its mooring. If so, he ought to try to recover it. He sat up and started to dress. But then, whatever it was, began to make its way back towards the bow – *against* the tide. It was alive. For a second, Kit froze and felt fear. He remembered Portsmouth Harbour. Had Commander Crabb come back to get him? Or was it Driscoll? Then he heard a voice – and someone knocking on the hull.

'Hello, can you help me?'

Kit went through the main cabin and outside into the cockpit. He looked around, but couldn't see anyone. Then the voice again: 'Hello.' Finally, in the glow of the anchor light, Kit saw the tips of four fingers, with bright red nails, clinging to the side-deck coaming. Someone was trying to climb aboard. Kit looked over the side, but it was too dark to make out a face. 'Wait a second,' he said, 'I'll get the boarding ladder.' Kit quickly unlashed the ladder and dropped the steps over the side.

As Natalya Voronova climbed aboard, it became apparent that she was stark naked. She sat in the cockpit dripping and breathing hard; her full breasts goose pimpled. 'Let me get you a towel,' said Kit, 'you must be freezing.' While the woman towelled herself dry, Kit put crumpled newspaper and kindling in the little stove. It wasn't long before the main cabin was a cosy nest with coffee percolating on the spirit cooker and Natalya wrapped in a white towel opposite him. 'I can't stay long,' she said.

'Have some coffee.' Kit began to feel pretty stupid – as if he were a lounge lizard trying to seduce a woman in his bachelor flat. He wished he hadn't offered the coffee.

Natalya seemed to sense his discomfort and smiled. 'Thank you.'

Kit could hear voices shouting from the beach. 'Nata-a-a-ly-a-a-a-a.'

'They're all drunk,' she said. 'I told them I was going for a swim. They must be worried.'

Kit didn't know how to play it. Something told him she was not trying to defect, but it was important not to turn her away if she was. He began to broach the question. 'We would be most happy to...'

'No, I don't want that.'

'Want what?'

'Political asylum.' Her voice seemed exasperated and annoyed.

'You must not be mistaken, I'm a loyal Soviet citizen.' She paused. 'But my husband is not.'

There was more shouting from the beach.

'Listen,' she said, 'there isn't much time. My husband, Viktor Voronov, worked with Zeldovich and Sakharov at Los Arzamas on – I don't know how to say in English – *Atomnoe Obzhatie*.' She began to move her hands together as if to crush something.

'Compression, fusion,'

'That's right. It's what you do to make hydrogen bomb.'

Kit nodded.

'Early this year my husband come to England, to Harwell – near Oxford.'

Kit had heard of Harwell. It was the nuclear centre where the British did their most advanced research. Aldermaston, by comparison, was a nuts-and-bolts engineering shed.

'Was it an official visit? Did the Kremlin allow him to come?'

'Of course, but it was very secret. He come to England to discuss *peaceful* use of nuclear, to build power stations for electricity.'

Kit sighed and smiled. Her news wasn't earth-shattering. Research on controlled fusion for cheap energy was almost declassified. 'Is that all?' he said.

'No, that is not all. My husband never came back.'

'What?' Something clicked at the back of Kit's brain.

'His friends say the British kidnapped him, but,' she said, 'I am sure he defected.'

'Why do you say that?'

'Because he was plotting with others.'

'Plotting to do what?'

'Viktor is a vulgar man, like a kulak. He dreams of driving Cadillac in California.'

Kit was tempted to say 'like Igor Stravinsky', but held his tongue.

'He and the others wanted to become rich, more rich than anyone could imagine – so they do this thing.'

'What did they do?'

Natalya smiled and let the towel drop off her shoulder. Her body was firm and sensual. 'I think maybe you prefer drive Cadillac too – or maybe boys.'

'No.'

'There isn't time. I must go back.'

Kit reached forward to brush the damp black hair from her face, then stroked her neck. 'What did they do, Natalya, please tell me?'

'Why don't you ask your British friends?'

Kit ran his fingers down the side of her neck – and paused with his thumb on her voice box. Maybe he should squeeze it out of her. He felt a frisson of excitement. It would be so easy to crush her larynx or pop a vertebra or two. 'Why won't you tell me?'

'Because I love my country and am afraid of being a traitor by talking too much. I have only told you what the British already know.' She touched the fingers Kit had placed on her neck. 'You want to choke me?'

'No.' Kit leaned forward, suddenly breathless and kissed her gently. 'Keep your secrets.'

'Thank you.' Natalya dropped the towel and left the warm fug of the cabin for the chill darkness. Kit watched her climb down the boarding ladder to slip into the dark river without a splash. 'By the way,' she said, 'how well do you know the Ninth?'

'I know that it was Beethoven's last symphony and that it ends with a choral section based on Schiller's *Ode an die Freude*. Why do you ask?'

Kit heard Natalya laughing from the river. She was invisible in the darkness. 'You obviously know nothing about the Ninth. Goodbye.' Her strokes gently splashed the water and stirred flashes of phosphorous that followed her as she swam to the shore.

Chapter Eleven

Kit didn't like the new office toy. It was an intercom that connected his desk with his new secretary. It made him feel more like a grey suit 'chicken and mayonnaise sandwich' Long Island commuter than a US diplomat. He was pretty snooty about business and US corporate 'style' – even though most of the world seemed to long for it. Kit looked at the intercom. It was a beige Bakelite box with brown trim containing speakers activated by a single button. He pressed the button and said, 'Ethel.'

'Good morning, Counsellor Fournier.'

'How are you? Have you settled in?'

'I'm fine, sir, and I have. Thank you for asking. How may I help you?'

Kit cringed and silently swore that he was going to get rid of 'the fucking thing'. 'Ethel, could you please ask Mr Perry to come to my office.'

'Yes, sir.' There was a pause filled with static. 'Deputy Counsellor Perry is on his way, sir.'

'Oh, for fuck's sake.' Kit immediately prayed the whisper had been inaudible. 'Ethel.'

'Sir.'

Kit was about to say that they should all address each other by their first names, but then realised that this would only embarrass Ethel. 'Nothing, I was just lost in thought.'

As Perry entered the office, Kit flourished the reports his deputy had prepared on UK dollar reserves, UK oil imports and Anglo-Egyptian relations. 'Excellent stuff, Tim, exactly what we wanted.'

'Thank you,' said Perry. He seemed mildly abashed by the use of his first name. He looked closely at Kit for a second, then added, 'Sir.'

Kit leaned back in his chair with his hands behind his head. 'What was she like?'

'Ethel?'

'No, Marilyn. Didn't you go to the party?'

'Oh, that. It was great.'

'So how was she?'

Perry sat down, folded his arms and looked sideways at Kit. 'You know when you see her close up, in real life, she doesn't look anything like she does in the movies.'

'Go on.'

'Very pretty face, but avoids eye contact, seems very shy. I suppose you could say that she has a good figure, but she's... pretty broad-beamed.'

Kit straightened up. 'Are you telling me that Marilyn Monroe has a fat ass? For Chrissake, Perry, you're supposed to be in the *diplomatic* corps.'

Perry looked closely at his boss. He never knew when Kit was joking. 'I suppose,' said Perry, 'that I should have said she wasn't very skinny.'

'No, what you *should* have said was that she's sensuous and womanly – like a Rubens. You ought to go to more art galleries – it might take off some of your rough edges.'

The deputy shifted nervously in his seat and began to redden.

'Sorry, Perry, I was being facetious. None of that stuff matters any more.'

'What stuff?'

'Culture. And speaking of culture, what did you think of Arthur Miller?'

'To be honest, Miller wasn't very grateful – considering that it was our embassy that laid on the reception.'

'What did he do? Piss in the punchbowl?'

'He said that President Eisenhower was in hock to big business and that he was going to vote for Adlai Stevenson in November. He also said that the Secretary of State was a danger to world peace.'

'He's allowed to have views. And what was Princess Margaret like?'

'She smoked a lot.'

'Right,' said Kit, 'thanks for covering that and thanks for these reports.'

Perry walked to the door, then stopped and turned around. 'By the way, Jeffers Cauldwell has gone AWOL. No one's seen him since last week.'

'Really.' Kit tried to look surprised. 'Who told you?'

'The DCM called me into his office. It was kind of weird – he wanted to know if I knew and if you had said anything.'

'Then what?'

'He told me to keep my mouth shut.'

'And you've just told me.'

'But you're my boss.'

'Thank you, Tim.'

As soon as Perry closed the door, the demons of paranoia and suspicion began to dance and leap around the office. Kit could almost feel their hot pointy fingers and hear their shrill laughter.

•

An hour later Kit was summoned to the DCM's office. Despite the summer heat, Birch was wearing his jacket – like a shield of office. He invited Kit to take a seat, but offered neither coffee nor water. There were newly hung photos on the wall behind the DCM. One photograph showed his sons paddling a canoe near their summerhouse in Maine, another was of Birch flanked by President Eisenhower and Secretary of State Dulles. All three men are laughing at a joke that would remain forever private. Pictures like that aren't just photos. They're power currency to let your visitors know who they're talking to. Kit had a few snaps like that himself, but he kept them filed away. It was one of the many games he wouldn't play.

'You did a fine job, Kit.' The DCM's face was impassive and impossible to read. 'Maybe too fine.' Birch slid the 8x10 glossies out of a buff envelope and put on his half-moon reading glasses to look at them. 'They certainly don't leave much to the imagination.'

'I wanted photo evidence that would stand up to any accusation of being doctored. A pair of naked men lying next to each other is fairly easy to fake – the KGB do it all the time. Sexually explicit ones, on the other hand, are impossible to counterfeit.'

Birch put the photos aside and steepled his fingers. 'In any case, we may no longer need them. Cauldwell and Knowles have disappeared.'

Kit looked at the DCM without blinking. 'That's always a danger with an operation like this. The targets' fear of exposure is so great they run away – it's a panic reaction. Quite often, they commit suicide.' Kit was surprised how calm and clinical his voice sounded.

'Do you think Cauldwell's a suicidal type?'

'No, I'm also surprised he did a runner. Jeffers is the type of guy who brazens things out. He's tough.'

Birch made a note on a pad, then said, 'When Cauldwell didn't turn up for work, I went around to his apartment with Hauser, the new FBI guy. No one answered the door, so Hauser picked the lock. I was primarily concerned that there might be classified documents lying around. So we had a really good search. Nothing. In fact, nothing at all – not even a birthday card or a scribbled phone number on the back of an envelope. Someone had scrubbed the place clean and done a very professional job: upholstery, floorboards, everything. On the other hand, they left his toothbrush and suitcase behind.'

'Have you informed the police?'

'No, I got the Ambassador to have a word with the British Foreign Secretary. We're claiming extra-territorial jurisdiction over Cauldwell's apartment and his disappearance. The Brits aren't too happy about it, but it is part of the international diplomatic protocol.'

'How do you know that Knowles is missing too?'

'It's in the press.'

'Could be messy if they link him to Jeffers.'

'Very, but I'm more worried about other things – like who turned over the apartment.'

'What about Cauldwell and Knowles?'

'Cauldwell is irrelevant, just an arts world gadfly. You're something of an arts man yourself, aren't you?' It sounded like an accusation.

'I like books and paintings – it gives you a perspective.'

'I don't know how you find the time. In any case, of the two, Knowles is the one who concerns me. Can you find out all you can about him?'

'Yes.' Kit stood up to leave. He wasn't sure that he should be taking orders from Birch. The DCM outranked him in the diplomatic hierarchy, but not – as far as Kit knew – on the intelligence side. 'Can I ask you something, sir?'

'Shoot.'

'Am I still Chief of Station?'

Birch smiled. 'You're still on the same pay grade.'

■

The basic facts about Henry Knowles were easy to find from press cuttings and documents in the public domain. He was born in Berkhamstead to an upper middle-class family. He could sight-read music by the age of five and was a prodigy on both strings and keyboard. When he was eleven, Henry won a violin and piano scholarship to Wells Cathedral School. He then went on to Balliol College, Oxford where he read PPE – Philosophy, Politics and Economics – and took a double first. Henry was offered jobs with the Treasury, several merchant banks, the Foreign Office (and presumably MI6), but turned them down to become a violinist with the BBC Symphony Orchestra. Meanwhile, he remained an active member of the Labour Party and had a seat on the National Executive. A true Renaissance man.

None of this struck Kit as terribly unusual. Jan Paderewski, the greatest piano virtuoso of his generation, became Prime Minister of Poland. But that was a passionate time in Polish history: it wasn't what you expected in 1950s England. Had Henry Knowles dreamed of becoming Prime Minister of Britain? If so, thought Kit, his little picture-taking session would have made him – and his country – forever a hostage of whoever had the negatives.

Kit was surprised, but not disappointed that they had run away. Sexual blackmail was the sleaziest trick in the espionage textbook. Kit liked the idea of meeting them in twenty or thirty years time in a mellow village in the south of France or Italy – where the locals shared knowing winks about their relationship but liked them all the same. Or maybe the bodies just hadn't turned up yet?

Kit needed to find out more than he could from press cuttings and concert programmes. He walked downstairs to the top secret archive vault. The stuff involved was too sensitive to keep in his own office safe – even though he had compiled much of it himself. It was a comprehensive list of the entire British Labour Party that rank-ordered its members from left-wingers like Aneurin Bevan, whom Allen Dulles described as 'the most dangerous extremist in Britain', to the anti-communist right of the party led by Hugh Gaitskell. The file contained a secret that no one must ever know: the extent to which the right wing of the Labour Party worked closely with MI5 and the CIA to undermine their own members on the left.

Kit sat at a bare desk and went through the file under the eyes of a marine guard. He was allowed to take notes, provided the notes remained in the vault. It was more practical to commit names and facts to memory. The stuff was dynamite. It contained the names of Labour politicians who received money from the CCF, the Congress for Cultural Freedom, a CIA front organisation aimed at spreading anti-communist propaganda. The demonising of communism was the Apostle's Creed of US foreign policy. It wasn't a free discussion of ideas. It was lavishly funded psychological warfare to achieve the military-diplomatic-financial goals of the United States. Kit tried not to laugh as he read through the CCF file. Once you knew who was pulling the strings, it was all so fucking obvious.

Kit skimmed the list of names to decide who was the best candidate to quiz about Henry Knowles. There was one name which stood out above the rest. It belonged to a backbench Labour MP who was even to the right of Gaitskell. The MP, owing to his love of fine wine and food, was codenamed Bacchus. Kit had met him a few times before at seminars and press conferences. In fact, Bacchus had entered politics from a background in newspapers – where, as a journalist, he had been notorious for accepting covert funding from the Congress for Cultural Freedom.

■

The restaurant was located a short walk from Lord's Cricket Ground and Bacchus arrived wearing a white linen jacket, a bow tie and a panama hat. It was, after all, one of the hottest days of the summer. Kit had already ordered a bottle of Montrachet which was cooling in the ice bucket. Bacchus came over to the table and twisted the bottle so he could read the label, 'Your wine tastes are pretty classy for a Yank.'

'I'm not a Yankee, I was born south of the Mason Dixon Line.'

Bacchus shook hands and sat down. 'It's still a very nice wine. Most people who want to show off order champagne and know fuck all about it.'

'I'm not showing off, I'm trying to bribe you.'

'That's even better. But I'm not on the Privy Council yet, so I can't tell the latest on HM's Suez policy.'

'I can. Eisenhower's just sent a very stern note to Eden, and Eden is going to ignore the warnings – or maybe he just didn't understand the President's prose.'

'Really.' Bacchus looked slightly abashed at the offhand way

Kit had passed on a piece of sensitive and classified information. The disclosure was, however, carefully calculated. It was in the US interest for the opposition to know what Eden was up to – and it was important for Kit to gain Bacchus's confidence by tossing a gem in his direction. The quickest way to gain intelligence was just to swap nuggets. 'So Washington thinks that Eden's going to go in.'

'Let's put it this way, he hasn't ruled it out – and he doesn't seem in a mood to take friendly advice.'

'Maybe his gall bladder – if he still has one – is playing up again. That's good. His government will fall and we'll end up in power.'

Kit smiled, but didn't comment. The view from E Street was that the Labour Party wasn't 'yet ready for power'. Although they were busy cultivating right-wingers like Bacchus and Gaitskell, there were still far too many dangerous left-wingers, like Aneurin Bevan and Tony Benn, in positions of influence. Not to mention the growing CND faction. 'Have some wine,' said Kit.

Bacchus sipped the wine slowly and rolled it around in his mouth. 'Lovely stuff.' He looked at the menu. 'I think I'll have the Cromer Crab salad.'

'Have the lobster. This meal's on Uncle Sugar.'

'Who?' Bacchus seemed confused.

'It's what we call Uncle Sam when the US taxpayer is footing the bill.'

'That's good. I'll remember that. What's that expression you use when someone totally fucks something up? I heard your military attaché use it.'

'"He stepped on his dick."'

'Like Eden will do over Suez.'

'And wearing spiked track shoes.'

'Ouch.'

The waiter came and they ordered lobster.

'Pity about that young candidate of yours that's gone missing.'

'I feel sorry for the family.' Bacchus emptied his glass and Kit topped it up. 'But,' said Bacchus, 'he wouldn't have been good for the party.'

'Why's that? He looked pretty bright.'

'Young Knowles was very bright indeed – and that made him even more dangerous. He was a protégé of the neutralist wing

– and a member of that new organisation called the Campaign for Nuclear Disarmament. They're getting too big for their boots.'

The food arrived and Kit ordered another bottle of wine.

'There was something else about Knowles that worried a lot of us.'

'His personal life?'

'Good lord, no. We're too grown up for that sort of thing to matter.'

Once again, Kit was reminded of his country's emotional and sexual immaturity. He felt ashamed that he had gone along with Birch's puerile blackmail operation – another layer of guilt.

'No,' Bacchus paused in thought; then speared a piece of lobster that he dipped in the melted garlic butter. 'I don't,' he said, 'want to say too much.'

'I notice,' said Kit, 'that you always refer to Henry Knowles in the past tense. Do you assume he's dead?'

'I think so.'

'Why?'

Bacchus touched his moustache and lips with his napkin before drinking his wine. Good manners, thought Kit, he knows that you shouldn't leave a greasy stain on the rim of your wineglass. He probably learned that in the officers' mess during the war – for Bacchus was not well born. 'You were a major, weren't you?'

'Intelligence Corps, SEAC.'

'I was in SEAC too,' Kit was trying the brothers-in-arms ploy, 'ended up under Gracey in Saigon.'

'Holding the fort for the French?'

Kit nodded.

'Must have been a messy business.'

'Pretty messy.'

'I was in India during the partition massacres. Whole trainloads full of corpses hacked to death. Sometimes giving up a colony makes things worse.'

Kit wasn't going to stoop to getting involved in a 'white man's burden' argument; he'd been there too many times before. He hated imperialism and all the patronising excuses of its apologists.

'Are you all right?' said Bacchus.

'Sorry, I was … thinking about things.'

'You asked me why I thought Henry Knowles was dead.'

'Yes.'

Bacchus lowered his voice, the wine was working. 'Young Knowles was playing some very dangerous games. As you know, he was a frequent traveller to the Soviet Union.'

'Wasn't it part of his job as a musician? Orchestra tours and master classes.'

'But there were other trips not many people know about. A very senior and left-wing member of my party is a director of a company that imports timber from the Soviet Union.'

'A closet capitalist?'

'Probably not. His reasoning, or excuse, is that trade links with the Soviet Union are good for international friendship and peaceful coexistence. But I think there's more to it than that.'

'You think he's a Soviet agent?'

'Rumours, just rumours – probably false ones. In truth, I think it's more complex.'

'How does Knowles tie in with this?'

'Money. Knowles may be a Marxist, but he's a very rich one – inherited family wealth. It was Knowles's money that set up the timber import company and, in consequence, young Henry is also a director of the company.'

'You're using the present tense again.'

'But that doesn't mean I've resurrected him.'

'How,' said Kit, 'does this company trade? Have they got their own ships?'

'No, all the timber is imported on Soviet merchant navy ships. The Russians wouldn't have it any other way – it gives them a chance to earn hard currency.'

'What are the trade routes?'

'The ships take on their cargo in Archangel in the far north of Russia and then sail to East Anglia. They disembark the timber in small ports – King's Lynn, Norwich, Lowestoft, Ipswich – those sorts of places. You can always check with your commercial attaché. Are you OK? You look like you've seen a ghost.'

'I'm fine.' Kit smiled. He really was fine. His brain had pocketed all the reds and was now working on the coloured balls: Vasili's apocalyptic message, Natalya's riddles, Knowles refusing the film bribe, the U2 photos of Los Arzamas. All the balls were whirring across the green baize to thunk in their appointed pockets. Kit already knew the answer, but he still asked the question. 'How then did Knowles's timber import business lead to his death?'

'Corruption.'

■

The next day, Kit attended a 'Soviet Studies' lecture at the Foreign and Commonwealth Office. Personnel from the US Embassy were invited to attend. The principal lecturer, an imposing woman with a severe haircut, was from the Department of Slavonic Studies at the London School of Economics. Part of the presentation was a slideshow of NKVD and KGB propaganda posters. It reminded Kit that the PSYOPS role of the KGB is much more overt than the CIA's. Kit's favourite poster was that of a broad-faced female factory worker. Her hair is tucked under a red scarf; she frowns severely at the onlooker with a finger over her lips. Beneath her is a message in Cyrillic script. A lean Englishman sitting next to Kit whispered, 'I say, do you know what that means?'

'I assume,' said Kit glancing at the lecturer, 'that it means keep your mouth shut.'

The Englishman sniggered. 'Or you'll end up like Trotsky.'

The lecturer shot a warning look in Kit's direction before continuing. For a second, her resemblance to the woman on the poster was stunning. The next slide was that of the Lubyanka itself – the KGB's Moscow headquarters. The speaker was now explaining how the KGB was a much more professional organisation than the NKVD it had replaced. Kit was bored. It was the same old stuff they'd learned as trainees. The lecturer then described how the modern KGB was divided into directorates. *The First Directorate is responsible for foreign operations and intelligence-gathering; the Second, internal political control within the Soviet Union itself. The Third Directorate controls military counter-intelligence and the political surveillance of the Soviet Armed Forces...* Kit tried not to nod off as the lecturer droned on. *The Ninth Directorate is a forty thousand-man uniformed force providing bodyguard services to the principal CPSU leaders. The Ninth also guards major Soviet government facilities – including nuclear weapons stocks. Other responsibilities include...*

Something made Kit sit up. He felt a live wire had come down on his head and a thousand volts were jolting through his brain. *The Ninth!* Why hadn't he realised then? As Natalya swam away, she hadn't been talking about Beethoven's *Ninth Symphony*. She had been tipping him off about the Ninth Directorate. Another billiard ball careened into a pocket. This ball had a name on it and wore little round glasses: Lavrenty Pavlovich Beria, former head of the secret police. Beria was dead, but his ghost was alive and wanting revenge.

∎

Kit didn't stay at the Foreign Office for drinks and nibbles, but went straight back to Grosvenor Square. As the taxi hurtled through Piccadilly Circus, Kit caught a glimpse of a face in the rear-view mirror. He was shocked when he realised that it was his own. He looked like a madman. Fear and paranoia seemed to be curling around his temples like wreaths of ectoplasm. He was carrying too much. And Kit knew that he had broken the rules: he had not reported things. He had told no one what Vasili had passed on – even though it was intelligence of vital importance to national security. Nor had he mentioned his meeting with Natalya. He knew that withholding information was an extremely serious offence. But, on the other hand, who could prove it? The Russians were hardly in a position to point the finger. Therefore, he was safe as long as he kept his mouth shut. Or was he? Had he been under surveillance when he met Vasili? Had someone observed Natalya swimming out to his boat?

Kit told the taxi driver to drop him off in Berkeley Square – one of those places that Americans always mispronounce – so that he could walk the remaining three blocks to the embassy. He didn't like people knowing that he was a diplomat. He also imagined, the paranoia again, that London cab drivers made a few extra pounds by reporting details of their passengers to the security services. It certainly happened in Moscow and Bonn. In any case, Kit liked walking in London – especially on the endless summer evenings. Few Americans realise how far England lies among the kingdoms of the north. The light summer evenings expose all, just as the winter murk hides all. As Kit scurried towards the embassy, he felt a hundred eyes boring into his back and a dozen cameras recording each guilty stride and backward glance.

As soon as Kit was ensconced in his office, he got out the maps and a pair of dividers to measure distances. It was, he thought, an awfully long fucking way. It was an enormous country – a vast land ocean. He then calculated driving times. It would have taken almost a week. Surely, it wouldn't have been possible. There would have been a security alert, check points and searches. But who would have manned the check points and carried out the searches? The Ninth Directorate. Was the entire unit part of the conspiracy?

Kit loosened his tie and stretched out in a chintz armchair that was placed next to his bookshelves. The chair had been among the furniture salvaged from Winfield House when it had been turned into a US Air Force Officers Club during the war. The Air Force guys made a mess of the house – and it had been bombed a bit too – so that at the end of the war the owner, Woolworth heiress Barbara Hutton, gifted it permanently to the US government for one gringo dollar. The mansion, phoney 1937 Georgian with high iron gates, sprawled over twelve acres of Regent's Park and was now the Ambassador's residence. There were, however, rescued bits and pieces of Hutton's Winfield House strewn throughout the embassy. She must have been trying for a fake English country-house look. It didn't work. The chintz roses looked even more out of place in Kit's office – but he liked it. Kit wished he had an open fire and a sleeping cat purring away on his knees.

Why, thought Kit, hadn't Vasili told him more? Was it because his Russian friend, in all honesty, did not know the whole truth? Kit committed the routes and rough figures to memory, then put the maps away. Kit knew that he was going to have to tell someone what he had learned and what he feared. But he wasn't sure who he should tell. Why was he keeping it all secret? Kit began an examination of conscience. Duty, honour, country. What about fairness and humanity? The problem was egotism: it could wear all those disguises.

Kit took off his tie and settled down for a long night. It was his turn in the rota to be embassy duty officer. Until eight the next morning, he was the chief representative of the United States of America in the United Kingdom. The official phrase was 'Envoy Plenipotentiary'. If, say, in the dark watches of the night, Washington declared war on Great Britain, it would be Kit who would have to don court dress – a tricorn hat and knee breeches – and trot over to the Foreign and Commonwealth Office to deliver the declaration that 'a state of hostilities existed'. Kit took off his jacket and shoes and sat down on the camp bed that the marine guards had set up in his office. The bed was made with such military perfection that he felt it a shame to ruin the immaculate tautness of hospital cornered sheets. But he needed sleep, so he peeled the blanket back. Before turning in, Kit carried the telephone over to the bed and dialled the night switchboard and communication centre to let them know he was there for the night.

Hours of deep dreamless sleep passed before Kit was jolted awake by a loud ringing. He fumbled for the phone and knocked it over. A voice from the disconnected receiver was saying, 'Hello, hello, hello, anyone there…' Kit finally recovered the phone and put the receiver to his ear. 'Hello, sorry, I was asleep.'

'Counsellor Fournier?'

'Yes.'

'Sorry to disturb you, sir, this is Lieutenant Buckley from the ODA. There's been a serious incident at Lakenheath Airbase in Suffolk.' The fear in Buckley's voice was making his voice waver. 'General Walsh has copied us the wire he's just sent to General LeMay's office at the Pentagon. Would you like to…'

'I'm coming to see you now.'

A minute later, Kit was standing in the harsh neon glare of the Office of the Defence Attaché. The walls were decorated with photos of aircraft carriers and gleaming jet fighters. Kit looked at the yellow paper in his hand, the perforated strip from the secure telex machine still clinging to its sides.

```
TOP SECRET
----------

PERSONAL FOR CINC LEMAY FROM WALSH. HAVE JUST COME
FROM WRECKAGE OF B-47 WHICH PLOUGHED INTO AN IGLOO IN
LAKENHEATH. THE B-47 TORE APART THE IGLOO AND KNOCKED
ABOUT 3 MARK SIXES. A/C THEN EXPLODED SHOWERING
BURNING FUEL OVER ALL. CREW PERISHED. MOST OF A/C
WRECKAGE PIVOTED ON IGLOO AND CAME TO REST WITH A/C
NOSE JUST BEYOND IGLOO BANK WHICH KEPT MAIN FUEL
FIRE OUTSIDE SMASHED IGLOO. PRELIMINARY EXAM BY BOMB
DISPOSAL OFFICER SAYS A MIRACLE THAT 1 MARK SIX WITH
EXPOSED DETONATORS SHEERED DIDN'T GO. FIRE FIGHTERS
EXTINGUISHED FIRE AROUND MARK SIXES FAST.
```

Kit reread the message. 'Mark sixes' were heavy-yield strategic nuclear weapons; the 'igloos', so named because of their shape, were the concrete bunkers used to store nuclear weapons. Kit remained staring at the stark words – *a miracle that one mark six didn't go*. The full meaning of what had happened finally sank in. The United States Air Force had, by a stupid accident, nearly turned the East of England into a nuclear desert.

Kit handed the message back to Buckley. 'Don't copy that and don't let anyone else see it. Have you rung your boss?'

'He's on leave in Arizona.'

'Shit. Well in that case, you'd better tell General Walsh to get his ass in here.'

'Sir.' Buckley looked pale and trembling. Walsh was, after all, the commander-in-chief of all US forces in Britain.

'Listen,' said Kit, 'you're not the one giving orders to the general, it's the US State Department. If he gives you any shit, pass the phone to me.' Meanwhile, Kit was personally dialling the home numbers of the DCM and the Ambassador. The situation was too sensitive to pass through the switchboard.

Chapter Twelve

The meeting began at quarter to nine in the morning. Attendance was on a strictly need-to-know basis. Kit sat bleary-eyed at the end of the conference table in the Blue Room. He was relieved to have kicked the Lakenheath incident upstairs and sideways. It was a matter far more relevant to the ODA, Office of the Defence Attaché, than to his own department. It was also a problem for the press attaché, who – if rumours stirred – would have to be adroit at deflecting, denying and outright lying. She was good at it.

At the start of the meeting General Walsh referred to the Lakenheath incident as a 'bent spear' – not as serious as a 'broken arrow', that's an accident when the nuclear weapon actually explodes. Other mishaps were known as 'empty quivers' and 'faded giants'. When pressed for more details about how the accident happened, the general admitted that the B-47 had crashed into the nuclear bunker while practising 'touch and go' landings. The Ambassador grimaced. Walsh said the practice was 'under review'.

At the conclusion of the meeting, it was agreed to issue a press release stating that there had been an accident at Lakenheath and that four US airmen had been killed. The accident had occurred *near* an area where *conventional* weapons were stored, but none of the weapons had been damaged and at no point was there the slightest risk of detonation. And finally, that *no* nuclear weapons were stored at Lakenheath and there were no plans to do so in the near future. The press attaché asked if she could release the names of the dead air crew. After a short discussion, it was agreed that openness in this regard would increase the credibility of the cover story. The general read and spelt the names: Captain Russell B. Bowling, 2nd Lieutenant Carroll W. Kalberg, 1st Lieutenant Michael J. Selmo, Technical Sergeant John Ulrich. Only Americans, thought Kit, had names like that: the deracinated roster of the melting pot. The words of a poem floated into his head like a flickering neon advert.

From my mother's sleep I fell into the State...
When I died they washed me out of the turret with a hose.

As Kit walked back to his office, the recollection of the general's use of nuclear weapons jargon made him smile: 'bent spears' and 'broken arrows'. And now, there's seems to be an 'empty quiver' too.

■

August had never been Kit's favourite month. When he was a child, it meant the summer vacation was coming to an end and heralded the arrival of Chesapeake Bay thunder showers and squalls. And for his father, it had meant Hiroshima and Nagasaki. And something in Kit's intuition told him that August 1956 wasn't going to be a good one either.

The international situation was dire because no one understood the consequences of what they were doing. Nasser had seized the Suez Canal and was stirring up pan-Arab nationalism. He didn't seem to realise that Israel, Britain and France were getting ready to thump him. On the other hand, Israel, Britain and France didn't seem to realise that America was going to thump them if they thumped Nasser. Meanwhile, the Hungarians were deluding themselves that they could break free of the Soviet bloc – and they were in for a thumping too. And all this was happening because people didn't read the signals or listen to any words other then their own voices. Too many foreign policy analysts spend so much time reading between the lines that they forget to read the lines that actually are on the page. That's how wars start.

And August, for Kit, looked bad in personal terms too. His mother was making a fool of herself with an electrician she had met in Bergerac. Caddie, his doctor sister, had written him about it. *He's not exactly a gigolo, he's only two years younger than Mom, but he's not exactly an intellectual either. He has a tattoo! In any case, Kit, it looks like we can kiss our inheritances good-bye. At least, you and I have decent jobs – as for poor Ginny, she's still 'writing' and hanging around with human spirochetes. I'm not going to look after her when she's old and indigent – you'll have to. By the way, do you see much of the fragrant Jennifer? I hear she's pregnant. Amazing news. A woman – who has never micturated nor defecated – appears to have fornicated! I won't believe it until I've seen the proof.*

Kit knew that Caddie would regret the bitchiness when she heard the latest news about her cousin. Kit had guessed what had happened as soon as Ethel, his secretary, told him that there had been a telephone call from Jennifer. She had never phoned him before at the embassy. 'Was there a message?' said Kit.

'She left a number, sir, and asked if you could ring back as soon as possible.' Ethel handed him the number.

When Kit saw that it wasn't Jennifer's home telephone, he felt a shiver run down his spine. As soon as he was alone in his office, he dialled the number. The voice that answered was full of starch and efficiency: 'Woodbridge Hospital.'

By the time Kit got to Suffolk, Jennifer had already been discharged from the emergency clinic and gone home. When Kit arrived at the cottage, she was sitting on a deck chair in the garden with a blanket over the lower part of her body. The pale yellow August sun seemed to jaundice her face and bare arms. There was a discarded book at her feet, a breeze rustling its pages. Jennifer was wide awake and staring blankly at the woods. As soon as she saw her cousin walking across the parched lawn, she spread her arms. At first Kit thought she was smiling, but then he saw that her face was distorted with pain and that tears were rolling down her cheeks.

Kit embraced her, then sat on the ground beside her and held her hand to his lips. She felt so feverish. 'Thank you for coming,' she said.

'I would do anything for you. Nothing or no one could stop me.'

'I lost the baby.'

'I know how much you wanted that child.'

'Do you?'

Kit was afraid to look into her eyes and buried his face in her lap. The rough blanket was wet with her tears. 'Perhaps I don't.'

'You didn't want me to have this baby, did you?'

'I wanted you to have the child because I wanted you to be happy.'

'You're lying.'

Kit looked into her eyes. It was like drowning in a whirlpool. 'Please, Jennie, please.'

'I'm sorry, Kit, I'm sorry. I shouldn't be a bitch to you.'

'Jennifer, I've always wanted to help you – but I've never known how.'

'Don't worry about me. I'm going to be all right.'

'You will, I'm sure.' Kit wanted to ask about her husband, but was afraid to say the words. 'You're not,' he said, 'going to be alone, are you?'

'Brian is away on Ministry business. I don't know where he is. I left a message at his office and they've promised to contact him.'

'I'll stay until he gets back. I'm sure they'll give him compassionate leave.'

'But what about your job?'

'It's not important. You are.'

∎

In the early evening a doctor stopped at the cottage to have a look at Jennifer. He said she was going to be 'fine', gave her medication and wrote a prescription. Meanwhile, Kit made a long-distance call to the States to break the news to Jennifer's parents. George answered the phone. 'Rideout's Landing, Colonel Calvert speaking.'

'Uncle George, it's me, Kit.'

'Golly, are you back in the States again?'

'No, I'm ringing from England.'

'Gosh, you sound like you're just down the road in Easton.'

Kit explained what had happened. It wasn't easy, but George seemed to understand – as if he had almost expected it. In the end, George was only concerned about his daughter. He only wanted to know that she was out of danger.

'She's fine, she's perfectly all right – but feeling awfully sad.'

'Does she want to talk? Please put her on.'

'Not now, she's not ready to talk now – and I think the doctor's given her some sedatives.'

'Poor thing. You must tell her not to fret, that it's not her fault. Sometimes nature knows best. I suppose that sounds hard – and I know that Jennie must be feeling so sad and so disappointed. I realise that she must be feeling just awful, but the important thing is that Jennifer is safe and out of danger. And you say that is so?'

'She is all right.' Kit prayed that, for once, he was telling the truth.

'Listen, I know that you're making the call because Jennie is not up to talking at the moment – so tell her that's OK, but that we're always here for her. But please look after her, Kit, and tell her how much we love her – and that when she wants to talk that she must telephone us. It doesn't matter when.'

'I'll have her ring you tomorrow. She'll be more rested and composed.'

'Thank you, Kit, you are a Godsend.'

'Do you want me to talk to Aunt Janet?'

'No, Kit, it's best that I tell her.'

'Give her my love. Goodbye for now.'

■

An hour later the phone rang and Kit answered. The line was bad. It was a ship to shore 'phone patch' that meant you had to use radio procedure, only one person could speak at a time. It was Brian. Kit started to say what had happened, but Jennifer was suddenly there beside him. 'Give me the phone,' she said.

'It's radio communication,' he whispered, 'you've got to say "over" whenever you finish speaking.'

'I know. I get a lot of those calls from Brian.'

Why, he thought, was Brian so often at sea? Kit left the room as soon as Jennifer began to speak. He could still hear her voice through the closed door, so he went for a walk in the garden. He didn't want to eavesdrop on marital intimacy during a time of sorrow. Once again, he was the outsider. Now that the summer sun had finally disappeared, the temperature began to drop. He shivered in the dank dark. There were noises from the trees and undergrowth: a rustling of feathers, calls and barks. The English night was a wild place. In tidewater Maryland, the night was sweaty and full of hungry mosquitoes and fat moths. Sometimes, the night was hotter than the day – and you tossed for hours, naked and awake on sweat-stained sheets. But England was different. After even the hottest summer's day, the chill of the North came back.

When Kit saw Jennifer's figure silhouetted in the light of the doorway, he went back to the house. She spoke first. 'Brian's coming back tomorrow.'

'That's good – you need him here.'

Kit watched Jennifer slowly lower herself on to a chair by the kitchen table. She held one hand to her stomach and looked like a person in pain. 'The doctor said the baby had been dead in my womb for some time. I think I knew, but didn't want to admit it. I hate to think of my body as a tomb, a sepulchre.' She put a hand to her mouth. 'It's too awful.'

Kit reached out and touched her other hand. 'Don't think that. You are life itself – it's the rest of us who belong to the shadows.'

'What did I do wrong? Did I eat the wrong food?'

'Nothing, Jennie, nothing. Look at grandmother, she had two babies that died and five that lived. It's nature – it's normal.'

'No, Kit, it isn't normal. There's something wrong, something on Orford Ness that Brian brings home with him – I think he's contaminated.'

Kit could see hate, anger and madness in his cousin's eyes. She wasn't thinking rationally.

'Look what's happened in Japan – after the atom bombs, all those birth defects. They won't tell us everything. There must be secret hospitals full of monsters – babies with two heads and no eyes, babies with flippers for arms and webbed feet. They want to throw us back in the sea.' She suddenly looked hard at Kit. 'You think I'm hysterical, don't you?'

'No, Jennifer, you're sane. We're the ones who are hysterical. We're the ones who made those bombs at Los Alamos – and there weren't any women politicians who decided to use them and there weren't any women pilots who dropped them.'

'But we would have, Kit. There are women who would have done that and more.'

'But not you.'

'No,' Jennifer squeezed his hand, 'and not you, Kit, not you.'

Kit leaned forward and kissed her brow. 'You're very tired, Jennie, I think you should go to bed.'

Later, Kit lay awake in the guest room and listened through the walls to hear his cousin's breathing. It was a way of being close: different rooms, but alone under the same roof. He wished that the night would last forever.

Kit thought about the things Jennifer had said. He wondered if it was possible that Brian's sperm had been damaged by radiation. Kit also thought that it was an ugly coincidence that the loss of Jennifer's baby had occurred at the same time as the nuclear accident – 'the bent spear' – at Lakenheath. Of course, if the bombs had actually gone off, then Suffolk would have become the English Hiroshima. How, he thought, how do you *really* get rid of those monsters?

■

The first thing that Kit did when he got back to London was to check a rubbish bin in Kensington Gardens for a fresh chalk mark. There wasn't one. Kit whispered, 'Fuck,' and continued walking. He came to a kiosk and bought a newspaper. He retraced his steps back to Kensington Gardens and sat on a bench near the Peter Pan statue. Kit opened his newspaper and wondered what he should do next. He felt that it was stupidly obvious that he was a spy trying to make contact with an agent. It was sort of funny: like the way a plainclothes policeman looks *more* like a cop than one in uniform. Kit looked at his watch, then began to read the paper. He'd give it ten more minutes.

On the inside pages, there was a brief reference to the accident at Lakenheath. The press office at the base had released the names of the airmen who had perished. The press attaché had certainly done a slick job. The British journalists were treating the incident as a tragic, but pretty humdrum accident. Not the least suspicion that a large chunk of England had so nearly been fried and radiated – Nagasakied. Kit wondered how long they could keep the story under wraps. He had since heard that a large number of American airmen had fled the airbase in a blind panic. They had commandeered cars and bicycles and tried to put as much distance between themselves and the smouldering atom bombs as they could. Surely, some of the Suffolk people – 'the indigenous personnel' – must have seen that terror-struck exodus. What did they think was going on? In any case, it wasn't the first time American troops had cut and run. Kit had done it himself – and the early days in Korea had been a disgrace. Americans, despite the Hollywood cover-up versions, were not very good soldiers. This was why they had to have nuclear bombs. No American army would have stood at Stalingrad. The Russian Army lost nine million soldiers – and fourteen million civilians – fighting the Nazis. What else can you say? How can anyone look a Soviet citizen in the face and not blush with shame?

Kit turned the page and found another story based in Suffolk. It was, he thought, odd for so rural a county to be mentioned twice the same day in the national press. The story was a macabre tabloid one.

CHAINED BODY FOUND ON BEACH.

Suffolk police are trying to solve the mystery behind a chained naked body found on a remote Suffolk beach. The badly decomposed body was found by a woman walking her dog near the coastal village of Shingle Street. Detective

Superintendent Tim Winter of the Suffolk Constabulary said: 'There are many unresolved issues surrounding this incident and we are treating the death as suspicious.' A Home Office pathologist has been called in to help determine the cause of death.

Kit folded the newspaper and thought about the Suffolk corpse. He felt sorry for the poor woman who had found it. She had probably enjoyed walking her dog along that beach for years. He doubted if she'd ever do it again. Dead bodies spoil the countryside. There was a beautiful Chesapeake Bay creek that everyone had shunned after the putrefied body of a tramp had been found tangled in the branches of a fallen tree – the soft tissue of his face eaten away by crabs. And, for a long while, crab cakes were off the menu too. The newsworthy thing about the Shingle Street body was the chains. Wrapping a body in chains was a method commonly used by gangsters and intelligence operatives to deep-six a corpse – so that it didn't become a 'floater'. During his OSS days Kit had helped dispose of a double agent in the South China Sea. The difficult thing was getting all that weight over the gunwales: you needed five or six gorillas. But maybe the Suffolk business wasn't murder at all. He'd heard about people committing suicide by weighting themselves down and walking into water. That's the way Virginia Woolf did it.

Kit leaned back and enjoyed the summer sun on his face. He wondered if Vasili had any of the chewing-gum left that Kit had given him. The fallback rendezvous signal was a piece of gum stuck on the inside windowpane of a phone kiosk on the Bayswater Road. It was, in fact, a far better way to arrange a meeting – but Vasili hated chewing gum. He said it made him feel like a Chicago gangster. Vasili simply preferred to chalk a Cyrillic 'K' – for Kit.

Kit left the park and walked the short distance to the kiosk. It was occupied by a young woman who seemed content to talk away the afternoon. Kit crossed the road and entered an off-licence. The stock was limited to ale, whisky and gin. If you wanted wine, you had to bring your own bottle and they filled it from a cask of sweet sherry. The shop assistant was bent over a crossword and didn't even look up. But Kit had the odd queasy feeling that someone else was looking at him. He went back into the street, almost running, and saw that the phone kiosk was free.

He crossed the road, dodging big London buses and black taxis that seemed to be aiming at him like hired assassins. Kit felt the paranoia rushing back. He opened the kiosk door and pretended to make a call while searching for the chewing-gum. There wasn't any gum, or a chalk mark, but there was a card stuck to the panel next to the phone. Was it Vasili's idea of a joke? The card said EMBASSY MASSAGE – and had Kit's own phone number. Kit was angry. It wasn't just a lousy joke, it was a dangerous joke. He unstuck the card and turned it over. There was another message. Kit read the words and broke into a cold sweat: *Under the spreading chestnut tree, I sold you and you sold me.* The frightening thing was the realisation that it wasn't a joke and that the card had not been left by Vasili. Someone else knew about his meetings with the Russian. And how much did they know?

Kit started to walk back to the embassy as rivulets of cold sweat dripped down his spine and funnelled into his butt cleavage. He felt a mess. Kit knew that, with a gun in his hand, he could put on a convincing tough guy pose, but he also knew that he went wobbly when his own life was in danger. He felt waves of nausea sweep up from his intestines and shake the rest of his body. He wanted to lie down in a safe dark place away from the eyes that seemed to be tracking him.

The rivulets of sweat had turned into a flood and Kit's shirt was soaked with sweat. A half-remembered address began to appear on the edge of his mind and then vanished again. He needed a new shirt. Kit turned into Bond Street. At the first shop he was greeted by a tailor with a measuring tape around his neck who asked if he had 'an appointment'? Kit smiled wanly and left. The next shop didn't require an appointment, but only made shirts to measure and they wouldn't be ready for a week. After being turned down by two more 'bespoke shirt-makers', Kit began to panic as waves of paranoia made him hyperventilate. He felt so dizzy he had to lean against a wall. Kit watched the people passing by. He envied them. They somehow belonged to the city and to England. He tried to explain in a faint pleading voice, 'They won't even let me buy a fucking shirt.'

A woman, wearing a floral dress and a broad hat, gave Kit a cutting look and said, 'Drunk in public. Disgraceful.'

Kit looked up and was about to say 'I'm sorry, I'm not very well' when he realised he had seen the woman before. Hadn't she been in the phone kiosk before him? But no, this one was older and wearing a hat. Kit wiped the sweat from his eyes, but when he opened them again the woman was gone.

The address started teasing Kit's mind again. It was somewhere near. Who had told him about it? A name began to form; then it was gone again. One half of Kit's brain was still normal and was watching the other half screaming out of control down a steep mountain gorge. He wanted to grab the steering wheel, but the mad half was strong as hell and kept giving him a sharp elbow in the face. It was like watching the blood drain out of your body. You know you have to tourniquet the wound, but your arms won't move. Kit closed his eyes and breathed deep. 'I don't care what they do. They're not going to have my mind.'

Kit felt a hand on his elbow. He opened his eyes. A man of middle-eastern appearance was smiling at him 'Are you looking for a shirt-maker?'

Kit nodded.

'My name is Youssef. I've been expecting you. My shop is just around the corner.'

■

Kit liked the shirts. They were well cut with the sort of long luxurious tails that hang down well below crotch and genitals. Shirttails like that stay tucked in and make you feel safe. They weren't Irish linen, but rich Egyptian cotton. The tailor was proud of his material and said that Egyptian was the best cotton in the world. 'But,' he said, raising his hands in a gesture of world-weary sadness, 'I don't know how much longer...' His voice trailed away. Kit sensed that the tailor, like himself, felt a stranger in a hostile land and didn't want to give too much away.

'Suez.' Kit whispered the word as if it were a secret code.

The tailor smiled and nodded.

'In that case, I'd better have two of them – no, make it three, it's best to stock up.' Kit felt dizzy again and smiled inanely. He sat down on a stiff-backed chair while the tailor carefully folded his purchases and wrapped them in brown paper.

Despite the origins of his cotton cloth, Youssef wasn't Egyptian; he was Syrian. When Kit tried to pay, Youssef motioned him to stay seated and to wait. The tailor pushed aside a brocade door curtain and said something in Arabic. A minute later, a tray arrived with an elaborate silver urn, plain glasses and a plate of

Turkish Delight. As Youssef poured the mint tea, he said that he had been born in Aleppo. Kit tried to follow the conversation, but there was a buzzing in his ears. As Youssef recited a litany of place names – from Thessaloniki to Marrakech – Kit began to forget where he was. The street sounds of London seemed to vanish. There had also been a Syrian tailor in Saigon, but his name had been Sharif. The OSS officers had used him to alter their field uniforms into a smarter cut: appearances mattered. Kit looked out the shop window and half expected to see trishaws pedalling past instead of black taxis. He wanted to be back in Vietnam, in the opium den in Cholon with Sophie, *la métisse*, making his pipe. Sophie used to sing to him in a voice so soft that you could barely hear the words.

The rest was a half-remembered dream.

The plasmodium falciparum is a cunning beast that sponges off both mosquitoes and humans to complete a life journey of wanton destruction. Falciparum is an unwanted guest, a parasite, that attacks red blood cells for their haemoglobin like an alcoholic drinking his way through your wine cellar. If you take your chloroquine primaquine, like you're supposed to, you'll probably get better. You'll probably even think that your bloodsucking visitor has packed his bags and left – but you're wrong. After drinking the best of your red stuff, he's decided to doss down in your liver cells. You won't know he's there because this is one drunk plasmodium that can pass out for a long time – years. And then one day, when you least expect it, plasmodium falciparum wakes up and decides he needs another drink. And once he's blotto on vintage haemoglobin, he decides to get laid – and, before you know it, your bloodstream has turned into a teeming nursery for falciparum's bastard brats. And suddenly you don't feel very well. You're burning with fever and pouring with sweat – and then you get the chills. You're freezing and can't get warm again. You want to lie down and curl into a ball. And then, for some reason, you try to get up again – and all the lights go out. You've lost consciousness because of orthostatic hypotension, a sudden decrease in blood pressure owing to low blood glucose levels. The malaria parasites have sucked the life out of your blood. You're pallid, faint and anaemic – you might even die.

■

When Kit woke up, he was lying on a narrow cot beneath a single white sheet – Egyptian cotton. The ceiling above him was grey and stained. He seemed to be in some sort of storeroom stacked high with shelves holding bolts of material. He was naked and his body felt dry and pleasantly cool. The fever and chills had gone, but there was a raw pain in his lower region. Kit closed his eyes again and tried to piece together what had happened. He remembered shirts, Syrians and mint tea – and worst of all, the card he'd found in the phone kiosk: *Under the spreading chestnut tree, I sold you and you sold me.*

Kit could now think clearly again and knew that it was all over. He'd been doubled, crossed and compromised. In a way, he was relieved. He lay back and felt the tension drain out of his body. The elaborate high wire act was over.

Kit longed to hear Sophie's soft voice and feel her body curling against his own. But the next words he heard were far from the sweet lilting French of Saigon. 'The photographs would have been much better if we had managed to wake you up.'

Kit opened his eyes and saw Jeffers Cauldwell seated on a chair beside him. He knew who it was even though the cultural attaché had dyed his hair black and grown a moustache. But Cauldwell's greatest disguise was a new face: one that was cold and devoid of expression. He had ceased to be a dandy affecting a camp Deep South accent. Cauldwell was what he had been for years: a serious player and Soviet spy.

'You were in a very deep coma. At one point we thought we were going to lose you. I told Youssef that necrophilia photos would be pretty damned kinky, but not much good for blackmail – you can't blackmail a corpse. When your pulse rate got down to thirty-eight, Youssef suggested we give you an intravenous adrenalin shot. I said, "No, let the bastard die." Youssef looked very distressed, I think he likes you. But you stabilised – and started to twitch about as if you were having a bad dream.' Cauldwell paused. 'What are you thinking, Kit?'

'Touché.'

'Touché indeed. I'm glad, Kit, that you're not taking it personally. Would you like to see the photos?'

'No.'

'No? What if you're pregnant? Wouldn't you like to know who the father is?'

'Can I have my clothes please?'

Cauldwell picked up a brown-paper package and tossed it to Kit. 'You ought to try one of your new shirts. I knew that you'd eventually come to Youssef's. I'd been telling you about his shirts for ages. In the end, you were going to come here for a fitting whether you liked it or not.'

'You were following me?'

'Of course. And if it hadn't been for your serendipitous attack of recurrent malaria, Youssef would have put a double dose of chloral hydrate in your mint tea. Go on, get dressed.'

Kit saw Cauldwell look away as he began to dress. Humiliation turned to anger. He wanted to attack Cauldwell while his back was turned and break his neck or choke him with his belt, but Kit wasn't sure they were alone in the shop. Or that the umbrella that Cauldwell was leaning on didn't have a ricin spike.

Cauldwell turned to face Kit. 'You deserve this, you bastard.'

'What happened to Henry Knowles?'

There was a hard glint in Cauldwell's eyes. 'You don't seem to have gotten the message, Kit. You're no longer the one who asks the questions. From now on, we tell you what you need to know and what you need to do.'

Kit knew it wasn't in his interest to show defiance. He wanted to stay alive and this meant he had to pretend that he was going to give in to blackmail. Why pretend? Kit thought about his job. It didn't matter: it was insignificant compared to whether he lived or died. But in his own mind, he had begun to draft a secret 'eyes only' cable to Allen Dulles confessing all his sins and explaining everything that had happened. Kit knew that his career was over. Not only was his cover blown, but his unauthorised and unreported meetings with Vasili lay somewhere on the misconduct scale between instant dismissal from the service and an indictment for treason. But the important thing now was to stay alive – and Jennifer too.

'By the way,' said Cauldwell, 'Vasili wasn't altogether pleased about the photos. He said he liked you and was sad about "the lack of dignity". He also wasn't sure that the photos, the ones of you I mean – even on top of all the unauthorised secrets you passed to the Sovs – are enough to compromise you. Vasili reckons that you're in so thick with Allen that you can 'fess up to everything and still bound free and smelling of lavender-scented Vaseline.'

Once again, Kit had the uncanny feeling that he had a neon sign on his forehead that kept flashing his thoughts.

'"Well, Vasili," says I, "you don't know the American system as well as you think. If a few backwoods American Congressmen become apprised of what Kitson Fournier has been up to, the shit is going to hit the fan. In those cases the boss always sacrifices the subordinate." Sadly, Vasili still didn't seem convinced that you could be turned. It was only then that I suggested the nuclear option – "Kit's dirty little secret". I suspected it for a long time – and it only took a burglary and simple search of your flat to find the evidence.'

Kit had begun to sweat again and this time it had nothing to do with recurrent malaria. For the first time, Kit saw the pistol handle sticking out of the waistband of Cauldwell's corduroy trousers. But it wasn't the gun that was making him sweat; it was the notebooks that Cauldwell was holding in his hands.

'I was,' said Cauldwell, 'surprised that there were so many of them and that they went back so many years. Jennifer must have been jailbait when you started keeping them.' Cauldwell smiled and began to flick through one of the notebooks. 'I can hardly claim to be an aficionado of heterosexual pornography, but this stuff does seem pretty hot and imaginative and more than a little perverse – especially the sections that you've written in French and Spanish, you clever dog. And I really like your drawings too. Look at this one. You ought to add speech bubbles, something like, "Try, Jennifer, to breathe through your nose, it helps suppress the gag reflex." At least, that's what I tell my pals.'

'Or they tell you.'

'They don't need to. I feel sorry for you, Kit, you don't know anything.'

'Then I can't be much use.'

Cauldwell picked up another notebook. 'It's not all erotic fantasy. Jennifer's more to you than an imaginary sex life – a substitute for the real one you never had. You really love her, don't you? In fact, she means more to you than your career, your country – or your own life. Jennifer is your religion. You would die for her, you would go on crusades for her. You would kill for her. In some ways, it's very moving – and almost cynical and immoral for us to use her to control you.' Cauldwell laughed.

Kit looked at the cold concrete floor. 'It is funny – in a way.'

'It's also tragic. Poor Kit, I wish that you could see your face. You look so drained and pale – like one of those sad saints lit by Lenten tapers in an Eyetie medieval church. You should have become a priest – or a pornographer.'

Kit looked at the notebooks: secret and black covered. He didn't understand either so he couldn't explain it to anyone else. When did the Virgin Mary become Mary Magdalene? Kit remembered the statue in the church in Managua. The Virgin, dressed in a gown of white and lapis lazuli blue, has rays of light emanating from her fingers. But when you kneel down in front of her, your face is inches away from her bare feet – and underneath her feet is a coiled serpent. The Managuan artist had painted her toenails scarlet red – and one beautiful foot seems to be trampling the serpent, but the other foot is stroking it. As a boy of thirteen Kit knelt before that statue and watched the serpent writhe beneath those beautiful feet in the flickering candlelight – hushed Spanish voices confessing their sins in the shadows – and as he raised his eyes the gown around her thighs seemed to part. And the Virgin was smiling, at him alone. You are my knight, my soldier. If you keep pure and slay my enemies, I will be here for you.

Cauldwell's voice came like a brick through a stained-glass window. 'Cousin Jennifer…'

'Shut up.'

'Wrong attitude, Kit, wrong attitude.'

'Leave her alone, show her those books if you must, but leave her alone. I beg you.'

'Kit, you're crying.'

'Listen, Jeffers, I plead with you – please, please don't let anyone hurt Jennifer. I'll do anything you want, but promise not to hurt her.'

'You're pathetic. You've lost your dignity too – and all because of your love for someone you don't even understand.'

Kit wiped his eyes, but still felt dirty and debased. Once again he felt a raw burning pain in his lower half. He tried to regain some dignity. 'I'm offering a deal – I provide information, you ensure that Jennifer doesn't get hurt.'

Cauldwell laughed. 'You really don't understand a thing.'

Kit suddenly caught the meaning and felt his heart race. With his new moustache and black hair Cauldwell looked like a devil pimp rising rich and immaculate from a sewer. 'How well do you know her?'

Cauldwell seemed to ignore the question. 'By the way, Kit, one of the last things I did as cultural attaché was to cable my counterpart in the Paris Embassy. I asked him to send you a novel. It's banned in Britain so he'll be sending you a sealed copy in the diplomatic pouch.'

Kit was tired of playing Cauldwell's game. 'I want to go. Is that all right?'

'That depends. But first, you listen and listen well. These are our conditions. You continue doing your job as if none of this has happened.' Cauldwell paused and stared at Kit. 'In fact, we're both looking for the same thing – it's just that you're much closer to finding it than we are.'

'What do you mean?' Kit did know, but the caginess of the career diplomat spy was inbred.

'Don't play games. Time is running out and you know it.'

'The bomb.'

'That's right, Kit, the bomb, the Russian hydrogen bomb – the one that's missing. We want to know where it is and the names of the traitors who provided it.'

'Why don't you ask Henry? He knows where it is.'

'Henry *did* know – and that's why he's dead. And if you don't tell us everything you know, I'm going to make one simple phone call and the same person who killed Henry is going to kill Jennifer too.' Cauldwell took out a writing pad and a pen. 'And you can begin with all the codes and agent names that you do know.'

■

Kit was surprised how easy it was to continue as if nothing had changed. He had been missing from the embassy for two days, but no one seemed to have taken much notice. Kit's only interrogator, the DCM, was on leave – and the rest of the staff assumed, as always, that Kit must be engaged on the spook side of his job. Perry handled daily routine more conscientiously than his boss. Meanwhile Ethel, Kit's secretary, covered his absences with convincing lies and credible excuses. No one, of course, dared speculate or whisper about Counsellor Fournier's whereabouts. In one way, it was comforting to know that his office functioned without him. On the other hand, it was worrying. How long could he be missing before anyone would notice something was wrong?

A week? Ten days? Kit had a chilling premonition of his body putrefying in a shallow grave while Ethel mouthed into the telephone: 'Thank you for calling, but Counsellor Fournier is temporarily out of the office. He should be back soon and will return your call.'

Kit was impressed by Perry's development as a diplomat and a political analyst. The deputy had such an excellent grasp of the unravelling Suez crisis that Kit allowed him to brief Ambassador Aldrich on the situation. Meanwhile, Kit had to prepare his own briefing – a top secret one – for Allen Dulles. Dulles was due to arrive in London in two weeks. It was going to be a difficult briefing. Kit was now working for two masters and couldn't lie to either. It was a tricky business. In Germany, Horst hadn't been the only agent who had tried working for both sides. There was another one who provided wonderful intelligence on the political opposition in East Germany. The stuff was fastidious in detail and totally reliable. It was so good the Russians wanted it too – so the agent gleefully sold his wares to both sides. His death hadn't been a pretty one – the hammer blows kept falling, but he refused to die. The agent was now part of West Germany's transport infrastructure.

The reverberations of Jeffers Cauldwell's disappearance were more nuisance than problem. The embassy was overrun with young intense counter-intelligence officers: CIA, FBI and Military Intelligence too. Kit was interviewed five times and kept to the script. Ironically, the counter-intell types seemed more interested in Cauldwell's sexuality than his ideology. It had recently been confirmed – thanks to a Home Office dental pathologist – that the body found on Shingle Street beach in Suffolk was that of Henry Knowles. There was an open verdict as to whether the death was suicide or murder. Some thought that Knowles had killed himself in such a bizarre way because he wanted to make it look like murder. The general assumption was that it was only a matter of time before Cauldwell's body turned up too – probably in equally bizarre circumstances. The counter-intelligence officers seemed to dismiss Cauldwell as too 'lightweight' to have been engaged in serious espionage. After all, he was only a 'cultural attaché' – and, as such, had no access to top secret information of relevance to national security. The visiting officers wanted to close the case and get back to an American summer. Meanwhile, thought Kit,

Jeffers Cauldwell is holed up in a KGB safe house somewhere in Greater London waiting for London's CIA Chief of Station to tell him where the Brits have stashed the missing Soviet H-bomb.

■

August was going to be a lousy month. July had ended with the lowest barometer reading ever recorded in a British summer. On the twenty-ninth, there had been violent gales on the south coast that had cancelled the yacht races at Cowes – and there were even winds of seventy miles per hour that had swept through London. The gale had struck London while Kit had lain comatose with acute recurrent malaria – as if the howling winds had been protesting his rape. It was the sort of thing that happened in a Shakespeare tragedy, dopey Lear out on the blasted heath. But Kit knew that it was just a coincidence because neither he nor his anal virginity was as important as a British king. Kit knew that the game was important – so important, that a misplaced card might mean the nuclear annihilation of millions of people – but that he was just a blundering bit player.

The worst thing was that he didn't know – in the purest moral and ethical sense – what was the right thing to do. Nuclear bombs were immoral and illegal weapons of indiscriminate and mass destruction, but countries had the right to defend themselves against these weapons – and, ultimately, the only way to do so was to have nuclear weapons of your own. But maybe that wasn't completely true. There was no way that the Soviet Union could attack Western Europe – the Russians were fully stretched controlling Eastern Europe. And Khrushchev's speech denouncing Stalin's 'grave abuse of power' had changed everything. In fact, it was doubtful for how much longer Moscow could control the Soviet Union itself. All the intelligence analysts and Soviet specialists knew this – but it had to be kept secret. If the ordinary people knew the facts, they would kick their rulers out of office and put them in jail. The arms race was a profiteering racket run by big business, a massive confidence trick. Everyone in the power elite knew this – except for the cretins who believed their own propaganda. Eisenhower knew it, and even said so in public: 'Beware the unwarranted influence of the military-industrial complex.' It was like Satan warning people about sin – it didn't matter, they never listened. But Kit had a job to do. He had to find a missing Soviet hydrogen bomb. But what then?

■

Kit arrived in Suffolk on a day of thunderstorms and hail. Bad omens for a brief sailing break. When he stopped at Jennifer's cottage to pick up his oars and oilskins – which he kept in a garden shed – the hail lay six inches deep on the ground. Kit crunched through the ice to the kitchen door. He looked through the window and was surprised to see Brian sitting at the table – it was early afternoon on a weekday. Brian seemed unaware of his presence. The scientist was staring at a pencil-drawn sketch containing various coils and formulae. There was a slide rule on the table and an open briefcase full of files with yellow security tags. Kit knew at once that he was staring at an intelligence goldmine. He backed away from the door – sure that Brian hadn't noticed his eavesdropping – and walked back to his car. There was a noisy farm tractor labouring down the lane. In order to mask the sound of his own engine, Kit waited for the tractor to pass the cottage before he turned the ignition key. He knew that someone was watching him. He looked back to the house. Jennifer was staring at him from her bedroom window. Kit put a finger to his lips; he sensed that Jennifer had nodded agreement; he put the car in gear and slunk away behind the tractor.

The Jolly Sailor was a good observation post. From a table by the window Kit could observe all traffic going to and from Orford Quay – and, more importantly, to the ferry to the Atomic Weapons Research Establishment on Orford Ness. The pub was full of fishermen and farm workers sheltering from the unseasonable weather. Kit knew he was an object of curiosity, but used his newspaper to avoid eye contact. He finished an article about the evacuation of British dependents from Egypt and then began the correspondence page. 'Letters to the Editor' are, as any intelligence officer knows, a more valuable source of information than the actual news articles. These pages provide, not only insight into what the 'educated classes' are thinking, but also contact names. It's a good way, once you've sifted out the cranks, to find useful agents. There were several letters complaining about the way Eden had compared Nasser to Hitler and Mussolini. Kit recognised the names of many of the anti-Suez correspondents – two were founding members of CND.

Kit folded the paper and pretended to begin the crossword, but was really eavesdropping on the conversations around him.

He knew one of the men at the next table because he worked on the estate that owned Jennifer's cottage. His name was Jack and he was head groom. Farming on the estate was now mechanised and there were no more working horses – only nimble Arab polo ponies, big hunters and point-to-point thoroughbreds. But Kit knew that Jack's first love were the Suffolk Punches, those great grey giants of the plough. He had once overheard Jack describe the Suffolk as, 'A horse with a face like an angel and a backside like a farmer's daughter, the gentlest animal I've ever known.' Kit liked hearing Suffolk people talk. You had to listen carefully, for their voices were soft and quiet. There was a ghostly stillness about them. Often, sitting in his boat on a gentle evening, Kit would be startled by a head suddenly appearing next to him as a fisherman or eel catcher passed close by leaning on silent muffled oars. They seemed to always be watching – the silent guardians of the sea frontier. Kit was a watcher too – but he hardly looked up as Brian's new Austin Devon motored by on the way to the Orford Ness ferry. Kit finished his drink and headed back to see Jennifer on her own.

■

'I've got something for you.'

Kit took a Hershey bar out of his jacket pocket. 'Look at this, American chocolate – I scooped up a dozen bars at the airbase.'

'I thought that you didn't like chocolate.'

'I don't. But I know that you do – your only vice.' Kit hid a smile as he handed over the packet. They had taken advantage of a brief sunny spell to have tea in the garden.

'You spoil me.'

'Have the rest of them.' As Kit pulled the Hershey bars out of his pocket, something metallic clattered on to the patio stone. 'Damn, where's it gone?'

Jennifer bent down and picked up a small rectangular object with aluminium casing. 'What's this,' she said, 'a make-up case?'

'It's a camera.' Kit seemed embarrassed.

'It seems an awfully small camera.'

Jennifer's hand shook as she held it, as if it were something about to explode. 'Do you take pictures of me when I'm not looking?'

'No, it's for copying documents.'

'Oh.'

Kit put the Minox III spy camera back in his pocket.

Jennifer looked across the garden into the dark wood dank with summer rain. The silence was eerie. There was no birdsong, only the chitter of swallows as they swooped and wheeled. She poured the last of the tea and gestured at the sky. 'Do you think those birds are evil spirits?'

'No, I think they are beautiful.'

'Don't be naive, Kit, you know as well as I do that evil can be beautiful – devastatingly beautiful. That's why the nuns made us cover our bodies.' Jennifer undid a button of her dress and looked inside. 'Do you think my breasts are nice? I think Brian wishes they were bigger. They plumped up nicely when I was pregnant, but now,' she put a hand inside her bra, 'they seem to have shrunk back to small apples.' She left the button undone and looked again at the diving swallows. 'They come all the way from Africa. Can you imagine how? They're so tiny. It must be witchcraft that brings them all that way.' Jennifer touched Kit's arm and whispered. 'Our cleaner is a Norfolk woman. She says that at the end of summer, when you see the swallows all perched together on the church roof, it's because they have to decide who in the parish has to die before they come back in the spring.'

'Spooky.'

'Not as spooky as the Russians.'

Kit looked closely at Jennifer. Her pupils were dilated and her lower lip was quivering. 'What about the Russians?' he said.

'In the old days...'

Jennifer's voice sounded so creepy – like a voiceover for a horror film – that Kit began to smile. But when he looked into her eyes, he realised that she wasn't joking – that she was close to madness. He reached out and put a hand over hers; her flesh felt clammy and feverish.

'In the old days,' she repeated, 'the Russians believed that swallows were dead children coming back to visit their parents.' Jennifer's eyes were shining with tears. Her arm swept an arc at the swallow-woven sky. 'Which one, Kit, which one is he?'

Kit knelt down beside her chair and put his arms around his cousin. He felt her lips gently kissing the back of his neck.

'Poor Kit,' she said, 'poor Kit. No one ever looks after you. What can I do for you – to make you happy.'

Kit stood up, trembling and unsteady. The garden around him seemed to be spinning out of control.

'Kit,' she said.

He never knew who moved first. He remembered only how their hungry mouths touched and everything else dissolved into a blur.

■

Promises were made, but not with words. As they lay together in bed, Kit knew – they both knew – that nothing else mattered. Everything that he had ever wanted lay alive and breathing within his arms. His career was an irrelevance. The worlds of diplomacy and espionage were already fading into half-remembered pantomimes. The missing Russian H-bomb could damn well stay missing; US Foreign Policy was a gangster racket best left to other gangsters; Allen and Foster Dulles were a pair of talking pigs' bladders on sticks – and the Brits could shift for themselves. Kit's only concern was planning an escape route and finding some place they could live. Where? It had to be somewhere beyond the reach of the KGB, the CIA and the British Secret Service. Kit closed his eyes and imagined a map of the world scrolling past. There wasn't a lot to choose from. Aside from Tito's Yugoslavia and Mao's China, there was only Albania. And how safe would any of those places be? It would be bad enough, if he was alone – but how could he expect Jennifer to live the gilded prison life of a Western defector cut off forever from family and friends?

Jennifer seemed to read his thoughts. She curled closer to him and kissed his shoulder. 'What do we do now?' she said.

'I don't know. My life isn't my own – yet.'

'What's that mean?'

'It means I can't just run away – go AWOL. There are too many knives out to get me – and if we're together you'll get hurt too.'

'I think, Kit, you have done some very bad things.'

'You don't know how bad.'

'Why can't we just drive to Dover and get on a ferry?'

'We wouldn't get past the first customs check. Have you ever seen my passport? It's a big black diplomatic one – it stands out like a thumb with gangrene. We'd need to get false papers – but all the forgers I know would sell us on to a higher bidder.'

Jennifer laughed. 'It's so awful, it's almost funny.'

Kit looked at his cousin. She was so beautiful, so perfect: too good for him. 'It's not going to work,' he said.

'What?'

'Us.'

She held him tight and buried her face into his neck. Suddenly her tongue was working down his body. She wanted him ready to make love again. Kit tried not to think of the Virgin of Managua. As Jennifer drew him into her she said, 'Do you believe me now, do you believe me now?'

Afterwards they fell asleep. When Kit woke the sky had darkened. Suddenly he sat up, then gently kissed Jennifer into waking. 'When,' he said, 'does Brian get home?'

'We've got another two hours.'

'I hate the thought of your being with him.'

'But what, poor Kit, can we do?'

'There's some things I need to clear up, and then I'm going to resign from the service. And then, Jennie – just to be safe – we're going to have to live outside the United States.'

'Why?'

'I don't want you to know – it's luggage that you best not carry.' But did it matter? Kit remembered the news photos of Ethel Rosenberg. She had only been indicted to put pressure on her husband to name names. She knew nothing, but they killed her too. 'Jennifer.'

'Yes.'

'We can't go on. It's got to end here.'

She embraced him and wrapped her legs around him. 'I'm a leech, Kit, you can't shake me off. I've loved you from the beginning – and I'm not going to stop loving you now.'

'Listen, Jennie, it's worse than you think. So bad, I'm going to have to research extradition treaties.'

'You have been naughty.'

'And if I don't finish the job I'm on now, it could be a lot worse.'

'How much worse?'

'I could be indicted for treason and, unless my lawyer is a whiz kid, found guilty and executed. Are you sure you want to be with me?'

'All the way.'

Kit lay back and thought about what he had to do. In order for him and Jennifer to be safe, he needed to satisfy both the Russians and the Americans – and keep one step ahead of the Brits. It was, he knew, almost impossible.

■

It was raining again. They both were sitting in the kitchen – the spy camera on the table between them.

'I've been unfaithful to my husband – and now you want me to spy on him too.'

'Yes.'

She turned the camera over in her hand and examined it closely. 'Look,' she said, 'the writing on the case, it's in Cyrillic script – Russian.' She looked up. 'Kit, *who* are you working for? Tell me the truth.'

'I'm not a double agent – I still work for Washington.'

'But how did you get this?'

'When I was in Bonn we took it off a German who tried to play a double game. Gerhard is now part of an autobahn bridge.'

At first, Jennifer held the camera as if it were a poison snake. Then she seemed to caress it with her eyes. Kit had seen it before, especially with guns, how repulsion turns into fascination. 'And now you've passed it to me.' She raised the camera to her face and sniffed it. 'I think I can smell the sweat and fear of the man you murdered.'

'It's not murder.'

'What is it then?'

'A sanction, a termination, a warning to others.'

'And that makes it all right.'

Kit looked away.

Jennifer stroked the camera with a finger. 'How do I use this thing?'

'It's not difficult, but you have to set the shutter speed and distance manually. It's best to take the photograph in normal daylight.'

'You mean I have to go into the garden?'

'Of course not, near a window would be good enough. If it's a sunny day, set the speed at 200, otherwise 100. For copying documents, you need to set the focal length – that's the other dial – to 0.2 m. And then hold the camera the same distance – about eight inches – above the stuff you're photographing.'

'How soon will all this be over?'

'I wish I knew – weeks I hope, maybe months.'

'Kit?'

'Yes.'

'Could we have babies?'

'Of course.'

'But being first cousins – isn't the blood line too close? It's illegal in most states, except for Tennessee.'

'We'll have to say we're "royal" – they get exemptions.'

Jennifer took his hand. 'I should be worried, Kit, but I'm not – I'm really happy. Nothing matters anymore.'

'There's one more thing. When you've taken a full roll of film, put it in this.' Kit took an object out of his pocket that was the size and shape of a fountain pen. 'This is called a "dead drop spike". You then stick it in the ground and I retrieve it by pulling up this loop – which looks like a grass cutting.'

'Where should I put it?'

'There's a grave in Orford churchyard of a young woman called Louise Whiting.'

'Billy's sister?'

'That's right. Place it near the foot of the grave – and leave a chalk mark on the churchyard gate to show you've left something.'

'Poor Louise, she was betrayed by an American airman – and now we're using her too. We shouldn't do that – she might put a curse on us.'

'But when I pick up the film, I'm going to leave flowers – white chrysanthemums.'

■

For Kit, the following week in London was living hell. His first night back he lay awake all night thinking of Jennifer. The jealousy was worse than ever. It corroded every corner of his mind. He couldn't bear to think of Jennifer still sharing a bed with Brian – and submitting to his bondage fantasies. He tried to understand why she did it, but that made his jealousy even worse.

The next day Kit sat at his desk and watched his in-tray overflow as he stared into space. At half past ten, he attended a heads-of-section meeting. The agenda was devoted to press and PR matters and was chaired by the press attaché. The new cultural attaché was present: a bear of a man with a Hollywood background. He was wearing a lightweight seersucker suit that looked woefully out of place in the wet London gloom.

When Kit got back to his office, he found a package on his desk with a diplomatic pouch receipt tag attached. Kit signed and dated the tag and put it in his out-tray. He opened the package and a book slid out: *Histoire d'O* by Pauline Réage. The promised farewell present from Jeffers Cauldwell. Kit opened the book and began to read: at first, it seemed to be S&M bondage pornography, except that it was much better written. The more Kit read the more he became inflamed with jealousy. He realised that it was a woman's book, written by a woman as a love letter. Kit knew that Cauldwell had sent the book as a taunt: its purpose was to mentally maim. He wasn't going to let the poison do its work. Kit got up and threw the book in the burn bag. He sat back down and opened the folder with the daily news briefing: Nasser had rejected the proposal for the Suez Canal to be managed by an international authority; plans had been unveiled to redevelop the Barbican bomb site. Kit closed the folder and retrieved the novel from the burn bag.

■

And who was O: Odile or Odette? Or did O mean she was nothing other than the O of her orifices? Or O for an object willing to be an object. Kit was back in his flat and it was just before midnight. Even though it was August, he had lit the gas fire. Was it cold? Or was he in for another bout of recurrent malaria? Kit poured himself another drink. He knew that Cauldwell had chosen the book to send him a message – a malignant message intended to undermine his sanity. It was like an MK-ULTRA experiment. Cauldwell wanted to cause disorientation. *Histoire d'O* was a drug intended to promote illogical thinking and impulsiveness in order to better manipulate and control. They wanted to shake his faith in Jennifer, like North Korean brainwashing had turned POWs. Kit poured another drink. The alcohol only made the doubt come back and grow like a torch-lit Tet dragon weaving through the streets of Cholon. Was Jennifer proud of her bondage and slavery? Was submission her way of showing love? He had to find out.

Kit stood up; he was unsteady on his feet. It had been a long time since he had been so drunk. He picked up a loose floorboard and retrieved his Smith & Wesson from its hiding place. He flicked out the chamber block to make sure it was still loaded. The rims of the six bullets glinted back at him. Good. Kit put on a leather jacket and dropped the gun into the right pocket. He wondered how to shoot Brian. The first two rounds would go into his sex organs. Kit would then let him suffer a while, so he could feel not only the pain, but also the realisation that he was no longer a man. How would Jennifer react to all this? Kit would have to play that by ear and instinct.

When Kit saw the signpost for Colchester he turned off the main road and stopped the car near a five-bar gate. The corn in the field on the other side of the gate had been beaten down by the summer storms. There was a rich malty smell. It was two o'clock in the morning and Kit had begun to sober up. He rolled the car window down so that the cool night air would make him even more sober. He now knew that he wasn't going to shoot anyone – or drive any further north. How, he thought, have I got into such a state? In any case, they were trapped on an island. Kit turned the car around. When he got back to London the eastern sky had turned into an angry dawn cauldron of orange and grey. The weather was getting worse.

■

The letter from Jennifer arrived via the second post. The message was encoded so Kit had to find his copy of *The Portrait of a Lady* to use as a key for decoding the message. The page used as the coding key was determined by how many days had elapsed since 1 September – the day that would have been the baby's birthday had he gone full term. Based on the note's date of composition, Kit turned to page 343. He wished he had chosen another book: the coincidence was too cruel.

> *"Her own children? Surely she has none."*
> *"She may have yet. She had a poor little boy, who died two years ago…"*

'Poor Jennifer,' said Kit, 'all the gods seemed ranged against you.' The deciphered message read: ETA ZERO ONE TWO SIX EIGHT BY SEA AWRE. Brief and telegraphic: Jennifer clearly remembered her training as a cipher clerk. The message implied that something was arriving on the sea side of Orford Ness at one o'clock in the morning of 26 August. Kit was certain that he knew what it was.

Kit picked up the book again and leafed through the pages. He had forgotten that Isabel Archer had lost a child. Those brief lines at the top of page 343 were the only reference that Henry James made to Isabel's tragic loss in the entire novel. What reticence, what understatement – and what other lessons, thought Kit, had Henry James learned from a lifetime in England? What a strange people – and the power of their unsaid words.

∎

It was a cold cloudy night and there was no moon. Despite the weather, there were still a few yachts on the river trying to salvage something of the season. *Louise* was on her mooring at Orford and Driscoll was slumped on a berth in the main saloon nursing a cup of tea laced with rum. The halyards rattled against the mast as squalls swept in from the south-west. 'I'd better tie those off,' said Kit. He put on an oilskin and went topside to silence the noisy lines. When he returned down below, he was dripping – and happy. Ops were dangerous for the body, but good for the soul. The adrenalin was pumping and driving the clouds away.

'There's something I don't understand,' said Driscoll.

'What's that?'

'This yachting thing. Is it supposed to be fun?'

Kit peeled off his oilskin and dropped it on the cabin sole. 'Fun? Of course it isn't fun. Fun is for lower-class people, like you, Driscoll.'

'Do you consider yourself a snob?'

'Not at all. In fact, Driscoll, I have socialist leanings – and I don't believe in inherited wealth.'

'Have you inherited a lot of money?'

'Quite a lot.'

'Since you think inherited wealth is wrong, why don't you give me yours?'

'Don't be silly, Driscoll, you'd just waste it having fun.' Kit looked at his watch. 'If we leave now, the tide will take us to the end of Havergate Island.'

'Do you think it's a good idea to go alone? If we both went, I could watch your back.'

'The problem is the tender. If a guard patrol sees it pulled up on the riverbank, they'll know they have uninvited guests. That's why I want you to drop me ashore and then hide up.' Kit left his oilskin dripping on the floor and put on a camouflage waterproof. He then covered his face and the backs of his hands with black greasepaint. He saw Driscoll shaking his head with disbelief. 'I know,' said Kit, 'all this commando stuff doesn't just make me look like an asshole, it makes me feel like one too. Let's go. I'll row back.' As Driscoll clambered into the tender, Kit checked his kitbag one last time: signal torch, automatic with silencer, wire cutters, binoculars, two hand grenades – one for them and one for himself. The idea was to blow off his head so the body couldn't be identified. And, of course, all the equipment – including the camouflage gear – was Russian. It was a false flag espionage op. If something went wrong, there wouldn't be any American finger-prints. Of course, anyone with half a brain would know the truth. The false flag paraphernalia was a fig leaf called 'plausible deni-ability'. It saved embarrassment for both sides.

The tender dropped down the river quickly on the tide and was soon hidden from Orford Ness by the low lying Havergate Island that split the river into two branches. Kit leaned back in the stern sheets and closed his eyes. It was very nice being rowed on a midnight river. Havergate, to their left, was a bird sanctuary with shallow lagoons. Kit hoped the Orford Ness guards wouldn't notice the warning calls of oystercatcher, curlew and avocet that followed their boat down the river.

When they got to the end of the island, Kit reminded Driscoll of his instructions and the emergency torch signals – three quick flashes at ten-minute intervals. Driscoll pulled the oars hard to row across the tide. When the boat crunched into the steep shin-gle of Orford Ness, Kit leapt out and ran for cover in the patchy vegetation at the top of the bank. He felt ashamed: he was enjoy-ing himself. Kit lay in a shingle hollow – the yellow blossoms of a horned poppy caressing his cheek. At first, the vast shingle spit seemed a barren desert of stone and salt spray, but there were many living things. The lonely sentinels of the sea frontier: cam-pion, pea, kale, stonecrop, hawk's-beard, toadflax and lavender. There was also a colony of lean hares that somehow survived and multiplied in the bleak wilderness. Kit could see them moving around. Their heads alert, still and listening.

The secret research base was a mile and a half to the north. Kit hoped that they didn't bother sending security patrols that far beyond the perimeter fence of barbwire and watchtowers. What he feared most were dogs. He got up and began to make his way towards the base. He kept in the middle of the spit where the shin-gle hollows and vegetation provided some scant cover. After every dash forward, he knelt and listened. The only sound he heard was the soft sough of the North Sea caressing the shingle spit. He was certain that he was alone. There was no sixth sense buzz warning him of another human presence. Kit moved quickly and half an hour later he was within a hundred metres of the barbwire fence. He crawled sixty metres closer, and then towards the sea. The last cover before the open beach was a clump of sea kale. He dared not go closer – the beam of Orford Ness lighthouse swept over the area at five-second intervals. He could also hear voices from the guard tower overlooking the beach.

It had stopped raining and the wind had shifted to the north. Although the night was cold and damp, Kit was sweating. He tried to burrow himself into the shingle behind the sea kale. His view of the beach behind the barbwire was excellent and the vegetation hid him from the guard tower. Kit took out his binoculars and began to scan the sea horizon. To the south was the ghostly loom of Sunk Sand Lightship. A few miles offshore were the slow moving running lights of a cargo ship heading towards Harwich. Nothing else. Kit continued to scan the empty sea. He wondered if Jennifer had given him the right information. Then something very odd happened. Orford Ness Lighthouse suddenly extinguished – and the sea and beach were as dark and unmarked as they had been in the days of the Iceni.

Kit heard noises out to sea – and they didn't sound very far away. They were the noises of ships' engines. He scanned the sea again. There weren't any lights, but there was a silhouette of a large vessel that was completely blacked out. She couldn't have been more than half a mile away – maybe closer. Suddenly her engine died and there was the rattle of an anchor chain paying out. Kit studied her shape as she swung to the tide – which had turned and was running south. Lying at anchor, the ship was only a couple of hundred yards from Kit's hiding place. She was a medium-sized cargo ship with her bridge and superstructure towards the stern. She belonged to the class of vessel used for transporting bulk goods: grain, iron ore, timber. Kit could see that the blackout wasn't perfect. There were a number of crew moving around the deck carrying hand torches. The ship was so close that Kit could hear voices – Russian voices.

The ship was fully laden and rode low in the water. There were two large cranes in the bows and a number of derricks further astern. Three crew, carrying tools, were walking forward towards the large crane. Two other men were walking behind them and talking – in English. One man spoke with a heavy Russian accent; the other man was obviously English. Kit recognised the voice – it was Brian's. The words travelled clearly across the night sea: 'Are you sure, Viktor, that the detonator has been made safe?'

'I'm pretty sure, but we need to remove it to make for certain. We've got the tools – we can do it now if you want.'

'No, I don't want to touch it until we get the bomb ashore and into one of those bunkers.'

Viktor turned and pointed towards the land. 'Your containment bunkers are different from the ones we have at Arzamas. Yours look like Buddhist pagodas – a good design for containing blast, but maybe not so good for stopping radiation. You should have asked for help.'

'The pagodas are fine, Viktor, they'll do the job.'

There was the noise of an engine starting in the bow of the ship and the silhouette of a crane began to move against the night sky. Brian's voice sounded worried. 'I only hope your crane will do the job – I'm not sure your detonator is stable enough to withstand being dropped from a height.'

'Not to worry. It's good crane. I check cable with my own hands.' Viktor shouted something in Russian and the crew on the crane laughed. Meanwhile, there was the slow thump of a ship's engine approaching from up the coast.

Kit scanned the sea horizon with his binoculars until he found a black lump coming in close to shore. The approaching ship flashed a brief signal and then her engines slowed. She was now so close that Kit no longer needed the binoculars to make out her shape and type. She was a large landing vessel: the type that the British had used to land tanks on the Normandy beaches. Kit watched as she manoeuvred astern of the Russian ship, slowed now to less than walking pace. The landing ship then spun around with a groaning of engines so that she lay abeam of the cargo vessel. Then there was a dull thud of steel on steel as the new arrival moored alongside.

The rest happened so quickly that it seemed practised and carefully choreographed. The crane motor whirred to a high pitch and the bomb rose out of the hold like an evil genie. It was lashed to a long pallet and was the size of a hearse. Kit felt his skin tingle. Mass death hung in solemn silhouette against the northern sky. Was this why we rose from the primal slime? Kit lay his face on his arm; he didn't want to see any more. He listened to the sounds as the landing ship headed into the beach and crunched on to the shingle. He heard the rattle of chains as the landing ramp thumped on to the stones. Then the sound of a tracked vehicle leaving the ship and climbing the steep bank of shingle. Britain now had its own hydrogen bomb. Kit lay still for five more minutes tasting the salt of his tears. He wanted out; he didn't care how. He just wanted out.

Kit crawled back the way he had come. When he was out of sight of the watchtowers, he got up and ran in short bursts crouching low. He was much more careful now than he had been coming. After each sprint he lay flat and listened to the night. He didn't want to get caught. Not now, now that he had something to live for. He had uncovered a conspiracy and he would soon have the names to go with it. Kit didn't care who used his secret once he had sold it. The secret was precious currency: the only currency powerful enough to buy him a life with Jennifer. Nothing else mattered.

Kit was less than two hundred yards from the point on the riverbank where Driscoll was supposed to pick him up. He halted and froze as soon as he heard the voices. One sounded London English, the other white South African – or maybe Rhodesian. The colonial voice spoke loudest. 'You're not fucking alone so don't tell me that. You're just a fucking colobus monkey. Where's your bwana and who is he?'

The next thing Kit heard wasn't Driscoll's voice, but Driscoll's scream. 'Not there, don't cut me there.' The scream was really bloodcurdling this time. 'Don't cut me any more, not there. Please, please, I'll talk.'

It was the London voice now. 'You'd better talk and you'd better not lie.' The two guards were now laughing. 'We'll know if you're lying, mate. And if you are, Johnnie's going to finish cutting your cock off and use it for fish bait – just like he used to do with those Mau Mau bastards in Kenya.'

Driscoll spoke next. Kit couldn't hear all the words, but he heard enough to know that Driscoll was spilling all the beans he had. And who, thought Kit, could blame him? That stuff about captured agents not talking was patriotic bullshit.

It was only afterwards that Kit thought that he should have tried to rescue Driscoll. He did have a gun and might have surprised them, but at the time he only wanted to save himself. While Driscoll was talking, Kit low-crawled to the river and slid down the bank and into the water as quietly as a snake. The tide was now flooding hard back to Orford. Kit kicked off his boots and let his bag sink to the bottom of the river. The incoming tide was so strong that Kit hardly needed to swim. As he drifted past the place where the guards were holding Driscoll, Kit couldn't see a thing, but he did hear them cutting off his head and Driscoll trying to scream through his gagged mouth. The decapitation wasn't a sawing sound, it was a hacking sound. They must have been using some sort of machete, thought Kit. He could hear the blade crunching through the cartilage and bone and then cracking on to the shingle below the severed neck. Kit bore the guards no malice. They were just players – as he had once been – and these were the rules of the game. It reminded him of a Stanley Spencer painting of Jesus being nailed to the cross. The village carpenter with a mouthful of nails and a hammer in his hand is just a tradesman doing his job. Crucifixions, kitchen shelves – all the same.

■

The Director of the CIA, Allen Dulles, had flown to London for the first stop of his world tour. He had taken over an Air Force DC-6 and turned it into a flying penthouse complete with a personal physician to look after his gout. The world tour was supposed to be secret, but Dulles expected welcoming parties to greet him on the airport tarmac. He was behaving more like a head of state than the head of a clandestine security service.

Dark clouds from the south-west scudded across the Heathrow sky as Dulles bounded down the boarding ladder – the gout seemed in remission. The first to greet the Director was Ambassador Aldrich who got a big bear hug. Kit was fourth in the protocol pecking order and had to be content with a wink rather than a hug. Allen Dulles still used his trademark wink as a seduction tool with devastating effect. The wink said, 'Those hugs and hearty laughs I give the bigwigs are just for show, the real business is between you and me.' Kit was ashamed that he still fell for it, for he had long known that 'wink' to be a whore. Nonetheless, Kit knew that a private meeting between himself and Director

Dulles was one of the principal reasons for the London visit – and Kit had prepared his lies with care. And when that meeting finally took place, two days later, Kit had even more lies to tell.

When Kit got back to his flat that evening, he picked up his post from the couple downstairs. There was a quarterly account statement from Medler and Gower about the family trust fund. It was more than he expected. Once again, Kit felt a wave of guilt and self-loathing. His wealth came from ancestors who had stolen land from one people and then enriched it by the slave labour of another. The money was cursed. Once again, Kit vowed that he would give it away. There was a letter from his sister, Caddie, with a New York postmark – and one from his mother postmarked from France. There were two postcards. One was from diplomatic friends on a mountain climbing holiday in Austria. They had addressed the card, presumably as a joke, to 'His Excellency Kitson Fournier, Envoy Plenipotentiary'. The other postcard was from Jennifer. It was a sepia view of Orford Castle. The message was deceptively bland: *Brian and I hope to see you before the end of the month – as you promised! Louise sends her love and is looking forward to seeing you again. All our love too. Jennifer and Brian, xxx.* Kit felt his heart begin to pound and his skin tingle. It was going to be a long night.

Kit arrived in Orford just after midnight and parked the car on a dark lane near the churchyard. He felt nervous: it was not an inconspicuous time to prowl among gravestones in a churchyard. He felt the shade of his ancestor, Tombstone Frank, sitting beside him with his grave-robbing spade. Kit had no idea what he would say if the vicar found him there. If anyone questioned him, he would hint at an adulterous rendezvous. In a way, it was true – and lies shaped from truth are always the best lies.

Kit sat in the car and watched moon shadows caress the ruins of the older larger church. It was often like that in Suffolk. When one church collapsed, they built a smaller church within the roof-less remains of its predecessor. It was as if the churches were shrinking in response to ebbing faith. Soon, thought Kit, the church would be the size of a doll's house with matchbox pews and thimbles for chalices. Kit rolled down a window and listened to the night. The wind was still blowing a force five; in the distance was the sound of a bell buoy. Kit wondered what it would be like to be out there – with 'those in peril on the sea'. He remembered the day that Jennifer had taken him to Orford Church to hear the rehearsal of *Noye's Fludde*.

Was that, he thought, the moment that he had fallen in love with this island – not its government and its policies – but its people and land? Kit left the car and walked to the churchyard gate past gardens heavy with runner beans and late summer roses. All around him were sleeping houses. 'I must,' he swore, 'never do anything that might bring them harm.'

It was easy to find Louise's grave. He flicked on his pocket torch and quickly played it over the grass. Jennifer had planted the dead drop spike at the foot of the grave as agreed. Kit quickly retrieved it and went back to the car. It was best not to hang around. He didn't bother to check what she had secreted in the spike until he got back to London – but he already had a good idea of what Jennifer had done.

It was after three in the morning when Kit got back to his flat. The first thing he did was take a double dose of amphetamines. This wasn't going to be a night for sleep. When he picked up the dead drop spike, his hand was shaking. Part of him hoped he wasn't going to find anything significant. He didn't want to be trapped in another dilemma – and he was afraid for Jennifer too. He took a breath, unscrewed the top of the spike and emptied the contents on to the kitchen table. There wasn't just one, there were two rolls of undeveloped film. What, thought Kit, has she done?

When the films were developed and fixed, Kit took them out of the tank and hung them above his bathtub. While he was waiting for them to dry, he opened the letter from Caddie.

35B 12th Street
Greenwich Village
New York, New York

Dear Kit,

I feel like a real bitch. I've just heard that Jennifer lost her baby. I'm so sorry that I said those awful things about her. Jennie's much better than any of us. She's kind, loving, full of generosity of spirit. And she's not stupid either. The trouble with our side of the family is that we always have to show off how clever and bright we are (and that applies to you too, big brother!). Maybe we're insecure and she isn't – because she

knows who she is and what she's worth. She's also very beau-
tiful – and some of us, who aren't beauties, don't always find
it easy to admit that she has everything else going for her too.
Except, of course, the thing she wants most: the ability to bear
a live child.

   I've written to her saying how sorry I am. When she's had
time to get over it, I'm going to suggest a consultation with a
friend of mine at Johns Hopkins who specialises in pre-natal
care.

   I miss you, Kit, even if you are a smart ass.

Love,
Caddie

Kit folded the letter and put it back in its envelope. He loved
Caddie – he loved them all. But he knew that it was unlikely that
he would ever see his family again. He went back into the bathroom to check the films. They were still wet. He went back to the
sitting room and opened the letter from his mother.

                              Château des Enfants
                              Antibes

Dear Kit,

   George wrote to tell me the dreadful news about Jennifer.
He said that you're on the scene and being a great help. I want
to do something too. I could come to England – or maybe it
would be best if Jennifer came here for a break. There's plenty
of room and she would be most welcome. Please advise.

Love,
Mother

Kit put the letter down and stared blankly into nothingness.
Nothing any longer connected with anything. His deracination
was as total as a summer rose hurled into the vacuum of outer
space. Kit went back into the bathroom. The negatives were dry.
He then took them into the kitchen where he laid them across
a white lit base normally used for making contact prints, and
studied them with a high-resolution magnifying class. At first,

he was amazed that Brian had left so much sensitive stuff in his briefcase, but then he realised that it was probably more secure to keep such documents close at hand rather then to leave them on Orford Ness.

The first roll of film had been used to copy technical and engineering reports. There were numerous sketches labelled with both English and Cyrillic script. The second roll of film contained densely copied tables, formulae and statistics – but also, and more importantly, names. Much of the information copied was in Russian. This, Kit knew instinctively, was a Holy Grail moment: the type of intelligence scoop that spies would, literally, die for. The film almost certainly contained the identities of the entire network of spies, agents, double agents and scientists that had conspired to steal and sell a hydrogen bomb to the British intelligence services – and Kit fervently wished that he didn't have it. Kit closed his eyes and prayed that he wouldn't have to use it. Jennifer had, with each click of the spy camera's shutter, lined up more than a hundred death sentences. The most important thing now was to arrange a rendezvous with Vasili – and let the bluffing and horse-trading commence. But time was running out – and, once he had had his meeting with Allen Dulles, Kit knew that the few hours remaining were going to be sprinting for the finish line.

■

'Have a look at this, Kit. These are the plans for our new headquarters in Langley.' Allen Dulles had spread out architects' drawings on the oak table in the Ambassador's committee room. It was the same table, a priceless antique from Jefferson's Monticello, that Allen and his brother Foster had sat around the last time they had briefed Kit. But this time Kit and Allen were alone. 'Have you been to Langley?'

'No, sir.'

'It's a beautiful sylvan place, low-wooded gently-rolling hills just south of the Potomac. Look at that.' Dulles pointed to a place on the drawing where there was a broadleaf copse next to a building. 'Clover is nagging the architects to keep as many trees as possible. It's going to be a veritable Arcadia, a university campus for intelligence studies and espionage. You know, Kit, I hate the image of spycraft as something dirty and sordid. I don't want my spies to be seedy perverts, I want them to be clean-limbed young men and women – looking forward with the open clear-eyed faces of freedom.'

Kit smiled wanly; he was lost for words. He was tempted to say something about nymphs and shepherds – or to suggest maypole dancing and campfire singing as training requisites. But he kept his mouth shut.

'What do you think?'

'It looks a lot nicer than E Street and should improve security too.'

'And the idea of a university campus?'

'Absolutely, sir, the intelligence trade is about acquiring knowledge – it's a higher form of learning.'

'Good, I'm glad you like it.' Dulles rolled up the drawings, then tapped them with a forefinger. 'If nothing else, Langley will be my legacy.'

There was a childlike innocence to Allen Dulles that made him difficult to dislike – but also made him dangerous. The world of espionage was just a 'game' to him. Allen knew, of course, that there was real blood and real suffering, but he never let himself get close enough to hear the screams and smell the bodily fluids. Kit felt sorry for Dulles, but he felt more sorry for the lives he ruined.

'Now, Kit, tell us about the Brits and their hydrogen bomb.'

'They haven't got one.'

Dulles made a steeple of his fingers and looked closely over them at Kit, as if sighting a rifle. 'There's something I don't understand, Kit.'

'Yes.'

'Can you think what it is?'

Kit had already calculated how much Dulles knew about his activities. He knew that if the Director had knowledge of his unauthorised and unreported meetings with Vasili, a confession wouldn't make any difference. In that case, Kit would be arrested that very afternoon and repatriated on a military flight in handcuffs. 'I think you can't understand why I've wasted so much time barking up the wrong tree.'

'Explicate.'

'I requested highly top secret U2 photographs of the secret Soviet nuclear installation known as Arzamas-16.'

'I know.'

'The problem is that I fooled myself into believing there was a far-fetched conspiracy involving rogue elements of the KGB and the British security services.'

'Which was?'

'I blush with shame to admit it, but I came to the conclusion that a ring of corrupt KGB officers and Russian nuclear scientists had stolen a Soviet hydrogen bomb to sell to the British.'

'What you're telling me is very interesting, but you tell me your story first and then I might tell you mine.'

'A number of loose threads and coincidences led me down this path. The first came from my cousin Jennifer who is married to the chief scientist at the Orford Ness Atomic Weapons Research Establishment.'

'George Calvert's daughter? You mentioned her when you were in Washington.'

'That's the one.'

'A very beautiful young lady.'

'She is stunning, but emotionally unstable. And because she's family, sir, I don't want any of this put in an official report.'

'I can understand.'

'I don't think Jennie ever got over her brother, Peter, being killed in that Saigon mess – and then her mother is a hopeless alcoholic. Maybe she came to England to get away from it all. In any case, she recently lost a baby – and that makes things worse. But even before that, Jennie had been telling me that something awfully strange and mysterious was going on at Orford Ness. She seemed so intense that I began to believe her. Ergo, I ordered aerial reconnaissance photographs of the site.'

'Yes, Kit, I have seen these photos and read the report. The analyst thinks the bunkers under construction are intended for containing a nuclear blast from within. So what? If the British are constructing a homemade H-bomb, they will still need containment bunkers.'

'That's true – I made a wrong assumption.'

'On the contrary, Kit, you were right. You have to take into account the urgency and speed with which they were building these bunkers. Why did the Brits have their H-bomb containment bunkers completed years before they could build an H-bomb?'

'I don't know.' Kit paused and pretended to think. 'Maybe it's a face-saving ruse. You're right, sir. They're years behind us and the Sovs.'

'Take me a bit more, Kit, through this corrupt KGB conspiracy theory you now seem to have discarded.'

'Three more threads. One, a conversation I had with a Russian cellist named Natalya Voronova whom I met at the Aldeburgh festival. She was trying to tell me that her husband, a nuclear physicist named Viktor Voronov, had defected to the Brits. But there's no evidence to corroborate this. I suspect that Natalya is a KGB agent herself and that she was passing on misinformation to create distrust between us and the British.'

'She is KGB, but that doesn't mean the information is false. Natalya might genuinely have been warning us about what our closest ally is up to behind our back.'

'In my view, unlikely. Second thread, a meeting I had with my contact, code-name Bacchus. You know who he is.'

Dulles nodded. 'A key member of the Labour shadow cabinet – and a right-winger.'

'That's the one. In any case, Bacchus tried spinning me a yarn full of cryptic innuendo about the shipping company that has a former Secretary of Trade as one of its directors. According to Bacchus, the company imports timber to England from the Soviet Union. The purpose of the company isn't so much profit, as the fostering of stronger Anglo-Soviet links. Bacchus tried to imply that the company was involved in some sort of conspiracy.'

'Such as using one of their ships to transport a stolen Soviet H-bomb to England hidden under piles of timber.'

Kit struggled to keep his composure. 'Frankly, sir, Bacchus is full of bullshit. There's a hidden civil war within the Labour Party. The right wing of that party, such as Bacchus, takes every opportunity to smear the left of the party. We shouldn't be naive about British game-playing. Bacchus was trying the same tactic as Voronova – misinformation. In any case, the implied smear is totally illogical. If the Labour left are controlled by the KGB, why on earth would they be conspiring with KGB traitors to nick an H-bomb?'

'Or perhaps the Labour left are British patriots who want a British nuclear deterrent independent of American control?'

'No, sir, the Labour left are nuclear disarmers – they don't want any sort of A or H-bomb.'

'And your third thread?'

'The disappearance of our cultural attaché, Jeffers Cauldwell, and the murder of his lover – if it was murder. Cauldwell's lover, Henry Knowles, was a rising member of the Labour Party – and, along with the former Secretary of Trade, a director of the timber import company. And, by the way, I bitterly regret my role in the attempted blackmail of the pair. In retrospect, I'm sure that the tragic outcome had nothing to do with politics or conspiracy.'

'I wish I had known about that blackmail business before it all began. Birch was wrong to give you those orders. I've had words with him.'

Kit felt a cold trickle of sweat run down his back. He suddenly realised that Allen Dulles didn't believe a single word he was saying – and, likewise, Kit realised that he was a trapped insect becoming more and more entwined in the Director's web. But he had to keep denying the truth. If Cauldwell or the bomb conspirators found that he had blabbed to the Americans, there was no telling how they would react. Kit's secret was intended for only one buyer and for only one price.

'So Kit, in your judgement, you are certain that there is no H-bomb – Russian or British – on Orford Ness?'

'None, sir, none at all.'

'And the conspiracy?'

'The only conspiracy is an attempt by the KGB to sow mistrust and friction between ourselves and our closest ally.'

'Sometimes, Kit, I almost have the impression that you might be working for the British.'

'To be honest, sir, MI6 would rather shoot me than recruit me.'

'Maybe so. But I hope that you're right about Britain not having an H-bomb, because if they did we would have to take some action – maybe even a covert raid to swipe it. You must never forget that the island of Britain is our unsinkable aircraft carrier – the cornerstone of US foreign and military policy. No British government should ever think that they can act independently of Washington – and that's why this one is about to get its fingers burned over this Suez nonsense.'

'By the way, I've got more information about Eden's health and state of mind. Liddel-Hart got so exasperated with the Prime Minister, he put a wastepaper bin over his head.'

'Sorry, Kit, I've still got some questions about you and the H-bomb business.'

'Sure.' Kit felt the sweat running down his back.

'Birch tells me that you were absent from your office for three days at the end of July. What on earth were you doing?'

'I was flat on my back in my apartment. It was my worst attack of recurrent malaria since coming back from Southeast Asia. And foolishly, I tried to treat it with large quantities of gin and tonic – used to work a treat in Saigon.'

'I think we're going to have to put you in for a medical, Kit. In fact, you're not looking very well at the moment. And something else,' Dulles reached in his jacket pocket and pulled out a press clipping. 'That girl that runs the embassy press office is awfully damned efficient. She found this and passed it on to Birch who in turn gave it to me. Have a look.'

Kit took the clipping. It was from the *East Anglian Daily Press*:

SECOND BODY FOUND ON SHINGLE STREET
Corpse Found Missing Head and Hands

Kit glanced at the article. The body had been found by a woman walking her dog. Kit wondered if it was the same woman who found Knowles. She must be getting fed up. He passed the clipping back. 'It's a strange piece of coast, sir, bodies are always getting washed up there.'

'You know what I'm thinking, Kit?'

'I'm not sure.'

'I think this body might belong to that frogman that you recruited for the *Ordzhonikidze* job in Portsmouth Harbour.'

'Or it could be a villain from the East End. London gangsters often use the sea as a dustbin for rivals.'

'In any case, we'll never find out who he was. MI5 has slapped a news blackout on the story. Why would they do that? Surely, underworld criminals are not a national security matter.'

'I don't know why. The Brits are often very secretive for no apparent reason.'

'Who knows?' Dulles looked at his watch. 'I've got to be off now. But I must say, Kit, you really must have a check-up, you're not looking at all well.'

Kit shook hands with Dulles, then began to walk down the two flights of stairs to his office. Halfway down, he felt nauseous and had to cling to the banister. He breathed deeply and tried to suppress an urge to be sick. There was something that Dulles had said which came back to Kit like regurgitated vomit: 'You tell me your story first and then I *might* tell you mine.' Dulles hadn't told *his* story – nor had he winked, not even once. Kit knew that he was no longer part of the inner circle. He had been discarded. He was a machine that could no longer be trusted.

■

Vasili was sitting on a bench in the shadow of the Peter Pan statue reading a book. At first, Kit didn't realise it was him: Vasili's features seemed so sharp and ascetic. The Russian looked like a poet-priest rather than a spy. 'Bless me father, bless me father,' thought Kit, 'for I have sinned and need absolution.'

As Kit sat down next to him, Vasili ignored him and continued reading. Finally the Russian spoke, but still didn't look up from his book. 'Rimbaud, do you know him?'

'A little.'

'Translate this, "*La dernière innocence et la dernière timidité.*"'

Kit looked up at Peter Pan. '"The last innocence and final timidity."'

'And this.' Vasili continued, '"*Ne pas porter au monde mes dégouts et mes trahisons.*"'

'"Not to carry my disgust and my treasons to the world."'

'Next, "*A qui me louer*?"' Vasili then paused. 'I like these lines, may I translate them myself?'

'Please.'

'"To whom shall I hire myself? What beast must I worship? What hearts shall I break? What lies must I believe – In what blood will I walk?"'

Kit put his hand in his pocket and looked up again at Peter Pan. There was no turning back; innocence was long buried. He took the film out of his pocket and handed it to Vasili.

The Russian closed the book of poems. His face seemed to harden. 'What do you want in exchange?'

'I want asylum and peace.'

'For yourself.'

'No, for two of us.'

'The scientist's wife?'

'Yes.'

Vasili closed his eyes and seemed to stare into an inner space. 'We'll need your passports – and recent photographs. Tape them to the bottom of the usual pew at Brompton Oratory – pretend you dropped your rosary. It will take about forty-eight hours to forge your new passports – we'll choose your new names. On Friday evening there's an Aeroflot service to Beirut from Gatwick. You'll be on that plane. You'll be met by an Englishman who will put you up for the weekend.'

'Kim Philby?'

'No questions, Kit, just follow instructions. On Monday morning you will board another Aeroflot flight to Moscow.' Vasili got up to go.

'Thank you.'

'Don't thank me, Kit. I'm not doing this out of friendship. I'm doing it out of duty. I wish this hadn't happened. Your country needs you more than we do.'

'What do you mean?'

'Are you blind, Kit, are you so in love with this woman that you are blind to your duty? Your country is going into a dark age. Big money buys power and office. The ignorant shout down the educated. You, as a person, had more power than you realised – the power of civilised thought and reason. How many like you are left? America is a drunken boat – adrift with no direction, laden with nuclear bombs primed to blow up the world five times over and madmen like General Curtis LeMay in charge of the gun decks. You could have tried to grab the tiller, but instead you chose a retirement dacha well stocked with vodka and caviar – and Comrades Burgess and Maclean as your regular dinner guests. Goodbye, Kit.'

Kit remained seated staring at the ground. He listened to the sound of Vasili's footsteps crunching through the gravel as he walked away. Kit wanted to run after him and tell him how wrong he was, but he knew that the Russian wouldn't understand – wouldn't understand how a person that you loved could be more important than the universe.

■

Kit knew that he was paying too much for the Austin A30, but there was no time to haggle – he needed a car quick. He usually drove a new Ford from the embassy motor pool, but he knew that driving a car with diplomatic number plates to Gatwick so that he could defect on a Russian Aeroflot plane was a shit idea. As Kit handed over the cash in crisp pound notes, the dealer assured him that the A30 was 'a real runner'.

'Do you mind,' said Kit, 'if I keep her here for a few days?'

The dealer could hardly say no because the garage on Manor Road was huge and mostly empty. While the dealer scratched his head, Kit peeled off another note and the garaging was agreed.

'What sort of business are you in... if you don't mind me asking?'

'I work in a bank in the City, I'm a commodities trader.'

'Well, I'm sure we can do you a better motor than this. Mind you the A30 is...'

'No, this car,' Kit gave a leering wink, 'isn't really for me – so we don't want anything too showy.'

'Sounds like there might be a young lady involved.'

'That might indeed be the case – so you can see why I want everything to be discreet, including the registration documents.'

∎

The next morning, when Kit handed his ID to the embassy doorman, he thought it received more than the usual scrutiny. And, as he made his way through the foyer, there was neither eye contact nor a salute from the marine on duty. As usual, Kit shunned the unwelcome camaraderie of the elevator. But as he bounded up the stairs he sensed the paranoia demon jogging and laughing beside him. When he got to his office, the DCM, Birch, was seated at Ethel's desk in the secretarial cubicle. Something was wrong, seriously wrong.

Birch looked up from a report he was reading. 'Good morning, Kit.'

'Good morning.'

'You don't need to be here today.'

Kit put his briefcase on the desk and looked down at Birch. 'Why don't I need to be here today?'

'Because you are on leave.'

'For how long?'

'That depends.'

'OK.' Kit picked up his briefcase and turned to leave.

'Kit.'

'I'll keep in touch.'

'Kit, can I have your keys please?'

Kit reached in his pocket and dropped his office key ring on the desk. 'Have I been suspended?'

'I haven't used that word.'

Kit turned to leave again.

'And your briefcase.'

'Sure, but can I keep my spare shirt?'

Birch nodded.

'Thanks.'

'You're welcome.'

Kit snapped open the case, took out a freshly laundered white shirt of Egyptian cotton and then left without looking back. As he walked back down the stairs, Kit felt awkward and embarrassed. He realised that he looked pretty silly carrying a shirt and nothing else. When he got to the door, a British doorman wearing a regimental blazer asked, 'Would you like a bag for that, sir.'

'Please.'

The doorman disappeared into a cubby hole and emerged with a small grey canvas holdall. 'Can't have a gentleman walking around carrying laundry. It's not dignified.' The doorman put the shirt in the holdall and did up the buttons. 'Here you go, sir, that's much better. Just drop the bag off next time you're here.'

'Thank you.'

Kit emerged blinking into the morning sunlight, his eyes dampened by the gentle gift of unexpected kindness.

■

Halfway between Colchester and Ipswich, Kit pulled into a garage to have the A30's oil and water checked. While the mechanic was looking after the car, Kit walked into the village to find a phone. When he finished dialling, he put a finger on the cradle. If Brian answered, he would hang up – he didn't care what suspicions he aroused.

'Sudbourne 234.' It was Jennifer.

'Can you talk?'

'Not for long,' she whispered, 'Brian's in his study. He's working from home.'

'Tell him you're going for a walk. Remember that abandoned boathouse I told you about on the Butley?'

'Yes.'

'There's a path to it through the marshes. Can you find your way there?'

'I think so.'

'I'll see there you in two hours – and bring your passport.'

'I'm not scared, Kit.'

'I love you. I must go now.'

As Kit walked back to the garage, he began to wonder why Brian was spending so much time at home. What did he know? Was he keeping an eye on Jennifer?

■

Kit turned off the main road after Woodbridge. As soon as he had crossed Wilford Bridge, where the headwaters of the Deben were dark and dappled by tree shadow, Kit knew that he was deep in hidden Suffolk. He loved that part of the county and wished that he could spend the rest of his life there. He wondered what Russia would be like. Maybe he could learn to love pure snow and endless birch forests too. Kit parked the car at a tiny hamlet called Chillesford where there was a church and five houses. The doorman's holdall was on the seat next to him: Kit had packed it with a Polaroid camera and a white sheet to use as a backdrop. The holdall bothered him. How would he ever get it back? Maybe he could send it to London in a Soviet Foreign Ministry diplomatic bag.

The path to the boathouse hadn't been used for years. There was marsh and river on one side, and sandy hills with heather on the other. It was the sort of place where children built dens and swore secret oaths. The boathouse itself had been built on one of a number of tidal islands. To get to it, one had to negotiate a series of single and double plank bridges that leapfrogged from one dry clump to another.

When Kit got to the boathouse, he checked his watch. He was five minutes late. He wondered if Jennifer would turn up. The call from the phone box had been reckless; it broke all the rules. It was likely that Jennifer's phone had been tapped – and she was now being interrogated by the Ministry of Defence security police. But supposing there had been a phone tap, why weren't the security guys at the boathouse too? On the other hand, what if it was only Brian – and the only thing he had discovered was marital unfaithfulness? What would he do? Would he shout at her? Beat her up? Lock her in the house? Kit closed his eyes, but couldn't block out the horror cinema of the mind: the torn clothing, the bleeding lip, the screams, the pounding fists. But maybe Brian wasn't like that. Maybe he would just brood his hurt as a silent inner lump. Kit pushed the rotten curtain material back from the door window and looked up the hill, to where the trees faded into heather. There she was: running and bounding down the path like a schoolchild released from a tedious lesson. She's so beautiful.

'I'm sorry I'm late,' she said, 'I got lost.'

'What did you tell him you were doing?'

'I didn't have to tell him anything. He left the house a few minutes after you rang?'

'Did he say where he was going?'

'No, but he took the car. He seemed in a grump – he often is these days.'

'Did you bring your passport?'

'Here it is.' She handed it over. 'Are we leaving soon, now?'

'Not now, on Friday – but when I tell you where we're going, you might not want to come. And I won't blame you if you change your mind.'

Jennifer put her arms around Kit and kissed him on the mouth. 'I'll go anywhere with you.'

'Even Russia.'

Jennifer brushed a hair from the side of her mouth and stared at her cousin. Then she smiled, 'You are joking.'

'No, Jennie, the only way we can be together is if I defect. My life isn't my own. I know too much. They can't risk my blabbing – or being kidnapped and forced to blab. Even after you retire, all your travel plans have to be approved. We belong to the State – until death do us part.'

Jennifer looked at the floor. 'I suppose I knew that all along.'

'And I've been a bad boy for a long time. It started with lies and omissions – and it's ended with treason. I've betrayed my country. They could hang me.'

'Kit?'

'Yes.'

'Did you do this for me?'

'Not just for you, but for me too – for my conscience.'

'What is your conscience?'

'A tangle of feelings and intuitions – it might be wrong. But it's my choice and the important thing is to choose.'

Jennifer put her hands on her cousin's shoulders. 'Look, I'm almost as tall as you.'

'It's wrong for me to ask you to come with me. Don't come.'

'Being the same height makes kissing better.'

Kit felt her mouth open against his and her tongue dart into his mouth like a demented serpent. She seemed more hungry and passionate than she had ever been before. Kit spread the sheet on the floor of the boathouse and they made love. Afterwards, when they still lay entwined, she said something to Kit – in a whisper – that disturbed him. It was a secret admission that, at first, made Kit give a nervous half-laugh. But when her words finally sunk in, they sent cold shudders up his spine. 'Kit,' she whispered, 'some-times… sometimes, I might want you to hurt me a bit.'

■

Afterwards, Kit pinned the sheet to a wall in the boathouse. 'What are you doing?' asked Jennifer.

'We need to take photos for our new passports.'

'Does this mean that we'll have to live forever and ever in Russia?'

'Not necessarily, the East bloc is big – East Germany, Czech-oslovakia, Bulgaria. There are many beautiful places – another world to discover. I hope someday that we'll be able to live in France. In any case, it will be easier for you to travel than me – you're not a traitor. You'll see your parents again.'

'I wonder what Mom and Dad will think of all this.'

'The important thing for them is that you're alive. Your life is the most important thing they have.'

'And my happiness – and I can only be happy with you. Hold me.'

Kit put his arms around her. 'You're shaking. What's wrong?'

'A shadow. I felt a cold shadow brush across my neck.'

■

After Jennifer had gone back to the house, Kit waited until it was dark before he went back to his car. The paranoia demon was back again and he felt eyes burning into his back. Darkness made it better. He had one more job to do before he returned to London – and he didn't want anyone to see him doing it.

Kit drove into Orford and parked the A30 in a quiet lane near the main square. He could see the tower of Orford Castle as a black silhouette against the blacker sky behind it. The Castle had been built in the twelfth century on the orders of Henry II – the same king who had ordered the goons to whack Thomas à Becket. Kit was sure that Henry hadn't meant the murder to be taken personally. It was about political independence: an English line in the sand against the power of Rome. Becket must have understood too. He was a seasoned player and knew the rules. The next morning the monks had to turn out with mops and buckets to clean up the blood, skull fragments and brain tissue that had sprayed all over the place.

Kit left the car and walked towards the castle. It had stood guard over the Suffolk coast for eight centuries, so it ought to manage looking after a much smaller package for another few decades. Kit put his hand in his coat pocket and felt the dead drop spike. The film that Kit had passed on to Vasili was the less important of the two. It was the one that confirmed that the Russian H-bomb was indeed on Orford Ness – and contained details and drawings of how the British were going to build their own version. It was a valuable piece of intelligence, but it contained no names, no agent network to be rolled up – and then tortured and shot in the basement of the Lubyanka. The second film, with its death sentence name list, was inside the dead drop spike that Kit was about to bury in the shadow of Orford Castle. He hoped it would stay there forever.

■

After Kit had dead lettered the passports and photographs in Brompton Oratory, he had been brush-passed a note by a woman who had almost knocked him down. She was reading a tourist map and pretended not to have seen Kit. 'Enschuldigen Sie, bitte… I mean excuse me.' For a second, Kit really believed that she was German, but as soon as she had gone on her way, he found a folded note in his hand. He slipped it into his pocket and continued walking until he found a phone kiosk. Kit went into the kiosk and got the note out, as if it were a phone number, so that he could read it without looking suspicious. Basic tradecraft. He read the note with the phone in his hand: '2200, Thurs. Tote dat barge on Abe's idea 'til yr cookin'.' It wasn't Vasili's writing, but whoever it was, wanted a rendezvous on the Grand Union Canal towing path near the gas works.

■

It was a dark and ugly place. There were railway sidings beside the gas works. The huff and wheeze of the shuttle engines and the clanking noise of metal on metal echoed like sounds from hell. The canal was a black greasy streak that stank of oily rot. The only sounds of life were the scurrying of rats in the undergrowth. From time to time, a rat belly-flopped into the canal for a midnight dip in the unspeakable filth. The grey walls of Wormwood Scrubs Prison loomed above the gas works: the prison, with its loom of white light, seemed warm and welcoming in comparison.

Kit checked his watch; his contact was five minutes late. He felt frightened, but didn't regret coming without a gun. There was no point in shooting his way out of a jam. If he had to do that, it meant it was all over and he was as good as dead anyway. Nonetheless, Kit kept himself hidden in the shadow of a chain link fence overgrown with convolvulus and rosebay willow herb.

It was a quarter past ten when Kit spotted a figure coming along the path. It was a tallish man who cast a swift and graceful silhouette against the white tombstones of Kensal Green Cemetery on the opposite side of the canal. For a few seconds, Kit wasn't sure that the figure was human – it seemed so quick-footed and smooth. As it came closer, it suddenly disappeared into the shadow of the fence. Kit instinctively reached deep in his pocket for the revolver that wasn't there. He heard the voice, before he saw the man. 'Kit, you've disappointed us.' It was Jeffers Cauldwell.

'You talk shit, Jeffers, I'm the biggest fish the Sovs have ever bagged and you know it.'

'The film you gave to Vasili is less than diddly squat.'

'It's a lot fucking more than you gave them. Don't play a game, Jeffers, that you don't know how to play. You're not even a junior varsity bench warmer.'

There was a faint pause, less than a second, before Cauldwell continued. 'Where's the other film, the one with the names?'

'There isn't one.'

'That's a lie and you know it. You're not stupid, Kit, you wouldn't be doing this if you hadn't taken out an insurance policy and stashed it away. All defectors do it.'

'Name one.'

'Maybe I ought to tell Vasili that you're doubled, that Allen Dulles is sending you to Moscow as a plant full of misinformation and bullshit.'

'No more games, Jeffers – just hand over the passports.'

'Where's the other film?'

'It's in my brain – with a hundred other rolls of film – and they're all going to stay there until Jennifer and I are safe in Moscow.'

Cauldwell put a hand in his jacket pocket and handed over the documents. 'I suggested your cover name be Zoltan R. Krumpecker III, but Vasili said it would attract too much attention.'

Kit looked at the new passports. 'So I'll have to be happy as Timothy Robin Wells, and Jennie will be Constance Wells. Good.'

Cauldwell smiled and said, 'No hard feelings?'

'None.'

'It's a scary business, isn't it?' Cauldwell put a hand on Kit's shoulder. 'If they catch us, we get extradited to New York. That means a roasting in the electric chair – like the Rosenbergs. You'll find that the Russians are more civilised. They just shoot you.'

■

When Kit got back to his flat, he poured himself a brandy and began to rehearse his final moves. The next morning he would pick up the car from the Manor Road garage and drive to Suffolk. His plan was to take single-lane country roads to make sure that he hadn't grown a tail. Kit wondered what he should do when he met up with Jennifer. The plan was to rendezvous at the boat-house at midday. If Brian was at home, her alibi was to be a shopping trip to Orford Quay for fresh fish. Kit had told Jennie not to pack a bag: it would be too conspicuous. They could buy whatever she would need en route. It would be like choosing her wedding trousseau. Kit knew that everything was going to be fine. He picked up the forged passports and examined them again. They were perfect. The Russian craftsmanship was far better than anything the CIA produced. Kit finished his brandy and smiled. Now that they had false passports for a new life, why go to Moscow? Instead of Gatwick, he and Jennifer could detour to Harwich or a channel port. The obvious problem was that the KGB knew the names and passport numbers. If Kit double-crossed his new masters, they would leak the passport details big time. It wouldn't be long before every immigration officer from Brindisi to Calais would join the hunt. On the other hand, it wouldn't happen immediately. It would take at least five days, maybe even a couple of weeks, before their passport details filtered down to frontier control level. Would that be long enough to buy new documents? The KGB were not the only forgers in Europe. Kit knew a half dozen of the best: Utrecht, Antwerp and Liège. Why, he thought, was this a craft at which the Low Countries excelled? Perhaps it was the tradition of Rembrandt, Vermeer and Van der Hals. They were consummate artists.

Kit poured another brandy. Double-crossing the Sovs was a tempting idea, but maybe it was wrong. Maybe their system, despite all its faults, was better. At least they had a vision – a vision based on reason and hope rather than superstition and greed. Maybe that's what turned Burgess and Maclean? And yet, part of Kit knew that what they did – and what he was doing – was deeply wrong. When you become an officer of the State – military, diplomatic or espionage – you sell your soul. The first thing you learn as a student of Foreign Policy is that nothing else matters except the survival and dominance of the State – 'the national interest'. It was more than an idea, it was sacred dogma. If the national interest required burning the faces off the children of Hiroshima and Nagasaki, you grilled those young faces until the soft tissue sizzled and caramelised into black ash. And now there was a bomb a thousand times more savage: his father had been one of its first victims. The State was a cruel cradle.

■

It was a beautiful Suffolk morning when Kit arrived at the boat-house. It was September, but the weather was warmer and clearer than it had been all summer – as if autumn had turned into spring. The reed beds were golden in the too bright sunlight. In a few weeks, the local thatcher and his apprentice would pole a flat-bottomed boat up the river and begin harvesting the reed. Kit knew both of them. They drank in the same pub where Brian and his henchmen went after work.

Kit checked his watch. It wasn't as early as he thought: Jennifer should be arriving any minute. He looked up the path towards the heather and tried to conjure Jennifer's figure emerging into the light. He wondered what she would be wearing and whether her hair would be free or tied back. He kept looking at his watch – then, after a while, stopped looking. She was already late, but only five minutes. Kit kept staring up the path, straining to see movement. His heart leapt when he saw a woodpigeon flushed from a fir tree at the top of the hill. Was she coming that way? He waited with his heart pounding. How long would it take her to walk from that tree? Five minutes? Kit began to count the seconds without looking at his watch. He'd begun to hate the lying minute hand. Kit stopped counting when he got to seven hundred. She was now twenty minutes late. He began to feel beads of panic sweat chilling his spine. Kit left the boathouse and started walking up the path. He had chosen the boathouse to provide shelter in case of rain or suspicious eyes – but now the only thing that mattered was meeting Jennifer and getting her to the car.

The wood that went up the back garden had been planted with giant Wellingtonia firs and redwoods by a Victorian lord. The non-native trees towered over the oak and silver poplars like freak aliens from outer space. The gardening lord had also introduced rhododendron that had now gone berserk, but provided cover for Kit as he worked his way to the edge of the garden. Kit kept deep in the shadows as he studied the house. There was washing on the line, but all else seemed quiet and empty. Brian's car was nowhere to be seen. 'Shit.' Kit swore under his breath. 'I bet she's gone another way, by the road.' Kit had noted that the wood was full of pheasants. The shooting season was about to begin. It was obvious: Jennifer had gone by road to avoid running into the gamekeeper. Kit swore at himself for leaving the boathouse and began to retrace his steps.

As soon as Kit emerged from the heather, he could see that the boathouse was empty, but something was different – someone had left the door open. So Jennifer had been there! He ran down the slope and across the plank bridges. He knew there would be a note – and it was easy to find it. She must not have had paper or anything to write with, so she had scrawled across the wall in block capitals with lipstick. I WAITED BUT YOU WEREN'T HERE. GONE BACK TO HOUSE. MEET ME THERE. J XXXX. Kit breathed deep and closed his eyes with relief. 'Stupid me,' he whispered, 'and poor you.' He then ran back to the road to where he had left the car in a lay-by. He needed to get to the house as quickly as possible. She was obviously alone, but Brian could turn up at any moment.

When Kit got to the house, he parked his car on the road. He didn't want to risk being blocked in on the drive. The washing was still hanging out to dry and everything seemed as still and quiet as it had before. He checked the drive: there was still no Brian. Kit walked around to the kitchen door and opened it slightly. 'Jennifer,' he said. There was no reply, he called more loudly, 'Jennie, where are you?' He looked on the kitchen table.

There was a copy of the *East Anglian Daily Times* open to the sports pages: Ipswich Town had signed a new centre forward. Kit had an impulse to pick up the paper and read the article. He wanted to be in a world where people did normal things – like hanging out the washing and following a team. Kit paused and looked around for the kettle. That's what the English always do in a crisis, they have a cup of tea. It seemed to work for them, but Kit knew it wasn't going to work for him. He came from a society driven by strong coffee and raw nerves.

Kit leaned on the back of a kitchen chair and listened to the silence. There must be a million different types of silence. There's the sweet silence of a summer garden on a still night. There's the adrenalin pumping silence before a battle's first shot. There's the punched-hard-in-the-stomach silence of a lover at the moment of betrayal. There's the silence of the stethoscope. But this one, Kit knew, was the worst silence of all: when the silence is listening to you.

Kit walked out of the kitchen into the darkness of the inner house. A bath tap was dripping and there was a copy of *Wisden Cricketers'Almanack* on Brian's desk. There was a musty smell of stale perfume. Kit knew that he wasn't alone. He stood in front of the bedroom door, the marital bedroom. On the other side was the private place of hushed pillow secrets, semen-stained sheets and knotty engenderings.

Kit turned the door handle and pushed the door open. The light from the bay window flooded the room and made Kit blink. Jennifer was lying on the bed with a white sheet pulled up to her neck and her eyes half-open. Her arms – white, slender and bowed like a wish bone – were lying on the crisp surface of the sheet. A single red rose lay across her cupped hands. The sunlight streamed through lace curtains and cast sombre patterns of grey flowers across her face. Kit whispered her name, 'Jennifer.' Each syllable palpable and heavy with longing. There was a musky smell in the room – and for a second Kit remembered Pepita lying in her coffin amid a riot of tropical flowers. You buried quick down there. A plump bluebottle fly landed on Jennifer's cheek. Kit winced as the fly crawled across the still luminous surface of her eye.

Kit moved into the room. He was desperate to hold her and to brush flies away from her face. He was dizzy with grief and his foot became entangled with a blanket that must have fallen from the end of the bed. As Kit bent down to free himself, he heard someone moving behind him – then a voice from the corridor. 'Take him, Johnnie.' Kit had heard that voice before. It was one that he would never forget. It belonged to the guard who had ordered Driscoll's beheading. There was a sharp pain above his right ear, a sudden reek of chloroform – and then all was blackness.

∎

'How's your head?' He was a nice man with a rugby-playing accent. He had brought Kit a pot of tea and a tray of digestive biscuits. 'Can you stand up and try walking around the room?'

'Could I have some clothes, please?'

The man handed Kit a dressing gown from a cabinet beside the bed. Kit stood up and put it on. The gown was grey and had blue trim; there was a Royal Air Force crest over the breast pocket.

'Do you feel any dizziness?'

'No.'

'Double or blurred vision?'

'No.'

'Have a little stroll.'

The room was functional and bare. The walls were painted institutional green and there were no paintings or books. The unusual thing was the hexagonal shape, as if the room were located in a tower or castle turret. There seemed to be windows in four of the walls, but they were covered by locked shutters. Presumably, thought Kit, to stop him jumping out. The closed shutters meant that it was impossible to tell the time of day. They had taken his watch, but his visitor was wearing one that said nine o'clock. Still, Kit had no way of knowing whether it was a.m. or p.m. He guessed there was another reason for the shutters: induced disorientation. It was a standard interrogation technique. Take away a person's perception of time and you rob him of his last reality anchor.

'How do you feel?'

'Fine.'

The man took an instrument out of a black bag and shone a light into Kit's pupil. He continued the eye and ear examination for some time. Kit wondered if he was trying to find his soul. At the end of the medical examination, the man had a look at Kit's head wound. 'Nasty haematoma, but no evidence of skull fracture or concussion. You're very lucky. Those fellows are animals.'

'Can you tell me anything else?'

'No.'

'Fine.'

'Good. I've got to go now, but if you experience nausea or vomiting, let someone know immediately.'

'How?'

'Shout loudly and rap on the door. Someone will hear you.' The man smiled, then got up and left the room. Kit heard two long heavy bolts slide into place on the other side of the door.

■

The food was English nursery stodge: Shepherd's Pie, Lancashire Hotpot, Toad in the Hole, over-boiled vegetables and lumpy steamed puddings. Although Kit ate very little, the plates continued to appear three times a day. At least it gave him a sense of time passing. After the first 'day', Kit asked the agent who brought his food if he could have some books. When the next meal came two Dickens novels – *The Old Curiosity Shop* and *Little Dorrit* – were on the tray next to the bangers and mash. There was also an anthology of Victorian poetry. Kit tried reading the novels, but the print was too small and the sentences too long. In any case, he found it difficult to concentrate. When he looked at a page, he didn't see the words – only images of Jennifer. It was worse than mourning. Mourning meant tears and relief, but what Kit felt was a stunned paralysis that locked every feeling in constant remorseless pain.

Kit thought it was odd that they left him alone with his food and cutlery. True, the table knives weren't very sharp, but the forks were. It would hurt a lot, but Kit was sure that he could dig out a wrist vein with a fork prong. If that didn't work, he could break a plate or a glass into sharp shards. The pain would be nothing compared to what was going on in his brain. Kit probed his left wrist with a sharp prong. Just do it, he thought, just do it.

■

Kit calculated that the visit came on the third day of his imprisonment. He knew that it was going to happen – they weren't going to try to stuff him with roly-poly pudding and treacle tart forever. Kit knew it was about to begin as soon as he heard the bolts being pulled back at what wasn't a normal feeding time. There were also muffled voices. On previous occasions, the doctor or tray-bearing agent had come alone. Kit thought he recognised one of the voices. It was a mandarin accent. The inflection was a world away from the London street urchin voice of the MoD security guard who had coshed him. The door opened a crack. The familiar voice said, 'I'll see him alone this time.'

The door opened fully and a man entered whom Kit knew only too well. He had fluffy white hair and was wearing a black lounge suit that was perfectly cut. The visitor put a small leather attaché case on a chair, then greeted Kit with a handshake and a warm smile. 'Counsellor Fournier, how do you do? Do you remember me?'

Kit nodded. 'Fine, thank you. And how are you?'

'Still settling in to my new job.' The visitor touched his hair. 'Do your colleagues still call me El Blanco?'

'I think we can now safely say that they're ex-colleagues – and if they call you that, it's very rude of them.'

'It doesn't much matter. We have our own nicknames – many of which are far more offensive. Would you like a drink? Beer, whisky?'

'I don't know. Is it after six o'clock?'

'It's about ten in the morning, but you deserve a drink after being banged up here for so long.'

'Whisky, please.'

While his visitor stepped out of the room to order the drinks, Kit recollected his last meeting with El Blanco. At the time Blanco, Sir Dick White, had still been head of MI5. A few weeks later, in the wake of the *Ordzhonikidze* debacle, White had taken over MI6 – a promotion owing partly to Kit's dirty tricks in Portsmouth Harbour. Kit wondered if that was why Blanco had preserved his life.

The whisky arrived with a pitcher of water and a bowl of ice. Blanco poured generous drinks and said, 'To your health.'

Kit drained the whisky without ice or water. 'Before we begin,' he said, 'I want to make one thing absolutely clear.'

'I'm listening.'

'I didn't kill her.'

'We know you didn't, but the Suffolk constabulary are not so sure.'

'Did the MoD goons do it?'

'No.'

Kit poured himself another whisky – and tried to stop his hand from shaking. He suddenly realised that MI6 must have known what she was doing – that's why White was being so 'nice'. Kit drank the whisky quickly and said, 'Don't fuck with me anymore.' He looked directly at Blanco, but the Director didn't flinch. 'You knew that she was passing on secrets – and you ordered your own guys to kill her.' Kit tried hard not to cry in front of Blanco.

What Blanco did next was so unexpected, so un-British. He reached out and put his hand over Kit's. 'I didn't want to hurt you. I was hoping you wouldn't have asked questions – just accepted her as being dead. It's OK, cry. Don't be ashamed of your grief.'

Kit wiped his eyes and stared into space. 'She was what I had instead of God, instead of country.' He paused and looked at White. 'Try to understand – I didn't believe in it any longer. That's why I became a traitor.'

Blanco nodded.

'We gave up everything so we could be together, and we almost pulled it off. But your boys got there first – and you had to kill her because she got involved in the game and broke the rule called "national security". The one rule you dare not break, the live centre rail. Fair enough, that's the way it has to be. The State is more important than any individual life.' Kit smiled and looked at White. 'I used to believe that too. But tell me, would you have killed your own wife, your own daughter, if she had broken that rule?'

'No, of course not. And I didn't kill Jennifer either.'

Kit poured himself another whisky. 'You're as convincing as a pig's bladder on a stick. We used to call it "plausible deniability". Then who did kill her?'

'No one killed her; she wasn't murdered. It was an accident.'

Kit put his face two inches from Blanco's and shouted. 'Stop lying to me!'

'I'm not lying to you, Kit, but…'

'But what?'

'But she did.'

Kit laughed. 'Oh, so you think she got cold feet – that she wouldn't have come with me?'

Dick White stood up and lifted the whisky bottle. 'I think I need a drink now too.' The Director poured himself two fingers of whisky and walked over to one of the shuttered windows. 'I think we need some light in here.' He reached into his pocket and pulled out a key ring. The Director unlocked and folded back the shutters while Kit stared into his whisky glass. 'Have a look, Kit, the view is spectacular, one of the best in England.'

The windows overlooked the point where the River Deben emptied into the North Sea. Longshore drift had created a long shingle bank that stretched a half-mile into the sea. The strong ebbing tide from the river crashed through breaches in the shingle. There were long lines of boiling white water where the river ebb collided with the sea waves. On the opposite bank were two squat Martello towers where ghost guards still kept a lookout for Napoleon's invasion fleet.

Kit joined White by the window. 'So this is where you brought me, so near.' Kit pointed across the river. 'That's Felixstowe Ferry over there – two pubs and a cafe. It's a good place to land – a steep clean shingle hard. And over there,' he gestured to a salt marsh behind the village, 'are the liveaboards. Those boats and barges never leave their mud berths. There must be twenty or so people who live on them all year round. Fishermen, poor families, old single men; there's an artist too who makes things out of driftwood and scrap.'

'You seem to know the area well.'

'You've brought me to Bawdsey Manor. We're on the top floor of a mock castle turret. This place is a Victorian folly that was built by a rich man who fell in love with this view. The RAF took it over in the 1930s and turned the whole estate into a secret research establishment. This is where you developed radar. They still do secret stuff, but I'm not sure what. In any case, it's a good safe house to stash people like me. You've got total isolation and layers and layers of no-questions-asked security. Why have you stopped telling me about Jennifer? You said she lied to me.'

'I don't think it would be fair – fair to you – to say more.'

'But, in the end, you intend to tell me whether I want to know or not. There's no need to dissemble. I know the game you're playing. You're giving me the long slow torture, like the Romans did to La Sainte Blandine at Lyons – and for the same reason, you want me to renounce my faith.'

White smiled. 'That's where they used, how do you say, *la chaise de fer rougie au feu.*'

'That's right, the red hot iron chair. We've got one like that in America, and that's where I'm going to be roasted if you hand me over – I know that game too. But let's get back to Jennifer. Tell me about her lies.'

'With both barrels?'

'Both barrels.'

'Jennifer was recruited by MI6 the same year she married Brian. She was a loyal and true agent – as she was, in her fashion, a loyal and true wife. You fell, Kit, head over heels into the oldest ensnarement trick in the espionage textbook – the honey trap. Would you like to see her agent reports on your lovemaking?'

'No.'

'In any case, things didn't work out as we had planned. The intelligence that Jennifer fed to you was intended, in the first case, to be passed on to the Americans.'

'You wanted them to know about the Orford Ness H-bomb?'

'Of course, there's no use in having these things if the people you want to influence don't know that you have them. For obvious reasons we couldn't go public about this device, but we certainly wanted Washington to know we had an H-bomb. And, of course, all the secrecy shrouding the Orford Ness project was bound to exaggerate our re-emergence as a world-class player in the arms race.' Blanco paused. 'Don't you see, Kit, these bombs are just as much status symbols as weapons? And we urgently needed H-bomb status to be taken seriously over Suez. And, of course, had we openly bragged about having one, then no one would have believed us.'

Kit finished his whisky. Truth is a chameleon that only shows its true colours when no one is looking.

'But then you went and spoiled things by not telling Washington that we had the big one. That's what Jennifer wanted you to do – that was her job.'

Kit looked away and shook his head. 'No, it wasn't…'

'Yes, it was. At first, she thought your defection story was a cover ploy to gain her sympathy. She thought you were still working for the Americans. Jennifer thought she could trick you into thinking that her love for you was so passionate that you could persuade her to do anything, even to spy on her husband. Jennifer thought it was all bluff and double bluff on both sides. Then the penny dropped. Jennifer realised that you weren't bluffing, that you really were planning to defect. She was shocked – we all were. We thought you were one of the hardest agents that Washington had ever sent out – a rising star headed for the cabinet or the NSC. In any case, when we realised you had been doubled we had to change our operational plan.'

'I need another drink.'

'In any case, we were cock-a-hoop when you gave Jennifer that Minox spy camera. We already knew that you were having unauthorised meetings with the KGB Chief of Residency, but still weren't sure what game you were playing.' Blanco refilled Kit's glass. 'So we called a meeting with Jennifer who convinced us, after some hefty questioning, that you really were going to defect. We were disappointed that our intelligence ruse – the covert nuclear message to Washington – had foundered, but we quickly realised there was another opportunity within our grasp. If we had failed to send a true – or true-ish – message to Washington, we could instead send lots of false ones to Moscow. We convened another meeting, a largish one, with several old colleagues from Five, including the Head of B Branch, and the Permanent Secretary who chairs JIC – that's how important it was. The purpose of the meeting was to rewrite Jennifer's script – and more importantly, to come up with a list of names.'

Kit looked into his glass. The dots were linking up. 'So you fed her false information to pass on to me, hoping that I would hand it over to the Sovs.'

'Precisely, but for some reason you failed to pass on the most valuable piece of artful misinformation, the microfilm with the names. Why not, Kit? Didn't you want to ingratiate yourself with your future employer?'

'I didn't want blood on my hands – all those midnight retributions in the cellars of the Lubyanka.'

'But, Kit, not any of the names on your microfilm were the ones guilty of selling us that bomb. It was a misinformation op. All the names we provided were loyal KGB agents whom we wanted to smear – one of the names was your friend, Vasili. I'm not sure that any of them would have been executed, but a few careers would have been ruined and a good many top secret security clearances cancelled. It would have caused organisational chaos. They do it to us all the time. They keep trying to frame Kim Philby as the "third man", but we're wise to their game of bluff and counter-bluff.'

Kit looked hard at White. More dots were joining up: the

message was as bleak as an unclaimed corpse. 'If I had handed over that film, and its list of fabricated traitors, it wouldn't have been long before the Russians spotted me as a doubled plant.'

'That's almost certainly true. They probably would have sent you back to America as part of a spy exchange.'

'To life imprisonment or the death penalty.'

'It's a rough trade, Kit. You know that better than anyone.'

Kit went back to the table to pour himself another whisky. 'Yeah, I know. And I know that the only reason Jennifer made love to me was because she was under operational instructions. Her lovemaking was tradecraft, her job as an intelligence officer.'

'I didn't say that. She might have had other reasons too. Jennifer liked sex. And so did Brian. He's dead you know.'

'Good.'

'We don't think so. He was an extremely talented scientist and administrator – and also one of ours.'

Kit stared into his drink. He felt the nausea of total confusion and deracination. 'So, Brian didn't kill Jennifer either.'

'Brian didn't murder Jennifer, but he was responsible for her death. It was an accident. We've just had the post-mortem report – from the chief Home Office pathologist working under the Official Secrets Act. The cause of death was postural asphyxia.'

'I don't know what that is.'

'It's the same reason people died when they were crucified. The body finds itself trapped in a position where the air passages are blocked or the diaphragm is unable to support lung function. The fact that Jennifer was tape-gagged contributed to her asphyxiation.'

'Couldn't that selfish bastard tell that she was in distress?'

'We'll never know. Brian hanged himself in one of the outbuildings. According to the pathologist, he must have done it within minutes of Jennifer dying.'

'You've tied up all the loose ends, haven't you? Open and shut case.'

Blanco flicked open the attaché case that he had left on a chair. He took out a file of documents and handed them to Kit. 'The post-mortem reports: you might find the photographs upsetting.'

Kit sat down at the table and began turning the pages. The first photos were of Brian hanging from a rafter with a purple bloated face. There was something strange about the rope. Kit peered closely. It wasn't a rope. Brian had hanged himself by knotting together Jennifer's underclothing. What else? There was a dark stain around the flies on Brian's moleskin trousers. Isn't it true, thought Kit, that people become incontinent when they're strangled? Had Brian wet himself? Or had he ejaculated a final gush of semen as he twisted in his death throes? Kit felt total exclusion: she had shared nothing with him. He was an outsider, never part of the secret; nothing more than a passing client. He looked at Brian again and felt his stomach churn with jealousy. Even death itself had been part of their marital love game.

The photos of Jennifer were heartbreaking: each organ dissected, measured and weighed – even her brain. Then they put everything back and sewed her up again. The stitched incision from pubes to throat looked like a bad repair on a canvas sail. When Kit had finished, he neatly gathered the documents, handed them back to White and said, 'There's a poem that goes:

Say I'm weary, say I'm sad,
Say that health and wealth have miss'd me,
Say I'm growing old, but add,
Jennie kiss'd me.

'Do you know it?'

'It sounds familiar.'

'How much did you pay her to kiss me?'

'We didn't need to pay her. She liked kissing you.'

'How do you know? Was that in one of her agent reports?'

Blanco sipped his whisky and looked directly at Kit, as if weighing up an angled shot at a driven pheasant. 'She liked kissing.'

Kit caught the nuance. 'What do you mean?'

'Jennifer had a lively appreciation of sexual pleasure in all its forms. She especially liked threesomes and dangerous sex. She liked feeling helpless and under restraint. She found struggling against her bonds intensified her orgasms. Maybe that's why she died: poor Brian thought she was struggling for pleasure, not for life itself. Very tragic for both.'

Kit got up and walked over to the window and leaned his forehead against the glass. Two long-liner fishing boats were leaving the river. The boats carried dan buoys that the fishermen used to mark where they laid their lines. The buoys were festooned with bright flags so they could be seen from afar. Those multi-coloured flags, fluttering and flapping in the sun, made the fishermen look like troops of knights riding off to battle. 'What,' said Kit, 'did you mean when you said that Jennifer liked threesomes?'

'She preferred the third person to be an extra man rather than another woman. She especially liked fellating one man while the other was inside her – fairly typical, I believe, for that sort of troilism.'

'Were there many lovers?'

'A few – one of the last was Henry Knowles. It started as a threesome, but then Jennifer started seeing him individually.'

'Who killed Knowles?'

'We honestly don't know. We think it was the Russians. They might have used that cultural attaché of yours who tried to defect.'

'Jeffers Cauldwell.'

'That's the one.'

'You said *tried* to defect.'

'We've arrested him and handed him over to the Americans – he was under surveillance for some time.'

'What's happened to your legal system? It used to be much admired. Have you dispensed with habeas corpus? Didn't Cauldwell have the right to an extradition hearing before a British judge?'

'It happened very quickly. Cauldwell was picked up at four in the morning and bundled out of the country on a US military transport plane from Lakenheath before midday. Lawyers were not involved. Spies don't have civil rights – that's why you're here.'

'You're sucking up to them, aren't you?'

'Who?'

'The Americans.'

'At the moment, it's not in our national interest to upset Washington.'

'In that case, why haven't you sent me to Lakenheath in a blacked-out van?'

White turned away from Kit and stared out to sea. A Sealink car ferry was steaming out of Harwich bound for Hoek Van Holland. 'Do you care, Kit, do you actually care what happens to you?'

'Not much, you've completely destroyed me – and you know

it. That's what you set out to do – and you did it with consummate skill.'

'You loved her.'

'You don't know when to stop, do you?' Kit paused. 'Why do
you keep twisting the knife? What's your next trick – a 3D film of
Jennifer's blow-job technique?'

'I haven't one, but I've heard that it was excellent – especially
well adapted for restarting a flaccid penis for more love. But I'm
sure you know that already.'

'Shut up.' Kit began to move forward; he wanted to choke the
life out of Blanco's mocking face. But the Director stopped him
with a single glance. The Englishman's eyes were cold, grey and
hypnotic.

'If it hadn't been for her, you would have been an excellent
intelligence officer.' Blanco's eyes had turned soft and caressing.

Kit looked away. 'I hated my job and I hated myself for doing it.'

'Pity.'

'It's not a pity.'

'I didn't mean for you, Kit, I meant a pity for me. I wanted you
to work for us.'

Kit laughed and poured himself another whisky. 'You must be
crazy if you think I would do that.'

'May I have some whisky too?'

Kit topped up White's glass.

'We're certainly knocking this bottle back – and I didn't have
a glass of olive oil to coat my stomach. You fellows use that trick
too, don't you?'

'You have to if you sup with the Sovs.'

'Mice,' said White, 'what about mice? Does that ring a bell?'

'Money, ideology, coercion and excitement or ego. They're the
hooks you use to recruit an agent.'

'I know. You stole that from us. We used the MICE acronym
to train SOE officers during the war.'

'So what?'

'You shouldn't be so dismissive, Kit, MICE always works.'

'That's what you think.'

Blanco smiled. 'Now, Kit, say I was trying to recruit you. I'm
absolutely sure that the M, the I and the E's would be non-starters.
Right so far?'

Kit slowly nodded.

Suddenly, the Englishman was no longer smiling. There seemed no emotion at all. 'So, Kit, let's talk about the C word, coercion.'

'Are you threatening me?'

'Yes.'

'You don't seem to understand.' Kit put on a twisted smile; the alcohol gave him a fake bravery. 'I don't care what you fucking do. Pack me off to Lakenheath like you did Cauldwell, fine. Or turn me over to the MoD goons so they can finish me off – that's even better.'

'No, Kit, we're not going to turn you over to the Americans – or to the MoD police. Why should we?' Blanco looked hard at Kit without blinking. 'You forgot about the third alternative, the Suffolk police. We're going to frame you, Kit, like no one's ever been framed before. It's going to be the perfect stitch-up, delivered from on high. You're going to be charged with the murder and rape of Jennifer. And, don't worry, that trial will go ahead, for the Ambassador will hold his nose and waive your diplomatic immunity. And Washington isn't going to raise a peep of protest either. In fact, it will save them the embarrassment of admitting that one of their most trusted diplomats was a spy who turned traitor.' The Director paused to tighten the screw. 'I wonder if your mother and sisters and Jennifer's father, your much loved Uncle George, will come to Ipswich to see you in the dock.'

Kit closed his eyes and spoke in a whisper. 'You win.' He opened his eyes and looked at the Director. 'You're a real master of the trade, Blanco, I hope you don't mind my calling you that. In fact, I was the one who coined your codename. Your full title was El Pene Blanco – the white prick. You've earned it.'

'Thank you.'

'You're welcome.'

Blanco looked at his watch. 'I've got to head back to London. You'll follow me in the morning. We're going to put you in a safe house in Croydon – sorry, it's a bit of a hole – for an initial debrief, but that will be only temporary. In the long term, it would be unwise to have you in the UK. But before you go, we'll be picking your brains about how Washington is likely to react to the Suez business.' A shadow came over Blanco's face. 'And the names of the people who have been leaking our plans.'

Chapter Thirteen

I think that I shall never see
A poem lovely as a tree.

A tree whose hungry mouth is prest
Against the earth's sweet flowing breast...

He used to think it was the sort of poem that gave poetry a bad name, but for months the words had been going round and round in Kit's head. He longed for trees – willow, oak, chestnut, ash, even scrub pine. But there weren't any trees, only rough tussac grass and clumps of small withered shrubs. The first impression was of an inhospitable island painted in shades of green, brown and grey – and that impression deepened every year. Kit sat down at an improvised desk in a wooden hut overlooking Queen Charlotte Bay and began to transcribe his rough shorthand notes. *Pond just by main road just east of bridge: water, colour of weak Earl Grey tea; depth, 40 cm; caddis, cladocerans, beetle larvae and adults. Lake Sullivan North: two zebra trout beheaded, heads placed in alcohol for otolithes. Guts examined, not much in them. Neither fish had much gonad. Possibly post-spawning fish.* He stopped writing to put on another jumper. It was the end of November and it had started off as a beautiful late spring day, but now turbulent squalls were sweeping in from the west and pelted the hut with sharp heavy hailstones. There was still a lot to write up – *Mickey Doolan's Ditch* and *Arroyo Malo* – before he could get out his hip flask and crawl into his sleeping bag. In the morning, he'd get a lift in the Camp House Land Rover to Warrah for another week of fishery assessment.

Kit pushed his notes aside and opened the poetry book. It was from the reading list that he had requested from his agent handler the last time they had met. It was certainly the only copy of Joyce Kilmer's collected poems on West Falkland. In fact, thought Kit, it might be the only copy of Kilmer's poems in the southern hemisphere. The light from the hurricane lamp flickered and hissed.

A tree that looks at God all day,
And lifts her leafy arms to pray;

A tree that may in Summer wear
A nest of robins in her hair;

Upon whose bosom snow has lain;
Who intimately lives with rain.

The tree was a woman. How many years? Ten years. It had been ten years since Kit had seen a tree or embraced a woman.

Kit had grown to like his cover as a naturalist. He could identify all sixty-four breeding species of birds. The Gentoo penguins and the flightless steam ducks were his favourites. The birds were trapped on the ground, like himself. The only native mammals were the elephant seals and the sea lions – he wasn't sure about the fur seal. In any case, he'd never seen one. Nor was Kit certain that the sheep farmers were totally convinced by his cover story. The sideways looks they sometimes gave him suggested they found something fishy about this lonely man with a strange accent. They certainly didn't find him friendly. Kit had been warned by each of his agent handlers not to say more to the islanders than was absolutely necessary. There were a hundred and fifty inhabitants on the island. And after ten years, Kit knew the names of only eight of them. He doubted that a transcript of his total conversation with his fellow islanders would fill four pages.

During his first three years on the island, Kit had been visited by an agent handler every seven or eight weeks. They brought him bags and bags of documents and photos to peruse and evaluate. The handler visits sometimes lasted more than a week. But, as is the nature of any intelligence asset, he was eventually squeezed dry. There just wasn't anything left to milk out of his brain and memory. Occasionally, there was a flurry of interest when one of Kit's former colleagues arose to prominence as a presidential advisor, ambassador, or as a member of the cabinet or the National Security Council. On these occasions, Kit was expected to profile the rising star in terms of strengths, weaknesses, character traits, psychology, personality, experience, vulnerabilities – and, of course, any useful dirt. Kit always complied – and sometimes enjoyed it. He especially enjoyed doing a job on one particular ex-colleague, who had come to be regarded as a possible CIA director or even a presidential candidate. But, as time passed, the rising colleagues began to pass into obscurity too – and the agent handler visits dwindled to a token annual event.

At the beginning of 1967, Kit was summoned to Port Stanley with the usual caveat that he wasn't to speak to anyone on the MV Tamar which ferried him across Falklands Sound or in the long base Land Rover that served as bus between the camp and the capital. Kit avoided conversation and eye contact by emerging himself in a tattered copy of Darwin's *The Voyage of the Beagle*. Nonetheless, a gregarious and unwashed sheep farmer tried to have a chat. 'Interesting book, mate?'

'Very. Listen to this, "The most curious fact with respect to this animal, is the overpoweringly strong and offensive odour which proceeds from the buck. It is quite indescribable..."'

The farmer turned away and left Kit in peace for the rest of the journey.

The only person on the islands who knew anything about Kit's past was the Governor. He didn't know much, but what little he did know was heavily wrapped with security cautions. Whenever Kit's agent handler arrived, the Governor provided accommodation for the handler at Government House and an abandoned sheep station ten miles outside of Stanley – far from prying eyes – for Kit's accommodation and his actual meetings with his handler.

Kit's quarters at the sheep station were Spartan: bed, table, two chairs, bottled-gas cooker, outside loo. He always arrived the night before his handler, then waited the following morning for the sound of the approaching Land Rover. His last handler had been named Martin, a quiet man in his late twenties who didn't seem to have a clue why he'd been sent eight thousand miles. It was obvious to Kit that his case officers were becoming younger and more junior. Last time, he and Martin had spent two days playing chess and birdwatching for sooty shearwaters and black-browed albatross.

When Kit heard the gears grinding in the distance, he put the kettle on. Five minutes later there was a knock on the door. Kit was brewing the tea. 'Come in, Martin.' The door opened and Kit looked up, it wasn't Martin.

The agent handler was wearing a tweed skirt and a grey sweater. Kit was speechless. She was much more of a woman now. There were even the beginnings of lines around her mouth. 'Good afternoon, Mr. Fournier. I believe we've met before.'

Kit was speechless. He couldn't believe it was her.

The woman laughed, it was the sort of refined, self-assured laugh that Kit often heard on the BBC World Service. 'Did you,' she said, 'did you really think that I was a French au pair? Can you remember what my name was, my cover name.'

'Françoise.'

'Excellent. I'm glad you haven't forgotten. How do you do? My real name is nearly the same, Frances – Frances Davison.'

They shook hands. Kit smiled and remembered how he had been duped by this same woman all those years ago on the train to Portsmouth. 'Your French accent was pretty convincing.'

'Remember how we sang 'La Mer' together?'

'I blush at the sentimentality.'

'It's a beautiful song. We must sing it again. In any case, we'd better get down to business. They want me to talk to you about Vietnam, you're supposed to be an expert.'

'May I ask who you were working for then, on the Portsmouth train?'

'I was MI5 then. Dick White took me with him when he went to Six. If you must know, it was a terribly botched surveillance operation. We didn't have enough operatives to cover all our targets. When I got to Portsmouth, I was supposed to hand you over to a second eyeball or a mobile backup, but none of them were there. But in any case, you were only second priority.'

'Who was first?'

'MI6, of course. Dick wanted to see how far they were going to drop themselves in the brown stuff. But come on, that's all in the past, we're supposed to be talking about Vietnam.'

'Don't go there. Let the Americans stew in their own juices.'

'That is the perceived wisdom back in London, but Lyndon Johnson is putting Wilson under an awful lot of pressure to send a token force. It doesn't even have to be a full battalion or company. Johnson told Harold he'd be happy with just a single Blackwatch piper – maybe he was joking.'

'Johnson doesn't want the firepower, he wants the symbol power – a Union Jack beside the Stars and Stripes over some bomb-blasted paddy field. They'd splash that image across every television screen and every front page. Don't do it.'

Frances spent the next three days interviewing Kit about Vietnam. She dragged hundred of names and memories out of his brain. She got him to evaluate and profile every official and officer that he knew, however remotely, who had anything to do with US policy in Southeast Asia. By the end of their time together, Frances had put together an impressive and factual briefing folder. 'This,' she said, 'is just what Control needs to stiffen Wilson's case. What's wrong Kit? You suddenly seem very far away.'

'I hope Wilson does stay out of Vietnam. If he does, it will be the first time that Britain has stood up against Washington since 1956. On the other hand, your policy on nuclear deterrence is one of complete submission to the US.'

'What do you mean?'

'One of your predecessors was kind enough to let me have a copy of the 1958 Mutual Defence Agreement that Britain signed with the USA. I've never seen such a total surrender of national sovereignty.'

'Macmillan was being pragmatic. He was bowing to necessity.'

'The French didn't find it a necessity.' Kit looked closely at his handler and wondered how far he could push her. 'What do you know about the Orford Ness H-bomb?'

Frances looked away, embarrassed.

'Don't pretend,' said Kit, 'that you don't know. They couldn't have made you my case officer without briefing you on the missing Sov bomb that, oops, just happened to come ashore in Suffolk.' He paused. 'If they didn't brief you, I will.'

'Listen, Kit, I know what happened – maybe even more than you do – but that whole business is something that no one talks about or even thinks about. It's one of those secrets that are so sensitive that even those of us who know can't admit we know.' Frances smiled. 'Even to the persons who know we know.'

'What happened to that bomb? I have a right to know, Frances, it's cost me eleven years of my life already? And I'll probably be stuck here until I die.'

'Probably. In fact, if they knew you wanted to talk about it, they might even end your life sooner.'

'The bomb didn't work, did it?' He paused. 'Otherwise, Macmillan wouldn't have gone hat in hand to sign that Mutual Defence Agreement.'

'Work it out yourself, Kit.'

'OK, the Sovs sold you a lousy H-bomb. It was like one of those "emergency capability" H-bombs that we deployed in '54 and '55. Sure, they would work, but they cut a lot of corners like safety, reliability and stockpile life expectancy.'

'It did work, but not brilliantly.' She reached out and touched Kit's hand. 'We shouldn't be having this conversation.'

'Then let's not have it.'

'No, Kit, you have a right to know. That bomb ruined your life and killed the person you loved.'

'Her death was an accident.'

Frances didn't say anything, she just looked at Kit. She waited for him to say something, but there were no words, only a look of pain that dulled his eyes and made him shrink within himself. She went back to the bomb question because it hurt him less. 'Have you heard of Operation Grapple?'

'Only what I read in six-month-old copies of *The Times*. Wasn't Grapple a series of bomb tests that you carried out in the Pacific? They were in the spring of '57, not long after Macmillan took over from Eden after the Suez humiliation.'

'That's right. But *The Times* didn't tell you that the test was faked.'

Kit smiled. 'Perfidious Albion.'

'We had two experimental H-bombs that were based on the second-hand Soviet one that was still stashed away on Orford Ness. The scientists even used some components from the Russian original – like the sheep farmers around here cannibalise worn-out Land Rovers. The trial H-bombs were called Green Granite Small and Purple Granite. The problem was that no one was sure that they were actually going to go boom. A failure would have been really embarrassing – and another British humiliation hard on the heels of Suez. So the scientists cooked up a massive old-fashioned atomic bomb that they named Orange Herald. The big A-bomb was dressed up as an H-bomb and guaranteed to show the world a super bang if the real H-bombs failed.'

'And the H-bombs did fail?'

'No, but they only went "pop" instead of "bang" and "kapow".'

In theory, an H-bomb should be a hundred times more power-ful than an A-bomb, but Green and Purple Granite produced a combined kiloton yield less than half that of Orange Herald. The Russian bomb failed us. They duped us for fifty million pounds in hard currency. There were no corrupt KGB agents – it was a con trick directed by the Kremlin.'

'But...'

'Poor you, Kit – the Russians fed stuff to you to make us think the Kremlin was panicking about a stolen bomb.'

'So after the Russians tricked you with a duff bomb, you swal-lowed your pride and went begging to the Americans.'

'That's your view, but in the meantime our scientists learned from failure and did explode some viable H-bombs by the end of '57.'

'But Blue Steel, the bomb you finally deployed, was just a US Mark 28 with a Union Jack logo.'

'How do you know?'

'I got one of your predecessors drunk.'

'I know you can't be trusted, but I still like you. Can I stay with you again tonight? It doesn't matter that the bed's so narrow.'

The affair continued for three years. Frances managed to per-suade her superiors that Kit's intelligence assessments and inside knowledge of the Washington establishment were worth three or four visits a year. Her marriage continued to deteriorate – and there were money problems too. The worse thing was that she saw the effect it was having on her children. They all needed a change. She left MI6 for a well-paid job in the City. They bought a farmhouse in Suffolk that they did up for weekends and holidays. Things were a little better. The marriage was stumbling along towards the finishing tape: that blessed day when the young-est finishes university. She wrote a long letter to Kit explaining all this. He didn't answer. His new agent handler only came to Stanley once every two years – and it was a welfare visit rather than an intelligence gathering one.

■

On the eve of his sixtieth birthday, Kit was summoned to Port Stanley. A lot of changes had occurred in the last two years. In the 1982 war there had been little action on West Falkland. In fact, there had been no fighting at all. Part of the reason for the peaceful outcome was that Kit had persuaded a vainglorious

Argentine colonel to surrender without firing a shot. The negotiations had taken place in the early hours of the morning over a bottle of Fundador Brandy. The colonel was convinced that Kit was a Guatemalan naturalist who had been stranded on the island when hostilities broke out. The British were grateful for Kit's intervention.

When Kit got to Port Stanley he was told to go to Government House instead of the usual sheep station. He was greeted by the Governor with a bottle of champagne. There was also a representative from MI6. It was a small birthday celebration – only the three of them. They had a present for Kit: a British passport and the freedom to leave.

∎

Kit's new passport was in the name of Patrick Louis Ferrar, although he still called himself Kit. He spoiled several cheques before he remembered to sign them P. L. Ferrar. He liked his new initials, PLF, the acronym for Parachute Landing Fall. The art of the PLF was landing on the balls of your feet with slightly bent knees, then twisting your body in a ballet gesture of consummate grace so that calf, thigh and the fleshy back muscles next to your armpit absorbed the force of your landing. PLF, how apt. The art of coming back to earth in one piece.

Kit spent a fortnight in a London safe house learning about his new identity and the precautions he would have to take. He felt uneasy in London after so many years. It was a different country and he knew no one. And there was also something that haunted him, something that he wanted to know. On the last day of the 're-orientation course', Kit began to ask his agent handler a question, but then stopped. 'No,' he said, 'it's not really any of my business.'

∎

Although Kit was twenty-eight years older and his black hair flecked with grey, he still was recognisable as Counsellor Fournier. Kit began to grow a beard and let his hair grow long to give himself the air of a retired academic or art lecturer. He wanted to slop about in a derelict farmhouse wearing espadrilles, torn jeans and a smock as he painted watercolours. With the help of an MI6 handler who had been brought up near Halesworth, Kit found a cottage overlooking a Suffolk river valley. He spent most of the first week just loving the trees. It had been so long since he had seen trees. He watched their branches tossing in the wind; he smelled them and caressed their trunks; he stroked their leaves and fondled their fruit.

Kit was picking plums when a car stopped at the bottom of his garden. He frowned. It was probably another nosey pest demanding something for the Harvest Festival or selling a ticket to some ghastly concert. He picked an overripe plum from his basket and began to take aim at the driver's window. He wanted to cultivate his image as a grumpy loner, but the plum was still in his hand when the woman started walking up the path. Frances was now in her fifties. 'Would you like a plum?' he said.

She put the fruit in her mouth, then removed the stone.

Kit reached forward. 'I'll take that.' The plum stone was warm and wet with her saliva. He closed his palm tight around it.

'They told me you were here – I don't live far myself.'

Kit looked away: his face was a blank.

Frances touched his arm. 'That empty look of yours frightens me.'

'Sorry, it's not meant to.'

'Why don't you have supper with me this evening?' She squeezed his arm. 'Don't look so nervous.'

'Why don't you come here instead? I like to cook.'

'Is it because you'll feel safer?'

'Yes.'

Frances looked closely at Kit and saw, for the first time, his fear and shame. His experiences hadn't broken him: he'd been broken from the start.

Epilogue

```
TO: SECURITY SERVICE 100 IMMEDIATE
LEDGER: S E C R E T/DELICATE SOURCE /UK EYES ALPHA
LEDGER DISTRIBUTION:
FCO - PUSD
CABINET OFFICE - JIC
REPORT NO: CX 82/80949 (R/UK/C)
TITLE: Guidelines for Directors Supervising Agent
Handlers Assigned to
PF/HAWKSBEARD
SUMMARY
```

HAWKSBEARD has been repatriated to the UK for humanitarian reasons. He was originally known as Kitson Fournier, but now goes under the name of Patrick Louis Ferrar for reasons of personal protection. During his recruitment process, and at various times since, Fournier/Farrar has been fed plausible explanations for events surrounding TURNSTONE. These explanations were largely based on half-truths and misinformation fabricated to create the atmosphere of 'trust' necessary to recruit Fournier/Farrar as a UK intelligence provider. It is essential that personnel working with Fournier/Farrar are familiar with his 'version of events' and do nothing to make him doubt their veracity. It is not our wish that Fournier/Farrar be detained in permanent isolation, but knowledge of any of the following areas of intelligence would make such detention inevitable.

During the recruitment of Fournier/Farrar, Director White truthfully revealed that Jennifer and Brian Handley were serving SIS officers. The Director did not, however, inform Fournier/Farrar that the couple were also part of the UK/USA spy ring that passed atom bomb secrets to the Soviet Union in the late 1940s. Brian Handley first came under suspicion in 1949, but betrayed his fellow scientist spy, Klaus Fuchs, to preserve his own cover and credibility. Handley's top secret security clearance was restored on the advice of Harold 'Kim' Philby, who was at the time SIS/CIA liaison. There is, however, no evidence that Brian Handley was a committed Marx-Leninist. He seems to have been motivated solely by greed.

Fournier/Farrar was also given misinformation concerning the deaths of Brian and Jennifer Handley. Their deaths had nothing to do with a bondage game that went wrong. They were executed by MOD security police who later claimed to have been acting under the instructions of (...*name removed to protect security...*). None of these executions was authorised by Director White – and, indeed, such non-judicial executions fall outside the guidelines by which all UK security services operate. The investigation carried out by the MOD Tribunal and Inquiries Unit decided that the security police could not offer sufficient evidence to prove that they were acting on the orders of (...*name removed to protect security...*). The security police were subsequently informed that they would be court-martialled for murder and rape. They were, however, offered the alternative of a resettlement package and new identities – which they accepted. It has since been verified that both men died while fighting as mercenaries in the Congo.

When (...*name removed to protect security...*) first came under suspicion of being a Soviet spy, he successfully denied all charges and continued in post until his retirement in (...*deleted...*). As more evidence came to light, (...*name removed to protect security...*) was again interrogated by D Branch – and finally confessed in exchange for immunity from prosecution. The following facts emerged from subsequent debriefings:

1 Brian and Jennifer Handley had been warned several weeks before their deaths that they were in danger of being named as spies by a KGB defector. The warning came from Vasili Galanin, the KGB London *rezidentura*, who also informed (...*name removed to protect security...*) of the situation.

2 The Handleys' escape plan to Moscow was delayed by Jennifer Handley who had fallen in love with Henry Knowles and was trying to persuade Knowles to accompany them to Moscow. (The Handleys believed in open marriage and sexual experimentation.)

3 Brian Handley reported to (...*name removed to protect security...*) that his wife had confided their situation to Knowles.

(...*name removed to protect security...*) denies that he knew of any plan to murder Knowles.

4 Before he was kidnapped and killed, Henry Knowles contacted the Security Service and fully reported the situation.

5 (...*name removed to protect security...*) soon learned of Knowles's report and knew that the Handleys would be unable to escape arrest. He knew that it was almost certain that one or both would break under interrogation and that he and others would be identified as Soviet agents. (...*name removed to protect security...*) therefore arranged their execution, an act that he describes as a 'regretful and awful decision'.

SOURCE COMMENT

The aim of any handler dealing with Fournier/Farrar is to assure that he live out his days anonymously and quietly. It is essential that the press and media remain unaware of his background and presence. Press speculation about 'vast conspiracies to deceive' or a 'Secret State' can only damage the image of the Security Service and the SIS – and, therefore, our ability to act effectively.

Fournier/Farrar seems to have developed an emotional attachment to his current agent handler. He appears to trust her and is willing to accept her advice and guidance.

Acknowledgements

First of all, I want to thank Dr John Puddifoot for suggesting Orford Ness as a setting for a novel. I am also grateful to David Davison for his insights about politicians in the 1950s and for books from his library. Likewise, I am indebted to Professor George Wickes for his accounts of the events that took place in Saigon in 1945. Anthony Parsons provided valuable recollections of Soviet musicians during the Cold War, as did Dr Chris Grogan at the Britten-Pears Library in Aldeburgh. John and Angie Gardiner must be mentioned for sharing the secrets of Butley Creek. And, of course, I must thank Angeline Rothermundt for her valuable editorial advice as well as Gary Pulsifer and Daniela de Groote for their continued support. Finally, I want to acknowledge the following books and sources. The one book for which I feel a particular debt is Peter Hennessey's excellent history of the 1950s, *Having It So Good*.

Britten, Benjamin. *Noye's Fludde, op.59, The Chester Miracle Play Set to Music*. Boosey & Hawkes, London, 1961

Davies, Barry; Gordievsky, Oleg; Tomlinson, Richard. *The Spycraft Manual: The Insider's Guide to Espionage Techniques*. Zenith Press, 2005

Eliot, T.S. *Collected Poems 1909-1962*. Faber and Faber, London, 1974

Hennessy, Peter. *Having it so Good: Britain in the Fifties*. Penguin Allen Lane, London, 2006

Grose, Peter. *Gentleman Spy: Life of Allen Dulles*. University of Massachusetts Press: New Ed. Edition, 1996

Henderson, Joe; Clark, Leslie; Clark, Petula; Valentine, David. 'Meet Me in Battersea Park', 1954

Hitchens, Christopher. *Blood, Class and Nostalgia: Anglo-American Ironies*. Vintage, London, 1991

James, Robert Rhodes. *Anthony Eden*. Macmillan PAPERMAC, London, 1987

Jarrell, Randall. *The Death of the Ball Turret Gunner*. From *The Penguin Book of Modern American Verse* edited by Geoffrey Moore. Penguin Books, London, 1954

Keever, Beverley Deepe. 'Un-Remembered Origins of "Nuclear Holocaust": World's First Thermonuclear Explosion of Nov. 1, 1952. Originally published by the *Honolulu Weekly*, October 30, 2002

Kilmer, Joyce. *Trees and Other Poems*, George H. Doran Company, 1914

Levy, Shaun. *The Last Playboy: The High Life of Porfirio Rubirosa*. Fourth Estate, London, 2005

Llosa, Mario Vargas, *The Feast of the Goat* (translated from the Spanish by Edith Grossman). Faber and Faber, London, 2003

McDowell, Dr R.M. 'West Falkland: field notes on sites selected for fishery assessment.' The National Institute of Water and Atmospheric Research, Christchurch, New Zealand, 1999

McTaggart, Lynne. *Kathleen Kennedy, The Untold Story of Jack's Favourite Sister*. Weidenfeld and Nicolson, London, 1984

Mailer, Norman. *Harlot's Ghost*. Michael Joseph, London, 1991

Marquez, Abelardo "Abe". 'Operation Ivy – The Testing of the Hydrogen Bomb' from Atomic Veterans History Project, March 29, 2007

Newall, Venetia. *Discovering the Folklore of Birds and Beasts*, Shire Publications, Tring, Herts, 1971

The Frank Olson Legacy Project Website, for its copy of the CIA Assassination Manual of 1953

Orwell, George. *1984*. Penguin Books, London, 1990

Owen, The Rt Hon Lord David, CH. 'Diseased, demented, depressed: serious illness in Heads of State'. An occasional paper based on a 2002 lecture published in QJM: An International Journal of Medicine, Volume 96, Number 5, Oxford, 2003

Réage, Pauline. *Histoire d'O*. Jean-Jacques Pauvert, Paris, 1954

Rimington, Stella. *Open Secret: The Autobiography of the Former Director General of MI5*. Arrow Books Ltd, 2002

Summers, Anthony. *Official and Confidential: The Secret Life of J. Edgar Hoover*. 1993

Taubman, William. *Khrushchev*. The Free Press, an imprint of Simon & Schuster UK Ltd. London, 2005

Trenet, Charles and Lasry, Albert. *La Mer*. Editions Raoul Breton, 1945

Wheeler, J. Craig. 'Sleet Sue.' From *The Wetokian: The Journal of the Atomic Weathermen*. Web Issue, Winter 2007

Whittle, Keith R. 'Anno Atomi: Growing Up With the Atom.' (Website)

Wright, Peter. *Spy Catcher*. Viking Penguin, New York, 1987

A number of real historical events are referred to in this book and real places are mentioned. A few real names are used, but no real people are portrayed. This is a work of fiction. When I have used official titles and positions, I do not suggest that the persons who held these positions in the past are the same persons portrayed in the novel or that they have spoken, thought or behaved in the way I have imagined.

Edward Wilson
Suffolk, England